The
BLIND
SIDE
of the
HEART

Also by Michael C. White

A Brother's Blood

The
BLIND
SIDE
of the
HEART

A *novel*

Michael C. White

Cliff Street Books
An Imprint of HarperCollins*Publishers*

HarperCollins books may be purchased for educational, business, or sales promotional use. For information please write: Special Markets Department, HarperCollins Publishers, Inc., 10 East 53rd Street, New York, NY 10022.

FIRST EDITION

Designed by Deirdre C. Amthor

Library of Congress Cataloging-in-Publication Data

ISBN 0-06-019431-6

99 00 01 02 03 ❖/RRD 10 9 8 7 6 5 4 3 2 1

This book is dedicated to Ken Childs—
minister to sick hearts,
soul of wit, friend
requiescat in pace

The thing on the blind side of the heart,
  On the wrong side of the door,
The green plant groweth, menacing
  Almighty lovers in the spring;
There is always a forgotten thing,
  And love is not secure.
—G. K. Chesterton

The mind of man is capable of anything—because
everything is in it.
—Joseph Conrad
The Heart of Darkness

Author's Note

This is a work of fiction. While some of the incidents in this book may bear a resemblance to events that have actually taken place, it is, finally, a work of the imagination. No character here is based on any person, living or dead. There are a number of real people, however, that I would like to acknowledge who helped me in the writing of this book. I would first like to thank Judge Kent Smith, Susan Fenton, Jonathan Elliot and Trant Campbell for their time and for the wonderful expert advice they provided on legal matters. I would also like to show my appreciation to the staff of Babson Library, Springfield College, for their invaluable assistance in getting research materials I needed, with a special thanks going to Bill Stetson for all of his help. As always, I want to thank Diane Reverand for her continued support and helpful advice. Once again, I'd like to express my deep gratitude to Nat Sobel—a better agent, editor, promoter and friend a writer couldn't ask for. And last, I'd like to thank my wife Karen, for all of her love, criticism, patience and support.

Prologue

It's been three years. It's time I should tell my side. After all, I knew Father as well as any, and a damn sight better than most of those birds who were so quick to condemn him. What did they know? What? I was there. I worked for the man going on eighteen years. Lived under the same roof. Made his meals and washed his clothes. Kept his house. Nursed him when he was feeling poorly. Eighteen years. That has to count for something. You know a thing or two about a person after that long. The man behind the collar. How he liked his eggs or the way he preferred his shirts to be ironed. The tang of his body after he went for his morning run. The way he was fond of joking with you. How he'd get these bad headaches, or the way he could fly off the handle sometimes. Mostly what I knew him to be was a decent man, gentle and compassionate: reassuring some girl who'd found herself pregnant and was afraid to tell her parents, or sitting by the bedside and holding the hand of a sick person till morning. Or how, after giving somebody the last rites, the way his light-blue eyes would take on that knife-edged faraway look, the pain etched on his face, that sad, lovely face of his. Or like when we heard about that poor boy's death, the way he'd cried like a baby. Just like a baby, he did. I was there. I saw that, too. Can any of them say as much?

And yet, what I probably know better than any is how much I didn't know, how much about the man was a mystery even to me. Even now. Still waters run deep they say, and with Father you surely couldn't see bottom. Aye, that too I knew about him.

Part I

1

As good a place as any to begin might be those Tuesdays. Right smack in the middle of Father's troubles. You might say it was like being in the eye of the storm. Behind us everything raging, ahead we could only guess what waited, but right there, a kind of quiet sanctuary, at least for an hour each week. On Tuesday, which has always been my day off, I'd get in my car and head down to visit Father Jack. Not every week, mind you, seeing as I had my responsibilities, but as often as I was able. I'd try to slip out of the rectory before half nine as Father Martin got back from early Mass then. By rights, it was my day off and none of his concern what I did on my own time. Still and all, I liked to be gone while he was over to the church. Otherwise, he'd give me some last-minute chore to do, some errand he wanted me to run, or at the very least, one of those censuring looks of his when he knew I was going to see his predecessor, almost as if to remind me who paid my wages now. Truth is, I never liked the man, though maybe I never gave him a fair shake.

It wasn't easy making those trips, especially for someone like myself who didn't learn to drive till she was nearly thirty—you know what they say about old dogs and new tricks. A half hour over the mountains just to get to the highway, then another hour down to the city. All the while worrying about bad weather, which you'd think twenty-five years in this cold, godforsaken New England would've cured me of. The worst of it came when I got there though: seeing Father like that, in that bloody, stinkin' place.

I used to bring him things to eat, home-baked treats to put some meat on him. Soda bread, scones with creamy icing, Irish whiskey cake from a recipe of my mother's. But he especially liked my zucchini bread. I grew the squash myself in a small garden behind the rectory. I'd make a dozen loaves and put them away in the freezer. On cold winter evenings, I used to warm a piece and serve it to him with some butter and a cup of tea while he worked in his study. He loved it. And though it wasn't the sort of topic to talk about in polite company, Father had always had problems moving his bowels and the zucchini kept him regular as the mail.

I was in the habit of stopping at a store and picking him up a few items—toiletries and mints and suchlike. And I'd bring him some clean socks and underwear I'd dug out of boxes Father Martin had had removed to the basement. Father Jack's underwear always used to be upstairs, in the second drawer of his bureau, where Father Martin's clothes were now: T-shirts on the left side, underwear on the right, dividing them, his socks, everything folded and neat as a pin. Sometimes I'd even sneak Father some parish stationery to write on, despite the fact he was forbidden to use it, per order of Monsignor Payne (Old Payne-in-the-arse, Father used to call him). But what would it hurt, a little paper to write on? Did they begrudge him that? Not that Father was much on writing letters, mind you.

And since Father had always been a great one for the books, I'd bring him things to read, too. You only had to hear him talk to know he was a person of great learning. Always with his nose in a book, that was Father for you. Many's the night he'd fall asleep in his study with a volume across his chest, his reading glasses resting on his nose. On my previous visit he'd give me a list of titles to pick up from his library, which also was stored in boxes in the basement, though I never let on to him, didn't see any cause to. I'd have to go hunting through box after box looking for things like *The Golden Legend* or Borromeo's *Instructions for the Building of Churches*, perhaps Augustine's *Confessions* or the *Summa Theologica*—in Latin no less! If he didn't tell me what to bring, I might pick him up a sporting magazine. Not quite the heady fare he was used to, but something to occupy himself. Besides, Father had always taken a lively interest in sports. He used to follow the Red Sox and the Celtics. From what I understand, he'd been quite a basketball player in college, and you'd often find him playing a pickup game with some of the lads out in the driveway. He'd been an avid golfer, too. In the old days, himself and Father Duncan and Pete Beaupre, close friends both, would play over at the country club. The old days indeed. Seems like a million years ago.

But I'm straying, which you'll notice I have a bad habit of doing. Anyway, on this particular Tuesday, I parked my Toyota and started walking across the lot. It was a cold and disagreeable morning, overcast and gray, with a raw March wind that cut you to the quick. It hinted at snow, and I was already worrying about the ride home. I had to hold my bandanna tight about my neck. As I approached the visitors' entrance, my eye caught, as it always seemed to, the large green sign to the right of the gate: HOLDEN COUNTY HOUSE OF CORRECTIONS. It never failed to send a tremor scooting up the back of my neck. Each time, it took a deliberate stiffening of the muscles in my lower back to go in. And once inside, there'd be that terrible odor I'd grown to know all too well: the sour stench of feet and sweat, of urine and shite and vomit, of bodies packed too close together. The smell of lost souls is the way it always struck me, like I was entering hell itself. It was an ugly, foul, depressing place, I don't mind saying. Yet I had only to stomach it an hour a week. I couldn't but wonder how Father, with his upbringing, endured it all the time. For, you see, he was not so much of a delicate constitution, I wouldn't put it that way. But there was no mistaking the fact he came from some money. What my mum, rest her soul, used to call lace-curtain Irish. A refined and cultured gentleman, one used to the finer things, such as listening to Mozart while he sipped his brandy of an evening. One used to his privacy and his quiet, to having things a certain way. I couldn't imagine what that place must have been like for someone of Father's temperament. I didn't allow myself to think much about it.

It's nothing like you'd imagine—prison. Forget about the movies showing the guards with their tommy guns and some fellow clanking his cup against the bars and all that rubbish. No sir. Everything was quite modern, quite up-to-date, with lots of glass and television cameras and brightly painted signs telling you what to do and how to behave (NO SMOKING, NO METAL OBJECTS, NO CONTRABAND)—all of which only served to make it that much more depressing. The room where the visitors sat would remind you a bit of a hospital waiting room, only bigger. It faced a glassed-in guard station where uniformed men were looking at television monitors and working switches that opened various doors. They had themselves a system. You reported to the window and then took a seat until your name was called over an intercom. When called, you had to go over and sign in and empty your pockets and allow your belongings to be searched by a guard. After that you had to walk through a metal detector, to make sure you weren't smuggling in a hacksaw or a gun, which, I'd heard, had actually happened on one occasion. Then, along with eight or ten other souls, you were herded like cattle into a cramped room no bigger than a large closet. I hated that part the most, as I have never been fond of tight places. I get claustrophobic. None too soon a buzzer would go off and a door opposite finally clanged open, and you were allowed to pass on down a corridor to another room where visitors met with their loved ones. All the while that smell kept getting worse, making you sick to your stomach.

But first, you had to take a seat and wait your turn. Sometimes you waited an hour, or even two, depending on how crowded it was and what sort of mood the guards happened to be in. I'd been coming here for well over a year, and I recognized a few of the Tuesday crowd. There was the heavyset Hispanic woman, Mrs. Ortiz; the gray-bearded black gentleman named Mr. Murphy, who came to see his grandson; the young, pregnant black girl, who sat with her eyes closed and listened to something on her headphones; and the others, mostly black or Hispanic, and mostly women, too, I noticed, some hardly more than girls, who passed the time watching the television in the corner as their kids ran about the room, some of the wee little ones being suckled at a mother's breast or sprawled asleep in a chair. It broke your heart to see all the children there. It wasn't a place for children.

One child I sometimes saw made me think of my Eion. Don't ask me why. He didn't look a thing like him, my son having been quite fair with strawberry-blond hair like his father's. While this little fellow had bronze skin and curly dark hair, eyes black as pitch. Perhaps it was a certain boldness in his gaze. Spunk, you could call it. This boy would come right up and stare at you the way my son used to, not shy in the least.

"What's your name?" he'd asked me one time.

"Maggie Quinn," I'd replied. "And yours?"

"Jesus Alvarez," he'd declared.

"Well, what do you know about that!" From my coat pocket I'd taken out the rosary beads with the small crucifix. I pointed at the tiny Jesus and said, "Jesus," pronouncing it as he had with an *h*. He nodded, smiling proudly.

"And how old are you, Jesus Alvarez?"

"I'm gonna be five," he said, holding up five fingers.

"Aren't we the big boy."

"How old are you?"

I laughed. "It's not polite to ask a woman of my years her age."

I like kids. Always have. If things had worked out different, I'd probably have had half a dozen. I'd be big as a house and no doubt right then I'd be sitting with Annie Harrigan in her kitchen, sipping tea and munching on scones, and going on about our kids. But things work out the way they do and that's that. When I visited the prison, I would try to remember to bring some sweets in my pocketbook so I'd have something to give Jesus. He liked Skittles especially. I looked around for him today, but the room was crowded and I couldn't make him out.

There was no place to sit so I was going to grab a section of wall to lean against when I happened to catch Mr. Murphy waving a hand at me.

"Saved you a seat, Miz Quinn," he said to me. "Figured you'd be here. Don't you look nice, all dressed up."

"Just some old things," I said. "But thank you all the same."

We'd chatted on occasion, this Mr. Murphy and myself. A decent sort. He must've come right from work, as he always wore the same soiled blue uniform with his name stitched over the breast pocket. He often shared his newspaper with me. Once when he had a button come off his shirtsleeve, I reached in my pocketbook and took out a needle and thread, which I always keep handy, and sewed it on for him in no time. He was so grateful.

"Sure is a cold one out there," he said.

"Aye, that it is, Mr. Murphy," I replied. "Thought as we might get a bit of snow on the way down."

"It feels like snow," he said. "Do you get much snow where you're from?"

"Indeed, we do. I'm way up north. Near the Vermont line."

"No, I meant where you come from. You got an accent."

"*Och*," I said, sometimes forgetting I had one. "I'm from Ireland originally. County Galway. No, we don't get much in the way of snow."

"With a name like Murphy, I must be Irish, too," he said with a wink.

"I've heard of black Irish before, Mr. Murphy, but you certainly take the cake," I joked right back. We both of us chuckled at that. "Well, they say everybody's got a wee bit of the Irish in 'em around St. Paddy's Day."

Which, as it happened, was only a week away. In years past I'd have been home getting things ready—cooking up a storm, making potato and leek soup, colcannon, corned beef and cabbage, cupcakes with green frosting, hanging shamrocks and leprechauns about the rectory, and cleaning like a house afire. Father used to have a little shindig, invite some people from the parish, some old friends of his. Afterward, he would play the piano and we'd sing all the old ballads. He'd insist I do "She Lived Beside the Anner" or "The Rose of Tralee." Used to say it wasn't St. Paddy's Day unless Margaret sang something, and I'd turn five shades of red because the truth is I can't carry a tune to save my life. Still and all, I'd give it a go. Somebody would say we'd missed our calling, should've gone into show business. Jack Devlin on piano and Maggie Quinn on vocals, they'd joke. We had some times, all right.

"What'd you bake your father today?" Mr. Murphy asked, glancing down at my bag.

"A zucchini bread. Can I interest you in a piece, Mr. Murphy?"

"No, thanks. You keep it for him."

I guess I ought to explain. On some previous visit to the prison, when Mr. Murphy asked me who I was seeing, I must've replied with "father" or perhaps "the father," something to that effect. I surely didn't say "*my* father," which would have been a boldface lie seeing as my own da passed on when I was ten. But it was also true, I must confess, that I didn't correct what I suspected—and perhaps secretly hoped—he'd think: that the *father* meant *my* father, not a priest. I told myself it was just to protect Father Jack. After all, hadn't Mr. Leo, his attorney, had him transferred down here for his own protection, where fewer people might know him and have a grudge against him? Threats had been made against his life, and they did keep him mostly isolated from the other prisoners for his own safety. The fewer knew he was here the better, was my thinking. So that part was true enough. But not the whole of it. You see, my letting Mr. Murphy think it was my father had less to do with Father Jack's welfare and more perhaps to do with my own. I figured Mr. Murphy might have seen the "Father Devlin" case in the news, and if he knew why I was there, it would have changed things, made it awkward between us, as it often did when people found out. Take, for instance, Mrs. Griffiths. She was the woman I started going to over in Montville to have my hair done. We were jabbering away once, friendly as could be, and I let slip something about Father Jack. Well, you should've seen the look on her face. Like I'd spit on her mother's grave or something. So the fact of the matter is I didn't go out of my way to let it be known who I was seeing.

The guards knew, of course. There was no fooling them. I could see it in the way they looked at me. I'd catch them trading glances or whispering on the sly. "See her," I could picture them saying to one another. "That one's here for the priest." Or, "She's the one testified for him." Yet for all I cared, the whole stinking lot of them could go jump in the lake. They were a mean, low-down class of men, rude and disrespectful, seeming to take pleasure in the suffering not only of their charges but of those of us who came to see them. They would stare down their noses at us and give us dirty looks and take their sweet-arse time letting us in. Like *we'd* committed a crime. Some weren't half bad though. One fellow named Officer Kozlowski, during Lent, handed me some palm leaves for Father's cell. "Give these to Father," he said.

"He's a lucky man got you for a daughter," Mr. Murphy continued. "What pod's he in? Maybe he knows my Junior."

Junior was his grandson, "in for," in the parlance of the waiting room, stealing cars. When the subject once came up I told Mr. Murphy that "father" was in for fraud. What was I supposed to say?

"Pod three," I replied. Father lived in a pod now. It made me think of a pea pod, one that might split open and out Father would fall to freedom. His was near the prison chapel where he assisted the chaplain. He wasn't permitted to say Mass, of course, could only help him by sweeping and cleaning up, ironically what Stanley Derenzy used to do for Father. Not wanting to pursue this line of conversation, I said, "Would you excuse me. I have to use the ladies' room."

"I'll watch your things," he said. "If they call your name, I'll tell 'em where you're at so you don't lose your place."

The bathroom was usually filled with chatty young girls primping in front of the mirrors, like they were going on a date instead of visiting criminals. But this day, thankfully, I had the room to myself.

I looked in the mirror. I removed my bandanna and ran a brush through my short, copper-colored hair. It used to be a fiery red, and I let it grow halfway down my back, but now it's the dull color of an old penny that has passed through many hands. I put some fresh lipstick on, dabbed a bit of Estée Lauder behind my ears, hoping to get the best of that prison stink. Then I got out my compact and had a go at covering the damage the years had done. All things considered, I'm still not a bad-looking woman, for all the good that fact has done me in my life. Though there's no mistaking it's the face of someone overly fond of her drink, mine has good lines, strong bones, which as anybody knows will serve you over the long haul. I got my looks from my mum, a handsome woman despite her not being well.

This day I had on my red pantsuit. My "courtroom threads," I called them, for it's what I wore when I took the witness stand. While neither loud nor gaudy, the pantsuit nonetheless showed my figure to advantage, still a size seven. And instead of the usual sneakers I wear when cleaning house, I had on the tight-fitting, uncomfortable dress shoes I wore to church, when I used to go, that is. It wasn't just vanity, though I suppose I'm as vain as the next person. You see, I always took great pains to look my best for Father. Out of respect naturally, but more out of gratitude for all he done for me. If it wasn't for him, I'd probably have ended up in the gutter somewhere. I never let Father see me without makeup or in curlers, even if it was just the two of us playing Scrabble of an evening. Besides, there was no telling when someone would come to the door and how would it look if I answered it in my nightgown? Or if I went into town in the clothes I'd scrubbed the floor in? *Would you look at Ma Quinn*, they'd say, *the drunken souse herself. And isn't it downright indecent, Father allowing a woman of her sort to live under the same roof.* For I knew what they whispered about me behind my back: drunkard, whore, crazy as a bedbug. It wasn't any secret about my past. No sir, no secrets in a loose-lipped, backbiting town like The Falls. When it'd just been myself to think about, why, I would thumb my nose at the lot of 'em, tell every last holier-than-thou son of a bitch to go blow it out their arses. Indeed, I would. Yet when I come to work for Father, I had to consider how my behavior would reflect on him. God bless the man, he'd stuck his neck out for me plenty enough times, so I tried to be careful, not wanting to cast him in a bad light. I don't want to give the impression I'd turned into a saint, far from it. But I tried my best to walk the straight and narrow, so Father would be proud of me.

· · ·

When I first laid eyes on him each visit, I had this little trick I played. I would give the inside of my cheek a good, hard bite. To fight back the urge to cry, you see. I'm not by nature a whiny, weak-willed sort of person, but it near broke my heart to see him like that. I mean I wanted to visit him, I dearly missed him from one meeting to the next. Yet at the same time, it was so painful to see him under such circumstances. There was no other way around it: he looked awful. Pale as death, he was, his hair turning ghostly white. And those once-lively, pale blue eyes of his haunted now. God strike me if the poor man hadn't aged a dozen years in the past two. The orange prison jumpsuit hung on him like a sack, and the bones in his cheeks stood out against the sallow skin of his face. His countenance was haggard and drawn. This visit he hadn't shaved for several days, the stubble coming in all white. He was usually clean-shaven for me. Before all this, he'd always been so fastidious, so careful about his person. He used to cut such a fine figure standing up there at the altar in his vestments, with that regal bearing he had. Now he reminded me of one of those bums he himself was always befriending, the ones who'd come to the back door of the rectory looking for a handout, saying Father had sent them.

We hugged briefly. Then, as the visitors' room was crowded, we made our way over to a table near where the guards sat, an unpopular spot for obvious reasons. I could sense Father Jack was in low spirits this day. Normally he seemed to welcome the company and made an effort at seeming animated, if only for my benefit. "Hello, Margaret," he'd say, his blue eyes turning lively, his smile temporarily sloughing off the dark shadows of his face. He'd eagerly inquire about parish news, how the Christmas pageant was coming, how his replacement, Father Martin, was doing, not in the least resentful, as most would surely have been in his shoes. He maintained at least a show of interest in things out in the world. And like a sighted person reading to a blind man, I'd become his eyes on that world. Yet this day, he just sat across the table from me, staring vacantly off into space the way he was apt to when he had something on his mind. I thought perhaps they'd changed his medication, as they had a few times before. Some tended to make him glassy-eyed and slow of speech, while others made him jumpy. Or maybe his heart was acting up again. With all the stress, he'd already had one heart attack a few months after coming here. It was a minor one, the doctors said. Still, it took its toll. He came out of the hospital sickly-looking and stooped over, and though it had happened nearly a year before, he'd never quite recovered. Yet I felt it was something else, not so much of the body as it was of the spirit.

"Here's the books you wanted, Father," I said. "And look, I brought your favorite. Zucchini bread."

I opened the aluminum foil I'd wrapped the bread in and slid it across the table. I could feel the guard, a burly, no-necked fellow with a shaved head, watching us like a hawk. Without tasting a piece, Father wrapped the bread up carefully and shoved it back into the bag.

"Thanks," he said. "Someone will eat it."

"But I made it for you, Father. Try a piece, why don't you?"

"I'm not hungry right now, Margaret." He called me that, never Maggie, as some did, or Ma Quinn as most in town knew me as. It was always Margaret. "Maybe later."

Occasionally he nodded or smiled at something I said, but I could tell his thoughts weren't in the room with us. It was the way he used to get after visiting a sick bed, off in his own world someplace. I considered his silence might've had to do with some bad news from Mr. Leo. Maybe something about the Blake investigation, perhaps to do with the blood business, a subject which worried Mr. Leo no end. Yet Father and myself hardly ever spoke about his case. Oh, in passing he might say Mr. Leo had just stopped by to see him. He might even allude to some new legal strategy his lawyer had begun, a new motion or appeal or whatnot. And once, by accident, I recall letting drop Justin's name. We were talking, about the old days and this and that, and the boy's name just sort of slipped out before I knew what I'd done. But normally we avoided the subject altogether. I didn't want to pry into what I considered his private affairs. Even if I was curious—and who wouldn't be?—I felt it wasn't my place. If he wanted to tell me, I figured he would. Looking back, even I think it odd that we didn't bring it up more. But like they say, hindsight is twenty-twenty, and I thought it best our visits ran smoothly. I wanted only to lift his spirits.

I jabbered on. For all his reading and intelligence, Father wasn't much for small talk, so even on his good days it would often fall to me to keep the conversation from lagging. I went on about how we might need a new boiler in the rectory. And how the religious supply company Father Martin had switched to to save money had once again sent the wrong candles. How the new choir director was getting on as well as the CYO basketball team Father used to coach. I talked for nearly the entire hour, which is all they allowed us. You see, during those visits, I tried to keep him connected, in touch with the outside world, so when he *was* finally freed and could begin his life anew, it wouldn't come as such a shock to his system. That too was a subject I came to view as being off-limits, dangerous, uncertain: the Future. His. Mine. Anything beyond the here and now, beyond the moments we shared during those Tuesday visits, was something I avoided.

No one from the diocesan office came to see him. No one visited him from town, not even his one-time pal Pete Beaupre. As soon as the going got rough, the lot of 'em had cut and run on him. He had no family to speak of. An only child, he'd lost his father when he was a boy, and his mother, who he'd been devoted to, had passed away some years before, a blessing in disguise that the poor woman didn't live to see her child reduced to this. He had some cousins in the Boston area, but Father told me they'd never been close, and not a one of them came to visit. Not counting the occasional reporter sniffing around for a story, his only visitors were Leo Manzetti, his attorney, and Father Duncan, who he'd gone to seminary with. And of course me.

Before it was time to go, I asked him something I had once or twice before. "You think you might hear my confession today, Father?"

"You know I'd like to, Margaret. But it wouldn't mean anything."

"You're wrong, Father. It would. Would mean an awful lot to me."

"Ask Father Martin."

"Him! Why, I wouldn't confess to passing wind to that one."

"Or Father Duncan. Go see him. You like him."

I hadn't been to confession in nearly two years. Not since Father's troubles began. I felt my sins piling up on me, weighing on me like the lead gown at the dentist's office. I'd asked Father before if he'd hear my confession, there in the prison. He said he couldn't. Said he no longer had the authority.

"Some other time maybe?" I asked.

He didn't say anything.

When it was time to leave, he gave me an awkward hug, his hands light as feathers on my back. I held onto him, pressing his bony ribs against me, not wanting to let go. I buried my face in his neck. That prison odor was on him, in his clothes. But beneath that, I could still smell Father, *his* odor: a sweet-sour fragrance of aftershave and sweat and something else, too, a man's smell, I guess you'd call it. What his clothes used to smell like when I put them in the washing machine. *Father's smell.* When we finally separated, he reached out and lightly brushed my face with the back of his knuckles. His fingers were cool against my skin and I shivered, felt goose bumps sprout on the backs of my arms.

"My dear, sweet Margaret," he said. "What would I ever do without you?"

"Oh, Father," I replied, biting my cheek again, feeling the pressure at the corners of my eyes. Don't you dare go blubbing on him, Maggie Quinn. The poor man's got enough on his mind.

"I want to thank you," he said.

"What for?" I asked. "Just brought you a few things."

"Not that. I mean for always being there. For your faith in me."

"*Pssh*. Get out with you now."

"No, it's true. How could I have gotten along without you all these years? You've always been a blessing to me."

"Sweet Jesus! Some blessing I been," I said, forcing a laugh.

"I told you, Margaret, that wasn't your fault."

"Oh no? You might not even be here if I hadn't made such a bloody mess of things in court. We both of us know that, Father."

"Forget about it. That's all in the past. You always believed in me. *Always*. No matter what happens, I just wanted you to know that."

No matter what happens, I thought, my guilt fluttering wildly in my chest like a bird with a broken wing. Though he wasn't one to complain, had the fortitude of a Job, Father sometimes worried me. After all, they'd stripped him of everything. Being a priest, helping people, relieving the suffering of others—that had been his life. *Who he was.* Sometimes, like today, he had the appearance of a man who'd traveled as far as he could, someone who couldn't take another step.

"Let's have none of that talk, Father," I said. I reminded him how hard Mr. Leo was working on his behalf. "What's that line you said once in a sermon. Let's see if I can get it right: 'Stand therefore, having your loins girt about with truth, and having on the breastplate of righteousness.' Something like that."

"Very good," he said, smiling. "Ephesians."

"That's what you need to do. Put on a breastplate of righteousness. Tell all them birds to go blow it out their arses—excuse my language, Father. Let 'em think what they will. Long's *we* know the truth, right?"

His eyes held me for a moment, probing me, then he looked off toward the windows, covered with wire mesh like the cage of a bird.

"Is everything all right?" I asked. "You seem not yourself today."

"Everything's just fine," he replied, but without the faintest trace of sarcasm. Father had a sarcastic streak, all right. An acid tongue that could cut to the quick when he wanted. But now he just seemed sort of resigned to whatever would happen next. In some ways, he looked as if the fight had gone out of him.

"I know it's hard, Father. But you mustn't get discouraged," I said, walking toward the door arm in arm with him. I could feel the bone beneath the fabric of his prison uniform. "Just be patient a bit more. Things'll work out. You'll see."

He nodded for my benefit. "Thanks for coming, Margaret."

"And try to eat more. You're too thin, Father. I'll bring you some oatmeal cookies next week, all right?"

He smiled. I turned and left the room. Yet, like Lot's wife, I couldn't help but glance back. There he was, walking away down the hall, toward his pod, carrying the bag of things I'd brought. His shoulders slumped, shuffling along like a weary old man. I called out to him "Father," then louder, "*Father Jack*!" But he mustn't have heard me for he just kept on walking, through the double set of doors, and was gone.

2

On the long ride back to Hebron Falls, I would always feel a bit depressed and lonely. I would feel as if I'd left a piece of me back at the prison. And this day was even worse. I couldn't shake that last image of Father, stooped over, shuffling along. It fairly haunted me. I thought how quiet he'd been, how broken in spirit he'd seemed. I wondered how much more he could endure, how much more he'd *have* to endure before it was all said and done. And then I fell to thinking how things could get a good deal *worse* before they got any better. My mind kept mulling things over, kept prying and prodding, like a willful tongue that wouldn't leave a toothache alone until it was throbbing to beat the band. I don't know why, but I had this terrible feeling that more bad news was bearing down on us. As I drove along everything got so jumbled up in my mind that my hands took to shaking, the way they're apt to when I get myself all worked up. Then the tears started; this time I couldn't stop them. They just poured out of me like a pipe inside me had burst. I couldn't hardly see to drive. I finally had to pull over on the side of the highway.

From the glove compartment I withdrew my trusty old friend, Mr. Boston, a half-pint I kept for just such emergencies. I'd been pretty good lately, at least since Father Martin said he'd had a complaint from someone who smelled booze on my breath when I was serving at a Catholic Women's Club luncheon. But my hands were atrembling like crazy and I couldn't stop crying, and I needed a wee bit in the worst way. There was only a couple of fingers' worth of ginger brandy left, and I polished it off in one draft. It did little to settle the raging in my head, though. My mind kept galloping on, which isn't always the best thing when you're in a black mood to start with. For as my mum used to say, if you dwell on your problems too much, they're likely to get worse, and there's wisdom in that for sure. I've always had this tendency, you see, to fall prey to these black moods, and that's when I hit the drink, thinking it'll help. But you might as well try to put out a fire with gasoline as do that.

I wondered if Mr. Leo *had* brought him some bad news. Maybe something about the Blake investigation, which was in the papers again. It had been quiet for a while, and now it was back. Perhaps there'd been a decision about the blood business. Aye, maybe it had to do with that. For the longest time, you see, Adams County D.A. Shelly Lassiter had been out for Father's blood. I mean this quite literally, as literally as a good Catholic believes the wine is changed into our Lord's blood during Holy Communion. Lassiter was a vindictive woman, one of those bony-arsed, hard-as-nails sorts who tries to out-man a man. She wanted to force Father to give them a blood sample. She'd been fighting Mr. Leo over this business since right after the trial. Wouldn't let it go, that woman. Kept hounding Father. Wasn't enough that he was in jail. That she'd ruined his life. No sir. Not for that woman. Mr. Leo said it was on account of her having big political ambitions, as he put it, and so she wanted to make a name for herself at Father's expense.

But Father, I kept having to tell myself, was in good hands. Mr. Leo knew what he was doing. And he was a battler, too. He wouldn't give up. He said over his dead body he'd let the other side have any blood samples. He said it was against Father's rights, that he'd fight the bastards all the way to the Supreme Court if necessary. Though quite honestly I sometimes wondered why we didn't just give them their blood and be done with it. Yet what did I know about such complicated matters? The moves by the D.A., the countermoves by Mr. Leo. The hearings and conferences, the motions and appeals. The decisions by this or that higher court. Why, the law was a complete and utter mystery to me, a puzzle with a thousand pieces. But if anyone knew how to fit those pieces together, that'd be Mr. Leo. The law wasn't just his job, it was, like Father Jack's own vocation, his passion, his calling, his very soul. An atheist, as he himself had once told me, he nonetheless had his faith and that was the law. He believed in it, in its holy intricacies, its formal rituals. He was a priest of the law, you might say. He could no more have been something other than a lawyer than Father Jack anything but a priest. I think that's why he fought so hard on Father's behalf. Both of them were so dedicated, so committed to what they believed in. So pigheaded, too. In most ways the two men—the tall, refined, lace-curtain-Irish priest from Boston and the short, street-tough, foulmouthed, Italian-atheist-lawyer from Providence—were about as different as day and night. Yet both lived their work, ate and breathed and slept their work. In fact, in some strange way I think Mr. Leo would have made a good priest, except for the part about not believing in God anymore.

Yes, Father was in good hands, I reassured myself. The best. If anyone could help him it'd be Mr. Leo. Sitting there crying like a damn fool wasn't going to help anybody at all, Maggie Quinn. So I wiped my eyes, gave the empty Mr. Boston the heave-ho out the window and got back on the highway.

• • •

I got off at the Montville exit—GATEWAY TO THE BERKSHIRES, the sign says, like it was the pearly gates and you were entering heaven itself. I drove west on Route 38, past the Kmart and the mall and the new Best Western, and started climbing up into the scruffy-looking, winter-scarred hills. Past the closed-for-the season tourist places and souvenir shops, past the naked apple orchards and the run-down farms and out-of-business cider mills. As I came down Mountain Road, the sky, a dingy gray, was sort of draped over Hebron Falls, like an old sheet over even older furniture. That winter, Father's second in jail, had been a bad one. Storm after storm had swept in from upstate New York, leaving everyone short-tempered as cats in heat, and several times making the drive down to Springfield impossible. And as the snow grudgingly gave up its hold, everything in town was left with this salt-dulled, shabby look about it—the mailboxes and road signs, the bushes and yards, the cars and houses and store-fronts, the war memorial on the village green and the grandstand in the park. Even the people walking along Main Street seemed grubby-

looking, hunkered down against the March wind. I was struck by
how grim and slovenly the whole place looked, how much it could
use a good scrubbing, which, when you keep a house for a living, is
the way you view things: clean or in need of cleaning, in order or
messy.

Let me tell you a thing or two about Hebron Falls—or just The
Falls, as most refer to it. The sort of place it is, the class of people we
have. It's way out in the boondocks, a small western Massachusetts
town that the Chamber of Commerce likes to paint in its brochures as
being "nestled" in the mountains—like it was an Easter egg sitting in
that fake green straw. And it certainly can be pretty up here, especially
in the fall, my favorite season, when the leaves turn and the smell of
apple orchards flavors the air. The Falls sits in a deep valley formed by
the Mashabaug River, with mountains completely ringing it like a pair
of cupped hands. But other times—winter, for instance, or mud season—it's not so pretty. In point of fact it's one of those dreary old
New England mill towns that's seen better days, especially with the
hanger factory having closed down a few years back and putting people out of work. There's a main drag with some stores and shops, the
CVS, Hodel's Market, Pelkey's Hardware, the weekly newspaper, a
couple of restaurants and a half-dozen gin mills, which do a thriving
business despite the unemployment. There's five churches, count 'em:
a Methodist, a Baptist, a Congregational, some ugly boxy affair out
on Route 38 where some of those TORCH members go. And of
course St. Luke's, the Catholic Church just across the river, where
Main runs into West Street.

The Falls is the sort of small place where, like it or not, everybody knows you, where if you had the runs on Monday, half the
town would know by Tuesday, and the other half would read about
it in the *Falls Sentinel* by Thursday. Before all this business with Father, though, it had felt like home. *My* home. I'd made myself a life
here. I had my work and my routines, my amusements. Mostly it was
keeping Father's house running smoothly: laundry on Wednesdays,
grocery shopping and my big baking on Thursdays, the floors and
such on Fridays. Church and then some people in on Sunday. Beyond
that I worked on the Christmas bazaar committee. Brought meals to
some of the old folks at the nursing home. Played rummy with a cou-

ple of the girls on Tuesday night. Worked in my garden or went for a walk after supper. Occasionally met my friend Cindy O'Connell at the Friendly's. Once or twice a week a quiet dinner for Father and me. If I thought about it at all, I guess I pictured staying here the rest of my days—or at least I didn't picture going anywhere else. It wasn't that The Falls had accepted me with open arms when I first come to work for Father. No sir, they surely did not and that's a fact. Like any small town, they don't take kindly to outsiders, and certainly not to outsiders with a past. Some put up with me only because of Father. Yet after a while, most grew to accept me, the way you might an unseemly wart on somebody's nose. You get so you avert your eyes. When I'd walk down Main with my shopping cart, they'd say, "Terrible weather we're having, eh, Ma." Or at the church bake sale someone might ask, "That was a lovely pie, Maggie. Could I get your recipe?" Things like that. Things that made you feel welcome. If you'd asked me before all this, I would have told you that despite its faults The Falls was a friendly enough sort of place. A nice, quiet kind of town. The people decent, mostly anyway. Be there if you ever needed them.

It's not the good times that tell you most about a person, or a town. It's the bad. Since all this, the blinders have been removed from my eyes. I've come to see this crummy little town for what it is. Not what folks would have you believe about themselves, but what they really are like. In their heart of hearts. I've come to see how vengeful and merciless and cruel they can be, especially when they decide to turn against you. I've learned what spineless hypocrites most people are, though I suppose it's not any worse here than anywhere else. But the thing about The Falls, you see, it has this grand, *la-de-dah*, our-shite-doesn't-stink opinion of itself. It likes to think it's real small-town, apple-pie, all's-right-with-the-world America, with its village green and its church suppers, its apple festival and its picture-postcard autumns. Likes to pretend it doesn't have its dirty laundry, its skeletons tucked neatly away in the closet. Likes to see itself as the kind of place the reporters—during Father's trial anyway—called "a sleepy little town nestled in the hills," or "a peaceful tight-knit community that stuck by its own." Stuck by it own, my arse! But to hear them tell it, everything was just fine and dandy, and

along comes this terrible ogre, Father Devlin. He had to go and
blacken the town's good name, so all you had to do was say Hebron
Falls to anybody, and right away they'd give you a funny look, because they knew you were from the town that Father Devlin came
from.

What about the rest of them, I want to say. Old Doc Kennedy,
for instance. A big muckety-muck, on the school committee and the
parish board. But everybody knows the doctor is nothing but a
drunk who nearly killed a woman because he gave her the wrong
drug when he was three sheets to the wind. Or what about Artie
LeBlanc, the former first selectman and lay deacon for St. Luke's? It
was hush-hush around town, but word was he'd got his stepdaugh-
ter in a family way and they'd had to send her to this home for girls.
Or Lucille Feola, who taught CCD classes and led a prayer group,
and who worked at the state home for the retarded down in
Holyoke. Everybody thought she was so nice and sweet. Turns out
the woman embezzled nearly a half million dollars, money that was
supposed to go for food and clothes for those people. Or the
Bassinger girl, daughter of Mel Bassinger, publisher of the town's
newspaper. She'd been arrested for selling crack in the high school,
and yet you never saw a word about it in the paper. Not one word.
Or John Granucci, who taught Bible study at St. Luke's. The fellow
had been caught in a motel room off the highway diddling some fifteen-year-old kid. I could go on, but you get the point. Come Sunday
though, you'd see these same upstanding citizens in church, looking
holier-than-thou, going up and receiving communion from Father's
hand. And yet when it came to him, how quick they were to believe
the worst, turn their backs on him and forget all he'd done for this
town and this parish. How quick indeed.

They won't tell you about him, but I will—I'll tell you about the
Father Jack I knew. He was the most selfless, hardworking, dedicated
man I ever saw. Priest or otherwise. He was always doing for people,
always on the go trying to help someone, support a cause, right an
injustice. He had this great abundance of energy. It was his idea to
set up a day-care center in the church community room for unwed
mothers so they could get a job, go back to school. He visited old
people in nursing homes. He made sick calls. He drove dirt roads

ten, fifteen miles up into the mountains to listen to bedside confessions. He helped get meals delivered to the elderly. He spent one day a week at a soup kitchen over in Montville. He started the shelter for runaway kids, and him and Rudy Lessard used to coach a CYO basketball team.

Kids especially liked him, I don't mind saying that even now. He understood them, could talk to them in their own language. He was always willing to listen, to help them if they had a problem. And when they got in trouble at school or with the law, he'd be there to go to bat for them. Every year he brought some of them, altar servers and CYO kids or those from the teen shelter, up to Fenway to see a baseball game or to his summer place up in New Hampshire fishing. He hired them to mow the rectory's lawn or to rake leaves. When they were in their teens, he helped them find jobs or he wrote letters of recommendation to get them into college, and later he married them or baptized their kids. When a lad needed a baseball glove or a pair of basketball shoes and there was no money at home, it was Father found it for him, often dipping into his own pocket. They would stop by the rectory. His door was always open to them. He'd have me give them milk and cookies, and then they might watch a ball game on the television in the den, hollering and whooping it up when the Red Sox scored. Or play a game of basketball or football out behind the rectory. I could still recall the way Father used to play after Saturday Mass, sometimes still in his vestments. How many times had I given him hell for that. "Don't be getting your good things all filthy, Father," I'd yell out the back door to him, like he was just another kid. Because I was the one responsible for cleaning them, and it'd be me who they'd whisper about in church if Father's things weren't spotless, the way you might look at the mother of some ragamuffin child and lay the blame at her doorstep.

•   •   •

Anyway, I happened to be going by Pratt's Cleaners in the center of town as I was thinking back about Father playing in his vestments, and that's when a bell went off in my mind. I suddenly remembered that Father Martin had left me a note on the kitchen table that very morning.

He wanted me to pick up his vestments at the cleaners. I'd nearly forgotten. So I pulled over and parked the car on Main. I hadn't been to Pratt's for a while. Those items of Father Martin's I couldn't do myself I'd been bringing over to a laundry in Montville. Though it was a half hour out of my way, I'd just as soon drive the extra distance, as there was little chance of my bumping into someone I knew over there. But Martin himself had dropped his things off at Pratt's and had said he needed them tomorrow for a Mass he was saying down in Springfield the next day. Though it was my day off, I couldn't very well say no.

I figured I'd slip in and out of the cleaners before anyone spotted me. I put on my sunglasses, which I wore whenever I had to go into town anymore. They were like a disguise. But wouldn't you know it, I couldn't find the bloody laundry ticket Martin had left me. I looked in all my pockets, went through my purse, hunted in all the compartments of my large handbag. Nothing. I wondered if I'd dropped it at the prison. Finally I decided to head in without it, figuring how hard would it be to find a priest's garments. Martin was the only priest in town.

Who should be standing at the counter, big as you please, but Mrs. Abruzzi. Just my luck, I thought. I used to clean house for the woman way back, before I worked for the parish. She lives in one of those big fancy homes up on Briarcliff Court, where the oldest and wealthiest families reside. Her husband's Joe Abruzzi, owns the only car dealership in town. He'd always been a thorn in Father Jack's side, even before all this. Now the Abruzzis were in tight as thieves with Father Martin. Abruzzi even donated a big new Buick to the parish, and Martin would invite them to the rectory for dinner. After the way they'd treated Father Jack, I had all I could do to keep a civil tongue in my head as I served them. Not only that, but on at least one occasion the Mister and I'd had words. So there was no love lost between the Abruzzis and myself.

We both of us stood there for a few minutes, neither saying a peep. Then from the back room I heard Josephine Pratt, the owner, say in a voice that suggested she thought they were alone: "Serve him right after what he did." Mrs. Abruzzi gave a phony little cough, trying to warn her they weren't alone, but Pratt kept right on. "He may have fooled everybody else but not me. I never liked the man." After a moment, she came out from behind a heavy gold curtain that served to divide the front and back rooms. She had a garment bag in her arms and she started to say, "I'd like to see them—" but froze when she saw me standing there. Josephine Pratt was a large, horsy woman with large, horsy features, a wide, loose mouth—*loose* in more ways than one, if you get my drift.

"Oh," she said, recovering. "I'll be with you in a minute."

She then went back to waiting on Mrs. Abruzzi. The two of them fell to whispering.

I didn't need two guesses to know what they'd been talking about before I came in, what most in town were talking about: Father Jack. They kept up their whispering, leaving me to stew in my own juices. Maybe they figured I'd up and leave if they just ignored me long enough. But to hell with them, I thought. I cleared my throat and said, as calm as you please, "Excuse me, ladies. I'm here for Father Martin's vestments."

That got their attention. Pratt traded can-you-believe-the-nerve-of-some-people looks with Mrs. Abruzzi before coming over to wait on me.

"All right," she snapped, "let's have your ticket."

"Seems I've misplaced it," I explained.

She *humphed* through her long nose. She was the class of woman that *humphed* a good deal, which I've noticed about women on the tall side, they tend to do that a lot. Then she pointed to a yellowed sign behind the counter: NOTICE TO PATRONS: ALL ARTICLES MUST HAVE A TICKET. THE MANAGEMENT. What management, I thought. It was just her.

"He was in just a couple days ago, Father Martin was," I explained.

"I can't keep track of everybody's items without a ticket."

"How many chasubles do you have back there?" I said, not liking her tone one little bit. But I changed tactics and added on a phony little smile, for as my mum used to say, you can get more flies with honey than you can vinegar. And I could remember Father Jack telling me not to pay any attention to what people in town said, that I should turn the other cheek. "If it's not too much trouble, Miss Pratt."

"No ticky no laundry," she replied, giving me my own phony

smile back and then some. She had a mouthful of long yellow teeth, like dried pumpkin seeds. She didn't call me by name, though I used to bring Father Jack's clothes here, his suits and vestments, things I couldn't do myself. She'd give me a ten percent discount on account it was for the church. Before all this, she'd say hello if she ran into me on the street. Since I'd testified at the trial though, she was like most—wouldn't give me spit if I was dying of thirst.

"Father Martin needs it for Mass tomorrow," I explained.

"I can't help that," she said. "Do you remember your number?"

"My number?" I said, unable to suppress a laugh.

"Can't have articles without a number."

I could feel the blood rising to my cheeks. It usually takes a good long while for my temper to percolate. Yet when it does, you'd better watch out. I'm not someone to be trifled with then.

"Miss Pratt," I began, "do you really expect people to go around with their laundry number committed to memory?"

"What we *expect*," she lectured, "is for people to remember their tickets in the first place. That's why we give them out."

"Hasn't anyone ever forgotten his ticket before?"

Bite your tongue, Maggie Quinn. You don't want to be shooting your big trap off and causing a scene. Father Martin wouldn't appreciate it if it got back to him, and Mrs. Abruzzi would surely see to that. He couldn't very well have his housekeeper getting into rows with his parishioners. That wouldn't look good, wouldn't help the church's image, no sir. But I also thought, *To hell with her. With the bloody lot of 'em.* I was tired of biting my tongue, of putting up with their snide comments. Tired of having people in town ignore me or avoid me if they saw me coming down the aisle of the grocery store. I was sick to death of turning the other cheek.

"What happens," I asked, "with people who forget their tickets?"

"What are you talking about?" she asked.

"Well, have you a room full of forgetful people's articles back there? You know, Miss Pratt, have you given any consideration to selling secondhand clothing? Just think of it now. What with all the people we have in The Falls whose memories aren't so very good. And we certainly have a lot of *that* sort, don't you think, Miss Pratt? People with short memories."

I gave her this prissy little smile, to make sure she got my drift.

She came right back though. "I thought *you're* the one with the good memory."

"How's that now?"

"Well, I just thought you're the one with the great memory." She glanced over at Mrs. Abruzzi again, winked at the woman.

"What do you mean by that?" I asked, though of course I knew exactly what she was getting at. The trial. My testifying for Father Jack. But I wanted the satisfaction of hearing her say it out loud.

Instead though, she suddenly gave in and said, "All right, what was it Father Martin brought in?"

"Just hold your horses a minute. What's this about my memory?"

"I don't have all day. Do you want your things or not?"

I had a good mind to tell her to stick Father Martin's vestments right up her big fat arse. But what was the use? So I told old horse-face Father Martin brought in an alb, a surplice, and a chasuble, all white, for Lenten season.

"Shouldn't be hard to spot," I said. "No sir. Not clothes like that."

"It might be a while," she warned sourly.

"I have all day. You take your sweet time, Miss Pratt."

She "humphed" again and ducked behind the curtain. I heard her back there shoving stuff around, the angry sound of hangers scraping a metal bar. Mrs. Abruzzi gave me a look intended to cut to the quick but I just stared right back. Let her tell Father Martin. Let him fire me for all I care. After a few minutes Pratt came out carrying a plastic garment bag with Father Martin's vestments.

"Well, what do you know?" I said. "That wasn't so hard."

"*Next* time you'll need your ticket."

"*Póg mo thón*," I said. When she raised an eyebrow, I told her it meant thanks for your kindness. What it actually means is kiss my arse.

I paid her, grabbed Father Martin's things, and headed for the door. Before I could get out though, I heard Pratt say to Mrs. Abruzzi, "I'd lock the bastard up and throw away the key."

I stopped and turned around.

"What's that now?" I asked.

"Nothing," she said.

"If it's Father Devlin you're talking about, kindly keep your bloody opinions to yourself, you horse-faced old bag you," I said, slamming the door for good measure.

Sitting in my car, I could see the two of them through the window, blathering away. I could just picture what they were saying, what people had been saying for months now: those whisperings I'd catch in the next aisle of the CVS, someone speaking in hushed tones in front of me at the checkout counter of Hodel's Market. Snippets of a conversation in the rectory as I served tea to a bunch of gossipy old hens: *I wouldn't think Father Martin would keep her on.* Or: *You can't tell me she didn't know anything. Right there in the same house with him.* Even worse than the whispers were those awkward silences that fell over people whenever I came into earshot. So you just knew.

I pulled out, drove west on Main toward the rectory—I used to call it "home" but somewhere along the line I'd stopped doing that. As I crossed Coffin's Bridge, a narrow, old, iron affair, I saw spray-painted on one of the girders, "Devlin's Guilty as Sin." Was it new? I wondered. Or hadn't I noticed it before? Maybe the same bunch that had tossed the rock through the rectory window. Instead of turning left toward the rectory, I turned right on West Street and headed for the Falls Tavern, a place I used to frequent in the "old" days. I'd not been there in months. I ordered a double whiskey from Reuben Belliveau, the owner, and took a seat over in a booth that looked out on the river. It was early yet. The place had only a few late-afternoon diehards sitting hunched over at the bar watching some talk show.

I downed my drink in two swallows and waved to Reuben for another. He brought a bottle over and another glass.

"Mind some company, Maggie?" he said. "Haven't seen you around in a while."

"No," I said. "I ain't been getting out much."

"How have you been?"

"Lousy."

Reuben was a decent sort. More than once when I hadn't the price of a drink, he'd let me put it on my tab. We went way back. Before I came to work for Father Jack, we'd been lovers for a while and had remained friends. Every now and then I'd drop in, have a Coke if I was on the wagon, a drink if I wasn't, and we'd talk. He was a good listener.

"What's the matter?" he asked.

"This bloody effing town is what's the matter," I said.

"Why?"

"The way they've treated that poor man," I replied. I gulped my drink, felt my throat burn as the whiskey went crashing down toward my stomach. "They're such stinkin' hypocrites, the lot of 'em."

"Don't let them get to you."

"After all he did for this place, it's a crying shame."

"Things'll work out," he said. It made me think of what I'd told Father earlier. How hollow it rang now. Something you'd tell a frightened child to help him sleep.

Reuben was one of the handful of people I could talk to about Father Jack, one of the few who hadn't already made up his mind. Not that he was on his side, but just that he hadn't already got the rope and picked out a tree.

"I feel so helpless," I said. "Not knowing what's going to happen. I just wish there was something I could do for him."

"You've done more than your share, Maggie. Let it rest."

"Easier said than done. I'm all he has. Me and Manzetti. He got railroaded the first time and if they have their way they'll do it again."

"He had a fair trial."

"Fair trial, my arse! You know as well as I do they'd all made up their minds long before he walked into that courtroom."

"Maybe. You want some advice? Stay out of it this time."

"How am I supposed to do that?"

"All's I'm saying is let whatever's going to happen happen."

"Abandon Father Jack!" I cried, louder than I should have. One or two at the bar looked away from the television and over at us. In a whisper I hissed, "Is that what you'd have me do? He had nothing to do with that boy's death, I tell you. *Nothing*. And yet the bloody bastards are trying to pin that on him, too."

Reuben reached across the table and patted my hand.

"Easy," he said. "I'm on your side. It's just that people come in and I hear things. Crazy things. How they'd like to get their hands on him. It's mostly just talk. Still, somebody gets boozed up you never know what they'll do."

"You think I'm afraid. They're all a bunch of gutless cowards."

"Just be careful, Maggie. I know you. Don't go looking for trouble."

"I didn't go looking for trouble last time. It found me. After all that man has done for me I can't just turn my back and walk away."

"No one's asking you to. But remember, however this turns out you still have to live here."

"Maybe," I said. I finished my drink. I took out some money and was going to pay, but Reuben said, "Put that away."

I thanked him and got up.

"You take care of yourself, Maggie," he said.

3

I guess you've a right to know something of me, how I came to know Father, how I got myself in the middle of this mess. It's a long story but I'll give you the short version.

As I said already, my own father passed on when I was just a girl. A man who liked his drink, my da was. He was three sheets to the wind one night when he stumbled out of Allen's pub in Galway and fell head-first under the wheels of a lorry. I once overheard Mrs. Coven, our neighbor, joking to the coal man, Mr. Heggarty, that my father hadn't a lick of brains to start with, so it wasn't no great loss his head getting run over like that. My da would come home buckled, in a foul temper, embittered at the world, his paycheck spent at some pub. My mum said he was nothing but a black Prod from up north, and what more could you expect from that class of man. He hated Catholics, and all the more when he was drunk. Though the man never attended any church, Protestant or otherwise, he didn't want my mother to baptize me or take me to Mass, calling it "popish foolery" and my mum's side "Catholic hoors." They'd have these terrible rows over it, but in the end she'd usually win out. How he and my mother, as Catholic as the Pope, ever got together is anybody's guess. When I'd ask her, she'd toss her head back and let out this fluttering girlish laugh. "They say love is blind, Maggie," she'd explain, at once wistful and bitter, as if that was the final word on it all.

Yet when he was sober, my da wasn't such a bad egg. It's true that kids remember what they want to, but I recall he could be gentle, soft-spoken, with a certain old-fashioned gallantry to him. A different man when he wasn't possessed by the drink. You could then understand what my mother had seen in him. For he was a good-looking fellow, raven-haired, with a lovely smile and fine white teeth all his own. When he was hung over I'd bring him some tea and milk crackers, and he'd pat my head and say, "There's my sweet girsha." That's what he called me, girsha. Sober, he could be loving and tender to my mother, attentive and caring to me. It was hard for a child to make sense of the two men he seemed to contain within himself: the one sober, the other drunk. I don't know if the drink put him in a black mood or if he drank because of it. The chicken or the egg, take your pick.

After his death, my mother, who cleaned houses during the day, took in laundry in the evening to make ends meet. She was never a well woman to begin with. She'd had scarlet fever as a girl and had a weak heart as a result of it. Nonetheless, she worked herself to the bone seeing to it I didn't go without: that I had a dress to wear for communion or a new pair of shoes, or that I had a few shillings in my pocket to take in a picture show. When I turned fourteen, I decided to quit school and help out. I couldn't see letting her work herself into an early grave on my account. Besides, I was never much on book-learning anyway. Not that I was stupid, mind you. I was clever enough. But it seemed all the things you learned in books never amounted to a good fart in a whirlwind. Books were one thing and the life you lived quite another. For when you finished a book, you were still your same old self, no better nor worse, though to my way of thinking you'd squandered a couple of hours you could've put to good use. Yet when I quit school it near broke my mum's heart entirely. You see, she'd dearly wanted me to get an education and go on to be something respectable, a schoolteacher or a nurse or even— God forbid—a nun.

Like her, I got a job cleaning houses. What the Irish are good for—breaking their backs in the service of others. I didn't really mind it though. There's something to be said about honest work and satisfaction in keeping a tidy house, even if it's not your own. By day, I scrubbed and dusted and polished the big fancy houses around Galway, and then I'd come home and make supper so my mum could sit and put up her aching feet for a bit. Sometimes she was so worn out she'd fall fast asleep. I'd do the wash and the ironing myself, and when she woke, I'd bring her a cup of tea.

"For goodness' sakes, child, why did you let me sleep?" she'd cry.

She'd had a tough go of it. As I said, she'd had had the scarlet fever, which gave to her eyes that distant, saintlike look they had. On top of that, she'd married a lazy sot of a husband who spent all his money in the pubs. She'd always had to work hard to make sure there was food on the table, clothes and shoes and whatnot for me. Before I come along, she'd had two babies, a boy and a girl, both of whom died in infancy. My father hadn't let her baptize them Catholic and that, I think, as much as their passing, was the great tragedy of her life. I remember her bringing me along when she visited their graves, her praying on her rosary and crying and asking God to watch over her little ones. She went to church every day to light a candle for their souls. I think it was through me she sought redemption. Unlike with her first two, she'd put her foot down and raised me strict Catholic. She never said as much, but I always got the feeling she thought I'd become the nun she herself had wanted to be as a young girl, before my father come along and spoilt things, as men have a habit of doing. She warned me about them. I can remember her telling me as we folded clothes together at night: "You're a lovely girl, Maggie, and there's many a fellow will be looking to undo you. Don't trust a one of 'em. Remember, the wages of sin is death." She was always going on about the wages of sin, almost like it was a full-time paying job.

I tried hard to be good, indeed I did. To be what my mother, rest her soul, wanted me to be. I loved her dearly and tried to plug the hole in her heart that the deaths of my brother and sister had ripped. I prayed for purity, longed for God's grace to enter my heart and carry me away. With my hands folded, on my knees, I pictured flying off somewhere on white wings. I asked Him to make me deserving. I went to church. I learned my catechism. I was confirmed and went to confession every week. I believed in heaven and hell and all the saints. At night I prayed for the souls of my brother and sister. I even prayed to the Blessed Virgin for my father's black Protestant soul.

But they say the acorn doesn't fall far from the tree, and that's true enough in my case. You see, I turned out more like my da than not. Despite all my attempts at goodness and purity, I was a wild, reckless youth, full of piss and vinegar. After my mum was asleep, I'd slip out of the house and meet up with Annie Harrigan, a girl from my street who was all for raising hell. We'd sneak off to the Claddagh House, a dance hall down near the Quay. I was a good dancer, light on my feet. I had no shortage of fellows, what with my long red hair, pretty complexion, green eyes. They gathered around me like bees to honey. Though I was underage—fifteen, sixteen at the time—they'd buy me a pint or let me have a drink from the bottle they carried in their pockets. While we danced, they would press close to me, and I could feel their business through their trousers. I don't mind saying I liked the sensation that I could do that to the lads. It gave me a feeling of power, and of being needed, too. The next day before heading to work I'd go and make confession to old Father Pearse, tell him how bad I'd been. Smelling of cigarette smoke and hair tonic, Father Pearse would warn me about sin and salvation. He'd have me say five Hail Marys and two Our Fathers and promise not to do it again. But that night I'd be back to my old tricks, drinking and letting the boys kiss me. There was a kind of wantonness in me I had no control over.

Then I met a lad by the name of Eion McGarrity, who played in a rock and roll band. I'd go and listen to him, and afterward he'd buy me a pint. We'd sit at a table and I'd let him run his hand up my dress. He had long curly blond hair and these frigid blue eyes you wanted to dive into, like cold water on a hot summer's day. When he touched me, I thought the skin of my thigh would blister for sure. He told me he loved me. He told me he'd never loved anyone the way he loved me. I believed him.

I forgot my mum's and the priest's warnings. What do the young know about death and sin? Death is for the old, and sin just something the priests throw at you to keep you in line. I thought myself in love, the way young empty-headed girls are apt to after a few pints and a tumble in the backseat of a Rover. When his band left for greener pastures, I found myself not only brokenhearted but with a big belly and no one to blame save myself.

My attitude was no sense crying over spilt milk. You've made your bed, Maggie Quinn, and now you have to lie in it. Whilst I didn't swallow all the business the Church dished out, I was enough of a Catholic to know that what I did couldn't be undone, despite word of women who did that sort of thing in back alleys. So at seventeen I became a mother. I named the child after his father, though I was never to hear from the lying blaggard again nor ever see a penny in support. In the eyes of the world, my son may've been born in sin, but he was the most darling child a mother could be blessed with. Had his father's blue eyes and curly blond hair, and a smile to melt the hearts of the wicked. He was my pride and joy, the love of my life. At first my mum was shamed by what I done. What would people say? What would they think? Yet when Eion came along, she quickly changed her tune. She doted on him entirely. She'd take him in the pram down our lane, showing him off to Mrs. Kavanagh and Mrs. Harrigan, proud as punch even though her grandson didn't have a father. I had him baptized and the three of us would go to church on Sunday, just like any other family. To hell with them as didn't like it. I thanked the Lord for giving me such a wondrous gift, and I put behind me my earlier, misspent days—or so I thought.

We decided that with her heart getting worse, it would be best if my mum stayed home and looked after Eion while I went to work. I'd come home at noon to nurse him. My mother would be playing with him, singing songs to him. When he was older, she taught him some words of Irish and the little charmer would say to me "*a chuisle mo chroi*," which is a term of endearment. In the evening I'd take Eion for a walk along the Quay, and on Sundays, if my mum was feeling up to it, the three of us would take the bus up to Lough Corrib for a picnic lunch. We'd have a grand time.

When my mum's heart got so bad she couldn't be chasing about after Eion, I had no choice but to bring him along with me to work. I explained to him how we needed the money and how he had to be quiet and not touch things and watch his manners around the people I was employed by. About this time I was working for a wealthy old widow lady by the name of Mrs. Burke. The missus was a snooty stick-up-your-arse old bird as ever you're likely to lay eyes on. Never smiled, expected everything just so. I had my doubts about things working out. But the funny thing was Eion had her eating out of his hand in no time. Her own children being all grown, she liked having a wee little one around again. The missus would be getting down on the floor and playing with him and buying him things like he was her own. He had the run of the place, a great big manor house out in the country. Besides me, she employed a cook and a groom for the stables and another fellow just to look after the grounds. There was fancy gardens to go walking in and fields for horseback riding and a pond out behind the carriage house with swans and a small rowboat. Whilst I went about my duties, Mrs. Burke would take Eion for walks or for a boat ride, or perhaps have him ride on the horses, though I always worried he might fall off and get hurt. But she assured me he'd be just fine. Sometimes she brought him into town with her when she did her shopping.

Eion, just shy of his fourth birthday, still took an afternoon nap. When he'd get tired, Mrs. Burke would let me put him down in one of the bedrooms. She didn't mind at all. She'd even fixed it up with toys, things she had from when hers were young. I'd put him down in there and go about my business. And when Eion would wake up he'd know to come looking for me or Mrs. Burke, whom he called "nana," which delighted her no end. The missus liked us so much, in fact, she even offered me a full-time live-in position, though I had to decline on account of my having to care for my mother.

Now Mrs. Burke had a son named Franny, and here's where things take a bad turn. About this time Franny came to stay with her. He was a loafer and a womanizer, and a great disappointment to the poor woman. She'd told me all about him. How she would give him money, and he'd go off and lose it on the ponies or on women and then crawl back with his tail between his legs looking for more. Franny wasn't bad-looking and a great one for talking up a storm. Thought himself quite a ladies' man, Franny did. He was forever coming around me and paying me compliments and offering me a drink from the silver flask he kept in his pocket. And if the missus wasn't in sight he'd try to get me to kiss him. But once burned, twice shy, was my feeling. I needed this job, being the sole support of my mum and the little one. Besides, I told him I wasn't that class of girl. His response was no sense of shutting the barn door once the horse was already out. Meaning that I'd already had a child.

One day the missus asked me to fetch some chairs in the attic of the carriage house for a lawn party she was having. She said she was going into town to do some shopping and wouldn't be back till late. I put Eion down for his nap and went upstairs in the carriage house to get the chairs. That's when Franny showed up. I could tell he'd had a few. He started in with his fancy talk, saying how pretty my hair looked and what a fine-looking woman I was and how he'd be the one to show me a good time. Like I came up the last road or something. But he was a foxy rogue, this Franny. He knew just what a girl wanted to hear. He offered me a drink, kept it up until I finally gave in. All right, just the one, I said. But then he tried to put his arms around me and kiss me. I told him that's quite enough, thank you very much. I have work to do. Yet he wasn't the sort that was used to taking no for an answer. Have another drink, why don't you? What's the harm? He told me I had the most lovely eyes. He said he knew just what a lonely woman like myself needed. And that would be you, I suppose, I told him. But he was right about one thing—I was lonely. Terribly lonely. I hadn't been with anyone since Eion Mc-Garrity. Just working and coming home and taking care of my mother and the little one. Franny said his mother wouldn't be back for a long while, and no one would be the wiser. And I thought to myself, what's so bad with having a bit of fun? I wasn't hurting anyone. Didn't I deserve it as much as the next person? I was still young. I still had a woman's needs. Was that such a crime? So I gave in and had another drink and then another after that. He started kissing me, and this time I didn't stop him. It felt good. It was like he'd stirred up some ache deep inside I didn't even know I'd had. I surrendered to it, to that ache. I'm not laying the blame on anybody's doorstep. No sir. It was my own fault. I knew what I was doing. I'm just trying to make you understand is all.

After that first time we took to meeting up in the carriage house. We'd sneak up there when the missus was away and Eion was down for his nap. We were careful. We made sure none of the other help saw us. I had Franny take precautions, too, as I couldn't very well get pregnant again. We carried on like this for some time. Franny was nice, a good lover, and fun to be with. He'd make me laugh. It wasn't love this time around. No sir. It was just need, a hunger that each of us were giving in to.

Then one afternoon Mrs. Burke was off somewhere visiting

friends and Eion was sleeping. Franny and myself were up there, do-ing what we did up there. That's when I heard the missus calling my name. Oh, my God! I thought. If she catches you, Maggie, she's sure to cashier you on the spot. And then where'd you be, no job and three mouths to feed? So I hurriedly got to my feet and straightened my blouse, put myself in order. I rushed down the stairs and out of the carriage house. My head was spinning crazily and my face was flushed with shame, and with fear, too. As I neared the stables I saw the missus walking briskly toward me. She had this pinched look on her face and I thought, Jesus, Mary and Joseph, she's on to us. Some-body saw us and must've told her. She said, "Where is he, Maggie?" I swallowed hard, thinking she meant her son. "Franny, ma'am?" "No," she said. "The lad. Where's Eion?" And I said, "Eion? Why, isn't he sleeping?" "No. He's not in the house."

The funny thing was at first I was relieved. She wasn't going to fire me, after all. So the two of us started calling Eion's name and looking for him. I thought he'd just wandered off a bit, nothing to fret over. We looked in the stables and in the gardens, searching high and low for him. After a while, he still didn't turn up, and I started to get a little worried. Any mother who's ever lost sight of her child for even a second knows what that feeling's like. It's then I saw Mr. Meakin, the man in charge of the stables, come running toward us in his manure-covered Wellies. "Come quick," he cried.

"What is it?" the missus asked.

"It's the lad, ma'am. He's fallen in the pond."

So I ran like the clappers and when I finally got there, I saw my baby floating face down in the middle of the pond, right beside the rowboat. Well, let me tell you, there's nothing in the whole wide world, probably nothing even in hell itself, to match the sight of that.

Franny, who'd followed us, jumped in, swam over, and pulled him out. But it was no use. His arms were limp and floppy, and his pretty eyes were open wide, the blue dulled to a slate gray and star-ing up at the bright sun. I could tell he was already gone. That his soul had slipped away. I didn't cry, I don't know why not.

Mrs. Burke showed up at the wake but not Franny, who, she said, had had to leave all of a sudden for England. I couldn't really blame him. It wasn't his fault. The missus tried to console me.

"These things happen, Maggie," she said. And Father Pearse called it "just a terrible accident." Which, I guess, it was. It could just as easily have happened when I was hanging out the clothes or making the beds. Or in church saying my prayers, for that matter. Yes, it could, I reasoned with myself. Except it didn't happen then. It happened when I was rolling around on the floor like a bitch in heat. My sweet child was breathing his last, perhaps calling out to me, needing me, when I was having my bit of fun, the slut that I was thinking only of herself. It seemed like a judgment from God, seemed like He was punishing me for my sins. People felt sorry for me. "Maggie Quinn's had such troubles, the poor girl," they'd say. "First her father and then that fellow running off on her. And now this." Others thought they were helping by saying, "You mustn't blame yourself, Maggie." But I did, of course. How could I not? The thing was they didn't know just how much I was to blame.

I told not a soul. Not my mother. Not Annie Harrigan. Not even Father Pearse. What was I supposed to say? How do you tell something like that? So for years I kept the secret inside, and like a hungry rat it gnawed away at my soul. There were those black years after the accident, when I thought I'd surely lose my mind out of grief and guilt. I took to the drink like a devil to sin, trying to forget. I lost my faith, or at least I tried to. I wouldn't so much as set foot in church. I cursed the Lord. I hated Him with all my heart. What sort of god would allow this to happen? If He'd wanted someone to punish why couldn't He have punished me? My mum kept giving me that the-Lord-works-in-mysterious-ways business, that it wasn't my place to question Him. She told me she knew what I was going through, having lost two babes herself. She told me to surrender myself to Him and He would help me, just as He had her. But I wouldn't surrender to Him. I was too pigheaded, I guess, too vain. It wasn't long afterward that He worked some more of His wonderful mysteries—He took my mother as well.

With her passing, there was nothing to keep me there anymore. I decided to pack up and leave Ireland altogether, a foul, stinking land that sucked the very marrow from your bones. I'd leave and never come back. I figured I'd try to make a new start for myself somewhere else. I was still young, I could begin over, I told myself. So I answered an advertisement by a Dublin firm that placed domestics in the States. That's how I wound up here, first in Springfield, Massachusetts, then later moving north to The Falls to work.

But I should've known running wouldn't do any good. Things here only went from bad to worse. I still had that rat inside, devouring me. I still had the craving for the drink, too. Oh, things might go fine for a while. I'd hold down a job. I wouldn't touch a drop for a few months, half a year sometimes. I'd start to put my life back in order. Then something, it didn't matter what, would always set me off—every drunk has her excuse. Mine might be some fellow reminding me of Franny Burke or seeing a child on the playground that put me in mind of my baby. Or that dream I'd sometimes have. In it, Eion would be in this great big house, which I took to be Mrs. Burke's, all alone and scared and calling out to me, and try as I might I could never get to him, the way it is in dreams. Even in my dreams I couldn't save my child. And when I'd wake up, that black mood would slip down over me like a hood on a condemned man and I'd fall to drinking again. I was let go from one job after another. Was down to renting a room at the Landmark Hotel down near the Mashabaug River, a flophouse for bums and drug addicts and whores. Whatever little cash I had went for the booze. And when I had no money, I'd go home with any fellow who had the price of a drink. A drunken whore is what I'd sunk to.

Finally, I reached the end of my tether. Things got so bad I couldn't see the use of waking to another day. One night I took a handful of sleeping pills and washed them down with a fifth of gin, figuring this was it. Before I passed out I remember waving my fist in the air and crying out, Take me now, you filthy bastard. That was the last thing I remembered. Somebody found me before the pills had a chance to do their work. Instead of hell, I woke in the loony bin down in Northampton, in a straitjacket and screaming my bloody head off. They'd later tell me I was carrying on about having killed some child, which to them only proved I was beyond the beyonds.

It's there I met Father Jack. He stopped by my room one day. He introduced himself only as Jack Devlin. He was dressed in trainers and a pair of sneakers. In those days he had the beard and the long hair, too. He didn't look nor act much like a priest. I hadn't been to church since coming to town, and wouldn't have recognized him anyway. He was tall and lean, with those striking blue eyes of his. Handsome in a severe sort of way. I took him for just another one of those shrinks who'd drop in to poke and prod you, trying to find out what made you tick. I was still in bad shape, my hands shaking, having those dreams. When he asked if I wanted to talk, I told him to get the fuck out and leave me be. The next time, don't you know, he showed up wearing his collar.

"You're a *priest*?" I said to him.

He nodded, smiling. "I should have warned you."

"Indeed, you should have, Father."

After that he would stop by to see how I was getting on. I had no other visitors. No one in the world who cared whether I lived or died. Why Father took an interest in me, I still don't know. Yet he was like that, always taking in strays, befriending those no one else saw fit to. He'd bring me something, a funny little card or some flowers perhaps, to try and cheer me up. He'd sit by the bed and keep me company. He didn't talk much though. Mostly he seemed content to sit there staring out the window. Truth is, Father wasn't what you'd call a good conversationalist. Oh, not that he couldn't talk on any number of subjects or speak up about something that mattered to him. It's just that he wasn't good at making up things to talk about. Silence didn't bother the man. That's the thing I would notice about him later on: how the two of us might be sitting in the den, me sewing and him reading a book, and not two words would pass between us some nights. Myself, on the other hand, I don't like silence, makes me uncomfortable. That's why we were born with a tongue in our heads. I thought, Jesus, is the man just going to sit there? So it was me who started jabbering. Soon I was telling him about growing up in Ireland, about my mother, about this and that. Running off at the mouth. The thing with Father, you see, without your even knowing it, he'd coax you out of yourself. Not with talking and asking you things and being nosy, but by holding his peace and letting you do the work. He was different from most priests I knew. He didn't lecture you, didn't tell you what to think or how to behave. How lacking you were in God's sight. No sir. What it was, I think, he was a plain ordinary man first and a priest second. When you talked to him you didn't feel like you were talking to God or some saint. It was like talking to a shy friend who just listened.

When I was feeling up to snuff, we might take a walk outside on the hospital grounds. It was spring then and we'd sit on a bench that looked out over a lovely apple orchard. We were sitting there one day when he told me his housekeeper had just given her notice. He said he didn't know how to boil water. Out of the blue he asked if I'd come to work for him.

"Me!" I said.

"You do have experience cleaning."

"I do. But I hardly think you want someone like myself, Father."

"Why not?"

"For one thing, I don't have the best of reputations. People'll talk."

"Let 'em. We can tell them to mind their own fucking business," he said with a playful wink, reminding my of how I'd cursed at him that first time. He never did give a tinker's fart what people thought. He did what he considered right and the rest be damned.

I told him I was willing to give it a go and see how things worked out. I said I couldn't promise anything. Couldn't guarantee I wouldn't be back to hitting the bottle the very next week. And I told him I wasn't much on religion and all, get that straight right away. He said that was fine by him. He said I was just to keep his house. I thought how my mum would've turned over in her grave to learn I'd ended up keeping the house of a priest.

I worked for him for eighteen years. My life didn't straighten out overnight. It took a long while, a lot of hard work, and even then there was the occasional rough patch, the times when I'd fall prey to those black moods and take to drinking again. More than once, Father had to make his own breakfast because I was hung over. And a couple of times he'd even had to pick me up at some gin mill because I was too drunk to drive. But with his help I was able to make a fresh start. No, I don't quite mean that. We none of us have the luxury to start fresh. The best we can do is just go on. Have the courage to put one foot in front of the next and keep on going. It was Father taught me that. Put one foot in front of the next. I don't know what I'd have done without him. He was always there for me, always my friend.

Was him that brought me back to church again. He didn't press me. For a priest he hardly spoke of God at all. He let me go at my own pace, let me return when I was good and ready. Ripe for the picking, he called it. When I was, I went to confession and told him about my son, about Franny, the whole sad, wretched story. Everything. It was the first time I'd told anyone. Why, it felt like a boil being lanced and all this foul, stinkin' pus come pouring out of me. I told him how I'd cursed God and turned my back on Him. Father just listened. When I was finished he didn't give me any penance. Not one Hail Mary or Our Father. Nothing. You see, he wasn't a believer in penances, which you might think kind of odd for a priest. But that was Father for you. Had his own notions about things, his own way of thinking. He said all of us did our own penance every day of our lives, in our own fashion. Said our salvation rested in our own hands, to make of it what we will, and that it was God who gave us the ability to choose His love or turn our backs on it. He told me I must have loved my child very much and I replied, indeed, I had. And then he said God knew how I felt, for hadn't He lost His only child, too?

That's how I come to know Father.

4

Father's troubles really began when those Roby brothers showed up back in town. I was taking my afternoon break, sitting in the den with my feet up and having myself a smoke. Usually I had to smoke on the sly, as Father wouldn't permit it in the house. No sir. A stickler about that, he was. Made his asthma flare up. Why, he wouldn't even bend the rules for Monsignor Payne himself when he came to dinner, and that man smoked like a chimney. If I wanted a cigarette, I'd have to go outside or sneak down into the basement, sometimes sharing one with Dina, the high school girl who worked afternoons. But Father was away and Dina had already left, so I wouldn't be breaking his rule in front of her and setting a bad example for the child. Besides, I'd give the place a good airing and no one would be the wiser.

Father had gone up to New Hampshire for a couple of days. He had a cabin where he went to relax. I'd never been there myself, but I'd seen pictures of it in Father's albums. On a lake, quiet and peaceful-looking. A place to get away. Father's job was stressful. Some people might think a priest lived on easy street. A free place to stay, meals provided, not a care in the world. But you couldn't pay me enough. He hardly had a moment's peace. There was always something, even in a small town like The Falls. Folks pestering him morning, noon and night. "Can Father come quick?" a frantic voice would plead on the phone in the middle of the night. An accident. Somebody taking a turn for the worse. Some kid high as a kite and threatening to hurt himself. Things needing the services of a priest.

It'd been a fine day all in all. It's funny how you recall the good times just before something bad comes along and changes things entirely. Like how you appreciate your health only after you've been sick. I'd finished my housework early, got the place looking sharp for Father's return, the following day. I did my big laundry, had hung the clothes out on the line. You can have your dryers. Nothing in the world the like of clean laundry snapping in the breeze. Makes a body think of the souls of children dancing in heaven. When Dina showed up at two, I went shopping in town for the big party we always had after First Communion, a little more than a week away. Then I drove to Heufelder's nursery out on Route 38 and picked up some tomato and pepper sets. I liked to garden a bit, had a little plot out behind the rectory Father let me cultivate. All winter I'd be looking through my catalogs, ordering things, getting ready for spring. I grew big beef tomatoes and wax beans, summer and butternut squash, bell peppers and eggplants and, of course, zucchini. I used to put up a lot of vegetables, make my own spaghetti sauce and succotash. While I was at the nursery I also bought some flowers, daylilies and mums, as Father preferred fresh flowers set out around the altar. He liked the church to smell like a garden, a living thing, and not some moldy old mausoleum, and I couldn't agree with him more.

While I was over to the church, I lit some candles and said prayers for my parents, for my brother and sister. And one for Eion, too. I'd not been to my son's grave in nearly twenty-five years and coming here was the next best thing. I'd sort of talk with him, ask how he was doing, if he was being a good boy. He'd have been a grown man by then, but I could still only think of him as my little boy. He seemed so real to me then, so close, as if I could reach out and brush his hair back from his face. Sometimes I'd have myself a bit of a cry but a happy sort of cry, which I always felt better for afterward.

Dina had left at five. Father Jack knew her family, the Ceruttis, and had hired the girl to come in afternoons to answer the phone, do some typing and filing, relieve me so I could go out and do my errands. She was a good kid, a little on the flighty side perhaps, but I liked having someone to gab with in that great big house. Especially if Father was out making his visits, it could get kind of lonely. Dina was full of piss and vinegar. A pretty girl with an eye for the boys—

reminded me a bit of myself when I was that age. She kind of thought of me like a big sister. Would tell me about her fellas, her problems. Sharing a cigarette in the basement, I'd giggle like a schoolgirl hearing her tales of young romance. How this boy was a good kisser, that one had himself a great arse. Another had broken her heart. Sometimes she'd get all teary-eyed on me, and I'd put my arms around her. "It's all right, love," I'd say. "There'll be others. Don't you worry none." The only thing was she was forever yakking with some boy on the telephone, which was supposed to be for parish business. I was always having to get on her about not tying up the phone with personal calls. That and remembering to write down messages while I was out.

"Oops," she'd said on her way out the door that very afternoon. "I almost forgot. Some woman called while you were gone. A reporter."

"Did you write it down?" I asked sharply.

She bit her lower lip. "Brian kept calling."

"Good heavens, child. Didn't we talk about this?"

"I'm sorry, Ma. I told him not to. But he just kept calling."

"Do you recall her name?"

"Something with an *L*, I think."

"That certainly clears things up," I said, trying to sound madder than I was. It was hard to stay mad at Dina. "This Lady L, did she say what she was wanting?"

"She wanted Father Jack. I told her he wasn't in and she just said she'd call back. If Brian calls, tell him it's over."

"Over," I said, with a smile. "Isn't that what you said last time?"

"But this time I *mean* it. Tell him I don't love him anymore."

"Tell him yourself. I'm not your social secretary."

Then she hurried out to the street where Mrs. Cerutti was waiting in the car. I think she confided in me more than she did her own mother, who she said used to hunt through her drawers looking for love letters and whatnot.

After she left, the place was stone-silent. Though I liked what I did and was never one afraid of hard work, I'd treat myself to a well-deserved late-afternoon break. Father was never a strict taskmaster, let me work at my own pace, for he knew I took care of business. I'd take off my sneakers and put my feet up. I had some problems with my feet, and being on them all day didn't help. I liked this part of the day, before having to get supper on the table but with my daily tasks all done, that feeling of accomplishment which comes after honest labor. Sometimes, I'd put a record on and listen to some Irish music, or perhaps I might write to my old friend Annie Harrigan, who still lived on the same street we grew up on in Galway. Occasionally, if Father was away somewhere, I might take a bit of Jameson, just a drop, mind you, to help me unwind. I'd sit there and sip my whiskey and kind of soak in the quiet like it was another sort of liquor. I liked the big old house, with its scent of floor polish and flowers. Liked its high, pressed-tin ceilings, its long, leisurely hallways, its ornate woodwork, worn smooth to the touch by so many hands.

I had my little room at the back of the rectory, where I slept and kept my things. It was a nice enough room, but when I took my afternoon break I liked sitting in the den. It was bright and airy, and had a lovely view of West Street and the river, and beyond that, you could look right up the entire length of Main Street, all the way to the war memorial, see people coming and going. On cold winter days, I liked the way the late-afternoon sunlight slanted into the room in broad, pleasant bolts, warming me, filling me. I liked, too, being surrounded by all the pictures on the walls and on the mantel. The ones of Father Jack—as a boy hugging a cocker spaniel, one in his Holy Cross basketball uniform shaking hands with some fellow who'd signed it at the bottom, "To Jack, Best wishes, Bob Cousy," another of him and his mother on his ordination day. Even a few of my own mingled in—a picture of my mum looking pretty and young in a summery dress, another of Eion wearing a cowboy hat Mrs. Burke had bought him and sitting astride one of her horses. Most of all, when I took my break at the end of a long day, I liked knowing that everything was as it should be, clean and orderly and in its rightful place. If Father had asked me where a certain shirt of his was or an umbrella or even a pair of cuff links, I could've told him like *that*. I wouldn't even have to think twice, no sir. *Oh, that's in the third drawer down in your bureau, sir.* Or, *Look in the upstairs hall closet.* And isn't that what home means when you really stop and think about it: knowing where things are, being able to put a finger on something without giving it a second thought.

You see, running the rectory wasn't just a job. It was *my* job. I did it well, too, and it kept me busy. Gave a certain order to my life. Cleaning and vacuuming, doing the wash and ironing Father Jack's clothes, grocery shopping and making meals, paying the household bills and seeing to it that things that needed doing around the place got done. Though it had grown in the eighteen years I'd worked there, St. Luke's was still a small parish. Except for Dina, it was always just Father and myself holding down the fort, as he liked to put it. I was pretty much in charge of the day-to-day running of the rectory, which is a full-time job and then some. But I wouldn't have had it any other way. I liked being busy. I liked thinking of it as my responsibility.

If he didn't have guests over for dinner, we'd take our meals together at the small table in the kitchen. It made more sense, just the two of us. When he wasn't out making his rounds or being called to someone's bedside, which was often, Father Jack and I would eat a quiet dinner together. We'd talk about the day, share our problems. Joke a little, too. Father was a big one for the jokes. You'd never know it later on, but he used to have himself quite a sense of humor. I guess you had to have one to deal with all the problems that came up in the course of a day in the life of a parish priest. After a particularly bad day, he'd come in the back door and say to me, in that terrible brogue he tried to put on, "How's about we chuck it all and run off together, Margaret Quinn? Buy a little hot-dog stand on the beach." He was always kidding around about how we would buy a hot-dog stand on the beach somewhere and live the life of Riley, just the two of us. Not a care in the world. And I'd give him the business right back, laying on the Galway brogue. "Get out with you now, Father. If you were me husband, I'd have you toeing the mark, I would for sure." "I bet you would, too," he'd say with a laugh, that big hearty laugh of his, his Adam's apple bobbing up and down. I meant no disrespect speaking this way to Father. It's just that's the way it was between us. Easy. Familiar. Yet I never overstepped the bounds, always maintained due reverence to his collar. While I knew there was always the possibility of him getting transferred to another parish and leaving me behind, after all these years I'd assumed this was the way it'd be. This was my life. Our life, if you will. My mistake, I guess, was picturing things going on like this, me taking care of him, growing old together. I tell you all this to show you how it was before, to give you a sense of what my life was like and what it was soon to become.

I'd just started a letter to Annie Harrigan. We still kept in touch. I'd ask about her family, the old neighborhood, how Mrs. Kavanagh and Mrs. Coven were getting on. I'd tell her about my life over here, my garden or something about Father or what I'd made for Christmas dinner. And a few weeks later I'd get a letter back, with some pictures of her kids. Funny how different our lives had turned out. Her staying put and now with a family and all, and me over here, an old maid taking care of a priest. My own feeling is you get the life you deserve, nine times out of ten anyway.

That's when the phone rang. It might as well have been a bomb exploding for the way it ripped into my life. I considered just letting it ring but I thought it might be Father Jack. Sometimes he'd call me from the cabin with errands he wanted me to do or to see if he had any important messages. I got up and went into the kitchen to answer it.

"St. Luke's. How may I help you?" I asked, which is how I always answered.

On the other end was a woman's husky voice, thick as maple syrup. She said, "May I speak to Reverend Devlin?"

"He's not in," I told her. "He won't be back till tomorrow. I can give him a message."

"You might want to watch the six o'clock news."

"Who—" But the person hung up on me. *What in blazes?* I thought. Somebody's idea of a prank? But whoever it was, she'd got me curious, I'll say that. I looked at the clock on the wall—it was a few minutes before six. I returned to the den and tuned in to Channel 9, a Springfield station, one of only two we get clearly up here in the hills.

After a while the news came on. The anchor had a deep tan and smiled too much to show his expensive dentalwork.

"Our top stories tonight," he said, smiling. "Governor Weld is in Holyoke to dedicate a new Vietnam Memorial. A tanker truck carrying liquid nitrogen overturns on the Mass Pike. And another Massachusetts priest is accused of sex abuse. More on those stories in a moment."

Was *that* what the caller had wanted me to see? I wondered. Because if it was, it didn't really come as a shock. No sir. At least not the way it once would have. As terrible as it was to admit, people were getting used to that sort of nasty business. You couldn't hardly open a paper these days without reading about some priest somewhere taking advantage of a child. Why, right here in Massachusetts we'd already had our share of priests diddling little boys, what with those three or four over in the Worcester area, and that one down in Springfield. Not to mention that Father Porter over in New Bedford. That fellow took the cake. They said he'd molested dozens of kids for years. That even made the national news. It was enough to turn your stomach, I swear. What in the hell was going on? What sort of riffraff were they letting into the seminaries these days that they couldn't keep their paws off little boys? If it had been my child, I'd have taken a baseball bat to them, priest or no priest.

I watched patiently as they showed the governor saying a few words in front of some statue. *Blah blah blah*, he went. Then they reported on the overturned tanker truck. From a helicopter, the camera showed the truck lying on its side and men spraying white foam on this big spill. Finally they got round to the story about the priest. I was listening close, as I thought Father would want to know the details when he got home. One of those convicted priests over in Worcester had gone to seminary with Father Jack.

"For more," the anchor continued, "we go live to Andrea Ladd at the Office of the Springfield Catholic Diocese."

"After years of tormented silence," said the reporter, a young woman with large doll-like eyes and blond hair sprayed into a tight helmet, "two brothers have come forward to accuse their former priest of sexually molesting them more than fifteen years ago when they were altar boys. The accused priest, Reverend John 'Jack' Devlin, pastor of St. Luke's Parish in Hebron Falls . . ."

For a moment I thought I hadn't heard it right, so I jumped up and went over and turned the volume up. But I had heard it right. They were talking about Father Jack. *Holy Mother of God*! It fairly knocked the wind out of me. Like somebody had come up and punched me in the stomach.

"Earlier today," continued this Andrea Ladd, "at a news conference in the law offices of Attorney Mason Elliott of Montville, the brothers made their accusations public for the first time."

They switched indoors then to an office. There were shelves of thick, leather-bound books in the background, and in front of the books a table was set up with microphones on it. And seated at the table were these two ordinary-looking fellows, adults, which took me a little by surprise. For some reason, I'd been expecting boys, altar boys, in their white surplices. But then I recalled that they said it had happened fifteen years ago. One of them was skinny, with a scruffy beard, long dirty-blond hair. The other one was heavier, with a pudgy face and dark hair and a scared-looking expression. They didn't look like brothers. And I didn't recognize either of them. I've a pretty good memory when it comes to faces but for the life of me I couldn't say I'd ever seen them around town.

After a while, the bearded one began to read from a sheet of paper in front of him. I don't recall everything he said. I didn't even catch his name, to tell you the truth. My head was reeling so. The words hardly made sense to me. Just these awful noises. What I do recall though was this one talking about shame. He said he couldn't bear the shame any longer. His voice broke and he started to cry, but he kept on reading from the paper. He said how *it*—he kept referring to this *it*—had ruined his life. How *it* had haunted him. How *it* had made his life unbearable. He may have said other things, I don't remember. Then right before he finished he used a word I do remember, one I'll certainly never forget: *rape*. When he said Father Devlin had raped him, it brought everything suddenly home to me. Abuse—what's that? Could be anything. But rape—that was a horse of a different color. I felt sick to my stomach. I felt like I was going to throw up. *Dear God in heaven*! Why are they saying these things about Father? I wanted to know.

Then I had an odd thought: What if someone's watching, say nosy old Mrs. Mueller from across the street, and she hears such terrible things being said about Father. Which of course was a silly notion indeed, as it was the six o'clock news. The whole bloody town would be watching. Reuben Belliveau would have the television on in the Falls Tavern, and all the people sitting around his bar would be watching and wondering what this was all about; it'd be on over at the seniors' center and in the American Legion hall and in Chub Feeney's barbershop; and as people were eating their supper, they'd stop chewing, freeze with their forks halfway to their mouths, and listen. Soon they'd be phoning their friends and neighbors, and blathering about it, and by morning everyone and his brother would know about it. It'd be all over town. There'd be no stopping it. It'd be like a wildfire. And Father would come home to this.

Andrea Ladd came back on. She was still standing in front of the diocesan offices down in Springfield. I'd had to run errands there for Father once or twice, and so I knew where the building was. She said a church spokesman told her the matter was "under investigation." She also said she'd tried to contact Father Devlin, but was told he wasn't available for comment. And then it was like a light going on in the old noggin: *L* for Ladd. *She* was the reporter Dina said had called. And it was her husky voice I'd heard on the phone just a little while ago.

I shut the television off and just sat stock still, not wanting to move. I knew it was bad. Just didn't realize how bad. Sort of like when you first cut yourself while peeling potatoes and you feel that initial shock of pain that takes your breath away, and yet you don't know how deep the knife went or how bad it is and you feel if you just don't move it will be all right. If you just stay completely still.

After I'd had a second to get over the initial shock, I thought, *There had to be a simple explanation.* Perhaps those two had mixed Father Jack up with some other priest. Maybe one from before Father's time here. Or maybe the one they had in mind was from another town even. Just looked like Father Jack or had a similar last name. Devlin was common enough. There had to be other Father Devlins. A simple case of mistaken identity. Things like that happened all the time. It'd be cleared up as soon as they had all the facts.

Then I decided I'd better call Father straightaway; he'd need to know. I went into the kitchen, got the number for the cabin, and dialed. I let it ring a good long while, but there was no answer. It was still light out. He was probably out on the lake in his boat. He liked to fish. I could picture him out there fishing right now, relaxing, not suspecting a thing. I wondered what I should do. Call someone else? Perhaps another priest, say Father Duncan, who lived in a monastery over in Worcester and used to fill in for Father from time to time? Or maybe his friend Pete Beaupre? I was about to pick up the phone when it rang, startling me.

"Hello," said a man's voice. "This is Taylor Bryant from the *Boston Globe.* Is Father Devlin in?"

"No . . ." I fumbled. "He's not."

"When do you expect him back?"

"I really couldn't say."

"Has he heard the allegations?"

"Allegations?" I asked.

"Of sexual abuse."

"Why . . . no. I mean, I don't know as he has."

"Is he going to deny them?"

"Is he *what*?"

"Is he going to deny he sexually abused those two men?"

"Why, of course, he's going to deny it."

"Can I quote you on that?"

"You listen to me, mister. He didn't do any such thing, and you can bloody quote me on it if you'd like," I said, slamming the phone down.

Watch your big mouth, I warned myself. Don't go saying anything that might hurt Father. This was serious. You had to be careful.

I tried his number several times, but still wasn't able to reach him. I went into the den, over to a front window, and peeked out. Mrs. Mueller was walking her dog past the rectory, on this side of the street. Her tiny rat-looking mutt stopped and shat right on rectory property, as if I hadn't told her a million times not to let him do that. She didn't so much as glance in this direction though, which meant she hadn't heard the news yet. Otherwise she'd be looking over here, maybe even coming up and knocking on the door. "What's all this about Father Devlin, Ma?" I could picture her saying. She was a meddling old bird.

The phone rang again, interrupting my thoughts. This time it was Pete Beaupre. I could tell by his high-pitched, nasally voice. Pete was a real estate agent in town. He was a good friend of Father's and I was glad he'd called. He might know what we should do till Father got back.

"Jesus, Maggie, did you hear?" he asked.

"I heard."

"Let me talk to Jack." Pete called him just by his Christian name, the only lay person I knew who did.

"He's not here."

"Where is he?"

"Up to his cabin. I tried calling. There's no answer."

"He needs to get back here. I mean, hell, did you hear the stuff those two are saying?"

"It's all rubbish, Pete."

"Of course, it is. But Jack should be here so he can defend himself," he said. "I bet you Abruzzi's somehow connected to this."

"No. You don't really think so, do you?"

"I wouldn't put it past him. You know how he is."

Like I said, Joe Abruzzi had always had it in for Father Jack. Abruzzi thought he was a disgrace to the Church. And to be honest, Father *had* ruffled some feathers with his different views on things. He was quite progressive in his thinking, especially for a priest. For instance, he was for the ordination of women and for gay rights. He supported abortion and birth control and divorce. And he wasn't one to keep his ideas to himself. Not Father Jack. For years he and Abruzzi had locked horns. Some time before this, Abruzzi and a few others, crackpots like Andy Sennett and Mrs. Vasse, had started this ultra-conservative Catholic splinter group called TORCH—as Father put it, a bunch of Nazi storm troopers. They distributed leaflets against homosexuality, premarital sex, contraceptives, divorce; they tried to get books banned in the high school. They made no bones about wanting Father out. They sent complaints to Monsignor Payne, who wasn't fond of Father to begin with. They tried to get the teen shelter Father had started over in Montville shut down because of a rumor drugs were being sold there. But the shite really hit the fan after it'd got out that Father had secretly performed the Sacrament of Marriage for Leah Bettancourt and Joan Kosnik, the two women who ran the bookstore in town. TORCH got up a petition to have Father removed as pastor, and they came damn close to pulling it off, too. So it was no secret that Abruzzi and his cronies would've liked nothing better than to see Father hurt. But *this*? It seemed even too much for them.

"He wouldn't go that far, would he, Pete?"

"I wouldn't be surprised," he said. "He's a nut-case. Anyway, we have to move fast. The longer we wait the worse it looks."

"I should get off the line, Pete. In case he tries calling."

"By the way, who are those Robys? They're not from town, are they?"

"Roby? Is that their name?"

"Yeah. Do you know them?"

Roby? I said to myself. The name had a familiar ring though I couldn't put a face to it. Certainly not those I'd seen on the television.

"I think I recall the name," I said.

"Has anybody contacted a lawyer?"

"Shouldn't we wait for Father to get home?" I said.

"We need to take the offensive, Maggie. I could write up a press release denying the charges."

"We should wait and see what Father wants to do."

The thing about Pete was he'd go off half-cocked and end up causing more harm than good. Take the money the parish was short that time. Father was terrible with his record-keeping, couldn't be bothered with it. Pete, who did the books, was always getting on him about it. This one year over three thousand dollars couldn't be accounted for. Admittedly, Pete was only trying to protect Father, fearing that his enemies would use it against him. So he tried to cover the missing funds by playing a shell game. However, when the books were finally audited by the diocese, it came out in the wash and made Father look even worse, like he'd nicked it and had tried to cover it up. But that's just what I mean about Pete.

"This thing'll snowball if we don't act fast," he said. "I'll make some calls. I got a friend who works in the D.A.'s office."

Yet in this instance, I almost had to agree with Pete—we had to do something, and quick, too. No sooner had I hung up than I got a flurry of phone calls: from TV stations in Worcester and Springfield; from an Associated Press reporter requesting an interview with Father Devlin; from a Florida lawyer offering his services, saying he had experience in "this sort of situation." How he'd learned about it down there so soon I'd never know. I also got one from a secretary in the Office of the Springfield Diocese, saying Monsignor Payne, the vicar for clergy, wanted to speak to Father. I told her he wasn't in. I received about a dozen calls from people in town. Some, like Judy

Moran, who ran the Christmas pageant, called asking what they could do to help.

"Bob and I are behind Father one hundred percent," she said. "Who's going to believe those Robys over Father Jack."

Roby, I said to myself several times, the name sounding more and more familiar. It rattled around in my head like a song whose words I couldn't quite remember but whose tune I recalled.

I tried calling Father again but still didn't have any luck. After I'd hung up, I stood there thinking about something he had said when the news first broke about Father Gallo, the priest convicted over in Worcester.

"My God, I knew him, Margaret," he said. "He seemed so holy. In seminary we used to go over to chapel for afternoon prayer together."

"There's some that can put on a good face to the world when underneath they're all rotten to the core."

"They'll think we're all like that now."

"Nonsense, Father," I said. "There's always one bad apple."

Though I wanted a nip in the worst way, I put on a pot of tea instead. I had to have my wits about me. I needed to be thinking straight. I was sitting at the table drinking my tea when Cindy O'Connell called.

"'Tis terrible, Maggie," she said. "Just terrible. Why would they be slanderin' a fine man like Father Jack?"

"How would I know, Cindy? Do you remember them? Roby."

"Sure I remember them. They lived down in Frog Hollow. The mother was one of those had men in and out all the time. Let them brats of hers run wild. Little hellions. Don't you remember them?"

"Maybe. I just can't place them."

"The older one was always in trouble."

"Wasn't one of them named Ryan or Richard? Something like that."

"Maybe," she replied.

We went way back, Cindy and myself. Like me, she'd come over from Ireland to find work here. She'd settled with relations in Boston before coming out here to work in the kitchen of the nursing home. We'd met in AA, birds of a feather as they say. A couple of us girls, Cindy and myself and sometimes Mrs. Fey, an older widowed lady, used to play rummy together. Cindy was a great one for the gossip, and I couldn't say as I wanted to be talking with her right then.

"What's Father saying?"

"He's out of town."

"Where on earth would they get these things from?"

"Who knows? Listen, I shouldn't tie up the line, Cindy."

"And to wait all these years," she continued.

"What do you mean?" I asked.

"Well, why would they wait all these years to bring it up? Don't you think that's a bit odd, Maggie?"

"The whole thing is odd, Cynthia. Listen, I have to go."

"It kinda makes you wonder though," she said. "Don't you think?"

I could tell she was fishing around, trying to find out if I knew more than I was letting on. Though she was my friend, Cindy sometimes rubbed me the wrong way. While I confess to savoring a juicy bit of gossip as much as the next person, she takes the cake. She's always talking about people, spreading rumors about this one and that. And yet, to see her in church! Goes to Mass every day and twice on Sunday. One of those weepy Catholics, which for my money is worse than a Baptist any day. The sort my mum used to call a crawthumper. And around Father she'd put on this coy little girl act. "That was such a lovely sermon, Father," she'd go, batting her eyes and flirting shamelessly with him.

So I took the bait. "What does, Cindy?"

"Why they'd make up such terrible things," she said. "After all this time, too."

"I wouldn't have any idea about that. No sir, I would not."

"You think he'll be saying Mass tomorrow?"

"And why shouldn't he?"

"Just with everything that's going on, I figured it'd be canceled."

"He'll be saying Mass, don't you worry none."

"Maybe I'll go over to St. Catherine's tomorrow. I don't care for Father Cetrone but he keeps it short."

"You do whatever you please, Cindy," I snapped at her.

"What are you getting all hot under the collar for? I'm just saying maybe I ought to make other plans in case Mass here is canceled.

"Good-bye, Cindy," I said and hung up.

That night the phone wouldn't stop ringing, people asking for Father or about what everyone began to refer to as "the news" or "Father Jack's situation." For months afterward, if you ran into people in the street they'd be talking about "the news." "What's the latest news on Father Jack's situation?" someone would ask me in Irene's Hair Emporium or when I was mailing something in the post office. As if I knew a whit more than they did, and would've told them if I had. After a while I decided to turn the answering machine on.

• • •

I kept trying to reach Father. I'd let it ring a couple of dozen times. Finally around two in the morning, for I happened to notice the clock on the kitchen wall which always tends to run fast, he picked up.

"Yeah?" he said, sounding groggy. A deep sleeper, Father Jack was. Though he didn't need more than a few hours a night, when he slept he slept soundly. Why, that man could sleep through a storm. How many times would he doze off on the couch, a book across his chest, and I'd throw a blanket over him, take his shoes off? Or the times I'd had to pound so hard on his door to wake him up, worrying that he'd be late for an appointment.

"Father," I whispered. "It's me. Sorry to be waking you."

"What time is it, Margaret?"

A calmness in his voice told me he hadn't heard a thing. I remember thinking: *Once I tell him why I was calling, he wouldn't sleep soundly again.* There'd always be something lurking at the edge of his mind, drawing him back from rest. My own opinion is that after we face some terrible tragedy in our lives, the most precious thing we lose is our ability to give ourselves completely over to sleep. I knew what that was like for sure. After my Eion passed away, I never slept soundly again—*ever*. A part of me would always remain awake, on the alert, as if expecting him to call out to me for help. And I knew it would be like this for Father. That what I was going to tell him, no matter how it turned out, would haunt him for the rest of his days. I hated to be the one to have to tell him, but that was the way of it, and I'd rather have it come from me than from some stranger.

"After two," I replied. "I tried to get you earlier."

"What's the matter? Did somebody die?"

I thought, *If only it were that simple.*

"No. You'd better come home right away, Father. There's been some trouble."

"What kind of trouble?"

"These men. They've said some things."

"What are you talking about? What kinds of things?"

"About you, Father."

"*Margaret*!" he said, annoyed. "For heaven's sakes, just tell me."

So I did. I blurted it all out, everything I could remember. I didn't use the exact words that Roby fellow had, but he got the drift of it. And I don't mind saying I felt ashamed telling him. Sick at heart, saying those things to a priest.

When I finished, I waited for him to speak. Yet nothing came from his end save this deathly silence. Like a hole had opened up on the other end, deep and dark, and I was standing on the very lip of it, looking down, and the only thing I could see was Father at the very bottom of it. I wasn't sure how I expected him to act. He didn't get mad very often. He was a person that usually kept his emotions tightly under wraps. However, when he did get angry, he could fly into a rage. Those blue eyes would flash and his usually soft, fleshy mouth turn hard as stone. Few had witnessed it except for me. I'd once seen him throw a Madonna statue across the room. Broke it into a million pieces. But he was quiet on the other end now, the way he was in his study at night listening to music or writing a sermon. Or the way he'd be after he came home from giving someone the last rites, when he'd just sort of stare off into space, looking lost and so forlorn.

"Father?" I said. Another second or two passed. I heard him take in a breath. "Are you all right, Father?"

"Yes."

"People've been calling."

"Of course," he finally said. His voice was detached, as if he were talking about something that had nothing to do with him.

"Nobody believes any of that rubbish, Father," I said. "Roby, their name was. Do you remember them, Father?"

"Yeah," he said without a moment's hesitation. "Bobby was the younger one. And the older one was Russell."

Aye, I thought, a light going off in my mind: *Russell Roby*. That was it. I remembered that name now. I still couldn't picture a face, though I did at least remember the name. *Russell Roby*. There was something about it. What it was I couldn't rightly say at the moment, but I knew it would come to me.

"Are you coming home, Father?"

"I'll leave right away. I should be there by six."

"What should I do, Father?"

"Do?" he said. "It's two in the morning. Go to bed."

Like I could actually sleep. I was a wreck. My nerves were shot all to hell. I'm not one who does well with a lot of commotion. I'm a creature of habit. I prefer my quiet routines, knowing one day will pretty much follow the one before like a tail chasing a dog. Though I knew I needed to keep my head clear, I got the bottle of Jameson from Father's liquor cabinet and poured myself a crapper's worth, to calm down. A wee bit wouldn't hurt a thing. Maybe even help me doze off. Then I got my rosary beads from the bedpost and climbed in bed. While I lay there sipping the whiskey I began saying the rosary. A decade of Hail Marys followed by an Our Father. My mum had given me the rosary when I was a girl. The beads were worn smooth as pebbles on the beach. Many's the time I found comfort in them. I didn't really think I'd sleep but I set the alarm anyway, as I always do. Like I said, I'm a creature of habit. I set it for five, an hour earlier than usual, so I'd be up and have coffee on when Father got home. I always liked to be up before him, get an early start on the day, have things ready for him.

In between saying "Hail Mary, full of grace, the Lord is with thee," I would say *Russell Roby* to myself. Like it was another kind of prayer almost.

5

That night I had all sorts of queer dreams, which is the way of it when your mind's uneasy. In one, I was washing a floor, down on my hands and knees, scrubbing away. Only thing is instead of soap and water I was pouring on the floor, it was broken glass. When I looked down at my hands, they were all cut and bleeding, don't you know, and the more I tried to clean the floor the more I made a mess of things. Everything was bloodied. Another dream was that one in which Eion was calling to me. As usual we were in this great big house, dark and empty, and from somewhere I could hear his voice, a child's voice, calling out. Like always, I'd go hunting from room to room, opening doors, trying to find where it was coming from. But my legs would hardly move, like walking through molasses. I could feel my heart beating with fear. *I'm coming, love,* I cried in the dream. *Just hold on, Mommy's coming.* But as with the other times I never made it. I never got there in time to do whatever it was I was trying to do. That's when the alarm woke me.

I got up and put on a pot of coffee, figuring Father surely would need it after driving all night. I sat at the kitchen table with only the night light on. It was still dark out and quiet. You could hear the mourning doves going *whoo whoo whoo.* The calm before the storm, I thought. I debated going out and seeing if the paper had come, thinking maybe there might be something in it about "the situation." But I worried about running into Mrs. Mueller, who often took her dog out before sunrise to do his business, usually on our lawn.

I'd had some time to sleep on it, to work things out in my head and see if there wasn't a simple explanation. I'm the sort as likes to start with a square peg in a square hole before getting fancy. As far as

I could see there was three possibilities. The first—and the easiest— was that those brothers had mixed Father Jack up with someone else. Which was surely possible. After all, it had happened years ago, when they were just kids. And people's memories played tricks on them, especially things that happened when you were a child. Take, for instance, how I used to swear I'd seen my da laid out in his coffin, even recollecting the charcoal-gray suit he wore. But my mum said that that was hardly possible as they'd had to have a closed coffin. I'd have sworn on a stack of Bibles I'd seen him though, which just goes to show you can't always trust your memory. Perhaps those Robys were mistaken, too. It was some other priest that looked a bit like Father Jack or had the same last name, and after a little digging they'd find the right one.

The second possibility took me some time to get my thoughts around entirely: *maybe they were lying, those two*. Perhaps they *knew* it wasn't Father Jack, and they were just making it up out of thin air. But why? I wondered. Why would anyone do that, especially to Father? I suppose they could've been in it for the money. That was one thought I had. Those people in the Porter case had settled with the Church for a hundred thousand dollars apiece, I'd read in the paper. That sort of money was enough to make a person lie. The Catholic Church was nervous and willing to settle at the drop of a hat. All's you had to do was cry "Father So-and-so touched me" and some lawyer with dollar signs for eyes came running. Father Jack had said as much. But why *him*, I wondered. Why Father Jack? Why not some other priest in some other parish, maybe one wealthier than ours? And those thoughts surely gave me pause. Maybe they'd had something against him. A grudge. An old score to settle. That might account for it. Or, as Pete Beaupre had suggested, perhaps somebody else had put them up to it. Somebody that didn't like him. Which seemed pretty far-fetched, even I had to admit that. Still and all, you could never tell what people would do for money. Or out of spite. The more I thought about it, the more I was able to convince myself that Joe Abruzzi and his lot were at least *capable* of pulling something like this. I wouldn't put it past them, that's for sure.

And then there was possibility number three. As soon as I opened my eyes that morning, it was there, complete and whole in my mind, so ripe and fully formed I had only to reach out and pluck it: what if Father *had* done those things? What if he *was* guilty of what they were saying? Everything is possible, I suppose. We are all of us, given the right conditions, capable of any manner of abomination. It was almost like I had to say it out loud, to get it out in the open so its foulness wouldn't sit and fester in secret and after a time smell up my mind, like a dead mouse under the sink. But no sooner had I allowed that notion entry into my thoughts, then I felt a wave of shame wash over me. How could you even think that, Maggie Quinn? After all that man has done for you, this is the way you repay him? Have you no sense of loyalty? Yet it was far more than loyalty keeping me from thinking it possible. I *knew* Father, the sort of person he was. Why, he was no more capable of doing that than I was. A kind and caring and decent man, Father Jack. I'm not saying he was perfect, mind you. He had his weaknesses, his flaws, just like you or me. But he was a good man, and a good priest, too. Wasn't he always helping youngsters and doing for them and sticking his neck out if they got in trouble? And didn't the kids love him? You never saw a priest so beloved by the young as Father Jack. So that was that.

Next, I turned my attention to the Robys themselves. Cindy had said she remembered them living over in Frog Hollow, those apartments by the river. Now they're called Riverview Terrace but everybody used to call them Frog Hollow because it's where the French-Canadians first settled in town. A rough section, it was, fights, drug busts, the police getting called down there all the time. *Russell Roby*, I thought, playing with the name, turning it over in my mind the way you would a coin in your pocket. I knew that name. At least I was pretty sure I did, though I still couldn't put a face to it. The ones I'd seen on the television didn't help me any. The Robys I'd have known would have been young kids. An altar boy, they'd said. *Russell Roby*. Where had I heard that name before?

Then I hit on an idea—maybe they'd be in Father's photo albums and I might recognize them and put a face to the name and recall what it was I remembered. So I went into the den and from the bookshelves started taking down the albums. About a dozen thick, dusty-smelling books filled with photos Father had collected over the years. He liked taking pictures of his parishioners. He had no family of his own so his flock became his family so to speak. There were pictures of First Communions and Confirmations, weddings and baptisms and birthdays. Pictures of Father toasting some beaming young bride and groom. Pictures of him and his good friend, the late Rudy Lessard, both of them coaches, standing with the team that won the CYO basketball championship one year. Pictures of little girls in their veils receiving First Communion. Pictures of former altar boys, most of whom I recognized immediately. Jason Thibodeau and Karl Whaley. Petey Lindstrom, who's now a town cop. The Santanelli twins, poor Joey having died in that car accident a few years back, and Jimmy whose son Father had baptized just last year. Brendon Flaherty. Gary Cerutti, Dina's older brother. They looked like angels, with their faces scrubbed clean and their long white surplices. Good kids, most of them anyway. I remember them stopping by the rectory before Mass or after school, maybe playing some basketball with Father out in the driveway. Afterward they'd come in and I'd serve them some pie and a glass of milk and they'd say, "Thank you, Ma Quinn." They were the ones started that, calling me Ma Quinn. I didn't mind. In fact, I kind of liked it. For many of them, especially those with family problems, the rectory became like a second home, a place to hang out. Father Jack's boys, people called them.

Of course you had your bad apples, the troublemakers, the wild ones, the back-talkers, all of whom Father had a soft spot in his heart for, saying they're the ones as needed his attention most. Like the parable of the sheep, he'd say, and they were the hundredth, the one lost lamb. Kids like Eric Soja, who stole a car and crashed it into a tree, or Matt Poulin, who set the middle school on fire. Or the Bassinger girl, the one who'd later be arrested for selling drugs. Or that snotty Villandry kid who had a mouth on him like a guttersnipe. Their pictures were there, too.

I thumbed through more pages. Some photos weren't very clear and took me a bit longer to place who it was. Like the youngest Pelkey boy, dressed as one of the Wise Men for the Christmas pageant, or Kyle What's-his-face, whose mother used to bake those awful pies no one bought at the bake sale. And some, no matter how long and hard I stared at them, I couldn't place at all. After all, I'd been there almost eighteen years and Father even longer. That was a lot of faces to recall. Maybe it was one of those? I opened another book, started flipping through its pages. A third of the way through I paused at one picture. It was of a young boy, a fine-looking lad, with strawberry blond hair falling to his blue eyes. He was in his altar boy clothes and was smiling shyly, as I could remember him doing in life. While I hadn't seen a picture of him in years, I knew right away who it was. Justin Blake. I felt a tightness in my chest on seeing the child. If I was a believer in omens or thought that misfortune was more than just rotten luck, I'd have said that seeing Justin right then and there was a sign. But of course I didn't think that. At least not right then anyway.

I was still looking at this picture when my eyes happened to fall on one of another boy on the opposite page. Must've been ten or eleven, and he was standing at the back door of the rectory, leaning against the porch railing. He was wearing his altar boy robes and smiling at the camera. Father must've taken the picture, from the driveway. Just another of Father Jack's boys, nothing special about him—except for one thing. His mouth. It was a narrow purplish line that curved in the corners into something you'd call a smirk. Yet as soon as I laid eyes on that mouth it all came back to me. That's all I needed, just one look at that mouth of his. With some people it's their eyes or a bump on their nose. Their hair perhaps or their voice. With him it was his mouth. I thought, *Why, that's him. That's Russell Roby right there*. No doubt about it. I could even recall the way he'd stare at you, sort of sizing you up. And always with that smirk on his puss, the way some kids do, as if they were laughing at you behind your back. As if they were too big for their britches. *Well well well*, I thought. *What do you know about that?* And as I looked at the picture some more I thought there was something else. Something that had happened with this Russell Roby. What? What was it? I couldn't remember then but I was sure it would come to me. And it would, too.

· · ·

While I waited for Father's return, I tried to keep busy, like I do when something's bothering me. No sense moping about is my view. Idle hands and all that. Since I already had the albums out, I took down the rest of the books and pictures and knickknacks from the shelves, and began dusting. I couldn't believe how filthy it was. Maggie, you're getting slack, for sure, I scolded myself. Can't keep a house so it doesn't look like a pigsty. While I was at it, I got a rag and some boiled linseed oil and polished the woodwork so it shone like a baby's rear end after a bath.

I heard a noise outside then. I went over to the kitchen window and peeked out. I saw Father's car pulling in the driveway. It was early still, about half six. The day was overcast, looking like it held the prospect of rain. I watched him ease his white Taurus into the garage, next to my Toyota. He got out but paused in the shadow of the doorway, right beneath the basketball hoop. He just stood there, staring up toward the house. For a moment I thought he'd seen me. I was going to rap on the window and wave to him, but I realized it wasn't me he was looking at. He was just sort of staring off into space, as was Father's way at times. For some reason I couldn't put my finger on, I didn't want him to know I'd been watching him. So I didn't wave, didn't so much as move. I froze. And I remember feeling my heart kind of stop when I realized I was spying on him.

When he came in the door, I didn't know what to say, so I said only "Good morning, Father. It's . . . good to have you back."

He looked a mess, he surely did. His beard had stuff in it, and his face was ashen, his eyes red-rimmed from lack of sleep. His hair was greasy and wild-looking, as if it hadn't been washed or combed in days. He was dressed in ripped jeans and the black hooded sweatshirt he wore when he went for his morning run. He smelled of the outdoors, of smoke and dampness, a woodsy odor. In his right hand he held a newspaper.

"Some coffee, Father?"

"No," he replied. He went over to the side window, which had a view of Main Street, and stared out, almost as if expecting someone.

"How about something to eat?" I asked. "You must be hungry."

"What?"

"Do you want me to fix you breakfast?"

"No. Anybody call this morning?"

"No."

"Anybody from the diocese?"

"Someone from there called yesterday. Your messages are in your study. Maybe I could fix you some eggs?"

"I'm not hungry."

"How about some toast, Father?"

"Goddamn it, Margaret, not now!" he snapped, startling me. I felt my face flush, like I'd been slapped. He headed out of the kitchen and down the hall to his study. As I said, he did have himself a bit of a temper, though he didn't show it often and hardly ever with me. With me he seldom raised his voice, even when I'd done something foolish, like the time I'd burned his stole while ironing it. Two people living under the same roof they're bound to get on each other's nerves now and again. That's only normal.

He returned in a few minutes.

"Forgive me, Margaret. It's just that I've a lot on my mind."

"*Och*! Don't give it another thought, Father."

"Maybe something later. If anybody calls, would you tell them I'm not here."

"If you don't mind my saying, Father. Do you really think that's such a good idea?"

"Why?"

"I mean, someone's bound to have seen your car drive through town. How would that look, me telling people you weren't in when they knew you were?" I could see he wasn't thinking straight. I thought a lie like that wouldn't be wise right then. I don't want to sound self-important or anything, but with all that he usually had on his mind, I took it as my job to watch out for his interests. Even at times if it meant speaking out of turn.

"I see your point." he said. "Just tell them I'm busy then."

"Certainly, Father," I said. Our eyes met for the briefest of moments, and then he looked away, no doubt with the shame of it all. I felt terrible for him, just terrible. Though I wanted to tell him I didn't believe none of that rubbish they were saying, nothing came out of my throat. Not a thing. What could I say after all that he didn't already know himself? He went back down the hall and into his study.

I washed some dishes. Outside, it was starting to rain, a light mist. I thought how it would be good for my garden. It's funny what comes wandering into your head at the oddest times. For instance, I can still recall something at my son's wake. I was sitting there with my mum, still in shock, gazing on Eion lying in this wee tiny white coffin we'd picked out, the smallest they had. Him looking so handsome and grown-up in the new sports jacket I'd bought him at Hearn's Clothing Store, as we didn't have anything decent to bury him in. And what I thought right then was what a shame it was he wouldn't get much use from that jacket. Can you fancy thinking such a thing at a time like that? About some bloody coat and your son's lying cold and dead in his coffin and it's *your* fault he's there. But that's what I mean about how the mind has a will of its own. Sometimes there's no sense even fighting it.

After a while Father came in the kitchen.

"I have a headache," he said. "I'm going to get some sleep."

"That's probably a good idea. You look awful tired."

"I don't want to be disturbed. Just make sure I'm up in plenty of time for Mass."

"Do you want me to rub your head, Father?"

When Father got one of his bad headaches, which he was prone to, I'd massage his temples for him. I'd place the fleshy part of my thumbs over his eyes and press down, while with my fingers I'd kind of rub his temples in circles. That was the ticket for his headaches.

"No," he said.

He went upstairs and into his room and shut the door. He didn't lay down though. I could hear him pacing around up there, back and forth, back and forth. The floorboards in the old house creaked when you walked on them. Sometimes when I couldn't sleep, from my bed I could hear him above me pacing back and forth, maybe thinking about a sermon or some problem that wouldn't let him sleep. I thought about what I had the previous night: that he would never sleep peacefully again in his life.

6

I recall when I had this lump in my breast. For the longest time—when I was taking a bath or getting dressed or going about my business—I'd pretend I hadn't noticed it. That it wasn't there. Even later, when I did finally admit that it was there, I told myself it was nothing. Just a lump. That's all it was. Nothing to get yourself all worked up about. Only when I'd finally gone to the doctor and was sitting in the waiting room looking at some magazine did I realize that my hands were shaking.

In the same way, I kept trying to convince myself it wasn't as bad as it seemed. Hadn't Father been through rough times before? There was the business with the missing money that Peter had tried to cover. After that the rumors started that Father had stolen it. Despite the fact that he had some family money, people wondered how he could afford a summer place and a boat on a priest's income. Or that time those kids got into the liquor cabinet up at his cabin. Some of the parents raised holy hell over that. Or the stink folks put up when it got out that he'd married Leah and Joan. Or take all the run-in's he'd had with Joe Abruzzi over the years. Though most folks liked him, Father surely wasn't without his enemies, and his time here hadn't always been smooth sailing. Far from it. Yet hadn't he weathered each storm? And I had every confidence he would this one. Once they got it all sorted out.

I went into the laundry room and started ironing. I let myself sink into the soothing ritual of moving the iron back and forth, the pleasant fragrance of starch and warm fabric a balm to my troubled spirit. From the hall closet I got Father's vestments and set them out for the Mass. I always set his things out, made sure everything was clean and ironed and just so, didn't have wine stains, checked to see he had the right colors for the various feast days. Rather than get dressed in the sacristy, he liked to change here and walk over to the church. Liked the fresh air, Father did.

Around ten I fixed him a little something to eat and was just heading up the stairs to wake him, when the doorbell rang. I peeked out the front window and saw these two men in dark gray suits standing there. They didn't look like those religious supply salesmen that came around peddling patens and cruets.

"May I help you?" I asked.

"We're looking for Father Devlin," the younger of the two explained, a good-looking fellow with dark skin and glossy black hair.

"And who might you be?"

"We're from the state police," the older one replied. This one had bushy eyebrows that grew unbroken above narrow, deep-set eyes. He was overweight, his belly tugging at the button of his suit coat. They may have said their names but the only thing I recall is the fat one showing me his badge. On seeing that, I knew things had passed on to another level. I knew it was more than just a little problem that needed to be sorted out.

"Is Father Devlin in, ma'am?" the younger one asked.

I considered telling them what Father had told me, that he didn't want to be disturbed, but figured he hadn't meant that for police. I told them to come in. I led them down the hall and was about to show them into the den when I remembered the albums. Sure enough I'd left them all out, some on the coffee table, some on the floor. It was a silly notion, but I thought I'd better put them away and tidy up. I didn't want them thinking I kept a messy house. No sir.

"Would you wait here a moment, please," I said.

One album on the coffee table was still open; it showed Father and an altar boy, Petey Lindstrom, in his cassock and white surplice in front of the altar. Father stood next to him with his arm around the boy's shoulders. They were both smiling, looking happy. I thought of leaving it out. I really did. *Look at that*, I felt like saying. *You want proof—there's your proof.* A picture's worth a thousand words. One look at how happy they were was enough to tell you Fa-

ther couldn't've done those things. But I gathered up the albums anyway and brought them over and put them back on the shelf. I
glanced around the room to be sure everything was in its place.

Only then did I show the two into the room and had them take a
seat. I said something about whether it was going to clear up outside,
as if I cared a fiddler's fart if it poured or no. Just friendly chitchat. I
even remembered to offer them some refreshments.

"Some coffee perhaps?"

"I'm already wired, ma'am," said the younger one, smiling. He
had a boyish smile, teeth white as pearls.

The fat one glanced around the room, casually, but in the manner of a woman looking for dirty corners or a carpenter checking for
bad miter joints. Someone used to sizing people up in a hurry. This
one's guilty, that one's not.

"I'll go get Father," I said. I went up and knocked on his door.
He was sleeping and I had to knock several times. Finally I heard this
groaning on the other side, like he'd taken ill.

"Father?" I asked through the door. "It's me, Father."

"I told you I didn't want to be disturbed."

"I think you'd better come down, Father. It's the police."

Still in his sweatshirt and jeans, he opened the door. His eyes
were bleary, unfocused. His face pale, like it gets when he's not feeling well. He didn't seem surprised so much as resigned to the news
that the police were there.

"I see," he said. "Tell them I'll be right down."

"He'll be down shortly," I explained to the police. I found the fat
one over near the mantel looking at a picture of Father and his
mother on the day of his ordination. You could tell it was spring because of the dogwood in bloom in the background. Father had his
arm around his mother, and she looked so proud of her son.

"Can I *help* you?" I asked. I wasn't sure what authority he had,
but I made it quite clear I didn't approve of him nosing around like
that.

He put the picture down and took his seat.

Father entered the room then and shook hands with them, as
cordially, I thought, as he would a couple coming in for a pre-cana
session. He looked grubby in his sweatshirt and dirty jeans, his hair

still uncombed and wild-looking. I could see how the two cops looked at him, thinking, *What sort of priest is this?*

Glancing over at me, Father said, "Have you offered our guests anything to drink, Margaret?"

The younger one replied, "She has, Father. We're all set."

I continued standing there, till the fat one said they would like to talk to Father. "Alone," he added, looking at me in case I was too dense to get his drift.

"I'll be in the kitchen, Father, if you need me," I answered.

While working on some oatmeal cookies for the communion party, I strained my ears trying decipher what they were saying. I couldn't make out much, though I did catch the younger detective ask, "Did you really meet Cousy?"

I went over to the window and looked out. I saw several cars parked out on West Street in front of the rectory. On the side of a van it said CHANNEL 9 ACTION NEWS. They were here already, I thought, swarming like vultures. It was going to be far worse than I'd imagined. It was starting to snowball, just like Pete had warned. I wanted to go back in the den and say to those fellows, *Hold on a minute. This is all wrong. It's all just a big mistake.*

After a bit Father came into the kitchen.

"They want me to go with them to the state police barracks."

"Why, for heaven's sakes?"

"They have some questions, I guess."

"Can't they ask their questions here?"

"I don't know. They said I could change first."

"That's a good idea. Are you gonna wear your collar, Father?"

"I suppose I should."

"And your navy-blue sports coat. That looks nice on you."

I thought how when he left here all those people outside would see him, and some would be taking his picture and he'd be on the six o'clock news and in the paper the next day. And people out there that didn't know him from Adam would see him for the first time and form opinions based on that. First impressions. I wanted him to look sharp.

"Go get changed," I said. "I'll bring your coat up."

I got his blue gabardine sports coat from the closet and gave it a quick once-over with the coat brush. Then I brought it up and knocked on the door. He opened it a crack and I handed the coat to him.

"What about Mass, Father?" I asked through the door.

"I think we'd better cancel it."

"Cancel it?" I repeated. I thought of Cindy O'Connell asking if Father would still be saying Mass. We'd had to cancel Mass only a handful of times since I'd been here. When Father was sick with pneumonia. Another time after he'd had the back surgery. Besides, I hated Cindy to be right. "I could call Father Duncan if you'd like."

"No, it's too late. I think we'd better just cancel it today, Margaret. Would you see to that?"

"Certainly, Father. And what should I say if someone calls?"

"Tell them the truth," he said.

"The truth?"

"That I'm being questioned by the police. If people don't know already, they will soon enough."

When he came out he looked a good deal more presentable, though he still didn't seem his normal self. He appeared tired and worn out.

"That's better," I said. "Wait, Father." I spit on my hand and smoothed down a cowlick that stuck up at the back of his head. We both kind of smiled at that despite the seriousness of the situation.

I watched as the police escorted him out to a black, unmarked cruiser. The mist had increased to a steady drizzle and several townspeople had gathered out at the sidewalk under umbrellas and raincoats. Mrs. Mueller was there, still dressed in her bathrobe. When the news people saw them, they rushed across the lawn like children playing some sort of game of tag, lugging their heavy cameras and microphones. That Andrea Ladd was among them. I was surprised at how fast she could run in a tight skirt and high heels across the rain-slick lawn. I watched them descend on Father, as the detectives guided him into the back of the car. They were snapping pictures and shoving their cameras and microphones at him. Poor Father, I thought.

• • •

All morning the phone fairly rang off the hook. People from town wanting to know what was going on. What was all this they were hearing about Father Jack. What was *he* saying? And who were those Robys anyway? Rumors were already flying. Some said they'd heard Father had been arrested and taken away, while others had him resigning or being forcibly removed from St. Luke's Parish. Some people, like Andy Sennett from the TORCH bunch, called to say he wasn't surprised at all. He said Father was an immoral man who was a disgrace to the collar. I hung up on him. Most from town though said they supported him, didn't believe a word of it. They said they thought Father was innocent. Reporters continued to call. Some fellow from the *New York Times* and another from a television station over in Albany wanted to interview Father. And Cardinal Stone's personal assistant called from Boston saying he had His Eminence on the line and he wanted to speak to Father. I told him Father Devlin wasn't here, but I'd be sure to have him call as soon as he got back.

I went about my tasks, trying as best I could to put the whole ugly affair out of my mind, figuring now that Father was back he'd know just what to do. Yet trying not to think about it was easier said than done. Like a fly buzzing around a piece of rotten meat, my thoughts kept coming back to it. I kept thinking about that picture of the young Roby at the back door and trying to recall what it was I remembered about him. And then I'd picture the other one, the adult I'd seen on the television, recalling how he'd said Father had *raped* him. Good Lord, it made me cringe just to think the word. I kept trying to make sense of it all. No doubt it was just a terrible mistake. The police would ask Father a few questions, realize it couldn't be him and let him go. And that'd be the end of it. I was so convinced, in fact, I went ahead and took out a pot roast from the freezer. I'd make Father a nice dinner as I had no doubt he'd straighten it all out and be home by suppertime.

I called over to the church several times, hoping to get ahold of Stanley Derenzy, the custodian, and have him put some signs up saying Mass was canceled. But I couldn't reach him, which didn't surprise me as the lazy bum could smell work a mile away and had a talent for making himself scarce. So I decided to head over myself. I put on a sweater and grabbed an umbrella, for the light drizzle had turned into a steady rain. While the church was a good quarter mile up West Street, I didn't drive. Instead I took the shortcut through the woods behind the rectory. In nice weather, I actually preferred it to driving. A lovely walk that cut through a grove of old cedars and some glossy-smooth beech trees, the oaths of lovers tattooed on their bark. Father often took the path through the woods, and sometimes the two of us would walk over to Mass together, chatting as we went. I chose it today, though, because I didn't want a soul to see me. It was as if, by canceling Mass, we—Father, myself—were admitting to a kind of defeat already. Yet by the time I arrived over to the church, my sneakers were muddy and soaking wet, and I was wondering if maybe I shouldn't've driven after all.

In the church, I said a prayer to the Virgin Mother. I asked her to watch over Father, to protect him against those that would seek to do him wrong. Then I went looking for Stanley. I checked in the community center for him, then poked my head in the classrooms, the offices, the sacristy. I even went to the door of the basement and called his name. It's where Stanley could often be found, sleeping one off on the old pews that were stored there. But I couldn't find hide nor hair of him. So I got some paper and tape from one of the classrooms and stuck up handwritten notices on the front and side doors. In large letters I wrote MASS CANCELED TODAY. That's all I said. I was cutting through the community center, intending to put a note on the back door, when I heard someone say, "What the fuck's going on, Maggie?"

I turned to see Stanley coming out of the kitchen. He walked over to me and stood there eating a sandwich. He was unshaven, his eyes rheumy as pond scum. He was younger than me by a few years, though he looked positively ancient. Most of his teeth were gone, and his face was caved in and pruny-looking. The fellow hardly bathed so you always tried to keep upwind from him. Father had hired him to sweep the floors and mow the lawn and do odd jobs around the church and the rectory—that is, when you could catch him.

"Mass is canceled," I explained.

"I mean with Devlin."

"Oh, 'tis nothing."

"Don't sound like nothing to me," he snorted.

He took another bite of his sandwich and mangled it with the few teeth he had left.

"It's just a mistake, don't you worry none."

"Mistake?"

"That's right. Father's at the police station right now straightening it all out."

"How in the hell can you mistake getting buggered by your priest? It's like being almost pregnant. You either are or you ain't."

"Well, you just keep your nose out of it. Father'll take care of it." I went over to the door and taped the last notice to the glass. "If anybody asks just tell 'em there's to be no Mass today."

"If he needed some, he should've got himself a piece of tail."

"Why don't you shut your filthy gob, Stanley."

"I got a right to my opinion."

"Well, keep your bloody opinions to yourself."

"Hell, I bet even the pope hisself's got some little honey he's dipping his holy wick into," he said, snickering.

I turned on him, for I was in no mood for his nonsense. "Why, you oughta be ashamed of yourself. After all Father's done for you."

Stanley was another of Father's "projects," like me for that matter. He was a bum and heroin addict when Father found him on the streets of Montville and took him in, gave him this job. Anyone else would have got down on his knees and kissed the very ground Father walked on for all he'd done for him. Not Stanley. He was an ungrateful whelp, the sort of cur who bit the hand that fed him. The more Father did for him in fact, the more he seemed to resent it. He used to grumble behind Father's back, say things about him. And I know he talked about me, too. I once overheard him say, "That bitch thinks she's so high and mighty. Living up in the big house with the padre like she was the queen bee." It was rumored, too, that he would buy booze for kids around town, in return for a couple of bucks. I told Father on more than one occasion he ought to get rid of him. Not only was he lazy as sin, he was nasty and spiteful. But Father said Stanley had had a hard life, that we needed to show him some compassion.

"Looks like the padre's got his ass caught in a crack this time," Stanley said, snickering.

"Shut up, Stanley," I said, pointing my umbrella at him. "I'm warning you."

I was almost out the door when he said, "You think you're so damn smart. Hell, you don't know the half of it."

I shouldn't have paid him no mind. Should've just chalked it up to his brain being so pickled and his heart so twisted and rotten. But for some reason I stopped and turned around.

"You'd better hope nothing happens to Father," I said.

"Why's that?"

"Who else would hire such a poor excuse for a man?"

Halfway home, I felt suddenly winded from the walk, and my feet, wet and cold, were aching. I paused momentarily, leaning against a beech tree. The skies were gray and low, as they often are up here in the mountains when it rains, with frayed wisps of clouds strung just above the treetops like batting. The rain had turned the May morning chilly, and I shivered. *You don't know the half of it.* What did Stanley mean by that? What didn't I know? But then I thought, Don't be paying that one any mind, Maggie. He was nothing but a damn fool. An ungrateful one at that. It'd be just like him to say something hateful, for no good reason other than spite. I'd known Father Jack almost twenty years. Knew him better, in fact, than anybody else. He was a good man. His whole life had been devoted to helping people, especially the young. They thought the world of him. In all the time I'd been here, I never heard any child have a bad word to say about him. Not a one.

Back home, I got out of my wet things and had myself a bit of Father's brandy to drive the chill out of my bones. Though it wasn't Saturday, the day I normally do the beds, I decided to change Father's sheets anyway. I figured he'd be tired after he was done straightening things out at the police station, and he might want to take a nap before dinner. He'd appreciate stretching out under nice crisp sheets. Nothing like clean sheets against your skin when you're tired. Besides, I wanted to be doing, not sitting around on my arse moping.

I went upstairs and into his room. I must've been in there a thousand times, maybe more—vacuuming or dusting, putting away his clothes, changing his sheets—but today it had a different feel to it. I don't know how to put it exactly. Father's was a spare, unadorned room, with faded, brown wallpaper that had been up since before I come to work here. There was the bed, a nightstand and bureau, a leather chair and reading lamp. A small bookcase with his favorite books. A few pictures here and there. Except for the gold-framed painting of the Lord over the headboard, there was nothing special about the room. Nothing that would lead you to believe it was a priest's quarters. Just some old bachelor's room, I suppose you would think it, the sort where little thought was paid to frills. Though Father wasn't sloppy, left to his own he would leave his bed unmade, and he was as likely to drop his dirty things on the floor as place them in the hamper. I didn't mind though, not really. I took that to be part of my job: picking up after him the way you might a slightly spoiled but very talented child. I can't tell you the times I'd found an orphaned sock of his under the bed or a slipper collecting dust beneath the bureau. Sometimes I would try to add a woman's touch. I'd put some flowers in a vase and set it on his nightstand, or I got him that pretty, black-laquered box to hold his jewelry. And once, I even went to the trouble of making him some new curtains. I bought some material at the Fabric Barn over in Montville, and I spent a couple days sewing them.

"How do you like your curtains, Father?" I asked.

"Curtains?" he said. He hadn't even noticed, which was just like a man for you. Not that Father wasn't appreciative. He was. It's just that he wasn't what you'd call observant. Details eluded him. He always had his head filled with more important things than a dirty sock or some curtains.

And I thought as well about the times I'd nursed him here when he was under the weather. How I would sit on the side of the bed and rub his temples when he had one of his bad headaches, or bring him some chicken broth after he was getting over the pneumonia that time. Or like when he was laid up with his back surgery. How I would bring his morning paper and his breakfast on a tray. The way I used to hold the mirror for him when he shaved or bring in a bowl of soapy water and wash his feet for him, trim his toenails, as he couldn't do it himself. How embarrassed he was. Yet who else did he have but me? I remembered all those things and wondered why. Why was I thinking about them now? Could it have been that already, even right then, I was afraid things might change, that all that was something of the past? I can't really say, except I knew I felt something different in his room that day.

I'd stripped his bed and was tucking in the sheets, drawing them snug the way Father prefers. That's when, out of the blue, it come to me: *Father's cross*. Why hadn't I remembered before? Just like now, I was making the bed when my eye caught something shiny on the floor near the nightstand. A solid gold cross with a gold chain, nothing fancy, but you knew it must've cost a pretty penny. When I gave it to Father, he looked kind of surprised and asked me where I'd found it. He said he'd been looking high and low for the thing. Told me it'd been a present from his late mother on his ordination day and so held a great deal of sentimental value for him, as you might well imagine. He even kissed me on the forehead in gratitude for having found it for him.

But the part I mean, the one involving the Roby boy, came some time later on. Maybe a month, two months later. I don't remember exactly and it's not really important. Anyway, I was over to the church. Father had sent me on an errand to pick something up in his office. I opened his door and who should I see in there but this very same Russell Roby. I remember it was him, all right. I'd seen him around before. He'd come over to the rectory a few times, to see Father. The truth of it was he was the sort of boy that rubbed me the wrong way. Just something about him. You know the sort I'm talking about. Always with that smirk on his face, like he was laughing at you behind your back. A little sneak I had him pegged for and I'm usually a good judge of character. And just recently some things had turned up missing, some cash from the petty cash box over in the rectory. An engraved fountain pen someone had given Father. Little things. So I asked him what he thought he was doing in Father's office. Nothing, he says, just waiting for Father. But what catches my attention is the cross hanging about his neck. If it wasn't the exact twin of Father's, why, I don't have eyes in my head. I play dumb, tell him, my, what a lovely cross you got yourself there and may I see it, pretending to take an interest in it. I just wanted to make sure it was Father's. Which it was, all right. The very same one I'd found. I ask him where he'd be getting something like that, and with that smirk on his face he tells me he got it as a present. Present, my arse. Did he think I was born yesterday? So I told him flat-out he wasn't pulling the wool over my eyes. Said we both of us knew it was Father's cross, and that he might as well come clean. At first, the little liar swore up and down he was telling the truth. But I'd have none of that. No sir. When I told him I was going to call the police on him and he'd be in hot water for sure, you should've seen how quick he changed his tune. He turned on the tears and begged me not to, said he didn't want to get in any trouble. You should've thought of that before you nicked it, I said to him. I put the fear of God in him.

When I gave Father his cross back I told him he ought to be more careful with it. I said if I was him I'd come down hard on that lad, too, to teach him a lesson. But Father held with sparing the rod. Was always too easy with some of those boys, if you want my opinion.

That was it. What I remembered about Russell Roby. I knew there was something. Wouldn't you know it, I thought: a thief and a liar was saying these terrible things about Father? Wouldn't you just know it?

• • •

Father didn't return until late that evening. Waiting for him, I sat at the kitchen table, glancing up at the clock. Every now and then I'd go to the kitchen door and look out, wondering what could possibly be keeping him. What would take this long? The nice pot roast I'd made him was cold and hard. When he finally got home, he looked a bit shaken by his meeting with the police. I asked if he wanted me to heat him up his supper, but he said he'd already eaten at the police station. He said he was exhausted and just going to go up to bed. I wanted to ask him how it had gone but I figured that could wait till morning.

"How's your headache, Father?"

"Not so bad."

Around ten-thirty, I made sure the place was locked up tight, got into my nightgown and crawled into bed. Though I hadn't slept more than an hour or two the previous night, I still couldn't sleep. I sometimes have trouble sleeping, especially when something's bothering me. I got up finally and threw on my robe. I went into the kitchen and made myself a cup of tea, adding a drop of brandy as I'd felt a chill in my bones ever since walking through the rain that morning. I headed into the den and turned the television on, making sure to keep the volume low. Soon the late news came on.

"Controversy continues to swirl around a Hebron Falls priest," said the anchor, not the smiley one, but an attractive, oriental woman. "For more on the story we go to Andrea Ladd in Hebron Falls."

I wondered if this Andrea Ladd specialized in this sort of thing, like some do sports or weather. She had her hair pulled back into a ponytail so she looked even more like a girl. She was standing on Main Street with Hodel's Market clearly in the background.

"Allegations of sexual abuse by a well-known priest have rocked this sleepy little town," she said. That was only the first time they'd call us a "sleepy-little-town." Before they got through with us though, we'd be the sleepiest little town on the map. "Earlier today," Andrea Ladd continued, "Reverend John Devlin was taken to the state police barracks in Montville for questioning."

It then showed Father getting out of the police cruiser and being led into the barracks, while a few reporters shoved microphones in his face. I almost didn't recognize him. He looked different, his face puffy and gray in the bright lights. I was thankful he'd changed into his collar and sports jacket at least.

This Andrea Ladd was next standing with St. Luke's in the background, the piece of paper I'd taped to the front door still visible.

"Reverend John Thomas Devlin, fifty-three, better known to his parishioners as 'Father Jack,' has been pastor at St. Luke's for the past twenty-three years. Though the priest is popular with many parishioners, he does have his detractors. Father Jack, a vocal critic of Church doctrine, was known to take controversial stands on issues ranging from gay rights to abortion, and was reprimanded by Church officials on several occasions, according to sources. At this point police have not charged Father Devlin with any crimes. However, a police spokesman did comment that the accusations are being seriously investigated and that Father Devlin is cooperating. Mass today at St. Luke's was canceled. When asked what he thought of the accusations, Father Devlin replied only with 'No comment.' This is Andrea Ladd reporting from Hebron Falls."

I dozed off in the chair and woke in the middle of the night. The television was still on. I turned it off and started for my room. That's when I heard the sound, like someone coughing. I listened carefully to determine where it was coming from. I headed past my bedroom and down the hall. I paused outside the door to Father's study. I could see this faint light seeping out from under it, which wasn't unusual as Father was often up late working. That's when I heard the noise again.

"Father?" I asked, knocking lightly on the door. "It's me."

"Come in," he said.

He was sitting at his desk, a brandy snifter in front of him. The reading lamp shaded his face but it was clear enough he'd been crying. He wore only a T-shirt and his pajama bottoms, no socks or slippers.

"Hope I'm not interrupting you, Father."

"No, no," he said, rubbing his eyes. "Please, sit down, Margaret. Can I get you a drink?"

"Oh, I'd better not," I said. "You know me."

"Just one? I hate to drink alone."

"Since you put it that way. Maybe a wee small one."

He went over to his liquor cabinet and poured me some Hennessey cognac from a fancy bottle. Father wasn't much of a drinker but his tastes were top-shelf.

"This is grand stuff," I exclaimed. "Couldn't sleep, eh, Father?"

"No."

"It's chilly. Oughtn't you to be wearing a robe? You don't want to catch cold, now do you?"

"I'm all right," he said.

"If you don't mind my asking, how'd things go today? With the police, I mean."

He shrugged. "I'm not really sure. They asked me some questions and I answered them."

"And that was it?"

"Pretty much."

"How come it took so long then?"

"I don't know."

"Did they say it's all straightened out?" I asked.

Father smiled at that, though I didn't see the humor in it. He rolled his cognac around in his glass, then took a sip.

"They said they'd be back in touch."

"Did it seem like . . . well, like they believed you?"

"Hard to say. They were pretty tight-lipped. I did offer to take a lie detector test if that would convince them I was telling the truth."

I felt something hard and tight inside me, like a clenched fist, loosen up a bit when he said this.

"Do you think they'll have you take one?"

"I don't know. I told them I was willing."

"That would pretty much put an end to all this, I suppose."

Father fell silent. He took a deep breath and sighed.

"I have no idea what's going to happen, Margaret," he said. "Let's hope nothing. But the last thing I want is to have my private life put under a microscope. Because that's what they'll do. I've seen it happen to other priests. They dig into your private business until they find something—*anything*. They'll twist things around so something that's perfectly innocent looks bad. It doesn't matter to them what it is. Just as long as they discredit you."

I wasn't quite sure what he meant, who the *they* were, but I nodded just the same. I figured it was the booze talking.

"I've made mistakes, Margaret. I'm not perfect."

"*Och*! Who of us are, Father?"

"Did you ever hear of Reverend Morandini?"

"No sir. Can't say I have."

"He was a priest in upstate New York. A dear friend of mine. A good priest. One of the nicest, kindest people I ever knew. Then somebody started these rumors about him and a married woman. None of it was true. They were just friends. But it didn't matter. They were just out to get him. They didn't like his politics. He'd made enemies in high places. When they were finished sifting through his personal life, he was ruined. He was forced to leave the priesthood. He moved around a lot, took odd jobs. He had a nervous breakdown. Twice he's tried to commit suicide."

"That's just terrible."

"I don't want that to happen to me."

"Aren't you jumping the gun a bit, Father?"

"Am I?" he said, looking into his glass. "I hate to drag you into this, Margaret."

"Don't worry about me."

"If you wanted to take a leave till this is all over, I'd understand."

"What?"

"I mean if you wanted to go away for a while. Till we see what's going to happen. The parish would continue to pay you, of course."

"And who would take care of things around here?"

"I could manage for a while."

"Do you *want* me to go, Father? Is that it?"

"No, of course not. It's just that things could get pretty ugly around here."

"I can take care of myself. This is where I belong."

"I just wanted you to know I'd understand if you wished to go away for a while."

"Nonsense. This is my place. Let's have no more of that now. Can I get you anything? Something to eat perhaps?"

"No, I'm fine."

"Get some sleep, Father. Things always have a way of looking worse at night."

"You know what Blake said about the night?"

"*Blake*?" I asked.

"William Blake. He was a poet."

"Oh," I said. I was going to say something but decided not to.

"He wrote, 'God appears and God is light, to those poor souls who dwell in night.'"

"I guess there's something to that, Father. Good night."

7

Though I hadn't slept much, I was up at the crack of dawn. First Communion was coming up and there'd be a lot to do. Cleaning and baking and getting everything shipshape for the party we had here afterward. Some of the mothers would be looking in the corners, seeing what sort of house I kept. And especially now I wanted the rectory to shine like a new penny. I wanted people to think, *That house was a well-run house. Could eat off the floors, you could.*

I put coffee on for Father and then went out and got the morning paper. At the bottom of the front page a headline read, CONTROVERSIAL PRIEST QUESTIONED ABOUT SEX ABUSE ALLEGATIONS. They had Father's picture, too, one from years ago when he was much younger. His hair was longer and the beard hadn't a trace of gray in it. He used to wear an earring in those days, though luckily you couldn't see it in the picture. The article said he was known for his "outspoken criticism of the Church," for the sometimes unpopular views he held. They made him sound like he was some kind of wild-eyed radical, like one of those IRA fellows ready to blow up a building. I gave some more thought to what Father had said the previous night. About how they would dig into his private life, try to make him look bad any way they could. Like they had with that other priest. It was already starting. I set the paper at his place, as I always do, though I put the article about him face down, so his own picture wouldn't be staring at him first thing.

I was in the kitchen baking pies when Father finally came downstairs. He looked in better spirits today. He'd showered, his hair and beard still wet and glistening, his cheeks beet red, the way they got when he took a hot shower. He was wearing his collar, so he must have had parish affairs to tend to.

"Top o' the mornin' to ye, Margaret," he said, putting on his bad Irish brogue, the way he would when feeling in a spirited mood.

"Why, hello, Father," I replied, wiping my hands on my apron. "Did you sleep well?"

"Like a log," he said, stretching. "I'll take those eggs now, if it's no trouble?"

"No trouble at all, Father," I replied, a bit surprised by the change in his manner.

"I'm famished."

Most mornings after he came back from his run, he'd have just a cup of black coffee, a bowl of cereal, and a piece of fruit. But today I whipped him up some eggs and rashers, home fries and toast. The works. I was glad to see his appetite back. A woman takes pleasure in making a meal for someone who likes to eat. I didn't quite know what to say so I figured I'd follow his lead. While I made his breakfast, I watched him out of the corner of my eye. He looked at the front page of the newspaper but then quickly turned to the inside section and started in with the crossword puzzle, as if it was any other day. I waited for him to say something. Anything. I didn't want to seem like I was prying, especially not after our talk last night about people digging into his private life. Yet when I realized he wasn't going to bring the subject up at all, my curiosity got the better of me.

"What happens now, Father?"

"What do you mean?" he said.

"About . . . well . . . with the Robys and all."

He shrugged his shoulders, then wrote something down on the crossword puzzle.

"Don't you think you ought to do something, Father?"

"Like what?"

"I don't know," I said. "*Something.*"

Father went back to working on his crossword puzzle.

"Maybe you ought to get yourself a lawyer," I ventured. When he didn't look up, I added, "A lawyer couldn't hurt none."

He nodded his head.

I brought his food over and set it down before him. He'd almost finished his puzzle.

"It's none of my concern, Father, but mightn't it be a good idea?"

"Uh-huh," he said.

"To look out for your interests."

"I suppose."

"Do you want me to call Pete? He says he knows a good one."

"What?" he asked, suddenly looking up, his reading glasses making his blue eyes appear puffy and loose.

"Jesus, Mary and Joseph!" I exclaimed. "Have you not been listening to a word I've said, Father?"

Two people living under the same roof, it's only natural they get on each other's nerves now and again. I know I have my annoying habits, like jabbering too much. With Father it was little things mostly. Like how he wouldn't lift the toilet seat when doing his business or how he'd leave a pen in his trousers' pocket and throw it in the hamper and after I did a wash the clothes would come out with ink stains on them. But what really got my goat was how preoccupied he could sometimes be, how wrapped up in his own world, you might say. For a man who was in most ways thoughtful and considerate, one who never once forgot my birthday, Father could be quite inconsiderate at times. Take, for instance, how he'd be hours late getting home and I'd be sitting there stewing, worried that something had happened, his car in a ditch somewhere. "Would it hurt you to call, Father?" I'd lay into him when he got home. Or like now, how he was more concerned about his bloody crossword than he was with the situation we found ourselves in. Father was a wonderful man in most respects, but I must confess there were times I felt like grabbing him by the shoulders and shaking some sense into him.

"A lawyer?" he said. "Whatever for?"

"A lawyer would look out for your interests."

"I can look out for my own interests."

"Pete thought it a good idea, too. He said you should have one."

"That sounds like Pete, all right. Besides, the diocese already has a lawyer. *If* I needed one, I could use him."

Father opened his daily calendar and wrote something down in it. He was so calm, so nonchalant this morning. Yet his calmness in

the face of what looked like certain disaster approaching had the opposite effect on me.

"I think Pete's right," I said. "A lawyer might not be such a bad
idea. What do you know about these things?"

"Margaret," he said, "I know what the truth is. I told the police
I had no idea what the Robys were talking about. And I don't."

"Why would they be doing this to you, Father?"

"The police have to investigate. It's their job."

"No, I meant those Robys."

"I don't know."

"Maybe they hold some grudge against you?"

"I can't think of any."

I paused for a moment, then asked, "Did you tell them about the
cross?"

"Cross? What cross?"

"Why, the one that Roby stole from you, Father." He looked at
me, perplexed. "Don't you remember? The older one. Russell. It was
him stole that cross of yours. The one your mother gave you. Don't
you remember, Father?"

"Oh, that's right. I almost forgot. And you think he's doing this
because of that?"

"I'm just thinking out loud is all. Trying to come up with some
reason for them to be doing this."

Father shrugged, then fell to perusing his calendar again.

After a while, I said, "Did you talk to Pete yet?"

"No."

"He thinks you should put out a press release denying everything."

"A press release! I'm not some politician running for office. I'm a
priest. Why should I have to defend myself against such baseless accusations?"

"It's just that there are people out there who'd like nothing better
than to see you hurt. Like yourself said, you have to be careful."

He got up and brought his plate over. He scraped what he hadn't
eaten into the garbage disposal, then put his dish in the sink. "*Magna
est veritas et praevalebit*, Margaret," he said, something he'd said
any number of times before. Great is truth and it prevails.

"In this world the truth isn't always enough."

"You know why they're even questioning me?"

"No, Father. I must say I don't have the foggiest notion."

"It's because of my views on things. They don't like my politics. What I stand for. That and because of all those other priests. The ones who did do terrible things. In people's eyes we're *all* guilty now. Not just the few but all of us. We've become society's scapegoats. Throughout history priests have been revered. They were the keepers of a society's values, its collective heart and soul. Did you know that in some cultures the priest is believed to be able to know the future?"

"No sir, I surely wouldn't know about all that." I thought how it would be just like Father to go rambling on at a time like this. "I'm just saying it mightn't hurt to get yourself a lawyer."

"But I don't need a lawyer, Margaret. I didn't do those things."

"I know you didn't. I know. Still, it wouldn't be a bad idea, Father. To protect yourself."

"I'll think about it. All right?" He looked out the window toward the garden and the woods beyond that. "I see you've set out your tomato plants," he said.

"That I have, Father."

"I'm looking forward to that tomato sauce of yours," he said, glancing at his watch. "I'd better get moving. I have to meet Terry Sabonis at the nursing home. Her mother's taken a turn for the worse. Don't bother with lunch. I'll grab a bite out."

He went into his study and returned with his prayer book and the silver pyx, which held the hosts for bedside communion.

"Father, I meant no disrespect talking out of turn like that."

"I know you didn't, Margaret. You're only watching out for my interests. And I do appreciate it. But please, let me handle this in my own way. Hold down the fort while I'm gone."

"What should I say if people call?"

"Just tell them I'm unavailable."

I watched him go out to his car, back out of the garage. He drove down West Street and turned right onto Main, heading for the nursing home.

• • •

Around mid-morning while I was baking pies, the doorbell rang. Wiping my hands on my apron, I went to answer it. Though it wasn't raining out, the sky was still overcast and gray. I peeked out the window. Who was standing there but those same two detectives.

"Good morning, Ms. Quinn," said the young one. I don't know how they'd got my name as I didn't recall giving it to them the day before. "We were here yesterday. I'm Detective Gomez and this is Detective Dufresne."

"I know who you are," I said. "Father's out."

"Actually, we'd like a few words with you," said the fat one, Detective Dufresne.

"With *me*?" I asked.

"If you have a minute," the younger one added.

"To tell you the truth, I'm kinda busy right now. Getting ready for our First Communion party and all."

"Boy, I still remember mine," said Detective Gomez, smiling proudly. "My family made a big deal of it."

"Well, if you don't mind, I have work to do," I replied and made as if to close the door.

"Do you believe he did those things?" Dufresne slipped in the crack, the way a salesman might slip in a free sample trying to get you to open the door.

"A course not," I replied.

"Did he tell you not to talk to us?"

"No," I said. "I mean, he didn't say anything one way or the other."

"You could help Father by answering some questions, Ms. Quinn," explained the younger one. "We'd sure like to clear this whole mess up. Father Devlin seems like a terrific guy."

"That he is," I replied.

"We'll only take a few minutes of your time, ma'am. An altar boy's promise," Gomez said, turning that nice smile of his on me.

"I suppose I could spare a few minutes," I replied. "Come in. But be sure to wipe your feet. I just waxed the floors."

I showed them into the den. They sat on the couch, myself across from them on the wing chair, with the coffee table between us. I kept my hands neatly folded in my lap so as not to give away the fact I was nervous. I felt like a little girl before them. I don't know why. I felt the way I used to when I was a child sitting in the confessional, waiting to begin, wondering what and how much to tell Father Pearse, if I'd say the wrong thing or forget something and go straight to hell for it. Detective Gomez glanced around the room, saw the small shrine to the Virgin in the corner.

"Reminds me of my house growing up," he said. "My mom used to have stuff like that all over the place. Candles, crucifixes, pictures of Jesus and the Madonna everywhere. The whole nine yards."

"Detective Gomez here's a good Catholic boy," said the fat one, grinning so his eyebrows bent into a thick *M* across his meaty face.

"A lapsed Catholic," the young one apologized. "And I married a Jewish girl. We couldn't get married in the Catholic Church. Broke my mother's heart."

"Depends on the priest nowadays. Father Jack would've married you."

"He would have?"

"Surely."

"I heard he was different like that," the older one broke in. "Liberal. Willing to bend the rules."

"I wouldn't know about that," I said. "He doesn't always agree with the Church's stand on things, if that's what you mean."

Dufresne took out a pad and a pen, and got right down to business. He asked most of the questions, while Gomez just sat there, occasionally throwing in a question or two, smiling to keep me at ease.

"Ms. Quinn, how long have you worked here?" asked Dufresne.

"Eighteen years. It'll be eighteen come December."

"All of that for Devlin?"

"For *Father* Devlin," I corrected. "Aye."

"That's a long time. You must like your job."

"I do."

"And how is it working for him?"

"What do you mean?"

"You know, is he a good man to work for?"

"Certainly. I'd hardly have stayed all that time if I didn't like working for him, now would I?"

I was going to say more but I warned myself not to go running off at the mouth. *Just answer their bloody questions, Maggie.* Not that I had anything to hide, mind you. Just that they were the police and certainly weren't looking out for Father's best interests.

"Would you say you know him well?"

"You can't hardly live in the same house with someone for all that time without getting to know him."

"What sort of man is Father Devlin?"

"A decent man. Hardworking. Kind and caring. And I can tell you right now he wouldn't of done those things."

"How can you be so sure?"

"Because I *know* him, that's why," I said forcefully.

"Would you mind taking a look at these, ma'am?" asked Detective Gomez. He slid two pictures across the coffee table. "Those are the Roby brothers."

The pictures showed two young boys. School pictures by the looks of them. One had short brown hair, pudgy cheeks, dark eyes shading toward black. I don't think I'd ever seen him before. The other had shoulder-length sandy-blond hair that framed a small, angular face, gaunt cheeks, eyes whose color fell somewhere between gray and blue. Not a homely child so much as plain, with forgettable features. Though his hair was longer here and he wasn't wearing his altar boy robes, it was the same boy I'd seen in the album. The same smirk. That was the thing you remembered about his face. When I was finished I put the pictures back on the coffee table.

"This one's Bobby," Detective Gomez explained, pointing at one of the photos. "The younger one. He'd have been about ten there. And that's his older brother Russell," he said, indicating at the other photo. "He would have been eleven in that picture. Do you recall either of these boys?"

"I remember that one," I said, pointing at the older Roby.

"Can you tell us anything about him?" Dufresne asked.

"There's not much to tell. He'd come around sometimes."

"What do you mean, come around?"

"He might drop by to see Father. Maybe stop in before Mass."

"So you *do* recall these particular boys coming around here then?" asked Dufresne.

"I can't say about the younger one. But the older one, he'd stop by sometimes."

"We heard that Father Devlin had kids over a lot. Is that true?"

"Some would stop by."

"What would they do here?"

"Watch a ball game on television or play some basketball outside. Help Father with the paper drive or car wash. Rake leaves. Things like that. It's not uncommon. Then or now. They like Father."

"Why?" Detective Dufresne asked.

"*Why?*" I said. "I guess because Father has a way with 'em."

"What sort of way?"

"He gets along with kids. He understands them. They feel they can trust him."

"Sounds like the Pied Piper," Dufresne tossed out. Everything the fat one said had this edge to it, like he was trying to bait me, trying to get me to say something I shouldn't.

"You wanted to know why they like him and I'm telling you," I snapped at him. "'*Suffer the little children to come unto me, and forbid them not,*' it says in the Bible." I saw the fat one write something down on his pad and I warned myself again not to lose my temper. But I didn't care for this one's attitude. No sir. Like he had something against Father, against Catholics for all I knew. How he'd called his partner a good Catholic boy. Growing up in Ireland, I knew what it was to have people look down their noses at you because of your religion. "They like him because he doesn't act like most priests."

"How's that, ma'am?" asked Detective Gomez. At least this one was polite, had some manners, showed some respect.

"He's not an old fogy," I explained. "Most priests are more concerned about all the rules. Don't do this, don't do that. Father's—"

But Dufresne cut me off. "So you're saying Father likes to break the rules? Is that it?"

"Don't be putting words in my mouth," I said to him. "I meant only that with Father people come first. That's why the kids like him. He thinks religion oughtn't to be just a bitter pill."

"He has a cabin up in New Hampshire. He ever take kids up there?"

"Sometimes," I said.

"Alone?"

I glanced from one to the other. "I'm wondering if I should even be talking to you like this? I don't have to, do I?"

"No, ma'am, you don't," replied Detective Gomez.

"Do you have anything to hide?" the fat one asked.

"Hide?" I said. "Why, of course not."

"Then why not talk to us? Help us get to the bottom of this."

Gomez said, "Ma'am, we don't like this any more than you. We don't want to make trouble for Father. You want to help him, don't you?"

"Certainly."

"Then talk to us. We're not looking to hurt Father Devlin. We're just asking for your help."

I began to like this Detective Gomez. He seemed sincere, with his boyish good looks and his glistening, dark eyes. He had nice hands, too—delicate yet not dainty, mahogany-colored, the nails almost pink.

"It's just so crazy," I said. "Father Jack would never of done anything like what they're saying."

"Why do *you* think they've made the accusations then?"

"Maybe they mixed Father Jack up with some other priest."

"Nope," Dufresne said. "We checked the records. They were altar boys here when Father Devlin was pastor. He was their priest, all right. No doubt about that."

"Then they're lying. They have to be."

"Why would they lie, Ms. Quinn?" Detective Gomez asked. "That's the thing we can't understand. What can they gain by coming out now?"

"There's the money for one thing. Besides, some people are just born liars. It's in their nature. *That one*," I said, pointing at the picture of Russell Roby, "I know for a fact is a liar."

"How do you know that?" Gomez asked.

"He stole something once and lied about it."

So I told them the story about Father's gold cross. How I'd caught him wearing it and when I confronted him at first he lied and said it was his. They didn't seem to think it was very important though.

They asked me some other things: if I ever recalled kids staying overnight; if boys were here without my being around; if Father had ever had kids up in his room. How many times did he take them up to his cabin in New Hampshire? Had any alcohol ever been consumed by children on parish property? This and that.

"To your knowledge did he ever take pictures of any boys?" asked Detective Dufresne.

"Pictures? Why, there's lots of pictures in the albums," I said, flicking my thumb toward the shelves.

"No, not those kinds of pictures," the fat one said. "I meant pictures of them naked. Pornographic pictures."

"Why, of course not!" I stammered. "Don't be ridiculous. Did they say that, too!"

"There's an accusation that Father Devlin took nude pictures of them," explained Gomez. "You wouldn't be aware of any such pictures?"

"Absolutely not! He's a priest, for heaven's sakes."

"I've worked with sexual offenders for years," Dufresne said. "I've seen Boy Scout leaders, teachers, CEO's, judges. You name it. Even a nun once. Pedophiles come in all shapes and sizes."

I got to my feet.

"I've said all I'm going to. Unless you got a paper or something saying I have to talk to you, you don't come back. You understand?"

"Thank you for your time, ma'am," said Detective Gomez, getting up and shaking my hand. His felt warm and smooth. "I know this hasn't been easy. We'll do our best to get to the bottom of it."

From behind the curtain I watched them pull out of the driveway. *To the bottom of it*, I thought. I pictured a hole, dark and bottomless as hell. The same sort of hole I'd pictured on the phone that night I had to tell Father about all this. Across the street I could see Mrs. Mueller peering out a window. The nosy old bird. A moment before the fire alarm went off I smelled something burning. I ran into the kitchen and opened the oven door. My pies were burnt black as pitch.

"Why you stinkin' sons of bitches," I cried.

8

For a few weeks nothing much happened, though as you can imagine the town continued to buzz with the news. Like I said, The Falls is a small place and not much happens. The last time anything near this big took place was when the Wohlers girl was found beaten and raped on the village green. Before that, you'd have to go back to the fire at the middle school. And before that I guess it'd be Justin Blake's murder.

When I went to Hodel's Market to do my shopping, people would inquire about "the situation." *Any news on the situation, Ma Quinn*? they'd ask, as if I knew anything more than they did. Or, *How was poor Father Jack bearing up*? they'd want to know. *It's a crying shame, a wonderful man like him to be dragged through the mud by those two.* Yet I noticed how after a moment or two they'd glance at their watches and exclaim, *Oh dear me, would you look at the time now*, saying they were late to such and such and hurry off, trying to put as much distance between themselves and yours truly as they could. Even then, I felt this subtle shift in things, in the way people acted around me. At first I thought it just my imagination. But it wasn't. No sir. People started giving me the cold shoulder. Standing in line at the post office once, I overheard Mrs. Silvera, the Catholic Women's Club president, talking to Jane Loiko.

"I could never put my finger on it," Mrs. Silvera said. "Just something about him."

"I know what you mean," Jane replied. "I always got that feeling, too, whenever I was around him."

When they happened to see me standing there, they nodded politely and fell silent. So I knew they'd just been talking about Father.

There was those began making themselves scarce, staying away from everything associated with Father Devlin—the rectory, the church, CCD, confession, Wednesday night bingo. Even me. They measured their comments, at least when I was in earshot, as if waiting to see which way the wind would blow. Others just wanted the inside dirt, and figuring as I worked for him I'd be the one in the know.

At Friendly's one evening I was having supper with Cindy O'Connell.

"Maggie," she said, "you think Father Jack's ever been with a woman?"

"What!" I exclaimed, almost choking on my food. "How in the blazes would I know?"

"You're *there* with him all the time."

"He's a priest, for God's sakes."

"Are you trying to tell me he's *never* had a woman?"

"I won't even dignify that with an answer. Eat your food."

"Don't be so naive. In his *whole* life. Think about it, Maggie."

"You think about it. He's married to the Church."

She stuffed her mouth with coleslaw. She likes to eat, Cindy does. She's as big as a house, and especially since she gave up the booze she packs it away like there's no tomorrow. When we went out to eat, she usually cleaned up her plate and then started in on whatever I couldn't finish. Like me, she's an old maid. Came over from Ireland when the troubles started back in the sixties. She lives in town in an apartment on Boylston Street with a couple of cats, works in the kitchen at the nursing home. She and I would get together on Fridays when Friendly's had all-you-can-eat fish and chips. Afterward we'd walk over to the park in the center of town and sit and gab. She was from up north, near Derry, and was always going on about the stinking Orangemen.

"You don't think . . ." she whispered. "He's not one of *those*?"

"One of what? What in the hell are you talking about?"

"That likes men. A queer."

"*Queer* is it now! This is beyond the beyonds, Cindy."

"Look how he married those two women."

"Father doesn't like men, I can assure you on that score. Now let's have no more of that rubbish."

But Cindy's the sort gets a bug up her arse and there's no stopping her. Especially when it comes to gossip! One time we were playing cards over at her apartment, and I'd tipped a couple glasses of sherry and it slipped out that I'd had a child. I'd never told her before. In fact, except for Father, I'd never told anyone in town. It wasn't anyone's business. After that, she wouldn't leave it alone. No sir. Like a dog with a bone. Always prying, asking questions. I didn't tell her everything of course. Just that my boy died. I told her to keep it to herself—after all, it wasn't the sort of thing you wanted everybody and his brother to know about. But don't you know the next time I ran into Mrs. Fey she comes up to me and says as how she feels so bad to hear about my son.

Cindy said, "I don't see what's wrong with asking if he's ever slept with a woman."

"You ought to be ashamed of yourself."

"He's a good-looking fellow. I've seen the way some of those women in the parish look at him."

I felt like saying that was like the pot calling the kettle black. Herself was the one always making eyes at Father, fawning over him. Like he'd even look at her, bloated up like she was.

"Just let it go, Cindy."

"I'm not saying anything bad about him. It's a compliment."

"A compliment! Whether a priest has slept with a woman or not doesn't seem like any compliment to me," I said, raising my voice.

"Ssh," she whispered, glancing around the restaurant. "Keep your voice down, Maggie."

"Then keep your filthy thoughts to yourself."

"All's I'm saying is, who's going to believe it?" she whispered. "Father Jack and a couple of boys. When he could have any woman he wanted."

"Cindy! Enough's enough. I'm warning you."

"You're going to sit there and tell me you never thought of him in that way."

"No, I haven't."

"If he wasn't a priest, you mean you wouldn't be thinkin' him good enough to park his shoes under your bed?"

"He's a fine-looking man, I'll grant you that," I told her. "But I never thought of him in *that* way. He's a priest, for Christ's sakes. A *priest*, don't you know."

"You're so full of it, Maggie Quinn, it's coming out your ears. I seen the way you act around him."

"What're you talking about?"

"What am I talking about, says she! Don't play dumb with me."

"I don't have the foggiest notion what you're jabbering about."

"I have eyes in my head, Maggie."

"Well, at least that's *one thing* you have in that head of yours."

"I wasn't born yesterday," she said, this leering smile carving her face in two. Winking at me she added, "Your secret's safe with me."

"What the hell're you talking about?"

"Like you don't know."

"That's it!" I cried, getting up. "You've gone too far, Cynthia."

"Where you going? Sit down and finish your supper."

"Since you can't speak with a civil tongue in your head I'm leaving," I said, hunting around in my pocketbook for money.

"I don't understand what you're getting so huffy about, Maggie. I didn't say anything bad about Father."

"Wondering if he's queer or having relations with women—that's not bad, I suppose."

I threw down just enough to cover my share of the check, not a penny for a tip, which I knew would get her goat. On the ride home, I got to thinking. How people, on seeing something that's decent and good, have to pull it down, drag it through the muck. So they can say, *See. He wasn't so special after all. He was just like us. His feet were made of clay.* Which says something about human nature, I suppose. That we're so used to filth we think everyone is mired in it.

● ● ●

Father tried to go about his work. Over the next couple of weeks he tried to act like nothing was the matter. He visited people in the hospital over in Montville, made his rounds at the nursing home, listened to confession, conducted Mass, went about the rest of his duties as pastor. He was called down to several meetings at the diocesan offices with Monsignor Payne, vicar for pastoral affairs. Father didn't like him, called him a bean counter, someone more concerned with financial statements than he was with souls. The muckety-mucks at the diocese had never been big supporters of Father Jack to begin with. Over the years, he'd been too outspoken for them, too lax with all the rules. He was always getting called on the carpet, having to defend himself. And now this.

For his part Father was pretty tight-lipped on the subject, kept it to himself, didn't like talking about it. He tried to pretend it didn't bother him. You see, there was Father the priest and Father the man. The priest was talkative and outgoing and self-confident. But the man was a private person, someone, as he himself had put it, that didn't like to have his personal life put under a microscope. But you could tell the things they were saying weighed heavily on him. How could they not? He'd lost his appetite, wasn't sleeping well. Dark circles formed under his eyes. I'd hear him upstairs pacing his room at night or find him in the morning asleep in the study. I tried to be supportive, tried to think positive. At breakfast one morning I told him, "Don't you worry, Father. This'll all blow over, you'll see."

"I certainly hope so," he said.

"Nobody believes those two."

"I wish I was as confident as you are, Margaret."

His sermon on the Sunday of the children's First Communion was one of the best he'd ever given. Though he looked haggard, his voice remained strong and steady, coming from some place deep inside himself that hadn't been affected by everything. If he had any private doubts about getting up before the congregation, you couldn't tell it by his voice. His homily was about the Good Samaritan. He talked about how the priest and the Levite had passed their half-dead neighbor by without offering help. But that the Samaritan had stopped and given succor to the man in need. Father talked about what it meant to give succor, how important it was to lend a helping hand when it was needed and not to turn your back. It wasn't hard to read between the lines. No sir. Still, many of us had hoped he'd get up there and talk about what was on everyone's mind. Come right out and say it was nothing but a pack of lies. Call those two the scoundrels they were. He didn't though. He didn't even mention it.

On the way out of church, I could hear someone whispering behind me. It was Edie Horvath, a woman who ran the Christmas craft fair.

"It's outrageous," she said to her husband, Walt.

"Edie, for heaven's sakes," he whispered, trying to shush her.

"I don't care who hears. He should just resign. He'll drag the entire parish through the mud."

"Father wouldn't have done that," said their daughter, Sharon.

"And how would *you* know?" the missus said.

"Because he's not like that. Father Jack's nice."

Sharon Horvath, a pale, thin girl with an gold hoop in her eyebrow and a tattoo on her arm, used to be an altar server. I recall her coming over to the rectory after Mass for cake and ice cream. She'd gone through a wild period when she hit her teenage years. Drinking, doing drugs, hanging out with a fast crew. A couple of years back she'd overdosed, and they had to rush her to the hospital over in Montville. They didn't think she'd make it. Father had sat with the Horvaths at her bed all night, comforting them, praying with them. Later, it was Father who got her into counseling, had her join the church youth group. And it was on account of him that she was going to church again.

"Thank God, he never tried anything with you," Edie said, well above a whisper.

We'd almost reached the front doors, where Father stood greeting people as they left. I'd heard as much as I could stomach. I turned to the woman and said, "You ought to be ashamed of yourself, Edie Horvath. After all that man has done for you and yours."

Let me tell you, that put her in her place, all right.

Yet just as Pete had predicted, there were signs that the tide *was* turning against Father Jack, and turning quickly, too. Only a few of the kids scheduled to receive First Communion in fact showed up that Sunday, and only a handful of adults came over to the rectory afterward for the party—the Beaupres, the Morans, Eileen Lessard, widow of Father's old friend Rudy, Father Duncan and a few other loyal families. And here I'd made all this food. It was awkward and embarrassing, and though no one said a thing about "the situation," it was obviously on everyone's mind.

Pete stayed afterward and spoke with Father Jack in his study.

Father and the Beaupres were good friends. They got together a lot socially. Pete and his wife, Becky, had Father to dinner and we'd have them here. The way other people have friends for dinner. As I cleaned up, I could hear Pete trying to convince Father to let him set up a committee to show the parish's support. But Father didn't want any committees.

"Jack," Pete cried, "don't be so goddamned stubborn."

"I'm not being stubborn. I'm innocent."

"You're sticking your head in the sand."

"I'm not going to dignify those accusations with a response. The facts will exonerate me."

"*I* know that and *you* know that. But if you sit back and let those bastards say those things without defending yourself, this whole damn town will turn on you . . . like *that*."

I heard the snap of his fingers.

"I have more faith in them than that."

"Tell me, how many showed up for the party, Jack?"

"People didn't want to spoil their kids' First Communion under this cloud. I can't blame them either."

"Don't be so naive."

"I'm not. Pete, I didn't *do* anything. They know that."

"Well, come out and say that then. Call a press conference like they did. Tell people in your next sermon that it's nothing but lies."

"No."

"Why not?"

"Because I'm not going to use the pulpit as a forum to promote my innocence. My years of service here should be enough proof."

"It's not that simple, Jack. If you tell a lie enough times, people start wondering if maybe there's not something to it."

"Pete, I know you're trying to help. I appreciate it. It's just that I prefer to handle things on my own."

"Would you at least let me contact a lawyer then. I know of this guy over in Montville. He's supposed to be really good. Was a trial lawyer with a big firm down in Providence."

"If I need a lawyer the Church has one."

"Are you crazy? They're going to be looking out for their own asses. They'll leave you hanging out to dry. You should have your own lawyer."

"But I don't *need* a lawyer," Father said. "I haven't even been charged with anything."

"You're making a big mistake, Jack. Mark my words."

But Father stuck by his guns, said no lawyer, no committees or press conferences and no public sermons protesting his innocence. He said the facts would show he'd done nothing wrong. On the way out Pete stopped in the kitchen. He's a tall, slender man, red-faced, with this perpetually surprised, almost embarrassed look to him like he'd just dropped an egg on the floor.

"He's so damn stubborn, Maggie," he said to me.

"You know him. Likes doing things his own way."

"Talk to him, Maggie. Maybe he'll listen to you."

"I doubt that very much."

"I don't think he appreciates the gravity of the situation."

At home, Father Jack began taking most of his meals upstairs in his room. Except for emergencies, he gave Dina and me specific instructions to say he was busy if anyone called for him.

While I tried not to put any stock in the things I heard, you couldn't hardly turn around without seeing or hearing something about it. It was *everywhere*—on the news or in the paper, the scuttle-butt swirling around town. Even in our weekly paper, the *Falls Sentinel*: FATHER DEVLIN QUESTIONED ABOUT SEXUAL MISCONDUCT, one headline read.

(May 28, 1993) Father John Devlin, pastor of St. Luke's Church, has been questioned by state police regarding alleged incidents of sexual improprieties involving two former Hebron Falls residents. The brothers, Russell Roby, 25, now of Brattle-boro, Vermont, and Robert Roby, 24, of Portland, Maine, allege they were sexually abused by Father Devlin on numerous occasions dating back to when they were altar boys at St. Luke's in the late seventies. A spokesman for the Adams County D.A.'s office wouldn't comment, except to confirm that the allegations were being investigated.

Mason Elliott, the attorney representing the brothers, has said that he fully expects Father Devlin to be indicted on criminal charges. "This has been a heinous breach of trust by both Mr. Devlin and by the Catholic Church. My clients have suffered irreparable harm at the hands of a deviant priest." Mr. Elliott also has plans to pursue a civil action against both Father Devlin and the diocese. "The Church was culpable for allowing a pedophile to violate these young boys." The *Sentinel* contacted Father Devlin but he refused comment. The investigation is ongoing. No charges as yet have been brought by the D.A.'s office.

Around town, you'd see news vans and reporters interviewing people. It got so bad I'd send poor Dina out if we needed some milk or something. I didn't feel much like speaking to anybody about it. Once she came back on the verge of tears.

"Everybody's talking about it, Ma," Dina told me. "I ran into Mrs. Wirstrom, and she goes, 'Dina, have you quit yet? You're *not* gonna keep working for that man, are you?' She's *such* a witch."

"Talk is cheap," I told her.

"But it's hard. Everybody's so mean to him."

"I know, love. Just keep a tight lip and don't pay 'em no mind."

On my day off, I called Cindy and asked her if she wanted to come over for lunch. We hadn't spoken since that time at the Friendly's. But she was very curt with me. She said, "I wouldn't be caught *dead* over there."

"Why not?"

"You kidding? With everything that's being said."

"It's not true. You know that."

"True or not, I wouldn't set foot in that *place*." She said "place" like it was some foul den filled with lepers.

We—Father and myself—found ourselves just sort of waiting for the next thing to happen, not knowing what that would be. We moved about the rectory on pins and needles, passing awkwardly by each other in the hall, our eyes not meeting when he came down for breakfast, being extra polite and distant with each other. This . . . *thing* had come between us, threw everything out of kilter. Father wouldn't talk about his situation, and I didn't feel it my place to bring it up. I stopped reading the paper and would shut off the television when something about it came on. And if someone in town did ask me about Father, I'd play dumb, say I didn't know any more than anybody else. Some part of me still liked to think it would all just blow over, that storm that was bearing down on us. Call it wishful thinking or stupidity, but I hoped that we'd wake up one fine morning and all this craziness would end and things would return to normal.

But what we woke to one morning in June wasn't that at all. The same two policemen showed up at the rectory just after nine.

"Where's Father Devlin?" the fat one asked.

"He's upstairs. Why?"

"We have a warrant for his arrest."

"Mother o' God!" I cried, looking at Detective Gomez.

"I'm sorry, Ms. Quinn," he said.

"I thought you said you weren't out to hurt Father."

"I'm just doing my job, ma'am. Would you have Father come down?"

I went upstairs and knocked on his door.

"It's the police, Father," I said when he opened the door. "They're back again."

"Did they say what they want?"

I started crying. "I'm afraid they want to arrest you."

"Damn it!" he cursed, his entire body seeming to sag with the news. He put his hand to his mouth, was quiet for a moment. "Tell them I'm getting dressed."

When Father came down, Dufresne said he was under arrest. He read him his rights like you see on the television shows, while Gomez took out his handcuffs. "I'm sorry, Father," the younger man said.

"Good Lord!" I exclaimed. "You're not going to put those bloody things on him, are you?"

"It's all right, Margaret," Father said.

"It's not all right, Father." I turned on the younger one. "You're a Catholic. Would you do this to your priest?"

"I'm sorry, Father," Detective Gomez said. "I have no choice."

"I understand," Father said. "He's only doing his job, Margaret."

They clamped the cuffs on him. As they got to the front door, I'm afraid I lost it and I caused a bit of a scene. I don't know what came over me. I threw my arms around Father Jack's neck and wouldn't let go.

"It's not right, Father, what they're doing to you."

"Margaret, it's okay," Father said. "Everything will be fine."

"No," I cried, holding on to him for dear life. It was as if I thought I could keep them from carting him away, as if I only had to hold him and not let him go and nothing would happen. Maybe it was that I thought if he left, he'd never be coming back again. Maybe I knew that even then. Finally, the fat one grabbed ahold of my arm and made as if to pry me loose.

"You'll please to get your stinkin' paws off me," I hissed at him.

"It's all right, Margaret," Father said, his face looking down into mine. "Margaret, listen to me. Everything'll be just fine. I promise."

"But, Father—"

"I promise. Have I ever lied to you?"

"You haven't."

"It'll be all right. I swear it will. I want you to do me a favor. Call Pete for me. Tell him I guess I'll need that lawyer after all."

"Certainly, Father," I said.

Outside, the reporters were ready to pounce on him; they must've been tipped off, knew he was going to be arrested. They rushed at him, surrounded him in a sea of microphones and cameras. I'd never seen the like of it, at least not in The Falls. A small crowd of townspeople had gathered, too, to catch the spectacle of a priest being hauled away in handcuffs: there was Mrs. Mueller, of course, and Marty Soja, little Kevin Tassinari, the paperboy, Blanche Panofski, on her way to work in her white hygienist outfit, a few others. Even Stanley, that disloyal cur, was among them. I could see the lot of 'em whispering among themselves, as the police put Father in the back of the unmarked cruiser and pulled out.

Pete helped Father make bail—a hundred thousand dollars! He put up his own house as collateral. That much money only drove home the seriousness of it all the more. Once out on bail though, Father didn't come home. Instead he went to stay with Father Duncan at the Jesuit monastery over near Worcester. It probably wasn't a good idea for him to come back to The Falls while awaiting his trial. The mood of the town had gone quickly from one of shock and disbelief to one of anger and outrage. Many were just plain mad at Father. The diocese also officially relieved him of his duties as pastor of St. Luke's.

Father Duncan stopped by to pick up some of Father's things. He was a short, pudgy fellow, with dark eyes and a quick wit. Father and he were close friends, went to seminary together. When Father had him to dinner the two would be up half the night swapping stories and telling jokes. "Maggie," Father Duncan would say to me, laughing, "did Jack ever tell you about what he did with the Bishop's underwear? Go ahead, tell her, Jack." He was going to be temporarily filling in at St. Luke's, though he wouldn't be staying at the rectory. In the past, when he'd filled in for Father Jack, parishioners grumbled that his sermons rambled, that he spoke too softly.

"How's he doing?" I asked. We were sitting in the kitchen. I'd made Father Duncan a cup of tea.

"You know Jack," he replied. "He's tough."

"Does he need anything?"

"I think he's all set. He said to say hi."

"What's going to come of all this?"

He shook his head. "I don't know, Maggie. I've known Jack for almost thirty years. He can be an arrogant son of a bitch. He can do stupid things. He doesn't know how to compromise. Most of the time he's his own worst enemy. But no one—*no one*—is more hardworking, more committed to helping people than Jack. I don't care what anybody says, there's no way I can believe he would have done something like this. No way. Jack loves kids."

"Then why are they saying those things?"

"I don't know. I just don't know."

"Would you give him my love?"

"I will."

The police returned again, this time with a search warrant. Detective Gomez was among them but not the fat one. They searched the house, went through Father's study and bedroom. They took his computer, several notebooks and stacks of papers, parish records, some books, as well as half a dozen boxes filled with personal items. They carried out his file cabinet. They even packed up all the photo albums from the den and took those.

"What do you want with them?" I asked.

"We have a search warrant for all this, Ms. Quinn," replied Detective Gomez.

"What is it you expect to find?"

"I'm not at liberty to discuss an ongoing investigation, ma'am," he replied, no longer with that smile of his. "Please stay back and let us do our work." He'd certainly had me fooled. Being so nice, and all that business about him being a Catholic. It was only to get me to talk. He was just like the other one.

When they were through, it took me the better part of the morning to put everything back in its place. The house felt so strange now that Father was gone. I didn't quite know what to do. Was I supposed to go about my business like nothing had happened? When would he be back? I wandered the empty, silent rooms. I went upstairs and into his bedroom. I looked around. They'd taken some things off his bureau, some photos. They'd ransacked his drawers and left his things a mess, so I straightened them out. Just before I left I happened to notice the faded square of wallpaper just above his headboard. It looked like the negative of something. It took me a moment to realize it was where the picture of the Lord had been. Now it was gone. My God, I thought. Was nothing sacred?

Part II

9

The summer before the trial was unbearably hot and muggy. Usually it's cooler up in the mountains. People come up here to get away from the heat down in the valley, but that year it was hotter than hell. If you took a cool shower in the morning, you'd need to take another one by noon. Even with the air-conditioner on full bore, I would sweat right through my housedress and have to change, it was that bad. When I'd go out to work in my garden or hang clothes on the line, I'd feel myself wilting under the heat. It was terrible, and I'm the sort will take hot weather over cold any day of the week.

On the evening news one night, I saw the lawyer who was going to defend Father. He held a press conference before the Superior Courthouse over in Montville. Leo J. Manzetti was a short but powerfully built fellow, with long, curly, graying hair down to his collar. He called the allegations "scurrilous," said his client was "innocent of any and all crimes he was being charged with." He said it was just a vicious attempt by certain "unnamed parties" opposed to Father Devlin to ruin his career. Manzetti had already filed motions to have all charges dismissed. Why, good for you, Leo J. Manzetti, I thought. About time someone stood up for Father.

A couple of days later I was vacuuming—no one told me otherwise, so I continued with my duties. That's when I got a call from Manzetti's office. His secretary explained that Mr. Manzetti had been retained as Father Devlin's defense counsel and that he had some things he wanted to discuss with me. She asked if I could stop by the next day. I said certainly. What did he want with me? I wondered.

His law practice was located on the third story of a building on Main Street in Montville, right next to the old Rivoli Theater, which was now a flea market. The building was stifling and didn't have an elevator, and I paused to catch my breath on the landing outside his office. It was only ten in the morning, but already it was ninety in the shade. I was sweating like a pig. On his door, it said LEONARDO J. MANZETTI, ATTORNEY-AT-LAW. I was wondering how good this Manzetti fellow could be if he couldn't afford an office with a proper elevator.

"Please have a seat," his secretary said to me. Her nameplate said Gina Demarco. I wondered if she was any relation to the Demarcos that lived over in The Falls. She was young, early twenties, I'd guess. Pretty in a cheap sort of way. Blond hair black at the roots. Hot pink lipstick, a skirt she'd need a crowbar to get in and out of. Now and then, she glanced over at me and kinda smiled. I wondered if she knew what I was there for and what she thought of someone who'd work for a man accused of such things. After a while she picked up the phone and spoke to her boss. She held back a smile at something he must've said. "Gimme a break, Lee. . . . Yeah, she's right here."

"Mr. Manzetti will see you now," she said to me in her official voice. She led me down a hall and opened a door to a room that smelled of rotting fruit.

The man I'd seen on the news was sitting behind his desk, eating an apple. He got up and came around to shake my hand. I was surprised at two things about him: just how runty he was in person and how strong his grip was. He was no taller than me, and I'm five-five in sneakers. I didn't like thinking Father had placed his future in the care of such a puny fellow. I guess I wanted someone tall enough to be imposing in court. But for a small fellow he had himself large, callused hands, a grip like a Connemara dairy farmer's.

"Manzetti," he said. "But call me Leo. I'll be handling Father Devlin's defense."

"Pleased to meet you, Mr. Leo," I said.

"Hot enough for you?" he asked, using his shirt as a bellows to cool himself off. He had dark sweat stains flowering under his arms.

"I'll say."

He asked, "Can I get you some coffee? Or maybe something cool?"

"No, thank you," I replied. "I'm fine."

Then to his secretary he said, "I think we're all set, Gina."

"I'll be working on the Lathrop file," she said, again holding back that smile, like I'd come in on a private joke.

I picked up on the way his gaze lingered on her rear end sashaying out the door. Wasn't just your casual, there-goes-a-nice-piece-of-arse kind of glance that a man will give a woman. No sir. It was more possessive, the sort a fellow gives to a car he's spent all day polishing. Also, I noticed how she seemed to know it and take her sweet time, the way women do when they know they got a man's attention.

After she left, Mr. Leo went back around behind his desk and sat down. His desk was cluttered with a mound of papers, file folders, books, coffee cups, crumbs, whatnot. You wondered how he could work, it was such a mess. He leaned back and put his cracked knuckles together, seemed as if he was trying to line them up.

"Father Devlin's told me a lot about you. Do you prefer Miss Quinn or Margaret?"

"Doesn't matter. Father's the only one calls me Margaret. Some, it's Ma Quinn. What friends I got call me just plain Maggie."

"Ma Quinn," he said, as if testing it out. "Has a nice maternal ring to it. It'll make the jury feel they're listening to their mother."

He took a bite of his apple. He had strong jaws. You could see the muscles working under the skin. I never did trust a man with a weak jaw. To my mind it shows a lack of character. If this fellow's jaw was any indication, he had plenty of character.

"So you think we'll be needing a jury, after all?" I ventured.

"More than likely," he replied.

"I saw you on the television. You said something about getting the charges dropped."

"Mostly that's just jockeying for position. Before a trial you try to gain whatever leverage you can," he explained, hunting for something on his desk. He selected a file folder, took out a yellow pad, and picked up a pen that had been badly gnawed on the end. "Father tells me he trusts you implicitly. That's the word he used, *implicitly*."

"That's good of him to say. I try to be deserving of his trust."

"And what about you?"

"Me?"

"Do you trust *him* implicitly?"

The question set me back on my heels, for sure.

"I'd do anything for Father Jack," I replied.

"That's not what I asked you. I asked you if you trusted him."

"Of course, I do."

"Why?"

"Why?" I said. "Because I know Father."

"You have no doubts he's telling the truth?"

"No sir. None. He'd never've done those things. Why it's just . . . unthinkable is what it is."

"Unthinkable—why? Because he's a priest?"

"Well, that too. But mostly because I know him to be a good man."

"It doesn't matter to me, one way or the other, Maggie," he explained. "Even if he did do those things, he'd still get my best. But I need to know how my witnesses feel."

"Witness?" I said.

"Potential witness. What is it exactly you do for him, Maggie?"

"Cook and clean. Laundry. This and that. Whatever needs doing. I take care of the running of the household so Father can tend to souls."

Mr. Leo smiled at that. "You cook, do you?"

"I try. Nothing fancy."

"Do you know how to make soda bread? Real Irish soda bread, with those little seeds?"

"Caraway seeds," I said. "I should say I do. And barm brack, too."

"What's that?"

"A cake made with yeast and fruit. An Irish fruitcake."

"You'd never guess with a name like Manzetti I'm part Irish. But my maternal grandmother was a Sullivan. She used to make soda bread. Delicious. With butter on it. Haven't had any since I was a kid."

"If you'd like, Mr. Leo, I could make you some."

"Would you really?"

"No trouble at all."

He riffled through some papers in the file folder, stopping now and then to peruse something. As he scanned the pages, I had an op-

portunity to look around what I considered a very unkempt room. A
sagging couch in one corner with clothes flung all over it, ties and
wrinkled shirts and whatnot. Bookcases that hadn't seen a dust cloth
in who knows when. Papers and books and more file folders strewn
on the floor. An apple core under the couch. A little fly cemetery over
on the windowsill. Good lord, I thought. In a glass cabinet to his
right were trophies showing two fellows going for each other's
throats. Wrestling trophies, they were. I would later learn Leonardo
J. Manzetti had been some sort of wrestling champ back in college.
At the bottom of the glass cabinet sat a fifth of Johnnie Walker, half
empty. Its sweet-looking, tawny-colored contents made me lick my
lips, a bad sign, for sure. I'd been a good girl, had had nothing pass
my lips that morning as I'd wanted to make a good impression.

"Let me start with the good news," began Mr. Leo. "These
charges against Father Devlin are pretty old. The jury will have to
wonder why they waited this long to come forward. And so far
there's no physical evidence to support the State's case. No physi-
cian's or police reports. No corroborating evidence. And no witnesses, which isn't unusual in cases like this. Let's just hope it stays
that way. It'll pretty much come down to their word against ours.
And unfortunately, that's the bad news, too."

"How's that?" I asked.

"Charges of sexual abuse are always tricky. Juries tend to believe
the victim and tend to doubt the word of an accused child-molester."

"But he's not a . . . he didn't do those things."

"That's not the point."

"Begging your pardon, Mr. Leo, what *is* the point then?"

His mouth curved into a haughty smile. A cocky little fellow, this
Leo J. Manzetti, one I wasn't sure I'd like. Even then, even before I
saw him operate in the courtroom, I got the impression he enjoyed
this, the sport of it. He seemed the class of man that liked a good
fight, enjoyed beating the lard out of his opponent.

"What I may believe or you may believe, Maggie, doesn't count
for diddly-squat. What counts is what twelve jurors believe. And in
sex abuse cases it's always hard to convince a jury that kids are lying."

"But they're hardly kids, those two."

"They were when they were abused."

"When they *say* they were abused."

"I'm just telling you it's going to be Father Devlin's word against theirs and the onus of proof is going to fall on us."

"I thought you were supposed to be innocent till proven guilty? Isn't that the way it works?"

"In theory, yes," Mr. Leo said. He swiveled in his chair to gaze out the window, which afforded a view of the black, greasy-looking rooftops of the buildings behind Main Street. The heat coming off the roofs made the air quiver and shimmy as it rose. In the distance was the hazy blue line of the Berkshires, fading as it blended with the sky. "In reality, Maggie, jurors tend to side with child victims—even if they are adults now. And especially when the defendant is a priest."

"They'd take the word of those two over a priest?" I said.

"Have you looked in the papers lately?" he asked. "It's not like it was in the good old days, twenty, thirty years ago. When the word of a priest was golden. Hell, back then even if a priest *was* guilty, it wouldn't have gone to trial. We wouldn't even be here. It would have all been hushed up. The Bishop would have handled it quietly. Soothed the parents. Packed the offending priest off to Timbuktu. And that would be it. But with all the sex abuse cases against priests coming out, people—potential jurors—are going to be very suspect of a priest saying he didn't do it. Right now, the pendulum has swung way over to the other side. Do you remember a few years ago with all those day-care places getting slammed with sex abuse charges?"

"Yes."

"It was like a witch-hunt. People just wanted to string 'em up. Nobody cared that the kids' stories were often contradictory. That the policework was shoddy. Half of those sent to prison have since had their convictions overturned on appeal. But that's buried on page ten. It's the same thing now with priests. Since that case down in Louisiana in the mid-eighties, and the Porter case right here in Massachusetts, the public wants blood. Hopefully, in time it will swing back toward the middle. But right now we have to face the fact that priests are our current bogeyman. There was a cartoon in the paper just the other day. A mother was teaching her kid to beware of strangers. The kid asked her what a stranger looked like and the mother said like Father O'Malley."

"What does that prove?"

"I'm just saying that's the climate we're facing. Particularly so if the trial is held in this county."

He anticipated my next question.

"Why this county? Well, any juror we get in Adams County is going to be thinking, he could have been *my* priest or *my* minister. There but for the grace of God, it could've been *my* kid he was doing that to. Especially with all the media attention. So I've filed a motion asking for a change of venue."

"Change of what?" I asked.

"To move the trial to another location. I don't think we can get a fair trial in this county. Probably not in all of western Mass."

"But Father Jack has a lot of friends around here."

"Once the prosecution gets into the particulars of what the Robys are alleging—and believe me the D.A. will get pretty graphic, I know the way she operates—any jury from around these parts isn't going to feel very friendly toward him. I've read the affidavits and they won't make for Sunday school reading. People will feel betrayed and threatened. They'll want to punish somebody. And they won't want to go back and face their neighbors if they didn't—even if he didn't do it."

"Why do you keep saying *if*?"

He drummed his pen against his cheek and made this annoying clucking noise in the back of his throat, a sound that made me think of a pigeon strutting around: *nnkkk-nnkkk-nnkkk.*

"It's just that I like to build a worst-case scenario." I would soon learn that was one of Mr. Leo's favorite expressions—*worst-case scenario.* "Everything's an *if.* That way there's no surprises," he explained. "We stand a better chance with a change of venue. But there's still an outside chance it won't go to trial. I've filed motions to dismiss on the grounds the indictments violate what was then the statute of limitations."

"What's all that mean?"

"Well, in Massachusetts there used to be a six-year statute of limitations for serious crimes, excluding homicide. That means you couldn't try somebody for a crime over six years old."

"But that was over six years ago, what they claim happened."

"Unfortunately, there's a catch. The law was amended in 1988 to make the statute for minors run ten years from the point when they turned sixteen or notified police. The clock, so to speak, didn't start ticking until the Robys turned sixteen. For the older brother the statute will run in November of this year, which I don't think is a coincidence. However, the earlier law was the one on the books when the alleged crimes took place. So I've filled a motion with Judge Askins to dismiss based on that earlier six-year statute."

"I'm afraid you've lost me, Mr. Leo. Can they try Father or not?"

"I'm hoping to get the charges thrown out, though I doubt Askins will go along with it. Still it's worth a try. Of course, there's another problem with going this route. If the charges *are* dismissed and we don't go to trial, it'll leave a cloud hanging over Father's head."

"You mean his name won't be cleared?"

"Exactly. To many he'll have gotten off on a technicality."

"Then he should go to trial and clear his name."

"If he does and we lose, he could be looking at a long jail term."

"How long?"

"Twenty to life for rape of a child, and the other counts. In a similar case over in Worcester, a priest got over two hundred years."

Mother o' God. My head swam with the thought.

Mr. Leo locked his fingers behind his head and leaned back in his chair.

"We do have some things working in our favor."

"Like what?" I asked.

"As I said, there's the length of time that's passed. A jury will wonder why they waited this long to press charges. The Robys are claiming 'retrieved memory syndrome'—about which there's a good deal of debate right now. Juries tend to be divided over that. Second is the character of the Robys themselves. They both have extensive criminal records. I'll be doing more digging into their background, hoping to impeach them as witnesses. In other words, make them look as if they're not credible. If you dig deep enough, there's always something, believe me. I've read over the younger one's statements and he seems the weaker link. He said he always liked Father Devlin and seems genuinely to feel bad about bringing charges. I think we can use that."

"Use it?" I asked.

"Yes, that he liked Father. We might be able to turn him. Play on his affection for him. And, of course, I'll paint Father Devlin as a cross between Mother Teresa and Mr. Roberts. That's where you come in, Maggie."

"Me?"

"Well, you've lived right in the rectory with him all that time. You must know him pretty well."

"As well as any, I imagine."

"Can you tell me a little bit about him? Do you mind if I tape our conversation?"

"No, I said.

He took a small black tape recorder out of his drawer and placed it on the desk in front of me. It made me a little uncomfortable, talking into that thing. I told him about Father. The sort of man he was. How hard he worked and how he was always going out of his way to help people. I told him about the teen shelter and the scholarship fund he'd started and the trips he took the kids on, and how he was always reaching out to those most in need. Funny, but telling it like that, it made Father seem like a nice man yet someone I barely knew. Just a list of good deeds. Though Mr. Leo had the tape recorder going all the while I spoke, he still wrote things down on his pad. Sometimes he'd stop and ask a question, or have me go back over something. But mostly he just listened.

"You've made Father Devlin out to be a very decent and holy man," he said.

"I thought that's what you wanted to hear."

"I do. But even good men have their—how shall we say?— quirks."

"I don't know what you mean by *quirks*. He isn't perfect, if that's what you're getting at. He's got himself a bit of a temper. And he can be quite absentminded."

"No. I mean does he get his kicks watching pornographic flicks or wearing women's clothing around the rectory?"

I felt the blood rise to my cheeks when he said this.

"If you don't mind, Mr. Leo, you're speaking about a priest."

"A priest accused of molesting kids. Does Father Devlin have *any* deep, dark secrets I should be aware of? Things that might hurt us if they came out in trial."

I thought of the night in Father's study. How he worried that they would dig into his private life, find something to use against him. People would be going through his life with a fine-tooth comb looking for dirt.

"Like all of us, Father's got his secrets, I suppose. But nothing 'dark,' like you're saying. Least not that I'm aware of."

"How about women?" he asked.

"Women?"

"Though it might hurt his standing as a priest, if Father Devlin had had sexual relations with adult women it might actually help us. Show he had a normal, healthy sex drive."

The question made me think of Cindy, her wondering if Father had ever slept with a woman. "Not that I ever knew of," I said.

"Did he ever make a pass at you?"

"*Me!*" I said, laughing out loud. "Hardly. Not Father Jack."

"I just meant an attractive woman living in the same house with him all those years. That would be understandable in my book."

Mr. Leo wore the vaguest hint of a smile, and I felt my face redden.

I replied, "Well, not in my book it wouldn't. We're just good friends."

"What about men?"

"He had men friends."

"I meant lovers," he said. "I don't mean to make you uncomfortable but I have to ask these things."

"He wasn't like that," I replied.

"How would you know? Priests are supposed to be celibate, right?"

"I'd have known, all right. I would have."

"So to your knowledge there was never any hanky-panky going on."

"No sir."

"Did Father ever exhibit *any* odd behavior? Anything at all?"

"No . . . not really."

"Maggie, please. Let's cut the crap with each other. You need to be completely forthright with me. Better I know something bad about Father Devlin now than in court. If you're holding anything back you won't be helping him. No matter what it is, I need to know. I don't want to be blindsided in court. I'm on his side, remember."

"It's just that he holds some peculiar notions for a priest."

"Like what?"

"He's got his own view on things. Gays and birth control and the like. And—how can I put this?—some might think he doesn't behave the way a priest ought to."

"Can you be more specific?"

"For instance, he'll fool around with the kids. Wrestling and horsing around with 'em."

"Did you ever see him behave in any way inappropriate with them?"

"No sir. Not really."

"What do you mean, 'not really'?"

"Well, Father likes to show his affection to the kids."

"In what way?" he asked, leaning forward.

"He'll hug 'em. Put his arm around a child. Sometimes . . . "

"Sometimes what?"

"He might kiss a child. On the forehead or the cheek."

"Did he ever kiss them on the lips?"

"I don't know. Maybe."

"Oh, Christ," Mr. Leo said, closing his eyes. "That's not good at all."

"He never meant anything by it. Just Father's way. Some of those kids never got much loving. 'Twas to show 'em somebody cared."

"But the prosecution will present things like that to show he acted inappropriately in his affection toward children," Mr. Leo said. "Were there ever any problems before this?"

"Never anything like this."

"No complaints from a parent or a kid about this sort of behavior?"

"Not to my knowledge."

"Any rumors? Something that floated around the parish?"

"There's always rumors. But like I said, nothing like this."

"And you'd have heard them? If something *had* made the rounds?"

"Oh, it'd have been hard for me *not* to hear a rumor. Being right there as I was."

"Good. That's very good. That'll work in our favor. Pedophiles usually have a history of this sort of behavior."

"Father's *not* that," I said. "He's not one of those. A pedophile." The very word tasted sour in my mouth, like milk gone bad.

"Did any boys ever spend the night at the rectory?"

"Aye, sometimes. Father would invite them, as kind of a treat for helping out around the church."

"Where did they sleep?"

"In the spare room downstairs."

"Never in Father Devlin's room?"

"No sir."

"How can you be so sure?"

"He'd have had to sneak 'em up right under my very nose. I'm a light sleeper, you see. And Father's room is right above mine."

"Did he ever give alcohol to kids?"

"I know what they said about that time up at his cabin. But I never saw him give booze to any kids."

"How about marijuana?"

"With his asthma? Father couldn't stand smoke of any kind."

"All right. To your knowledge, did he ever take nude photos of boys?"

"To my *knowledge*?" I said. "Do you think I'd have kept quiet if I'd known about something like *that*?"

"I don't know. Would you?"

"Certainly not. What do you take me for?"

"No offense, Maggie. I'm just trying to connect the dots. Trying to form a picture of Father Devlin. Were boys ever allowed to go around the rectory without clothes?"

"Of course not," I said. But he must've read something in my face. I never knew a body could look at you the way Mr. Leo could. Like he had X-ray vision. Look right into the darkest corner of your heart.

"What?" he asked. "Don't hold anything back. I need to know *everything*. Think of this as being in the confessional, Maggie."

"Something happened once. But not like what you're getting at."

"Tell me anyway. It might be important."

I told him how one time a couple of boys and Father had played a game of football out behind the rectory and had gotten their things all filthy dirty. There was Petey Lindstrom and Drew Thibodeau, the Santanelli boys, some others, too. Even little Justin Blake, may he rest in peace. As some of them were to help him serve five o'clock Mass, Father had them come inside and take showers, and I was to wash their clothes. Father had some work to attend to over at the church, and when their things were dried they were to change and come over and meet him there. So I gave them towels and told them to wait in the spare room till their clothes were ready. That's when the doorbell rang. It was Mrs. Mueller, from across the street. She'd brought something for our bake sale. I was chitchatting with her when Justin ran screaming past, not a stitch on him, the others chasing after him with towels, giving him the business. It wasn't anything really. Just boys feeling their oats is all. Still, you could see the shocked look on Mrs. Mueller's face, and though I explained about their things being in the wash I don't know as she believed me.

"It may have looked bad but I assure you, nothing happened," I said. "That's the God's honest truth."

"But this is exactly the sort of thing they'll try to use against us. As they say, the devil is in the details, and Lassiter will bring in as many details as she can to paint Father as capable of doing this."

He started gnawing on his pen again. His yellowish-green eyes narrowed, lighting on something on his pad. "Do you remember either of the Robys spending the night at the rectory?"

"They may have. I couldn't really say."

"Do you remember them at all?"

I told him what I remembered. I told him about the gold cross the older one had stolen, same as I had those detectives. But Mr. Leo seemed a lot more interested. As I spoke he rubbed a hand across the angle of his jaw so I could hear a spot he'd missed shaving.

"Are you positive he stole it?"

"I saw it on him with my own two eyes. He was sneaking around in Father's office. Caught him red-handed, you might say. He lied about it till I said I was going to call the police on him. Then he owned up to it and damn quick, too."

"Do you think he harbored a grudge against Father over it?"

"I don't know. I suppose it's possible."

"That's good, Maggie," he said. "Whatever we can do to show they have a history of deceptive behavior or have something against Father Devlin is going to help us. Anything else?"

"I don't believe so. No."

He paused for a moment. "I have to ask you this, Maggie. Is there anything I should know about *you*?"

"*Me*? Have those two said something about me, too?"

"No, no. Nothing like that. I just need to know anything that might impeach your testimony."

"I've had a bit of a problem with the bottle, as far as that goes."

"So have we all, Maggie," Mr. Leo added, smiling.

"More'n a bit, I'm afraid. The long and short of it, I was a drunk. It's no secret. Other things I did, too. I tried to commit suicide. I ain't up for sainthood, that's for sure. But I got nothing to hide neither. That was mostly before Father took me in."

"And now?"

"I have the occasional drink or two."

"Anything else that might challenge your credibility as a witness?"

I thought for a moment. It *was* sort of like being in confession with the priest asking for more sins. You knew there probably was something else hiding in a corner or swept under the carpet, but you couldn't think of it right then. Or at least *told* yourself you couldn't.

"That's about it."

"Okay. We'll stop for now," Mr. Leo said, putting his pen down and closing his folder. "As we get closer to trial, we'll meet again. I should warn you that some questions I'll have to ask you may be very unpleasant. I just want to prepare you."

"If it'll help Father, I'll do whatever I can."

"Don't talk to anyone about the case," he said. "And here's my card. If you remember anything else in the meantime give me a call."

"About them Robys, you mean?"

"Anything really. No matter how small, it still might be important. It's been my experience that things come back to people once they start thinking about them. It's like priming a pump."

He came around his desk and escorted me to the door.

"Oh, one last thing," he said, leaning into me so I could smell his too-sweet cologne. "When I used to wrestle, I always liked to know what my opponent's best moves were *before* I stepped onto the mat. Some like to know the weaknesses and exploit them. Me, I like to know what my opponent's strengths are. Which in a trial means knowing where *I'm* weak. Speaking strictly hypothetically, if you *were* to remember something that might prove damaging to Father, under oath would you tell it anyway?"

"Father wouldn't want me to lie," I replied.

"Very good," he said, almost like I was a student and had given him the right answer. Yet why did I get the impression it wasn't exactly the answer he was hoping for? For a moment, Leonardo J. Manzetti searched my face with those yellowish cat eyes of his. It was the look of someone, I don't know, someone who was hunting for something, not just *anything*, but something he *already* knew was there, something he'd misplaced or momentarily couldn't lay his hand on but which he nonetheless was sure existed and all's he had do was look closely enough. *What?* I thought. *What did he want?* Up close I noticed a pale scar over the bridge of his nose and wondered if he'd gotten it finding out his opponent's strengths.

"May I pay you a compliment, Maggie?"

"I guess so."

"You have very pretty eyes," he said.

This caught me completely by surprise. I didn't know what to say. I found myself looking down at my toes.

"And if you get a chance, don't forget that soda bread."

That was the first of many meetings I would have with Leo J. Manzetti.

10

While Father was away, I followed the case in the news. I saw a picture of Shelly Lassiter in the paper one morning under a headline that read, D.A. SEEKS MAXIMUM AGAINST PRIEST. Lassiter was a thin, pinched-looking woman of early middle age. She had short dark hair and was wearing glasses in the picture. She talked about all the recent scandals involving clergy in the state and said that no one, not even a priest, was above the law. She called Father a "monster" hiding behind a priest's collar.

Mr. Leo, not one to be outdone, got in a few licks of his own. He was able to get some of the counts dropped, others reduced, though Judge Askins wouldn't buy the statute of limitations business. The judge ruled that Father would stand trial. In the news one evening, I saw Mr. Leo, in front of his office on Main Street, reading a statement. "Father Devlin categorically denies these slanderous attacks," he said. "He has faithfully discharged his pastoral duties for close to a quarter of a century. In that time he has gained not only the respect and love but the trust of the parishioners of St. Luke's and of the people of Hebron Falls. And I am confident that after a jury hears all the facts, they will acquit my client of all charges so he can get back to where he belongs—serving his flock."

We didn't hear much from the Robys that summer. Mr. Leo said that the D.A. and their own attorney Mason Elliott would keep them quiet and "under wraps" until the trial. Just as he'd predicted, Mr. Leo was able to uncover some dirt on the brothers. He'd hired a private detective to do some snooping. They had lived in town only two years, which explained why I didn't recall them clearly. After they moved away, they'd had their problems, all right. They'd both been in and out of foster homes and reform schools and prison. The older one, Russell, had a record longer than your arm. He'd been arrested for shoplifting, breaking and entering, stealing a car, insurance fraud, you name it. The younger one, Bobby, wasn't any sweetheart either. He'd been locked up for assault, once for hitting his wife, another time for attempted rape. And both had had their problems with drugs. They'd been in and out of detox several times. They surely weren't the little angels their lawyer, Mason Elliott, had painted them to be.

Even the Church got in the act, though they tried to hedge their bets, play the safe middle ground. A spokesman for the diocese, Father Wozniak, a young fellow with curly blond hair and wire-rim glasses, appeared on the television with that Andrea Ladd: "Our legal counsel is in a dialogue with Mr. Elliott in hopes of getting help for the Robys," he said. "They are, of course, in our prayers. At the same time the Church steadfastly supports Father Devlin's contention of innocence." Contention of innocence indeed, I thought. The gutless bastards. Pete was right. If push come to shove they'd hang him out to dry quicker than you could say "Hail Mary full of grace." When Andrea Ladd asked Wozniak about the priest's removal as pastor of St. Luke's before the trial, he said only that Father Devlin was being relieved of his duties until the "situation" was resolved. He called it was a much-deserved rest. Some rest, I thought.

During the months leading up to the trial, I continued to get phone calls from people in town. Some were still supportive. There were those who offered money for the legal defense fund Pete and a few others had set up. Others donated their time licking envelopes or making phone calls or volunteering to go door to door getting names on a petition asking that Father be allowed to continue in some capacity until the trial. We had a pancake breakfast and several car washes to raise money. We even held a prayer vigil in front of St. Luke's one night. People showed up, though much fewer than we'd hoped. Still and all, it was good to see them there. We held candles and locked arms. We prayed for Father. Several of the young folk played guitar and sang songs. One song was "We Shall Overcome." When I walked back to the rectory that night, I felt good for a change. People were still behind Father.

But a growing number of folks in town weren't so supportive. In fact, just the opposite. Many, including some who'd supposedly been Father's "good" friends, thought he should just resign for the good of the parish. They said a trial would only drag the church through the mud. Whether he was innocent or guilty, some wanted him simply to go away. At a meeting of the parish board over in the community center, there was a heated debate between those that backed Father Jack and those that wanted him to step down. It got pretty ugly, with people not only attacking Father but each other as well. A young man who was new to the parish and had small children in Bible study class, accused Josh Pelkey, whose children were grown, of not caring about kids.

"It's damn easy for you to back Father Devlin," said the man, "it's not your kids that'll suffer."

Some phoned the rectory to cancel their financial contributions, others to put a stop to wedding or baptism plans, and still others to say they were switching parishes, going over to St. Catherine's in Montville or to Our Lady of Hope down in Belmont. Despite it being Father Duncan who was now handling the altar server training, parents called to say their kids wouldn't be coming anymore. They gave various excuses. Only Lillian Hodel, who along with her husband Clifford ran Hodel's Market, came out and said it was because of Father's situation. "Don't get me wrong. I've always liked Father Jack," Lillian told me. "But I have to think of my daughter." Masses now were sparsely attended, even the big Sunday one at half nine, which used to overflow the main church and spill over into the annex. Now it had fewer than a hundred people, and hardly any children to speak of. People squirmed in the pews as they tried to hear Father Duncan, who spoke just above a whisper. That was of course when I still bothered to go to church, back before Father's permanent replacement arrived.

This whole thing was beginning to tear the parish—in fact, the entire town—apart. There were editorials in the newspaper. Some backed Father, referring to all the good he'd done during his time here or asking that we suspend judgment till he had his day in court. But even more took the opposite view. As Mr. Leo had warned, they assumed Father was guilty just because he was a priest. And they thought it scandalous that such a thing had gone on in their town, in their church, or that anybody, least of all a Catholic, would lift a finger to help such a man. Here and there around The Falls, you'd see signs up calling for Father's permanent removal or one of those TORCH leaflets tacked to a phone pole with some quote from the Bible about sin: THEN THE LORD RAINED UPON SODOM AND UPON GOMORRAH BRIMSTONE AND FIRE. One afternoon I came out of Hodel's Market to find one jammed under my windshield wiper: CASTRATE THE BASTARD.

As the weeks rolled by that summer, I found myself staying in the rectory more and more. Before all this, I liked getting out, getting some exercise. Walking into town to do my shopping or to mail something for Father. Or in the evening, after I cleaned up from supper and while Father was working in his study, I might walk over to the park and watch the kids playing on the swings. But no more. I didn't like bumping into folks and having them give me the third degree about Father. What did I think? And what was going to happen? And had I heard Mrs. Such-and-such had said So-and-so told her this or that or some other bloody nonsense. Why I couldn't stand listening to all that rubbish. No sir, I could not. Besides, Mr. Leo had told me to keep my mouth shut about the case and that's what I aimed to do. I even avoided working in my garden. I worried that someone passing by out on the street would see me and take it as an open invitation to come over and start jabbering. Weeds overtook it and with a lack of water the heat scorched my plants. They withered, turned yellow, and slowly died.

I tried to keep busy, but without Father around there wasn't a whole lot needed doing. I realized it wasn't so much a house I looked after as the man who lived in it. So I'd make up these lists of jobs just to keep myself out of trouble. I went through all of Father's things— straightening out his drawers, arranging his shirts by color, tossing out a ratty old sweatshirt or a sock lacking its mate. Father tended to wear things till he was coming out at the elbows and every now and then while he was away, I liked to go through his things, weeding stuff out for the Goodwill box. I ironed his trousers and hunted for missing buttons and loose threads. I packed his winter clothes in boxes, threw in some mothballs, and brought it all up to the cedar closet in the attic.

I cleaned the house with a vengeance. I did things I'd been meaning to get to for ages. I got up on a stepladder and dusted the chandelier in the foyer. I scrubbed all the venetian blinds, every last one. I removed the food and condiments from the kitchen cabinets and put down new shelf liners. I finally got around to cleaning out the hall closet. I took some paste wax and had a go at the banisters, buffing them till I could see my distorted face in them staring back at me.

When I did go out it was usually only to drive over to Montville, where I'd taken to doing most of my shopping, though with just me and occasionally Father Duncan staying for dinner, I didn't need much in the way of groceries. Once, seeing as I was going to be over there on some errand anyway, I decided to bake a soda bread and bring it to Mr. Leo. I was hoping to use it as an excuse to find out how Father's case was coming along. He wasn't in though, and I ended up giving it to his secretary.

"This is for Mr. Leo," I said.

"Who?" replied Gina Demarco. She was seated at her desk and reading one of those supermarket checkout magazines, the sort where some woman's always getting herself pregnant by a chimpanzee or some such nonsense. "Oh, you mean Mr. Manzetti."

"Would you see he gets that?" I said. "By the way, any news on Father Devlin's case?"

"I'm afraid I can't give out information about clients," she said.

"But he's a close friend, Father Jack."

"I'm sorry. You'll have to ask Lee—I mean, Mr. Manzetti."

Mostly though I stayed cooped up in the rectory. Sometimes entire days would slip by and except for a phone call or Dina, I wouldn't hear another human voice. Although Father Duncan filled in for Mass and heard confession, he didn't stay at the rectory but would drive over from Worcester and then head back after performing his duties. He said he had other commitments at the monastery, and I believed him, though I couldn't help but wonder if I was in his shoes would I like staying here, what with everything going on. Rumor had it they were going to send us a full-time replacement but weeks passed and no one came. It was almost as if the diocese just wanted to forget about us entirely. The big house suddenly felt like an enormous cave with just me in it, sounds echoing throughout the place. During the day it wasn't so bad. I had my work. I'd keep busy, going from one mindless task to the next. Trying not to stop. Trying to lose myself in my work. So I wouldn't fall into one of my moods and start hitting the bottle.

But the nights were another story altogether. There was nothing to do, no one to talk to. Nothing to keep me from chewing on my own morbid thoughts, till they left a foul taste in my mouth. One evening, I decided I couldn't stand it any longer. I needed to get out, be with people. I got cleaned up, put on some makeup and walked down West Street to the Falls Tavern. It felt good to be out of the house. The day had been hot and oppressive, but the summer evening had turned cooler the way it does up in the mountains. There was even a light breeze blowing. Walking down the street in the dark, peering into the windows at families doing ordinary things like watching television or eating supper, I felt a little better. Things weren't as bad as they seemed. When this business was over, I told myself, Father would come back and everything would return to normal.

Inside the Falls Tavern, I took a seat at the bar near Reuben. He was doing paperwork, and Ed, who worked nights, was tending bar.

"She'll have a Jameson straight up," he said to Ed.

"No, no," I said. "Make that a ginger ale."

"So how's it going?" Reuben asked.

I shrugged.

"They have a date for the trial?"

"It was supposed to be in September. But last I heard it was postponed again."

"Somebody told me you're going to testify for him?" he asked, looking up from his paperwork.

"And why shouldn't I?"

"Just wondering."

"Someone needs to stick up for him."

"I got nothing personally against the man, Maggie. You know that."

"But most around here would just as soon skip the trial altogether," I said, raising my voice. "Go straight to lynching him."

"Easy," Reuben said. He nodded his head toward a table over in the corner. "See who's over there?"

It was Joe Abruzzi and a couple of the salesmen from the dealership he owned.

"Let the bastard hear me," I said. "I don't care a fiddler's fart."

"Maggie, don't go out of your way to make trouble for yourself."

"I changed my mind, Ed. I'll take that drink after all."

I was on my third glass of Jameson when I felt this tap on my shoulder. I turned to see Joe Abruzzi.

"How are you, Ma Quinn?"

I recovered enough to say, "Just fine."

Abruzzi was a tall, thin man with narrow, stooped shoulders. He had a year-round, orangish tan he got from going down to Florida all the time.

"And Father Devlin?"

Reuben cut in. "I don't want any trouble here, okay, Mr. Abruzzi?"

"No trouble," the man said. "Just asking her how Father is."

"Oh, he's fine and dandy," I said. "Couldn't be better."

"It's just terrible what's happening," he said, somehow managing a straight face. "I know we've had our differences in the past, he and I. Tell him he's in my prayers."

"You know what you can damn well do with your prayers, Mr. Abruzzi."

"What kind of way is that to talk?"

"Don't be trying to cover up your spots with me."

"What's that supposed to mean?"

"We both know where you stand. You've never liked Father Jack and you'd like nothing better than to see him run out of town."

"No, I don't like him. And yes, I do want him out. But not like this."

I warned myself to let it go. But the drink, as it has a way of doing, had loosened my tongue. As my father was wont to say, *in vino veritas.*

"You mean to stand there and tell me you're not pleased as punch this is happening to him?"

"No, I'm not. This is bad for everybody. The whole town."

"Huh! And I suppose you had nothing to do with those two?"

"What?" he said, his eyebrows arching so you could see these white lines along his lids that the sun hadn't reached.

"You didn't put them up to saying those things?"

"Are you crazy? Of course, not! Why would I do that?"

"Why, indeed," I said.

He stared at me for a moment.

"You ever consider they're telling the truth?"

"In the pig's bloody arse," I said.

• • •

After that I didn't go out if I could help it. I found myself looking forward to Dina coming in in the afternoon. Somebody to talk to. We'd sit at the table having a smoke and jabbering about her social life. Some party she'd been to out at the reservoir or necking with this Brian fellow up at Pelham's Overlook. Like I said, she was a hot ticket, put me in mind of my own greener days. No matter what sort of mood I was in she usually cheered me up.

We were sitting there one afternoon right before her mother picked her up.

"Brian's older brother remembers them," she said.

"Who?"

"Those Robys."

"What's he say about them?"

"He didn't know them real well. He remembers the older one getting sent down to the principal's office a lot."

I took a drag on my cigarette.

"Tell me, love," I said. "What do the kids say?"

"About the Robys?"

"About all of it."

"I don't know. They think it's kind of weird."

"Do they believe it?"

She shook her head. "No. They believe Father Jack."

"All of 'em?"

"My friends anyway."

"But there are some that don't?"

"I guess so. They know I work here. They don't say much around me."

"You must hear things."

Dina shrugged.

I told myself to let it drop, that there was no sense going on. What was I looking for? What did I want to hear? I felt sort of like I was in the dark groping around in a box of needles looking for a certain one. I was just as likely to get myself pricked as find it. But there's a stubborn, pigheaded streak in me that sometimes doesn't leave well enough alone.

"What do you hear?" I asked.

"I should get my stuff," Dina said. "My mom'll be here any minute."

"Hold on. What do they say, love?"

Dina fidgeted nervously in her seat. Finally she said, "The usual stuff."

"And what's the usual stuff?" I asked.

"Some of the kids say, well . . . that Father Jack's . . . you know, gay."

"Gay!" I exclaimed. "They say that, do they?"

"Some do."

"Because of all this business with the Robys?"

"It was going around before that."

"Before that?"

"Yeah. That's the rumor anyway. You never heard that?"

"Of course not. Father Jack's not gay," I said. "How long has that been going on?"

"I don't know. Awhile."

"Why on earth would they say such a thing?"

"I guess because he married those two women. And he supports all that gay rights stuff."

"So because he believes in doing what he feels is right, they think he's gay?"

"No, not just that."

"Then why?"

"Because he's kind of like . . . well, you know."

"No, I don't know. Tell me."

"Well. Friendly with kids."

"And that makes him gay?" I said, raising my voice. "Because he's friendly."

"I didn't say that, Ma. I'm just telling you what some say."

Right then we heard a car horn honk out at the road. Dina hurried into the office, got her things and started for the door. Yet she stopped before she left.

"If you talk to Father, please don't tell him I said those things."

After she was gone, I chewed on what she'd said. That some thought Father gay. How ridiculous! Yet she'd said that had been going around long before the trouble with the Robys. Why had I never heard it before? I was right here. I was always talking to the kids that came around. How come I never heard that rumor? I thought how Dina had said some considered Father too friendly, as if being friendly was a crime. And yet, in some ways I guess I knew what she was getting at. When I first come to work for him, I must confess I thought some of his ways a bit peculiar for a priest. How he let kids hang out at the rectory or was always taking them places. Or the way he'd fool around with them, wrestling and being playful. And how he was always hugging them, putting his hands on them. Touching them. Till I got to know Father anyway, I admit I didn't think it looked right.

The thing is, you were brought up to think a priest should act a certain way. Priestly, I guess you'd call it. He was supposed to be formal and reserved. He was supposed to make sure the rules were followed and those that broke them were punished. I could never remember touching or being touched by old Father Pearse, except occasionally when he grabbed you by the scruff of the neck when you'd done something wrong. Though well respected, even well loved by many, Father Pearse was a strict, exacting class of man, who'd just as soon box your ears as look at you. He kept his distance. You didn't want to get too close, nor did he allow you. You didn't think much about his private life, what went on behind the rectory's door. You were always a bit afraid of him, too, the way you are around a policeman. But Father Jack was different. He was friendly and warm, especially to the kids. Like I'd told those detectives, he didn't care a fig for all the Church rules and regulations, or for how things looked. It was people he cared about.

Take this one time. It's hardly worth relating but I will all the same to make my point. Father and I had gone to Ginny Nolan's funeral. Ginny, who used to sing in the church choir, died in a car accident out on Route 38. We were at the cemetery. Her youngest, Katie, was taking it pretty hard. I was standing right next to Father. I remember him putting his arm around the girl, trying to console her, saying not to worry, that her mother was in heaven. What any priest might do. Nothing out of the ordinary. But the thing I remember most was how Father got down on his knees, took the little girl's face in his hands, and kissed her ever so lovingly on each cheek. Kissed away the child's tears. I glanced around. I saw people sort of exchanging looks. I saw that. But I don't think in all my days I'd ever seen a more tender, a more loving and compassionate gesture from anyone. Not from a priest. Not even from a mother toward her child. And if you'd been there, seen the trusting sort of way Katie looked up at Father, as if surrendering her pain to him, then you'd have felt that way too.

Or take the time up at Father's cabin, when those boys got their hands on some booze. I never heard all the details, but as I understood it they got themselves liquored up and went swimming bare-arsed in the lake. Nothing more than what boys do, but it happened to be while they were with Father. He found himself in hot water that time, though he said it wasn't any big deal. Just boys having themselves a bit of fun.

"I don't mean to stick my nose in, Father," I told him later on. "But hadn't you ought to be more careful?"

"Careful?"

"You know. Those boys doing what they did up to your cabin."

"They're just kids, Margaret. Just kicking up their heels."

"I know, Father. It's just that it might give some the wrong impression."

"Wrong impression?" he said, staring at me.

"Well, you know how they like to talk around here."

"Let them. Do you think I care what those small-minded fools think? Nothing wrong happened up there. Nothing."

You see, the thing about Father was he could be naive. Smart as he was, he didn't always know how people thought, the way they looked at things. How the world worked. But I think it wasn't just being naive. Truth is he had what you might call a certain arrogant streak to him. That's a fact. I want to give you as true a picture of the man as I can, warts and all. Maybe it was that blue-blood upbringing of his or that he thought himself smarter than most people, which he was. In any case, he wasn't one to suffer fools gladly, not Father

Jack. If he thought he was right, the rest be damned. Sometimes that put him on thin ice. You see, most don't mind if their priests are cold fishes or dumb as doorknobs or give boring sermons, or if they're a tad too fond of their vino. But they don't like them to be smarter than they are, and they surely don't like them to be upsetting the settled way they think about things. They want their priest to be a bit like a train conductor—to give them a nice smooth ride from baptism to last rites.

One late summer day several weeks before the trial was to start, I took some brass cleaner and went around polishing the doorknobs. The house has all these antique brass doorknobs, and you wouldn't believe how grimy they get from people's hands. So I like to have at them every once in a while. I was in the downstairs hall when I heard Dina call me from the kitchen. As soon as I saw her, I could tell something was wrong. She looked about like she was going to start crying any minute.

"What's the matter, love?" I said, thinking it was boy problems.

"I . . . my parents . . ."

The poor thing suddenly burst into tears.

"There now," I said, going over and hugging her.

"My parents. They . . . won't let me . . . work here anymore," she said between sobs. "I tried to tell them Father didn't . . . do those things. But they wouldn't listen."

"It's all right," I said, comforting her. "When are you leaving?"

"Right now. My mom's waiting out in the car. I have to go."

As I stroked her hair, I realized she was in some ways like a daughter to me. And like her mother, I, too, would want to protect her, even if it meant hurting others' feelings.

"I'll miss you," I said.

"I hate to do this . . . to Father. And to you, Ma."

"I understand, Dina. Don't worry. We'll manage."

"Tell him . . ." she said. "Tell Father it wasn't me."

"I will, love. He'll understand. When this is all over, you come back, okay?"

"I will," she said.

I watched her walk out to the car and get in. I knew she'd never be coming back.

11

After Dina stopped coming to the rectory and before they got a full-time replacement for Father Jack, I was alone in that big house most days. Waiting for the trial, biding my time. A watched pot never boils, and that's true enough. The quiet of the place, something I used to appreciate, now just got on my nerves.

One day, having nothing better to do, I headed up into the attic. You could hardly put one foot in front of the other, the place was such a mess. Father being the pack rat he is, he never got rid of a thing. There was all manner of junk up there. Gifts people had given him years ago, which he hadn't the heart to throw out. Christmas decorations. Lamps and fans that didn't work. Old books and newspapers. Stacks of *National Geographic* and *Time* and *Catholic Digest*. Boxes and boxes of papers: flyers he'd had made up for some car wash and never got around to throwing out, old receipts and invoices, estimates by contractors, canceled checks and bank statements, exams and themes written by his former students when Father had taught at the community college over in Montville. Clothes, too: old coats hanging on hangers and boxes filled with sweaters and shirts and trousers long out of style. I didn't know where to start. Many's the time I'd ask him if he wanted me to get up here and get a handle on things, but we never seemed to get around to it. There was always something more pressing needed tending to. So my figuring was what better time than the present?

It took me the better part of a day. The attic was hot and stuffy. The dust made me cough, and I felt the sweat running down my back. But it felt good to be getting things under control finally. Creating order out of the chaos up there. When Father got back, he'd be surprised for sure. I sifted and sorted. I organized. I threw out stuff he'd never miss. I got rid of junk. I divided it into piles: one I intended for the dump, the other I planned on dropping off at Goodwill. Anything I wasn't sure whether Father would want I left. I called over to the church looking for Stanley to help me with the heavy things. As per usual, when there was work to be done, he wasn't to be found. So I ended up lugging the stuff out to the parish van myself.

I came across things I hadn't seen in years. A plaid shirt I'd given Father one year for his birthday. A pair of cracked brogues I could remember bringing over to the shoe repair shop in Montville to have resoled. Socks I'd darned till I couldn't darn them anymore. Trousers that Father used to wear when he played golf with Peter Beaupre and Father Duncan. A plastic creche, minus the figures, someone had given us for Christmas. An awful portrait of Father that Mrs. Pelkey, who considered herself something of an artist, had presented as a gift to him. Father and myself used to have quite a laugh over it. Didn't look a bleeding thing like Father. There was even my old phonograph, the one I used before Father bought me a stereo for my room. Each article brought back a certain memory, made me think of better days.

Over near the chimney where the roof had leaked before we'd had it reshingled, I came across about a dozen boxes of old, musty-smelling books. Father was always buying books at tag sales and flea markets. Like I said, he was grand one for the books. Besides that, those volumes we didn't sell at the church book sale usually wound up up here. There were hardcovers and paperbacks, works on theology as well as children's books and classics and whatnot. Some had titles like *The Collected Works of St. John of the Cross* or *The Faith of Our Fathers.* Many had been damaged by water, their pages puffy and discolored, some with their covers ripped off or their spines cracked and pages spilling out. I knelt on the floor and began going through them. The books worth saving I put to one side. Many though were beyond salvaging, and those I tossed straightaway into a garbage bag. Father no doubt would have been fit to be tied, throwing away books like that, but my feeling was what he didn't know wouldn't hurt him.

I'd just grabbed ahold of several books, when something slipped out of one of them and fell to the floor. I picked it up. It was a picture, a small wallet-sized photograph. As the light in the attic wasn't very good, I brought it over to the dormer window on the south end of the house, to get a better look. It was a photograph of Father Jack and some young boy. They were standing with St. Luke's in the background. Father had on his vestments, and stood behind the boy, his hands on the child's shoulders. The boy was wearing an altar server's white surplice and black cassock. He had blond hair, which fell to his eyes, pretty features, his small, delicate mouth shaped into the faintest hint of a smile. I looked at the picture for another moment or two before it registered: *Why, for goodness' sakes*, I thought. *It was Justin. Little Justin Blake.* I flipped it over. In blue ink, which had bled into the paper, it said, *With love, Just.* The picture brought back a flood of memories. He'd been a friend of ours, of Father's and mine. More than a friend. Like family almost. The boy used to come around a lot. A darling, sweet child. Then he died. I still had a hard time putting it the other way: *murdered.* It'd happened years ago. I thought I'd gotten over it, the pain of his death. The *way* he died. As with my own son, I'd thought I could remember him without the ache, thought I could think of him, *just* him, the good memories, without dredging up all the rest. But I was wrong. Seeing his picture now brought on a sudden painful fullness in my breast, the way it is when you're nursing and it's been too long and you feel your breasts about to explode.

The air up in the attic had suddenly become dry and rough. It felt like I was swallowing sandpaper whole. I decided to call it a day. I slipped the picture into my breast pocket, right over where it hurt. I picked up a couple of garbage bags and headed down.

I first drove over to Montville to drop off the clothes at the Goodwill box in the Kmart parking lot. I was glad to be out of the stuffy attic. Though the day was hot, the air was crisp with the smell of new-mown hay from the farms along Route 38. The sky was a deep, expansive blue, highlighting the green of the mountains. After depositing the clothes, I realized I was hungry. I hadn't eaten breakfast or lunch, so I stopped at the bakery in the plaza and bought a scone and a glass of iced tea. On the way back I took a left on New Falls Road heading south, toward the town dump. From the van, I emptied the garbage bags and boxes of junk and piles of papers.

"Hey, Maggie," someone called. It was Pete Beaupre. He came walking over.

"Hello, Pete," I said.

"We're having a meeting next week at the community center." Pete and a few others had started a group called "Friends of Father Devlin." They'd raised money for his legal defense, sent out letters in support. "I was wondering if you could make some coffee."

"I'd be glad to."

"Leo Manzetti's going to come. He'll fill us in on how our side's doing."

"I'll be there."

• • •

At night, I'd wander the house unable to sleep. So I'd take a drop, you know. Just to help me relax. But a drop had a way of turning into two and then three, and before I knew it, I was three sheets to the wind and sailing. I'd sit there in the den without any lights on, gazing out the window at Coffin's Bridge. Thinking. This and that. On the one hand, I still felt it was all just too incredible to believe. To even consider Father capable of doing that. It was crazy is what it was. It had to be those two Robys, I figured. And I'd wonder why they were doing it. What in the world did they have against Father Jack, especially now after all these years? Did they hold a grudge against him? Or was it the money, as Mr. Leo had said? There had to be a simple enough answer, which no doubt would come out at the trial.

But then, my thoughts wouldn't stop there, would keep on nosing around the subject. I'd get to thinking about what Dina had said, how some of the kids thought Father was gay. *Father*, I thought, *gay?* How could that be? Just because he didn't flirt with women, the way some of the priests did? Take that Father Malicki down in Our Lady of Hope Parish. When he come to dinner, why, he'd be giving me the eye and letting his hand linger on my back and saying something about my hair. Because Father Jack behaved himself, or because he showed some simple affection to kids, did that make him gay? In all the time I'd been here, I'd never once heard any such thing. And wouldn't *I* be the one to know? A woman can tell that sort of thing about a man. Can feel it. To me, Father was as normal as the next fellow—except that he was a priest and had taken a vow of celibacy. Just because he held the vow sacred and couldn't have relations with a woman, did that make him any less of a man?

Then I'd start thinking about what Mr. Leo had said, how even good men have—what was his word?—their *quirks*. Their secrets. *Does Father Devlin have any deep, dark secrets?* he'd asked. It wasn't that I was beginning to buy any of that rubbish. Certainly not. But all his questions, they'd sort of put a bee in my bonnet, and it buzzed around there and wouldn't leave me alone. *Could* there have been a secret part of Father I didn't know of? A part he kept hidden from everyone, including myself? We all of us had our secrets, those dark places in our hearts we wanted to keep dark. Places we allowed no entry into, no light or communion. The heart, after all, wasn't a simple thing. It was enormous, boundless. It was like a huge mansion, with all these rooms to it, one room leading to another and then another after that, behind every door something we least expected.

But then, I thought, let's say for a moment it *was* true. Of course it wasn't, but just say for argument's sake it was. Wouldn't I have seen something? Heard something? How could he have kept that a secret from *me*, of all people? I was right *here*. I washed his things and made his bed. I knew things about him no one else did, things probably his own mother—rest her soul—hadn't known. If he'd had a dark side to his nature, one that desired little boys, wouldn't I have known? Wouldn't I?

Sometimes when I was feeling poorly, questioning everything I'd once believed, everything I knew in my heart to be true, I'd take that picture out of my purse, the one I'd found up in the attic. The one of Father and Justin Blake. I'd just stare at it for a long while. Both of them were smiling at the camera. They looked so happy, so innocent. Friends. *With love, Just*, the boy had written. Yet Father had said how he was afraid they would take something that was innocent and pure, and twist it around until it didn't look innocent. And of course he was right. I could see his point. Even something as innocent as this picture, I suppose. *With love, Just.* I could imagine them taking that and twisting it all out of shape. Of course they wouldn't know the half of it. Not the half.

I'd sit there pondering these things, sipping my glass of Jameson, my mind going every which way. And the next morning I'd wake up, my head aching and the house as quiet as a tomb.

• • •

With the trial still some weeks off, things in The Falls settled into a tense but quiet sort of mood. Oh, people still continued to gossip about "Father's situation." You'd have had to be deaf not to hear 'em. And you'd see some reporter nosing around, asking questions. On the evening news there'd be somebody you recognized from town. One night there was big, fat Cindy O'Connell flapping her lips like she was the last word on it: "We're all just shocked as could be," she said. "Everybody thought he was a good man, too. And now to hear this, why it shakes your confidence in the Church." *Everybody thought he was a good man.*

Despite the quiet, there were a couple of incidents though. On a billboard out on Route 38 somebody had spray-painted an obscenity using Father Jack's name. And one night some idiot chucked that rock right through the rectory window. Woke me out of a sound sleep. Scared the living daylights out of me. A note attached said, "Death to Preverts." Which is the way the ignorant bastard spelled it. Petey Lindstrom, the town cop, came by and asked me some questions

"I wouldn't worry, Ma," Petey said. "But just to be on the safe side, you ought to keep your door locked all the same."

"What's gonna happen to Father Jack?" I asked.

"Sorry. I can't discuss it."

"You knew him, Petey. You don't think he did those things, do you?"

"I'm really not supposed to talk about it, Ma," he said, heading down the front steps. He turned around, though, and said, "He was always good to me. I'm praying for him, Ma."

Father Jack continued to stay away from The Falls. Mr. Leo thought it better if he kept out of sight. I would write him letters that I'd have Father Duncan take back with him when he returned to the monastery. Yet he never wrote back. I figured the man had a lot on his mind.

Father's replacement, a Reverend Daniel Martin, arrived that September, a few weeks before the trial. The new priest was a very particular sort, and it took me some time to adjust to his ways. Martin was a small, frail fellow, with a bald noggin shiny as a brass doorknob. He had this long puss on him usually, a glum, hadn't-a-good-BM-in-days sort of expression. Finicky as an old lady, he was. Expected his shirts ironed just so and meals prepared special since his stomach was quite sensitive. Nor did he like my things all over the house, my photographs and my cigarette lighter and my "private items" (which meant, I suppose, hanging my undergarments over the shower stall). He thought it didn't look professional. I was to keep them in my room, thank you very much. And I wasn't to enter his room, not even to make his bed. About the upcoming trial, he gave me very explicit instructions: "There is to be no talking with the media about the Father Devlin matter, do I make myself clear, Miss Quinn?" That's what he called me, Miss Quinn. Right off the bat I knew he didn't like Father Jack—or me for that matter—so I had to watch what I said around him. Our conversations usually amounted only to "Yes sir" or "No sir" or "I'll see to that right away, Father." I tried to stay out of his way, step lightly when he was about. Keep my thoughts to myself. Like they say, it's hard serving two masters, which is what I felt I had.

This Father Martin had some muckety-mucks from the diocese for lunch one day. There was Monsignor Payne-in-the-arse himself, some fellow dressed in a business suit and the young blond-haired priest I'd seen speaking on television. I was bringing them coffee when I overheard them talking. I paused out in the hallway.

"I always thought he was a loose cannon," said the Monsignor, a heavyset man with silvery hair and thick glasses. He was puffing on a big cigar, something he hadn't been able to do when Father was here. "He was always stirring up trouble."

The young priest, Father Wozniak, said, "We have to be concerned about damage control. The last thing we want is another Porter situation here."

"Is he amenable to accepting a plea bargain?" asked the one in a business suit, a tall man with a high, bony forehead and slippery eyes. "It'll be better all around if he pleaded rather than dragging this through a trial. Who knows what sort of dirt this could stir up."

"I doubt it," groaned Payne. "He's not a team player. I should've shipped him out long ago. Then he'd be somebody else's headache."

"I agree with Ralph, sir," offered the young priest. "The best course we can follow is to try to get him to plead guilty and avoid an inflammatory trial. The media will crucify us. Do you think we can settle with those two out of court?"

"That shouldn't be a problem," said the one in a suit.

I entered the room then. The smoke was so thick you could cut it with a knife. I began to pour their coffee.

"Ralph," said the Monsignor, directing his question to the one in the suit, "what do you think it'll cost us?"

"Depends," he said. "Out of court we might be able to offer fifty and settle for eighty each, plus medical expenses."

"Damn," the Monsignor cursed. "And if we go to trial?"

"Six figures if we lost. Though if we took them on in court, we could make them look pretty bad. I have their files here. They're a couple of bad boys."

"I'd recommend we settle," the young priest said. "But first we should try to talk some sense into Devlin."

They continued jabbering away right in front of me, like I wasn't even there.

"Excuse me," I said finally. They all sort of looked up at me, as if they hadn't noticed me before. "I don't mean to be sticking my nose in where it don't belong. But Father hasn't been convicted yet."

"Of course not," said the Monsignor. "Mary—"

"It's Maggie, sir."

"Maggie, of course. We have the utmost faith in Father Devlin."

"Have you now, indeed?"

"Absolutely," the young blond one cut in.

"You've a funny way of showing it then," I said.

"That'll be quite enough, Miss Quinn!" Father Martin warned.

"No, it's all right, Dan," the Monsignor said to him. "We're behind him one hundred percent, Maggie. It's just that we have to be prepared for every contingency. We've already been hard hit by, well, similar cases."

"You know more'n I do about these things," I said. "But seems to me Father's innocent till a jury says otherwise."

Father Martin, his bald dome turning bright red, was embarrassed that his housekeeper would speak out of turn like that. "This really doesn't concern you, Miss Quinn," he said. "This is a Church matter."

"Begging your pardon, sir," I said. "But I've worked for Father for eighteen years, and he's a dear friend, not to mention my priest. As a Catholic, it *does* concern me."

"Of course," said the Monsignor. "We appreciate your thoughts. And rest assured, Maggie, we'll do everything in our power to see that Father Devlin receives the Church's support."

Support, I thought. Fat chance of that. Father had made enemies in high places because he'd never been one to keep his mouth shut. He'd spoken out in the Porter case, saying the Church was as much to blame for molesting those kids as Porter. Said how the Church kept transferring him from one parish to another, hoping to pass the buck, keep it quiet. That sort of thing didn't win Father Jack many friends with the muckety-mucks at the diocese.

After his guests had left, Father Martin came into the kitchen where I was cleaning up. I thought there'd be hell to pay now.

"I understand your loyalty to Father Devlin. But you report to me now. So in the future I would appreciate if you would refrain from involving yourself in Church matters. Do I make myself clear?"

"Oh, quite clear, sir," I replied. "Couldn't be any clearer."

• • •

In the community center one night, the group supporting Father met. There were about twenty of us true-blue and loyal supporters. Others may still have believed him innocent, but they didn't want to show their faces and risk having people think they supported a child-molester. I made coffee and brownies and even a soda bread, knowing as Mr. Leo was so fond of it. I sat in the back.

Fifteen minutes into the meeting, Mr. Leo finally arrived. When he got up in front to speak, he looked kind of rumpled. His trousers could have used pressing and his tie was askew and his shirt had these sweat stains under the arms. While he said he couldn't get into the particulars, he explained in general how the defense's side was shaping up, how Father Jack was doing, how people could help. He thought the State's case wasn't that strong. He explained about "re-trieved memory syndrome." He said it was when a person suddenly remembers something awful that happened to them from long ago.

"Sexual abuse victims are supposed to experience it," Mr. Leo said. "It's what some of the people in the Porter case claimed. And it's what the Robys are claiming. The prosecution is going to bring in an expert to testify on the validity of retrieved memories."

"You ask me that's just a crock of bull," yelled Mossy Vogel, who owned Vogel's Newsstand on Main. Several people nodded in agreement.

"How could you *not* remember something like that?" cried Judy Moran, director of the choir.

"It's certainly controversial," said Mr. Leo. "In fact, a couple who were accused by their daughter of sexual abuse have started a False Memory Syndrome Foundation. Of course, we'll have our own expert to refute it."

"Just have Father Jack get up on the stand and call them two the liars they are," Nathan Heufelder said.

"I doubt if Father Devlin's going to testify," Mr. Leo explained.

"Why not?" said Pete, who sat up front.

"In a case like this, I just don't think it would be in his best inter-ests."

"He's got nothing to hide."

"Remember, if I put him on the stand the prosecution will get their crack at him, too. It's too risky."

Some at the meeting exchanged looks of disbelief at the fact that Father wouldn't be testifying in his own behalf. Somebody asked how Father was holding up, and Mr. Leo said he was doing fine, was understandably under some stress but was optimistic and ready for the trial. He said he just wanted to clear his name.

"He asked me to thank everyone for their loyal support and for their prayers. Said he only wished he could be here in person to do it."

Most of those present applauded at this.

"One other thing," Mr. Leo said. "I probably should tell you the prosecution has put a deal on the table."

"What sort of deal?" Pete asked.

"It's actually pretty good. They'd drop the rape charges. Father would plead guilty to indecent assault," Mr. Leo replied. "He'd get off with no jail time. Ten years probation. Some time at a psychiatric facility of *our* choosing. In exchange, the Church would pick up the tab for treatment for the two brothers—as well as offering them a generous cash settlement. That way we avoid a protracted civil suit later."

I recalled the conversation by the Monsignor and the others.

"I knew they were just in it for the money," Judy Moran said.

"Sounds like they're running scared," offered Leah Bettancourt, who was seated next to her partner, Joan. In the window of their bookstore, as in several other businesses in town, they displayed a sign that said, "FATHER JACK IS INNOCENT."

"What the hell sort of deal is that?" someone yelled.

"No way," cried another.

"You didn't advise Jack to take it, did you?" scoffed Pete. "It'd be the end of his career. He'd be ruined."

"It has to be his decision," said Mr. Leo. "If we go to trial and lose, he could get a stiff jail term. I would be remiss as his counsel if I didn't make him aware of all of his options."

"That's not an option. He's innocent," Pete said. "Everybody knows those bastards are just in it for the money. And everybody here knows who put them up to it, too."

Several chipped in with, "You're damn right." Another yelled, "I heard Abruzzi's paying Elliott's legal fees. Is that true?"

Despite what Mr. Leo said about the defense case looking up, I had a bad feeling, as if he was holding something back. Mr. Leo, I noticed, didn't act so animated this night. It seemed as if some of the starch had gone out of him.

I met him outside afterward.

"How are you, Maggie?" he asked.

"I'm all right."

"Did you make the soda bread?"

"I did."

"Boy, that was good. Just like my grandmother's."

I walked him over to his car. The night was clear and warm, and smelled of pine from the woods behind the church. The crickets were making an awful metallic racket. They sounded like a fat man trying to clear his throat.

"I don't know about you," Mr. Leo said, "but I could sure as hell use a drink. Anywhere we could get one?"

"We?" I replied. I thought of our last meeting. The way he'd stared at me, what he'd said about my eyes.

"You look like you could use one too," he said.

"I suppose you could come over to the house."

"House?"

"The rectory, I mean."

We got in his car, an old Mercedes with a clanking diesel motor, and drove over to the rectory. I grabbed the bottle of Jameson from the liquor cabinet and poured us both a good stiff one. From the freezer, I got us some ice.

"Have you eaten supper?" I asked.

"No."

"I could make you a sandwich."

"I don't want to trouble you."

"No trouble," I said. I fixed him a tuna fish sandwich and we sat at the small kitchen table, our knees bumping.

"How's Father *really* doing?" I asked.

"He's pretty exhausted. But you know him. He's tough."

"That memory business."

"Retrieved memory syndrome."

"Aye. Do you buy it?"

He lifted one upturned palm, kind of shrugged. "It's whether a jury buys it," he said. "Whether they believe those lying bastards."

"What I mean is, do you think a person can really forget about something like that and then all of a sudden remember it years later?"

"I'm not a psychologist, Maggie. If you're asking if I believe the Robys, no, I don't. But if you're asking if I think people are capable of hiding things from themselves—yes, I do. We do it all the time. We're actually very good at it."

He took a bite of his sandwich.

"Is everything all right, Mr. Leo?"

"It's very good," he said, thinking I meant the sandwich.

"No, I was speaking of Father's case."

"Oh. I think we're in pretty good shape. I got statements from a couple of dozen people. Former altar boys. Kids he helped at the shelter. Boys he coached. All are willing to swear that Father Jack never even looked at them cross-eyed. That he was the greatest thing since sliced bread. It's basically going to come down to their word against ours, and when I get through with those two little pricks—pardon my French—their word won't look so good, believe me," he said, smiling at the thought.

His smile revealed a mouthful of crooked and chipped teeth—teeth that had been on the receiving end of a lick or two. From the wrestling, his nose had been broken and his ears were cauliflowered and ugly as sin, which I guess was why he wore his hair long. Mr. Leo wasn't handsome in the usual sense of the word, but he did have a strong jaw, those peculiar yellow eyes, and the sort of rugged looks that grew on you the longer you stared at him. Some people look better at a distance and when you get close up you see the flaws. Others, like Mr. Leo, look better up close, the flaws giving them a certain character.

He wasn't like any lawyer I'd ever known, though I can't lay claim to having many lawyer acquaintances in my circle. Still, he was different from what I *pictured* lawyers being like. Was a bit rough around the edges, that long hair, a slightly disheveled look. The way he swore like a trooper. If you bumped into him in some pub, why you'd take him for a plumber or a truck driver. The thing I found most surprising—he gave you the sense that you could trust him. I thought all lawyers were just a pack of lying scoundrels with their eye on the buck. But this Mr. Leo seemed like you could believe what he told you. The sort of fellow you'd want in your corner when the chips were down.

I asked, "Then why'd you bring up that business about the prosecution wanting to make a deal?"

"Because these are serious charges and if we lose, Father could spend a long time in jail. A *very* long time."

He'd finished his drink so I poured him another, got him some more ice cubes. He dipped his finger in the glass, swirled it around. Then he crossed himself.

"*In Nomine Patris, et Filii, et Spiritus Sancti,*" he intoned, the singsongy inflections those of someone who'd had training.

"So you were an altar boy."

"You betcha. Old Father Kupek. Tough as nails. Fought for the

Polish resistance. A great guy though. Taught me to wrestle. Helped me get a wrestling scholarship to go to college. If it wasn't for him I'd probably be on the other side of the law right now."

"Where do you go to church?"

"I don't. I don't believe anymore."

"In the Church?"

"In any of it."

"There was a time I lost my faith, too," I said. "Sometimes it takes a while to find it again."

"I'm not really looking for it," he said. He took a sip of his drink, let it linger on his tongue for a moment, like it was the host and he was an altar boy once again taking communion. "Tell me, Maggie, how in the hell did you wind up here?"

"*Och*. It's a long story. Came over in 'sixty-nine. Been here ever since."

"Do you get back to Ireland much?"

"Actually, I've never been back."

"Really? Why?"

"I don't know. I suppose there's nothing there for me."

"No family or anything?"

"They're all gone. I keep in touch with a friend. Maybe someday I'll go for a visit. Who knows?"

"Was there never anyone special in your life?"

"Special?" I asked, a little surprised by the question, but less so than I would have been the first time I'd met him. Mr. Leo made it a habit of asking questions that took you by surprise. I guess the lawyer in him. "I suppose there was."

"How come you never married?"

"Am I on the bloody witness stand already?" I asked, frowning. Mr. Leo laughed.

"Sorry," he said. "I'll withdraw the question."

"It's all right. I guess it was on account of no one ever asking me."

"I find that hard to believe."

"Do you now? And just what do you know about me?"

"An attractive woman like yourself. I would imagine she had plenty of opportunities."

"Would you listen to him. If I didn't know better, Mr. Leo, I'd say you were trying to sweet-talk me."

"Surely you had your chances."

"I might've. I'm not saying I didn't."

"Nothing serious?"

"Nothing that amounted to anything."

"I can picture you having a family of your own. I bet you'd have been a good mother."

I shrugged, wondering where all these questions were leading. Was he just trying to see what sort of witness I'd make? Checking my background the way he had the Robys'?

I said, "Besides, I was too busy looking after Father Jack."

"He could've hired another housekeeper."

"It's not just the cleaning, I'm talking about. Father's the sort needs tending to. Someone to watch over him." Mr. Leo looked at me like he expected me to go on, perhaps to tell him something about Father I hadn't already. Maybe those deep dark secrets he'd been so interested in knowing. I filled my mouth with whiskey instead.

"Do you care for Irish music, Maggie?" he asked.

"Is the Pope Catholic," I replied. "Not all this new stuff. The old sort. Red Hurley. John McCormack singing 'My Wild Irish Rose.'"

"I know this place down in Springfield where they play Irish music. Maybe we could go sometime. When this is all over, I mean."

"Is it a date you're asking me on, Mr. Leo?"

"I guess you could call it that."

"We'll see. Let's get through this first."

We sat for a while in silence. He finished his whiskey and said, "I should be shoving off. Thanks for the sandwich and the drinks."

From the kitchen door, I watched him go down the steps. He walked over to his car, opened the door, but paused before getting in.

"Oh, Maggie," he said. "What do you know about a Justin Blake?"

Blake? I thought. At the mention of his name, I felt that same stirring in my chest, a subtle ache that rose from my stomach and settled in a spot right behind my sternum. It sat there rigid and firm as a tumor. I thought of that picture in my purse, of Justin and Father standing in front of St. Luke's in their robes. I thought of it then, just as I would continue to think about it during and after the trial. "He was the boy I told you about. The one the others chased through the rectory."

"You didn't tell me the rest of it."

"What rest?"

"That he was murdered."

"I didn't think it mattered. What's that got to do with anything?"

"Nothing," he said.

"They why did you bring it up?"

"It's just that I like to know *everything*. I don't like to be surprised. Do me a favor, don't mention it to anybody else."

"I won't."

"Good night, Maggie."

As he drove down West Street, I couldn't help but wonder what his questions about the Blake boy meant. What did *that* have to do with the Robys? Or with Father? I didn't see the connection. Maybe I should have, even then. Maybe I was just looking the other way. I don't know.

12

In October, after several delays, the trial finally got under way. Mr. Leo had told me since I was going to be called as a witness I wasn't allowed in the courtroom. Some rule they had. They had more rules than the Catholic Church, I swear. I decided to go over anyways, to show my support. I planned on waiting outside in the hall with the intention of catching Father when he was going in. Figured they wouldn't mind that. I'd packed him some clean underwear, thinking he might need it, and baked him some scones. The pictures I'd seen of him in the paper made him look like he'd lost weight. I told Father Martin I had some personal affairs to tend to and that I'd be needing the day off. I had the time coming to me after all. Except for once when I'd had a touch of the flu, I was never sick a day in eighteen years, and I never went away on holiday. Father was always after me to take some time off. You deserve it, he'd say. Go away and relax for a few days, Margaret. I'm relaxed right here, I'd tell him. Why do I need to go away to relax?

Superior Court was in a dreary old granite building on the east end of Main Street. From the outside, it would remind you of a museum and the inside wasn't much livelier. On the opening day of the trial, all these people were milling about out front, some carrying signs, a few for Father but mostly I'd say against. Some of those TORCH folks were there, like Andy Sennett. He carried a sign which said, CHURCH A HAVEN FOR HOMOSEXUALS AND PERVERTS. Another sign said, DEVLIN'S GUILTY AS *SIN*. Luckily, I wore a bandanna and sunglasses so no one would recognize me. I was able to push past them and go in. A guard searched my belongings and then made me walk through a metal detector.

"What are these?" he asked, holding up the aluminum-foil-covered scones.

"Scones," I replied.

Inside it was crowded, too. Reporters and cameramen and police were standing around. A few people I recognized from town, but most I figured were just Nosey Parkers wanting to gawk at Father, like he was some sort of freak. Others must've been waiting for their own day in court, and a scruffy-looking lot they were, too. I asked some fellow with tattoos and a ring in his nose where I might find the Father Devlin trial. You'd have thought I'd called his mother a whore. "Superior Court's on the third floor, lady," he grunted at me.

While waiting in the hall outside the courtroom, I saw that Andrea Ladd interviewing someone. She had herself all decked out like there was no tomorrow, wearing this short yellow skirt and a couple pounds of makeup. I hunted in my pocketbook for a mint to cover the smell on my breath. I'd had a nip on the way over, just a wee small one to smooth out my nerves. I was on the lookout for Father, hoping to catch him before he went in. Wish him good luck. The next thing I knew that reporter woman was shoving her bloody microphone in my face.

"You're the housekeeper, aren't you?" she asked. Don't ask me how she knew, especially with the sunglasses and bandanna.

In person she looked older, hardly a spring chicken anymore. Her neck gave her away. A woman's neck never lies and that's the truth.

"Do you have any comment about the trial?" said Miss Television Reporter.

I shook my head, recalling Father Martin's warning to keep my trap shut. Yet she didn't give up that easy.

"Do you think he's innocent?" she asked.

"Why a course he's innocent."

"Then why do you think they're bringing charges?"

"Ask them, why don't you."

"Have you heard the rumors that there are others?"

"Others?" I said.

"Other people who are going to come forward with accusations of abuse."

"I've said all I'm going to," I replied. "Now if you'll excuse me."

People were streaming into the courtroom. Though I kept looking for Father I didn't see him anywhere. I peeked through a small window in the swinging doors at the back of the courtroom. The room was packed. You'd have thought it was a football match they were watching. I figured I had as much right as those birds to be there. Besides, who's going to notice you, I thought. So I took a chance. I slipped in the door and took a seat in the back, kept my head down so I wouldn't be seen. Hell with their bloody rules.

It was only the third time I'd ever been in a courtroom, the first being for jury duty ages ago and the second when I'd been arrested for DWI some years back. It was a large formal room, with high ornate ceilings, dark woodwork, and, despite the four paddle fans circling lazily overhead, hot as hades. The benches would remind you of church pews, worn smooth and hard on your bottom, but with every class of obscenity carved in them. Right in front of me somebody had written, "Just hang the motherfucker." It was old, from some long-ago trial.

I glanced around. In the aisles were several television cameras recording the whole thing for the six o'clock news. Up front, I saw those two detectives, Gomez and the fat one, talking with D.A. Lassiter. I recognized her from the news. She wore a gray plaid suit and had her short dark hair all puffed out like a poodle's going to a dog show. I looked over at the jury but didn't know a soul. Three men and nine women, which I wasn't sure was good for us or not. The women, I mean. I wondered if any was from The Falls, or if there was a Catholic in the lot. Only one priest showed up, Father Duncan, who was sitting up front with Pete Beaupre and Judy Moran and a few other Father Devlin supporters. I saw Mr. Leo. He was calmly writing something on a pad, almost unaware of all the commotion swirling around him. When he glanced up and gazed around the courtroom, I pretended I dropped something on the floor and bent to pick it up. I was pretty sure he hadn't seen me. Next, I caught sight of the Roby brothers, seated right behind the D.A. The scrawny, older one was looking around the courtroom, smiling and enjoying himself, while his younger brother sat hunched over, staring at the floor, looking for all the world like he was going to be sick. I looked for Father but didn't see hide nor hair of him. Where was he? I wondered. Why wasn't he here?

But just as I was thinking that, a door opened on the left and two guards came out escorting Father over to where Mr. Leo sat. I hadn't seen him since that time they led him away in handcuffs. He was wearing a dark suit, a new one, for I'd never seen it in his closet. No collar though, nothing to show he was a priest. That had to have been Mr. Leo's idea. Some sort of angle, I figured. Maybe he thought being seen in a collar might have struck the jury as somehow worse. But it seemed to me Father ought to have been dressed like who he was, not trying to hide it. He glanced around once and I tried to catch his eye, but he didn't see me with all the people there. He looked as if he hadn't been sleeping well, bags having formed under his eyes, and I could tell the food they were serving at that monastery hadn't agreed with him as his face was drawn and thin.

A man called out, "All rise!" and the black-robed judge came out from another door, after which we sat down. The same fellow as told us to rise mumbled a few words and the show got under way. (Funny how it would sort of remind you a bit of being in church. What with all the standing-up and sitting-down business, the solemn intoning of words and invoking of the Lord's name, the formal ritual of the thing.) Judge Askins was an older gentleman, in his late sixties, with receding gray hair and tired, slightly protruding eyes that made him resemble a sleepy frog. He said a few things to the jury, and then to the D.A. and Mr. Leo.

D.A. Lassiter got first crack. She rose and walked stiff as a board over to the jury. In person she was a small, bony woman, with no hips or bosom to speak of, and these sharp features that had the same effect on your nerves as would a dentist taking a drill bit to your teeth. But I had to give her her due: she could talk with the best of 'em. Just looking at her you knew she was going to be a tough one to beat. Mr. Leo would have his hands full, all right.

"Good morning, Madam Foreperson, members of the jury," she began, her voice sounding put on, that of a actress saying her lines. "What we have here is the difference between what we see on the surface and what's beneath that surface. On the surface, the defendant, Father Devlin, appears to be a wonderful man. A remarkable man in most respects. Well educated. A priest. Teacher. Counselor. Coach. A pillar of the community. Someone who helps troubled youths. Someone you'd trust with your own children. Father Jack, he's known to the young people of his parish. Good old Father Jack.

"But as anyone knows looks can be deceiving. There's another side to Father Devlin. A darker side. An evil side. A side he has kept carefully hidden away. The Commonwealth will show that Mr. Devlin had a penchant for pornography. That he took pornographic pictures of young boys. We will show you a deeply troubled man who had a drinking problem, and who, while under the influence, acted immaturely and impulsively with young boys, on occasion even violently. Finally, we plan to show that beneath all the other faces he presents to the world, Father Devlin was, and is, a *pedophile*. Yes, ladies and gentlemen. A man who has molested children for his own sexual gratification. He may not resemble one of those dirty old men who hang around playgrounds looking to grab a child, but, in fact, he's worse. He's far more dangerous, for he hid his evil lusts behind the collar of a priest. He violated the sacred trust that was placed in his hands. The Commonwealth will show that the defendant is what psychiatrists call a preferential child molester. That is, one who abuses children not by using brute force, but by gradually seducing them using a ritualized pattern aimed at gaining their friendship and confidence. We will show that Father Devlin befriended young boys, that he gave them presents, took them places, plied then with alcohol and drugs, and then, when they trusted him, he abused that trust to make them become sex slaves to satisfy his depraved lusts.

"Father Devlin here is a thief. He stole something from these two young men," the D.A. explained, pointing at the Robys. "What he stole was something far more precious than all the wealth in the world. Something that could never be given back to them, not even now. For Mr. Devlin stole their *innocence*. That's right: their innocence. He robbed Russell Roby and Robert Roby of their childhood, and they have paid a heavy price for it. A heavy price indeed. They have grown into unhappy and troubled adults. Their lives have been racked by silent suffering and by secret shame, by drug abuse and crime and failed relationships, by anger and by violence. And, not least, by a loss of faith in the Catholic Church. And it's all due to *that* man," she said, now pointing at Father Devlin. "In the Bible it says, 'Whoso shall receive one such little child in my name receiveth me.

But whoso shall offend one of these little ones which believe in me, it were better for him that a millstone were hanged about his neck, and that he were drowned in the depth of the sea.' Ladies and gentlemen of the jury, that's what God says we are to do with those who offend the little ones. Hang a millstone around their neck and drown them in the depth of the sea."

When she was finished, the courtroom was silent. You could hear a bee whacking into the high windows, trying to escape. Mr. Leo got up then, buttoned his coat, and strutted over to the jury box confident as a gamecock about to enter the pit. Slowly, he looked at each member of the jury, giving each that penetrating stare of his. When he began to speak, he talked of Father Devlin's distinguished career, his years of service, his work with young children. He said how Father had been a priest for almost thirty years and never once, *not once*, in all that time had he been accused of anything like this. He said it would come down finally to a question of belief.

"It's really quite simple," offered Mr. Leo, going over and resting both hands on Father's shoulders. "Are we to believe my client? A man who has given his life for his town, his parish, his Church. A man beloved and respected. A man who worked with troubled youths, who helped and befriended them, who was dearly loved by them. A man of God! Are we to believe him? Or are we to believe the word of . . . of *those* two?" Mr. Leo pointed with great disdain at the brothers. "Both convicted felons, substance abusers. One man a thief, a drug addict and pusher. The other, someone who abused his own wife, who spent time in jail for attempted rape. *These . . . men* have the audacity to sit before us and besmirch the good name and sterling character of my client. In the more than twenty years he's served this parish, no one has ever brought such charges against my client. Why? Because he never did anything like this. I know what you must be thinking. Another priest accused of abusing children, of breaking his vows. When will it stop? What can we do? I understand your feeling that. But don't make my client pay for the sins of those others priests. Remember this, ladies and gentlemen: Father Devlin doesn't have to prove anything. *Not one thing.* The burden will be on the State to prove—beyond a shadow of a doubt—that my client is guilty of the crimes for which he is being charged. Who are *you* going to believe? For when all is said and done, that's what it will come down to. Their word against my client's. Thank you."

The prosecution then began calling witnesses. Each one had to raise his right hand and say "I do" and then climb up into that little wooden box of a witness stand. The first, Mrs. Broadmoor, a former teacher, testified that she'd had the younger Roby in her class. She recalled him as a quiet boy, one who never caused any problems. Henry Schoerner got up next. He'd been a Cub Scout leader, said he remembered the older one being in his troop for a little while. He said Russell Roby liked to fool around, but he wasn't a bad kid. Other witnesses testified to having gone to church with the Robys while some recalled one or the other of the brothers helping Father Jack serve Mass. You could see what the prosecution was up to. Trying to paint them as innocent little angels who'd never done a bad thing in all their days. Helping old ladies across the street and being kind to dogs.

Next, the D.A. called Mrs. Mueller to the stand. In her seventies, she had a bad widow's hump and ill-fitting false teeth that clattered when she spoke into the microphone. She wore a blue print dress, this little box of a hat, and these white gloves, like she was going to a party. Lassiter began by asking her how long she belonged to the parish and how well she knew the defendant.

"I knew Father Devlin well enough. I was secretary of the Women's Club for years. And before that treasurer."

"Where do you live?" D.A. Lassiter inquired.

"Seventy-eight West Street."

"And where is that in relation to the rectory?"

"Kitty-corner across the street."

"Did you know Father Devlin to have boys over to the rectory?"

"Why, all the time," she replied. "*All* the time."

"Did you think that was strange?"

Up to this point Mr. Leo had just sat there, listening, occasionally writing something down. Now he stood up and said, "Objection, Your Honor."

"Sustained," replied the judge, his chin resting on his palms. Judge Askins sat through much of the trial like that, looking bored to death with the whole affair. There was, I would soon realize, a good bit of this objecting and sustaining as well as some overruling thrown in too, and when both sides couldn't agree they'd have themselves a little private gab session over on the side of the judge's bench to straighten it all out.

"All right, Mrs. Mueller," Lassiter tried again, "what did *you* think of Father Devlin's having boys over to the rectory all the time?"

"I thought it very strange."

"Why did you think that?"

"What good reason could there be for a priest having young boys over there all hours of the day and night?"

"Did Father Devlin ever act in a manner you thought inappropriate with children?"

"He certainly did. He was always grabbing them and fooling around. Especially if he'd had a few."

"Objection, Your Honor," said Mr. Leo.

"I'm going to let Ms. Lassiter have that one," said the judge.

"Did you know Father Devlin to drink?"

"Oh yes. It was common knowledge," replied Mrs. Mueller. "Everybody in the parish knew he had his problems with the bottle."

"Objection," Mr. Leo repeated. "Hearsay."

"Sustained," Judge Askins said. "The jury will disregard the witness's last response."

"Mrs. Mueller," the D.A. continued, "did you ever see—with your own eyes, that is—Father Devlin in a state of intoxication."

"Yes, I did."

"Could you tell us when and where?"

"It was at a St. Patrick's Day party over at the rectory. Father was slurring his words and singing in quite a loud voice. In general, not acting the way a priest ought to act, that's for sure."

"Did you see something else on that occasion?"

Mrs. Mueller looked over at Father and gave this prim little smile before answering.

"I was coming out of the bathroom and I was passing by his study. I saw him in there with this boy—"

"Objection, Your Honor," Mr. Leo interrupted. "*Commonwealth v. Welcome—*"

But the judge cut Mr. Leo short. "I'm going to allow the State some latitude to pursue this line of questioning. Continue, Ms. Lassiter."

"What did you see them doing, Mrs. Mueller?"

"Kissing."

"You saw Father Devlin kissing a boy?" Lassiter said.

"Yes."

"What sort of kiss was it?"

"Objection, Your Honor," Mr. Leo said.

"Overruled."

"The sort of kiss a father might give a son?" Lassiter continued.

"Not to my way of thinking. It was right on the mouth."

"On the mouth?"

"Yes. *Right* on the mouth."

The D.A. went on to ask Mrs. Mueller about loud parties at the rectory, about boys running around unsupervised, about Father allowing sleepovers. The old bag, you could tell, was in her glory, ripping into Father like that.

"Mrs. Mueller, did you ever see boys naked in the rectory?"

"Once," she replied. "I knocked on the rectory door and Ma Quinn—she's the housekeeper—answered the door." I felt my face redden but no one took the slightest notice. "We were standing there talking, and these boys came running past. They were in their birthday suits."

"They were naked, you mean?"

"Naked as the day they were born."

"What did you think of that?"

"Why, I thought it was disgraceful. Right there in the rectory."

"Thank you, Mrs. Mueller. No more questions, Your Honor," said the D.A., who sat down.

Mr. Leo rose, still looking at some papers he held in his hand.

"Mrs. Mueller," Mr. Leo began, "you said you've known the defendant for many years, correct?"

"That's right."

"Did you know that among his many academic honors Father Devlin has a master's degree in counseling? And another master's in psychology. And that he has worked with and counseled youths for many years. Did you know that, Mrs. Mueller?"

"I knew he had all these fancy degrees," she replied.

"And since he counsels young people, wouldn't that be a legitimate reason for kids being over at the rectory?"

"Not at two in the morning," Mrs. Mueller replied, looking self-righteously around the courthouse.

"Are you aware that Father operates a house for runaway children? The Father Devlin Shelter I believe it's called."

"I heard something about that."

"Well, Mrs. Mueller, wouldn't that explain children being around at 'all hours'? After all, runaway kids don't run away just during the daytime, right?"

"You ask me, they were up to no good."

"What did they do over at the rectory that you would classify as 'up to no good'?"

"I'd say running around naked was up to no good," she replied, drawing a tight smile over her dentures.

"Mrs. Mueller, you seem to spend an awful lot of time watching what goes on over at the rectory."

"I'm not *watching* anything," she said, indignant. "I live across the street, and I see what I see. Anyone with eyes in his head would."

"You testified that Father once kissed a boy, correct?"

"That's correct."

"To your knowledge, did Father do this—kissing a child—just this one time? Or were there other times as well?"

"Other times, too."

"In fact, Mrs. Mueller, wasn't he in the habit of kissing kids right in church? In front of the entire congregation?"

"That's just what I mean. If I were their parents, I wouldn't have stood for it."

"But no other parents ever complained about it before now. Isn't that correct?"

"I couldn't say. Maybe they didn't have the nerve."

"Or maybe they didn't see anything wrong with it. Wasn't Father Devlin just an affectionate person?"

"I never thought it was right."

"Do you consider showing affection wrong?"

"Certainly not. There's a time and a place for it. But not right out in front of everybody like that."

"So you're saying Father Devlin didn't try to *hide* his affection toward kids."

"He didn't know where to draw the line."

"Do you consider yourself a religious person, Mrs. Mueller?"

"I like to think I am."

"Are you familiar with Paul's Epistle to the Romans?"

"Not with all of it. It's been a while."

"Let me refresh your memory then. In his letter Paul instructed fellow Christians to, and I quote, 'Salute one another with an holy kiss.' Wasn't that what Father was doing? Just greeting fellow Christians with a holy kiss."

"It wasn't holy to my way of thinking."

"Mrs. Mueller, you said boys were over at the rectory 'all hours of the day and night.' Was Father Devlin alone in the rectory with these boys?"

"I couldn't say. I wasn't there."

"Of course, you weren't. So you couldn't really say what went on *inside* because you weren't there. But someone *was* usually in the rectory. Doesn't St. Luke's employ a full-time housekeeper, one who resides at the rectory?"

"I guess so. Yes."

"And do you know who that is?"

"That'd be Ma Quinn," she said. "If she's sober."

Why the filthy bitch, I thought, feeling the blood rise in my cheeks.

"Your Honor," Mr. Leo protested.

"The jury will disregard the witness's last statement. Mrs. Mueller, please confine your comments to answering the questions."

"So, Mrs. Mueller, Father wasn't *alone* in the rectory with those boys, now was he?"

"I guess not."

"Thank you. No further questions, Your Honor."

"We'll take a short recess," said Judge Askins.

•   •   •

Out in the hallway, I ran into Pete Beaupre.

"I told you he was good," he said.

"Who?" I asked.

"Manzetti. Remember that case down in Northampton where the woman supposedly hired a hit man to kill her husband."

"Sort of."

"That was Manzetti who got her off."

"Let's hope he can do the same for Father. Do you know where a bathroom is?"

"First floor there's one."

I headed down. I entered one of the stalls and sat on the pot. While I relieved my bladder I thought on what old lady Mueller had said. I was still fuming, not only over what she'd said about me but what she's said about Father. Sure, he was affectionate. He might hug a child, even kiss him. That wasn't any secret. But it wasn't at all like she tried to make out. It was just his way, you see. He said too many of those kids had never had anyone show them they cared. He was just showing them that they were loved. That Christ loved them. And what was so bad about that? Wasn't that the Lord's message all along? To love thy neighbor.

I also thought how she'd said Father used to drink and carry on when he'd had a few. Which was a boldface lie if ever there was. Sure Father liked his wine, and he might have an after-dinner brandy or two. He wasn't any teetotaler. And after a drink, it was true he'd laugh and loosen up a bit, sit down at the piano and sing a song, tell an off-color joke that might make the likes of some fussy old bird like Mrs. Mueller blush. But what was the harm of it? Someone like Father, who was by nature somewhat reserved, it did him a world of good. Yet in all the time I worked for him, I only saw Father Jack really buckled once, which is more than most men can say.

I remember he'd come home from playing golf with Pete Beaupre and Father Duncan, and he was feeling no pain. Couldn't even make it up the stairs he was so far gone. Had himself a wedding to do that evening too, I recall. "Goodness' sakes, Father, did you drink Lough Erne dry?" I joked, which is what my mum used to say to my da when he'd had too many. I helped him into the bathroom and got him undressed and stuck him in the shower. At first, I felt sort of odd seeing him like that. His nakedness. But then I thought, I was just helping him. Nothing wrong in that. After I got him straightened out, I went downstairs and made a pot of coffee, to sober him up.

When I come back up, there's Father sitting on the floor of the shower, don't you know, sobbing away. Going on about how much he missed him and how he wished he had him back. I figured he was talking about his own father, who'd passed away when he was but a lad, a blow he never fully recovered from. Sometimes, when the rectory was quiet and I couldn't sleep, I'd hear him talking in his sleep like this. I said, "It's all right, Father. Everything's just fine." While I was getting him dried off, he hugged me awkwardly, his lips brushing against my ear. "Margaret," he said, "are we ever going to buy that hot-dog stand?" "You and your hot-dog stands," I said. "Shut your trap and get a move on. You got a wedding to perform." He said some other stuff, too, which I chalked up to the booze. And he had himself a bit of a bugle, which embarrassed me a little, though it was only his body acting on its own and had nothing at all to do with his head. Nothing more than goose bumps in the cold.

But that was the only time I ever knew him to drink more than he should've.

• • •

There were a few other witnesses before the prosecution called Teddy Villandry. I recall he played Joseph in the Christmas pageant one year, a tall, lanky boy with curly hair. Villandry had filled out a lot since I'd last seen him, and he'd lost some hair, but I could tell right off it was him. He used to hang around with the older Roby. This Villandry was a foulmouthed little brat, the class of boy that used to bully the others smaller than him.

"Mr. Villandry," the D.A. began, "what did you think of Father Devlin?"

"I didn't like him."

"Why?"

"He was always trying to be one of the guys," Villandry said. "You know, patting you on the back. Wrestling. Tickling you."

"And you didn't like that physical contact?"

"No way. I thought it was queer."

"Objection, Your Honor," said Mr. Leo.

"Sustained."

I was looking at Father when he happened to turn around. He scanned the courtroom. For a moment, he seemed to look right at me, but I couldn't say whether or not he recognized me.

"Did Father Devlin ever take you and some other altar boys up to his summer place in New Hampshire?"

"Sure. A few times."

"What would you do there?"

"Go fishing. Swim. Go out on his boat."

"Would you tell the jury about an incident that took place up at Father Devlin's summer place involving alcohol?"

"A few of us kids got drunk."

"Where did you get the alcohol?" the D.A. asked.

"From Father Devlin."

"*Father Devlin* provided you boys with alcohol?"

"We helped ourselves from his liquor cabinet."

"And he didn't mind?"

"No."

"Was he drinking, too, Mr. Villandry?"

"Yes."

"Did you often see Father Devlin drink alcohol?"

"All the time," Villandry replied.

I saw Father lean toward Mr. Leo and whisper something to him, and then Mr. Leo nodded and wrote something down on his pad.

"Now going back to that time at the cabin when you boys got drunk," Lassiter continued, "did something else happen up there?"

"Yeah. We went skinny dipping," said the former Joseph.

"Who's we?"

"A bunch of us. Russ Roby," he said, pointing at the older Roby. "Bugsy Taylor. Myself. I don't remember who else."

"Did the skinny dipping include Father Devlin?"

"Objection, Your Honor," said Mr. Leo. "Relevancy."

"I'm going to allow it," the judge replied. "You may answer the question."

"Yeah, it included Father Devlin," Villandry replied.

"What did you think of a priest going skinny dipping with boys?"

"I thought it was pretty weird."

"And when you got back home, did Father tell you anything in regards to this drinking and skinny dipping activity?"

"Yeah. He told us not to say anything about it."

"Why do you think he told you to keep quiet about it?"

"I guess he thought he'd get in trouble. But somebody squealed."

"And what happened, Mr. Villandry?"

"We all got in trouble. Even Father Devlin."

The D.A. went over to her desk and picked up a piece of paper.

"Your Honor," she said, "I'd like to enter into evidence an official letter of reprimand from the Springfield Diocese. Now, Mr. Villandry, would you describe Father Devlin's behavior after he'd been drinking."

"That was just the thing. You never knew what he'd do. Sometimes he'd get silly. Other times he'd get real mad. Once I remember he slapped Bugsy Taylor in the face. Knocked him down."

"Did he scare you?"

"Sometimes. He had a temper."

Lassiter asked a few more questions, then sat down. Mr. Leo stood up and walked over to the witness stand.

"Mr. Villandry," he began, "about the alcohol up at Father Devlin's cabin. You said you got it from a liquor cabinet, correct?"

"Yes."

"Was the liquor cabinet just left open?"

"I don't remember."

"In fact, wasn't there a lock on the cabinet?"

"There may have been. Yeah, I think there was."

"Isn't it true that Father Devlin kept the liquor cabinet locked up?"

"Yeah, but—"

"Just a *yes* or *no*, please."

"I suppose."

"And did Father Devlin ever give you boys permission to go into that cabinet? To help yourselves. I'll remind you you're under oath."

"No. But we knew where he hid the key. And Father Jack sort of just looked the other way. It was understood."

"But he never *explicitly* gave you permission. In other words, he never gave you the key and said, 'Help yourself.' Isn't that true?"

"I guess not. It was a long time ago."

"Yes, it certainly *was* a long time, wasn't it?" Mr. Leo said. "Now about the skinny dipping incident, whose idea was it?"

"I don't know. I can't remember."

"Well, was it Father's?"

"I don't know."

"Tell me then, was it *after* you boys had raided Father's liquor cabinet? In other words, was it *after* you'd been drinking?"

"I guess so. It was late at night and we snuck out of the cabin and jumped in the water."

"You say you 'snuck out' of the cabin. Why did you sneak out?"

"I don't know."

"To sneak implies stealth. Was it so Father Devlin wouldn't hear you?"

"Yeah, I guess so."

"Then Father Devlin wasn't with you when you boys first went out, was he?"

"No."

"So it couldn't have been his idea, could it?"

"Probably not."

"He came out later, correct?"

"Yes."

"Was he naked or was he wearing a bathing suit?"

"I think he was wearing a bathing suit."

"You *think* he was, Mr. Villandry? Was he or wasn't he?"

"Like I said, it was a long time ago. But I remember he jumped off the dock and into the water with us."

"Mr. Villandry, while you were skinning-dipping, did Father *do* anything?"

"I don't understand the question?"

"Well, did he make any overt sexual advances toward you or any of your friends? In other words, did he try to touch any of you in a way that would be considered inappropriate?"

"Not with all of us there, he wouldn't."

"So in other words, nothing happened?"

"No, not that time."

"Mr. Villandry, did Father *ever* try anything of a sexual nature with you on *any* other occasion?"

"No, not with me, he didn't. But I heard things."

"Your Honor, I ask that that be stricken."

"Strike that from the record," ordered Askins. "The jury will disregard that last comment by the witness."

"Mr. Villandry—and I'd like a simple yes or no—I ask you again: did Father *ever* make any sexual advances to you or anybody in your presence?"

"No."

"Thank you, Mr. Villandry," said Mr. Leo. "No more questions."

As it was close to four, the judge said he was going to adjourn for the day. While he was giving some instructions to the jury, I slipped out of the courtroom and took a seat on a bench in the hallway. I figured I'd wait there and give Father the things I brought. Yet he never came out. Finally, I caught sight of Pete.

"Where's Father?" I asked him.

"They took him out another way."

"Why?"

"For his protection. There's been a threat against his life."

"Oh, my God."

"Manzetti said it's just a precaution. Better safe than sorry though. Especially with all those crackpots out there."

On the ride home I thought about the time those boys had got into Father's liquor and the big stink it caused. People had called the rectory, wondering what had gone on up there. Others I bumped into around town would ask me about it. I told them it wasn't anything. Just boys being boys. Having themselves a bit of fun and things had got out of hand. Still and all, my own personal opinion was that Father should have been more careful. He had an image to uphold. He should've known how something like that would look, how in a town like The Falls it would set the tongues to wagging.

13

The next morning I got up at the crack of dawn to get an early start on my chores. I didn't want to fall behind in my duties and have Father Martin have an excuse to cashier me. Afterward, I got cleaned up and changed, left a note for Martin saying I needed another day off, and then headed over to the courthouse. I wore the sunglasses and bandanna again. I felt like a spy or something. While I worried about causing problems for Father, I felt I had as much right as anybody to be there. I wanted to hear with my own two ears what they had to say. As the previous day, I took a seat way in back and was careful not to let Mr. Leo spot me.

The D.A. brought in a Dr. Somebody-or-other with a dozen degrees from Harvard or some such place, to talk about retrieved memories. Mostly I didn't understand him. But from what I could make out, he said we had what he called "defense mechanisms," ways of hiding things from ourselves and making up all these lies that we convince ourselves is the truth. Which sounded like a lot of fancy drivel to my way of thinking. This Dr. Somebody-or-other jabbered on all morning, the sort of big blowhard who liked to hear himself talk. It was hot and stuffy in the courtroom, and I hadn't slept well the night before and I'd not had my tea that morning. And then that blasted bee—or maybe it was his brother or cousin, I don't know which—started up again. He was bumping against the glass. *Bzzzzzz-tck, bzzzzzz-tck*, he'd go, over and over again. Nearly drove me crazy, it did. So I closed my eyes, just figuring to rest them for a moment.

I must've dozed off. I had a dream about a little boy. He was way up high somewhere, sort of like on a rooftop of a very tall building. Right on the edge, he was, and looking down at me. He was all in white, a long robe like a surplice. I was afraid he might get hurt. In the dream I called to him to be careful, not to move. Then, don't you know, he was falling through the air, dropping toward me headfirst, his arms out in front of him like he was diving into water. In the dream I made as if to catch him, but before he got to me he started floating, light as a feather. His robe was spread out to the sides like the wings of some beautiful white bird. When I looked up at him he spread his wings and flew off.

I must've started snoring or making noises in my sleep, for this fellow next to me gave me a bit of a nudge with his elbow, and all of a sudden I was back in the courtroom. When I looked up, the older Roby was on the witness stand. His hair was cropped close to his head, no doubt to make him look younger. He had a pale bony face and eyes set too close together. He wore a brown jacket, a shirt open at the neck.

"Mr. Roby, the abuse happened over fifteen years ago," the D.A. was saying. She was pacing in front of the witness stand. "Can you tell the court why you're just now coming forward?"

"I didn't remember it," Roby said.

"You didn't remember it? How could you not remember something like that?"

"I guess I blocked it out. I didn't want to think about it."

"Mr. Roby, you heard Dr. Merriwether testify that children who experience severe trauma often repress memories of that trauma. That is, as a defense mechanism, they push the memory from their conscious minds and refuse to acknowledge it. Would you say that's what happened to you?"

"Yes, I would."

"When did you first remember that you'd been abused?"

"About seven months ago was the first time. I was in rehab. For my drug problem. My therapist helped me remember it."

"And that was the very first time?"

"Yes."

"And before that you hadn't the slightest idea?"

"I used to have a lot of bad dreams. Nightmares of somebody

dressed all in black chasing me. But I didn't connect the two."

"Mr. Roby, how old were you when the abuse started?"

"Ten or eleven, I guess. It was right after we moved to town."

"How did you feel toward Father Devlin before the abuse began?"

"I liked him. My old man had left us and I was lonely and Father Jack acted really nice to us. Me and my brother."

"What did he do that was so nice?"

"He'd play ball with us. Take us places. Bowling or to a ball game. Just spend time with us."

"So at first you liked him?"

"Yes."

"Then the abuse started?"

"That's right."

"Do you recall the first time Father Devlin molested you?"

"I do. It was in the sacristy before Mass," Roby said, looking over at Father Jack. An audible sigh went up from the courtroom when he said this. The judge sort of knitted his brows and frowned at everyone the way a father would at a child who'd belched at the supper table. I looked over at the jury, tried to read their reaction. But they just sat there stony-faced. One woman, about my own age I'd say, had even brought along her crocheting and calmly worked on it throughout all of the trial, sweet as you please.

"Were you alone in the sacristy? When he molested you?"

"Yeah. We got dressed in there for Mass. Father Jack would make sure we looked okay. He came up behind me and put his arms around me."

"Was that unusual, for him to hug you, I mean?"

"No, he used to do that all the time. But this time he lifted up my surplice and he started rubbing me."

"Rubbing you how?"

"My penis."

Again there was a sigh. This time the judge pounded his gavel and warned everybody to be quiet. I glanced around the courtroom. One of the jurors, a heavyset fellow, sat there with a scowl on his face. In the row in front of me, a woman with short dark hair was pecking away at one of those small computers. A reporter, I figured.

Across the aisle on the other side of the courtroom, I saw a blond man, balding, maybe thirty. He looked vaguely familiar though I couldn't place him.

"Then what happened?" Lassiter asked.

"He kept rubbing me until . . . well, until I came."

"You were eleven. Was this the first time you'd reached orgasm?"

Roby smiled, and when he did, I saw that same smile he'd had as a boy. A smirk. That cocky little smirk I remembered.

"No," he said. "It wasn't the first time."

"And how did you feel?"

"Kind of grossed out, I guess. Dirty."

"Why did you feel dirty?"

"Because he was my priest. And I knew it was wrong."

"Did Father Devlin want you to keep what he did quiet?"

"Of course. He said it was our little secret."

"Did he say what would happen to you if you told anyone?"

"He said I'd go to hell."

"A priest said you'd go to *hell* if you told anybody?" D.A. Lassiter repeated for emphasis, glancing over at the jury.

"Yes."

I saw the woman who was crocheting look up, first at Roby and then over at Father, as if she was trying to figure out who to believe. Father sat there rubbing his temples, like he had one of his headaches, and staring off into space. During most of Roby's testimony, he hardly changed expressions. I couldn't help but wonder if that would look good for the jury. Shouldn't he appear outraged? Indignant? Then again, maybe Mr. Leo had told him just to sit there, pay Roby no mind at all.

"Did he threaten you in other ways?" the D.A. asked.

"Not in so many words. But I was always kind of afraid of him."

"Why?"

"On the outside he was really nice. But there was something about him that was scary. I don't know how to explain it. I guess it was that you never knew what he'd do."

"What do you mean by that?"

"Well, he could just change all of a sudden. One minute everything's great, he's laughing and in a good mood, and the next he's screaming at you."

"Did you ever see him get violent?"

"He hit Bugsy Taylor this one time. Made his nose bleed. Another time he grabbed my brother by the hair and shook his head."

"Was he ever violent with you?"

"Yeah. He slapped me once. Or if people were around, he'd grab you by the arm and squeeze it. So no one could tell."

"What else did he do to ensure your 'little secret' would stay quiet?"

"He used to give me things. Candy or cigarettes. Presents. He bought my brother a bike."

"And he took you places, didn't he?"

"Yeah. To the movies. Up to his cabin a few times. Once he took me up to Fenway to see the Red Sox play in the World Series."

"And during these trips would Father Devlin abuse you?"

"Sometimes. If we were alone."

"All told, how many times would you say he abused you?"

"You mean actual sex or just kissing and touching?"

"Some sort of genital contact."

"I don't know exactly. A dozen times. Maybe more."

The testimony went on and on. I wondered if it would ever stop. I started to feel a bit light-headed, dizzy almost. It was so hot in the courtroom, must have been eighty degrees. All the windows were closed tight, and I could hear that bee buzzing away, whacking into the panes. Only it seemed for all the world like it was *inside* my skull. Trapped there and trying to get out. While I wanted to get up and leave, I felt I couldn't. I felt I had to hear it all, as terrible as it was.

"Where else did the abuse take place?" Lassiter asked.

"Once or twice up at his cabin. A few times in his car. We'd go up to Pelham's Overlook."

"Where's that?"

"Up on Pelham Mountain over in Hebron Falls. A lover's lane, I guess you'd call it."

"Where else, Mr. Roby?"

"A few times at the rectory."

"He abused you right at the rectory?"

"Yes. Up in his bedroom. We used to go up there and he'd give me a beer or we'd smoke some cigarettes. Maybe do some marijuana."

"Did Father Devlin smoke marijuana, too?" Lassiter asked, raising her eyebrows for effect.

"Yes."

Why, the filthy liar. Him saying that only proved he was lying. Father couldn't stand smoke. Anybody who knew Father knew that.

"So Father Devlin," Lassiter continued, "would give you a beer or some marijuana. And then what?"

"We'd have sex."

"Where?"

"In his bed."

"Do remember anything about the room?"

"There was a picture of Jesus over the headboard."

"Can you describe it?"

"It was just a regular picture of Jesus. It had a gold frame."

The D.A. went over to her desk and picked up a small painting. It was the one that had hung over Father's bed.

"The police took this picture from Father Devlin's bedroom in the rectory," Lassiter offered. "Is this the picture you remember?"

Roby looked at it for a moment, then said, "It is."

"Wasn't Father Devlin afraid someone might catch the two of you in his room?"

"I don't know. I think it turned him on. The danger."

"There was a housekeeper, wasn't there?"

As I had the day before when my name was mentioned, I sort of lowered my head, put my hand to my face so no one would recognize me.

"Yes."

"Where was she all this time?"

"She was usually in her room getting snockered."

"Objection, Your Honor," said Mr. Leo.

"Sustained," replied the judge.

The lying little bastard, I cursed under my breath.

"Did she ever catch you and Father Devlin in his room?" Lassiter asked.

"I was up there with Father Jack this one time. He wanted to do it, have sex, and I didn't, and when I refused, he slapped me. I guess I yelled at him. A little while later there was a knock on the door. It was the housekeeper. I remember being real scared."

"What were you afraid of?" Lassiter asked.

"Getting caught. Having everybody find out."

"And what happened?"

"She knocked on the door and said something like, 'Is everything all right in there, Father?'"

"Do you have any idea why she said that?"

"I think she knew something was going on."

"Objection, Your Honor," said Mr. Leo. "It's asking the witness to speculate about what someone was thinking."

"Sustained. The jury will disregard the last exchange."

"What happened next?" Lassiter continued.

"Father said everything was fine, and she left."

That low-down filthy scum. I never did any such thing. He was lying through his teeth. He'd lied about Father smoking, and he was lying now. Everything he said was a bleeding lie. They had to see that.

"Mr. Roby," the D.A. continued, "would you tell the court, in your own words, what exactly Father Devlin would do to you?"

"It started with masturbation. Later we got into oral sex."

"Did he perform fellatio on you or would he have you do it to him?"

"Both ways."

"Did Father Devlin ever ejaculate in your mouth, Mr. Roby?"

God save us, I thought. I looked over at Father, but he was staring straight ahead, his demeanor unchanged. I was glad he didn't know I was there, listening to all that rubbish. That dizzy feeling I had was getting worse, and my stomach was starting to feel funny, too. I wasn't sure how much longer I could sit through it. I felt I couldn't breathe, that I was underwater and couldn't get air into my lungs.

Roby nodded. His eyes became moist. He coughed, cleared his throat, then said, "Yes."

"I know this must be very painful, Mr. Roby. I have only a few more questions. Was Father Devlin circumcised?"

"No, he wasn't."

"Are you sure?"

"Yes. You don't forget something like that."

My head was spinning faster and faster, and I had this terrible burning sensation in my stomach. I feared I was going faint dead away if I didn't get some fresh air. Wouldn't that be just grand? Making a scene like that. Mr. Leo would kill me.

I stood up. "Excuse me," I whispered to the woman next to me.

"Mr. Roby," Lassiter continued, "confession is an important ritual in the Catholic Church, is it not?"

"It is."

I reached the aisle and headed for the door.

"Did you make confession with Father Devlin?"

The last thing I heard before the doors shut behind me was Roby saying, "How was I going to tell my sins to *that* man?"

In the hall, I bumped into some woman with a little child, and she gave me a dirty look. I rushed down the two flights of stairs and into the bathroom, where I barely made the stall before I started retching. I vomited till nothing came up anymore. When I was done, I washed my face and dried it with some paper towels. I glanced at myself in the mirror. *Och*! I looked terrible, pale, my mascara all smeared. After I finished getting myself in order, I headed out the front door and into the bright fall afternoon. Unsteadily I walked across the street to the parking lot and got in my car. There, I reached into the glove compartment and took out the pint of Mr. Boston. I had a good nip and then another and only then did things begin to settle down a bit.

As I sat there, I wondered how that Roby could get up there and say such stinkin' lies with a straight face. I never knew Father to have kids in his room. Never. And I surely never knocked on his door and asked if everything was all right. No sir. The closest I could come up with to something like that was once when Father'd been laid up in bed. Had himself a fever, couldn't hold anything down. I'd bring him cold presses for his head and some weak tea with just a bit of honey. Starve a fever, as they say. I do recall hearing him moaning and carrying on on the other side of the door. I was worried about him. So I knocked and asked, "Should I call Doc Kennedy?" I said. I might've said something like, "Are you all right, Father?" Which would make sense. I might have said that. But it was nothing like that Roby was saying. Why, he made it seem like I knew there was something going on on the other side of the door, when the fact of the matter was that was as far from the truth as you could get.

• • •

When I was feeling a little better, I went back into the courtroom. Mr. Leo was already questioning Roby. He spent a long time asking him about his past, his criminal record, his taking drugs, his ability to remember things clearly. Several times the D.A. objected, though in all but one instance Judge Askins overruled her.

"Mr. Roby, you testified that until a few months ago you didn't even *remember* the abuse you now allege as having taken place. Correct?"

"That's right. I didn't remember."

"And you expect this court to believe that all of a sudden, out of nowhere, it's all coming back to you. As if a cloud covering your memory suddenly vanished, and you can recall everything so clearly. Do you really expect us to believe that, Mr. Roby?"

"It's the truth."

"So things you had no recollection of, before this miraculous recovery of memory, you now remember with remarkable clarity."

"Some things, yes."

Mr. Leo nodded pensively, glancing around the courtroom.

"You testified that Father Devlin took you places, correct?"

"Correct."

"And that on some of these outings you claim he abused you?"

"I don't claim anything. He did."

"And where would it happen? This alleged abuse."

"In his car sometimes."

"In his car. Do you recall what kind of car Father had?"

"I don't know. I was just a kid."

"Do you recall anything about it? What color it was? Or what kind of seats it had."

"I think they were leather. Maybe red. I don't know."

"I see. Do you follow baseball, Mr. Roby?"

Roby looked a bit confused. "Sure. A little."

"Well, would you consider yourself a Red Sox fan?"

"I guess so. Who's not in New England?"

"I'm a Yankees fan myself," Mr. Leo said. "Now you testified that Father Devlin brought you to see the Sox play in the Series."

"That's right."

"Was it just the two of you?"

"Yes."

"Did Father Devlin abuse you on this trip?"

"I don't remember."

"But you said he *did* abuse you sometimes when he'd take you places, correct?"

"That's right. I just don't remember if he did that time or not."

"Do you remember who the Red Sox played?"

"Cincinnati."

"Of course. The Big Red Machine. Johnny Bench and Pete Rose. Who could ever forget that one? Like I said, I'm not a Sox fan but what New Englander can ever forget Carlton Fisk hitting that home run in game six," said Mr. Leo. "Was it that game you went to?"

"No."

"I suppose you'd have remembered if it had been. But you know what's funny, Mr. Roby, I've seen that tape of Fisk hopping down the baseline waving the ball fair so many times I'd almost swear *I* was there. Even though I wasn't. Are you absolutely sure you weren't there for Fisk's home run?"

"Yes, I'm sure."

"Do you remember which game Father Devlin took you to?"

"No, I don't."

"But you *were* there for one game of that Series, correct?"

"*Yes*," Roby replied, getting annoyed.

"Do you recall if the Red Sox won or lost?"

Lassiter got to her feet and said, "Objection, Your Honor. What's the relevance of Mr. Manzetti's line of questioning?"

To tell you the truth, I had to wonder myself what all this business about baseball had to do with anything at all.

"Overruled," said the judge. "But get to your point, Mr.

Manzetti. You're trying my patience and I *am* a Sox fan. The witness will answer the question."

"I think they won," Roby replied. "But I'm not sure."

"But you *do* remember Father Devlin bringing you to a game against Cincinnati, correct?"

"That's correct."

"Do you remember where you sat?"

"No."

"Well, was it behind home plate? Or out in the bleachers?"

"I don't remember."

"Do you remember *anything* about the game."

"No, I don't."

"Frankly, I find that a little hard to believe. I mean, how many times does a Red Sox fan get to see his team play in the Series? Now, if it were me and I was lucky enough to go to a World Series game, I think I'd have remembered everything about the day."

"Well, I didn't," Roby said, that smirk on his face.

Lassiter said, "He's already answered his questions, Your Honor."

"Yes, Mr. Manzetti," said the judge. "We've enjoyed your little Fenway Park tour. Now let's move along, shall we."

Mr. Leo went back to his desk and picked up a thick book. From where I sat I couldn't make out what it was. He showed it to Lassiter. She nodded, and then Mr. Leo went to the witness stand again. What in blazes was all this about, I wondered.

"Now, Mr. Roby, when did you move into town?"

"The summer before I started fifth grade."

"Do you recall what year that was?"

"Nineteen seventy-seven."

"And would that have been the first time you met Father Devlin?"

"Yes."

"You're quite sure about that?"

Roby looked over at the D.A. before saying, "Yes, I said."

"Mr. Roby, this is a baseball almanac. Unlike people, it doesn't lie, and it doesn't claim to have retrieved memory either. Would you do me a favor? Would you read to yourself what it says right *there*,"

Mr. Leo asked, opening the book and placing it in front of Roby. Roby was quiet for a moment, and when he looked up you could tell something was terribly wrong with him. The smirk had left his face, and he glanced nervously around the courtroom.

Mr. Leo was now the one who was smiling.

"Please tell the court when the Red Sox played in the Series against Cincinnati? What year?"

"'Seventy-five," he whispered.

"A little louder, Mr. Roby?"

"'Seventy-five," he said, louder. You could hear people whispering.

Well, what do you know, I thought.

"That was two years *before* you met Father Devlin, wasn't it?" asked Mr. Leo. "Two whole years before. And yet you said you clearly remember Father bringing you to the World Series against Cincinnati. I'm a little confused, Mr. Roby. Could you clear things up for us?"

Roby stared at Lassiter, as if waiting for her to help him out.

"Maybe it was some other team," he conceded.

"But just a moment ago, Mr. Roby, you testified, *under oath*, that you clearly recall seeing the Red Sox play Cincinnati."

"I remember he brought me is all."

"But how's that possible?"

"I don't know. It just is."

"Isn't it funny, Mr. Roby, how your mind plays tricks on you? You swear something happened and it's just your imagination."

"It wasn't my imagination. He abused me," Roby cried, pointing a finger at Father.

"So you say, Mr. Roby. So you say."

"The bastard did. He did."

"That'll be enough, Mr. Roby," Judge Askins warned. "The jury will disregard the witness's last statement.

"That's all, Your Honor," Mr. Leo said. He started back to his desk but stopped and turned around. "Oh, there is one more thing, Mr. Roby."

Roby was halfway out of his seat and had to sit down again.

"Did you ever steal anything from Father Devlin?"

"No."

"You're sure about that?"

"Yes. I'm positive."

"Thank you. No more questions, Your Honor."

"Since it's getting late," said Judge Askins, "we'll adjourn until tomorrow morning."

Driving home that afternoon, I thought how Mr. Leo had made Roby look like the lying scoundrel he was. Why, when he'd finished with him he had him all twisted up in knots. Who would believe him now? On the six o'clock news that evening, Andrea Ladd, wearing a blue blazer and a white turtleneck, reported the following: "Today in the Father Devlin trial, both sides landed impressive blows. For the prosecution, Russell Roby gave graphic and painful testimony of abuse he claims having suffered at the hands of Father Devlin. However, the defense scored big as Roby contradicted himself several times during a grueling cross-examination by Leonardo Manzetti. The trial resumes tomorrow in Montville Superior Court."

• • •

That night Father Martin told me he was having some guests for lunch the next day. People on the parish board.

He said to me, "I'll need you to stick around tomorrow. I hope that won't be a problem, Miss Quinn."

"Actually, sir, I do have some plans."

"Well, I'm afraid you'll have to change your plans."

I still needed this job so I bit my tongue and did what I was told. Besides, would it have done Father any good at all if I dug in and got myself canned? Certainly not. And after today, I felt a little better about his chances. Though he wasn't out of the woods yet—I dared not be *that* optimistic—at least he was in good shape.

So I stayed home the next day and got the place shipshape for Martin's guests. I set the dining room table and placed some flowers about in vases. For the luncheon, Father Martin wanted me to make these fancy little crabmeat sandwiches—tuna or egg salad, what I usually made, wouldn't do, it *had* to be crabmeat. I served lunch to the board, which included Mrs. Silvera and Mrs. Kennedy, Doc

Kennedy's wife, Mel Bassinger from the newspaper, and Mrs. Abruzzi. Except for Mel, who was a decent skin, not a one of them had ever had a good word to say about Father Jack. Yet I was as polite as polite could be. It was yes sir and no sir, and could I be getting you any more coffee, ma'am. Even when that old bag Mrs. Abruzzi referred to "the deplorable situation," I just continued about my business. I tried not to think about what was happening over in the courthouse. Or if I did give it any thought, it was only to assure myself that soon it would all be over and Father would be coming home.

But that evening I couldn't hardly wait to turn on the news.

"There was startling testimony today in the Father Devlin sex abuse trial," said Andrea Ladd, who stood on the front lawn before the Superior Courthouse. "Robert Roby, the younger of the two Roby brothers, took the stand to testify. He accused Devlin, the fifty-three-year-old Roman Catholic priest, of abusing him, including having taken naked pictures of him. And in a stunning revelation that had the packed courtroom buzzing, Roby said that he had seen similar photographs of another boy. That other boy was Justin Blake, the Hebron Falls youth whose brutal murder fifteen years ago rocked this quiet little town. A murder which remains unsolved to this day."

Justin, I thought. *Sweet Jesus, no.*

Next, they showed the boy's picture, the one they always used to show whenever they mentioned his case. Him in his altar boy robes, smiling, his pretty eyes sparkling and his blond hair falling loosely in his face.

Andrea Ladd continued: "Defense counsel Leonardo Manzetti vehemently objected to Roby's testimony, but he was repeatedly overruled by Judge Askins. At one point, the judge threatened him with contempt. When asked to comment about today's shocking testimony, Manzetti said only that he was filing a motion to have the case declared a mistrial. Regarding the revelations, Adams County D.A. Shelly Lassiter replied that an unsolved murder case is never closed. She said that her office is prepared to 'pursue the investigation wherever it leads us.' What this means for Father Devlin remains unclear. What is clear, however, is that Father Devlin's troubles are far from over. Reporting live from Hebron Falls, this is Andrea Ladd, Channel 9 Action News."

As soon as it was over, I called Pete Beaupre.

"Pete, I just saw the news. What in hell's going on?"

"It was awful, Maggie. Just awful. The younger Roby claims Jack took pictures of him. Pornographic pictures."

"Did they have them? The pictures."

"No. But did you hear about the Blake kid? That Jack supposedly took pictures of him, too?"

"I heard. They won't believe that. No bloody way."

"You should've seen Manzetti. He went ballistic. He got in a shouting match with the judge."

Pete fell silent on the other end. Finally he said, "You know what this means, don't you? They'll try to connect Jack to that."

"Get out!" I said.

"Think about it."

"Listen to what you're saying, for God's sake!"

"That's what people were whispering outside the courtroom."

"Come on, Pete. You're talking about Father Jack. *Father Jack*."

"I know, Maggie. I know. But six months ago who could've pictured *any* of this happening?"

I could sense the subtle change in his voice. Even then I could hear the doubt creeping it.

"You don't believe any of that, do you, Pete?"

"No," he said. "Of course not." But it was there, the change.

Late that night, Mr. Leo phoned to say he'd be calling me as a witness at the end of the week. I could tell he was mad.

"It'll probably be either late Thursday afternoon or Friday morning. In the meantime, Maggie, stay the hell out of court."

"You knew?"

"Of course I knew. I told you witnesses aren't supposed to be in court. The last thing I need right now is Askins finding out you've been attending the trial. He'll throw the goddamn book at me."

"Sorry," I said. "How're things looking for us?"

"You heard about Robert Roby's testimony?"

"I did."

"Before today, I thought we were holding our own. I thought we had a decent chance for acquittal. Better than decent. But with this stuff about Justin Blake, who the fuck knows."

I remembered our conversation out in the driveway after the

meeting at the community center. Mr. Leo asking me what I knew about the boy. I should've known something was up.

"Frankly it was what I feared the most," Mr. Leo said. "I was worried Lassiter would drag the kid's name into it."

"You knew she would?"

"Let's say I'd heard a rumor. That Askins allowed her to bring it up at all is outrageous. They don't have the damn photos. And that fucking Askins just let her get away with it. It's extremely prejudicial to our case. I've already filed motions for a mistrial."

"If we get it, they'll let Father go?"

"Not quite. What it means is I've asked Askins to declare this a mistrial. If he rules in our favor—which to my mind he has no choice but to declare a mistrial—they'll have to drop the charges or retry him. There's no way Father can get a fair trial now. Not with the jurors hearing that he may have taken pictures of a boy who was subsequently murdered. At the very least, if Askins rules against my motion, it'll be grounds for an appeal later. So it's not all bad news."

"It sounds that way to me."

"We're not finished yet. We still have a few punches to throw."

"So I should plan on you calling me? To testify?"

"Yes. And no booze, Maggie. All right? I need you to look sharp and credible on the stand."

• • •

I knew it was looking bad. Just didn't know how bad till the next day. The headlines in the paper read, "WITNESS SAYS PRIEST TOOK NUDE PHOTOS OF MURDERED BOY." It would be the first time they'd have both their pictures, Father Jack's and Justin's, side by side. Justin looked like an angel in his altar boy robes, while Father was caught coming out of the courthouse, his face drawn, bags under his eyes, his lips parted. I went into my bedroom and from my purse got out the photograph I'd found in the attic. The one of Father and Justin standing in front of St. Luke's. Justin was smiling and Father stood proudly behind him, his hands on the boy's shoulders. They'd been such dear friends. I turned it over: *With love, Just*. I couldn't believe any of this was happening. No sir. How in the name of God anyone could think such a thing was beyond me.

14

For the next couple of days I stayed away from the court. I followed things in the news as best I could. Mr. Leo didn't get his mistrial. "JUDGE RULES PRIEST'S TRIAL TO CONTINUE," I read in the paper. The prosecution had rested its case, and now it was the defense's turn. I knew Mr. Leo would come out swinging, that, as he'd put it, he still had a few punches to throw. He brought in a string of witnesses to testify for Father Jack. There was several former altar boys, among them fellows like Freddy Mayette, Jimmy Santanelli, whose son Father had baptized, as well as Drew Thibodeau and Karl Whaley and several others. I read how they all said Father was a wonderful man who had helped them in any number of ways, was there for them if they ever had a problem, and never so much as harmed a hair on their heads. Even Dina Cerutti, bless her heart, testified. She said Father Jack was a kind and sweet man, always nice to her. Several people who'd spent time at the teen shelter testified, too, saying if it wasn't for Father Jack, why, they'd have ended up in trouble for sure. I saw on the news how one young girl said she'd been a drug addict and was supporting her habit by selling her body on the street. Father had helped her get off the drugs, had counseled her, helped her get a job. Now she was a dental hygienist and was going to get married and attended church on a regular basis—all of it thanks to Father Jack.

Several priests also took the stand to testify for him. Some had known him from back in the seminary. They described him as a bright student, hardworking, dedicated, a man committed to helping people. Father Duncan said he'd never heard a bad word spoken about Father Jack. He knew him as someone people trusted, someone who loved kids.

Mr. Leo also called several witnesses that didn't have much good to say about either of them Robys. One fellow, the probation officer of the younger brother, testified that Robert Roby had given a false statement to police about violating a restraining order his ex-wife had taken out against him, but that he was found out and sent back to prison. Another witness, who they showed on the news in prisoner's clothes and manacles, testified that he'd once helped Russell Roby in a credit card scheme and when they were caught Roby lied and said he'd had nothing to do with it, tried to leave him holding the bag. Which just proves there's no honor among thieves. Mr. Leo even brought in his own memory expert, another Dr. Somebody-or-other. Unlike the other fellow, this one said how people's memories were *not* always reliable. He said there was lots of cases of people bringing charges against perfectly innocent people, only to have it turn out it was a pack of lies.

The day before I was to testify, Mr. Leo had me come to his office again, to "prep me," as he put it, like I was going in for surgery or something. Which, as it turned out, wasn't too far off the mark. He told me to put some makeup on but not to overdo it, get my hair done, wear something modest but nice. "You don't want the women on the jury to get jealous if the men stare at your ass," he said matter-of-factly. Though when I described the four plain dresses I had to my name, he thought they were too "old-maidish." He felt I needed something a tad flashier. He said the jury expected court to be a little "sexy" after all. He had Gina Demarco go out and buy me a red, figure-hugging pantsuit at the J. C. Penney's in Montville.

He told me when I took the stand I was to relax and speak in a loud, clear voice just as we'd practiced. But not too loud, nor was I to talk in such a way as to make it look as if I'd rehearsed my lines, which of course I had. He said it was important to appear natural, that everything seem to come directly from the heart and didn't look forced or contrived. He told me not to stare at the jury so it seemed like I was challenging them, but on the other hand not to look away either so it made them think I was avoiding them. He told me to keep my answers with Lassiter short, yes or no, if possible. He warned that she'd try to get me jabbering and get me tangled up in my own words. And most important, he advised, I was not, under any circumstances, to get angry with the woman, even though she would surely try to get my goat and make me look bad.

"Just tell the truth, Maggie," Mr. Leo told me. "That's all."

That's bloody all! I thought, as I drove over to the courthouse one crisp fall morning. The truth of it was, all of his instructions and his prepping and his warnings had got me so jumpy I didn't know whether to shit or go blind. I hadn't slept a wink the night before, even though I'd taken a sleeping pill and had downed a couple of drinks to boot. Out in the car before I went inside, I opened the glove compartment and helped myself to a wee bit of the oul' Mr. Boston, on account of my nerves. My throat was so dry I feared I'd get up there on the witness stand and my mouth would open but nothing would come out. What would it hurt? And then I figured if one was good, two would be even better. The drink calmed the blood that was pulsing in my neck. *There*, I thought. Now you're ready. I took a couple of breath mints to cover the smell, got out of the car, and headed in.

I went up to the third floor and took a seat on one of the benches outside Superior Court. They had me wait a very long time. I hadn't noticed before, but on the wall opposite were dark-hued portraits of these sour-pussed old farts, judges and the like. Directly across from me one stern-looking old bastard wearing a white wig seemed to be staring at me. *What in bloody hell are you looking at?* I felt like saying. My hands were still twitching a bit, and I wished I'd taken another belt of the brandy. Or none at all. As it was, I was sort of betwixt and between, not quite relaxed but feeling my neck a little wobbly. *Take it easy,* I said. *Just tell the truth*.

After a while the bailiff come out and called my name. I had to walk right past everybody, feeling the eyes of all those birds on me— the judge and D.A. Lassiter, those people on the jury, the reporters and the cameramen, and all those other folks in the court, the lot of 'em no doubt thinking, *Would you look at herself, strutting up there grand as you please in her new J. C. Penney outfit*. It was all sort of a blur. I felt this weakness in the knees and my stomach was churning, my face flushed. I knew then I shouldn't have had anything to drink. Before I sat, that fellow asked me to put my hand on the Bible and swear that every last word that came out of my mouth was the whole truth and nothing but so help me God. "I do," I said.

Once I was seated, I felt kind of trapped, claustrophobic, like an animal in a cage with everybody gawking at me. And that blasted microphone made every little noise resound throughout the courtroom like it came from the mouth of God Himself. But when I glanced over and saw Father sitting there, looking tenderly at me the way he might if we were playing Scrabble some evening, I knew I'd rather be no other place than where I was—trying to help him if it was in my power.

Mr. Leo got up and walked over and stood in front of me. He smiled, showing his crooked teeth.

"Would you tell the court your whole name?" he asked.

"Margaret Kathleen Quinn," I replied, my name sounding strange and unfamiliar saying it out loud like that in front of everyone.

"What do people call you?" Mr. Leo asked, though of course he already knew the answer to that. While never in my entire life had I been on a stage, being up on that witness stand is what it must be like. All those people gawking at you and you saying lines you already knew by heart and trying to make it sound natural—*from the heart.*

"Some call me Maggie. Others it's Ma Quinn."

"Do you mind if I call you Ma Quinn?"

"Go right ahead."

"Where do you work, Ma Quinn?"

"Why I work at the rectory, of course."

"For the record, that would be St. Luke's rectory in Hebron Falls, correct?"

"It would."

"And you reside there as well?"

"I do."

He went on to ask me questions in this vein—how long I lived there and who I was employed by and what my duties were and this and that. Which I couldn't see the point of, if you want my opinion. What I learned about the law is that it's a lot like life: most of it don't add up to a fiddler's fart, it's just there to fill in between the big things. Now and again I'd look over at Father Jack. He sat straight up, still as a statue, his face expressionless, though occasionally I thought I detected a bit of a smile intended just for me. I might glance over at the jury, too, to see how they were taking in what I was saying. That woman with the crocheting was still at it, hardly looked up. But I remembered Mr. Leo telling me not to stare at them so I didn't. And once, I happened to catch D.A. Lassiter writing something down after I'd answered one of Mr. Leo's questions. I got nervous just thinking how she'd lay into me when it came her turn. *Just relax*, I kept saying to myself. *Easy does it*.

"Ma Quinn," Mr. Leo said, "there's been testimony that Father Devlin had a drinking problem. In your opinion, based on what you personally observed of the defendant, did he have a drinking problem?"

"Certainly not. He may have had a drink now and again, like anybody, but it wasn't a problem. Wasn't even *close* to a problem."

"Did he keep alcohol in the house?"

"He did."

"To your knowledge, did he ever give alcohol to children?"

"No sir. He did not."

"You're certain about that?"

"Not to my knowledge, he didn't."

"Did Father Devlin have boys over to the rectory?"

"Why, sure he did."

"How often?"

"On many occasions. They were always coming over."

"For what reason?"

"Would depend. He might invite some kids over for supper. Or sometimes a few of 'em and Father would watch a ball game on the television or play basketball out in the driveway. Or to help them with homework. Other times he just had 'em over, no reason at all. Especially those in need of his attention," I said, staring right at the Robys in the front row.

"What do you mean, those in need of attention?"

"The ones with problems at home. In trouble with the law."

"An eyewitness testified that she came to the rectory door one time and saw boys running around in their 'birthday suits.' Is that true?"

"Yes," I replied. You could hear people shifting about in their seats and this low sort of murmur when I said that.

"Would you explain why they were naked, Ma Quinn?"

"They'd got their clothes dirty and they were supposed to help Father over to the church. So he had them clean up while I washed their clothes. And, well, they come running out chasing each other with towels, like boys'll do. It was my fault. I should've been watching 'em."

"So nothing happened?"

"No, nothing happened. Father wasn't even home. He was over to the church then."

Mr. Leo paused for a moment to look at his notes. While he did I gazed out over the courtroom. I looked for Pete but didn't see him. He probably couldn't take any more time off from work, I thought. I did spot Father Duncan though, seated right behind Father Jack. And way in the back I happened to notice that blond fellow I'd seen there before. He was sitting by himself.

"All right, Ma Quinn," Mr. Leo began again, "did Father Devlin take pictures of his parishioners?"

"Why, all the time. He likes keepin' pictures in his albums. They're like his family, you see."

"Did he own a Polaroid camera?"

"Polaroid?" I asked.

"You know. One that takes instant pictures."

"No sir. Just a regular one. I don't know what kind it is. The sort you had to get the pictures developed. In fact, Father used to have me bring 'em down to the drugstore for him."

"You're quite sure he didn't own a Polaroid camera?"

"I never saw one around."

"Ma Quinn, are you usually home?"

"Aye, usually. Unless I'm doing errands."

"Don't you ever take some time off? Go away on vacation?"

"I like sleeping in my own bed."

"So you're on duty at the rectory all the time?"

"I have Tuesdays off. But the rest of the time I wouldn't call it 'on duty.' It's my home, you see. A body's not on duty in her own home."

I looked over and saw Father smile at that.

"Where's your room?" Mr. Leo asked.

"At the back of the house. Near the kitchen."

"And where is Father's bedroom?"

"Second floor. Right above . . ." I got a frog caught in my throat then and I started to cough. Mr. Leo walked over to his table, poured me a glass of water from a pitcher he had and brought it over to me. "Thank you," I said, when my throat was clear. "Father's room is right above mine."

"If you're in your room, can you hear Father up in his room?"

"That I can. When he plays his music I can hear it. Or even when he's pacing up there. He's right above me. And the floors are old and squeak when you walk on them."

"So would it be fair to say if someone were up there with him, you would hear them?"

"Objection, Your Honor," said Lassiter. "Asking for an opinion."

"I'm going to let Mr. Manzetti have that one," declared the judge. "You may answer the question, Ms. Quinn."

"It'd be hard for me not to," I said. "Right below him like I am."

"To the best of your knowledge, did Father Devlin ever have boys up in his room?"

"He most certainly did not."

"How can you be so sure?"

"Like I said, I'd have heard 'em."

"Ma Quinn, do you remember either of the Robys being in the rectory?"

"The older one, I do."

"To your knowledge was he ever in Father Devlin's bedroom?"

"No sir, not to my knowledge, he wasn't."

"Did you ever knock on Father Devlin's door and say . . ." Mr. Leo looked down at his yellow pad. "'Is everything all right in there, Father?'"

I stared right at that Roby before answering. "I most *certainly* did not."

Mr. Leo walked over to the jury box, rested his hand on the railing.

"Ma Quinn, did you ever have occasion to question the truth and veracity of the plaintiff, Russell Roby?"

"I did, yes."

"Do you recall an incident involving Mr. Roby and a certain gold cross of Father Devlin's?"

"Indeed, I do."

"Can you tell the jury about it?"

"Father had this gold cross, you see," I explained, looking over at them. "His late mother gave it to him for his ordination. It was very special to him. And then one day I see *that* one," I said, pointing at the older Roby, "wearing it around his neck."

"Are you sure it was the same one? Could it have been another one that just looked like it?"

"It was the very same. I'd held it in my hands before. It was Father's all right. No doubt on that score."

"And how do you think he got it?"

"I'll tell you how he got it. He stole it, that's how. I saw him coming out of Father's office over at the church and the cross was around his neck."

"And did you confront him about it?"

"I did."

"Did he deny it?"

"At first. He gave me some cock-and-bull story saying it was his."

"So in other words, he lied to you?"

"That he did."

"And what did you do?"

"Why I told him I was going to call the police."

"And then what did he do?"

"He started crying and begging me not to. He didn't want to get in trouble, you see."

As I was speaking, I saw Lassiter turn around and begin talking with Russell Roby, who sat right behind her.

"While under oath, Mr. Roby denied ever having stolen anything from the rectory. Was that a true statement, Ma Quinn?"

"It was not."

"So he perjured himself. In other words, Mr. Roby lied under oath?"

"He did."

"Ma Quinn, in all the years you were employed by the parish, did you ever see Father do anything inappropriate with these two boys?"

"No sir."

"How about with any *other* children?"

"I did not."

"Nothing at all?"

"No sir. Never. Not once. And believe me, if something had happened in that house I'd have known about it. I *would*, for sure."

"And in all those years did you form an opinion regarding the character of the defendant?"

"Indeed I did."

"And what is your opinion?"

"That he's a good and decent man. As fine a priest as you're ever likely to meet. And he would *not* have done what those two are saying."

"Thank you, Ma Quinn. No further questions, Your Honor," said Mr. Leo.

15

D.A. *Lassiter* asked for a short recess, which the judge granted. I went to the bathroom, then headed out to my car for a smoke. The day had warmed up some, though there was still the feel of autumn in the air, as if summer had finally surrendered. I thought I'd done all right. I had followed all of Mr. Leo's instructions. Yet I was nervous about the prospect of facing that Lassiter woman. Scared the day- lights out of me, she did. I made sure nobody was looking and had a quick one to settle my nerves a bit.

When court resumed, I took the stand again. Lassiter came over to me, close enough that I caught a whiff of her perfume, something expensive yet subtle. She held a manila folder in one hand, her glasses in the other. She wore a sharp-looking gray suit and a white blouse, open at the neck, which exposed these pointy little bones in her chest, made me think of fish bones. Her mouth was hard, with these deep grooves on either side like cracks, as if her face might break if she so much as smiled. Was a tightly wound sort of woman you could see— her back ramrod straight, her makeup done just so, not a hair out of place. What surprised me though was up close she looked actually pretty, far prettier than she had from the back of the court. Except for her mouth, she had a girlish sort of face. Straight white teeth, attrac- tive dark brown eyes. She'd have been a nice-looking woman, I thought, if she'd let herself.

"How are we today, Ms. Quinn?" she began, all lovey-dovey, like we were a couple of girls under the hair dryer at Irene's Hair Em- porium.

"Middling," I replied coolly.

"Just middling?"

"I'll feel a good sight better when this is over."

"That makes two of us," she said, smiling. Her face didn't crack, though the smile seemed to hurt her. "You testified that you worked for Father Devlin since 1975, correct?"

"Yes. I started in December of that year."

"How did you come to be in his employ?"

"How? He needed a housekeeper and I needed a job."

"What I mean is, how did you meet him, Ms. Quinn? Did you respond to an ad in the paper, say?"

"No, I didn't answer any advertisement. I was down to the hospital in Northampton, and that's where we met."

She slipped her glasses on and looked over some papers in her file folder. She turned so her back was to me. "Would that be the psychiatric hospital, Ms. Quinn?"

"'Twould."

"And were you employed in a housekeeping capacity there as well?"

"No, ma'am," I said. "I was a patient there."

"A patient?" she repeated, facing the jury.

"Yes."

"Would you kindly tell the court what you were there for?"

"Objection, Your Honor," Mr. Leo complained. "Relevance?"

"May we approach?" said Lassiter.

They had one of their little powwows off to one side. While they were at it, I glanced over at Father. I wanted to smile at him but I thought I shouldn't. His face was haggard, his eyes exhausted. After a bit the lawyers and the judge finished up their jabbering.

"I'm going to allow the question," explained the judge.

Lassiter said, "Please tell the court what you were in the hospital for, Ms. Quinn."

"I had a bad cases of nerves."

"A bad case of nerves? Ms. Quinn, isn't it true that you tried to commit suicide? That you took an overdose of sleeping pills? That, in fact, you'd had a complete nervous breakdown?"

"I guess that's what they called it."

"That *is* what they called it. Your Honor, I would like Ms. Quinn's hospital records entered into evidence," Lassiter said. "And isn't it also true that you were suffering from acute alcohol withdrawal?"

"I don't deny I had a problem with the drink in those days. But that was before I got myself straightened out."

"And just when was that, Ms. Quinn, that you got yourself *straightened out?*"

"When I come to work for Father. With his help, I was able to put my affairs in order."

"And since then, you've never had a problem with alcohol?"

"Objection," Mr. Leo said. "Again, what's the relevance here?"

"Clearly, Your Honor," Lassiter countered, "the witness's substance abuse problems have a direct impact on her credibility. On her ability to perceive and be aware of things going on around her."

"Overruled," Judge Askins said. "I'm going to allow it."

Lassiter said, "Ms. Quinn, since the time that, as you put it, you got yourself straightened out, you've never had a problem with alcohol?"

I started to wonder if she hadn't had somebody watching me out in the parking lot. What if she asked if I'd had a nip out there? What would I say? I couldn't lie. I'd sworn on the Bible to tell the truth.

"I have a drink now and again."

"Just one now and again, Ms. Quinn?"

"Sometimes a bit more, I suppose."

"Do you drink in the rectory?"

I looked over at Father. "Sometimes. But it's on my own time."

"You mean when you're off duty?"

"That's right."

"But, Ms. Quinn, earlier you told us you don't see yourself as being on or off duty. Because it's 'your home,' I think you put it."

"What I mean to say is, after all my work is done, I might have a glass. It helps me relax. Helps me fall asleep."

"So you have trouble sleeping, Ms. Quinn?"

"Now and then."

Lassiter glanced at her notes. "Do you ever take sleeping pills?"

"Sometimes."

"So to help you sleep you might take sleeping pills or have a glass of whiskey, correct?"

"That's right."

"Do you ever take both sleeping pills *and* whiskey at the same time?"

"When I can't sleep, on occasion I might."

"And does it work? Help you sleep, that is?"

"Usually."

"And where in the rectory do you drink?" she asked.

"I don't know. I suppose my room mostly."

"And when you're drinking in your room, do you have your door open or shut?"

"I guess I'd have it shut."

"Why?"

"Why? It wouldn't look right, I guess."

"So you don't think it's proper to be doing that in the rectory?"

"Just a drink or two. I didn't think it any big deal."

"Still, you kept your door shut, correct?"

"Yes."

"Was Father Devlin aware you drank in the rectory?"

I didn't quite know how to answer that one. If I said no, it'd look like I was being sneaky, trying to cover up what I was doing. But if I said yes, people would think Father didn't mind that was going on right under his roof. Lassiter was a foxy one, all right. My face started to get warm.

"I don't know," I replied. "He may have."

"But it's obvious from what you said, you didn't *want* him to know. Otherwise why would you shut the door, right?"

"I suppose."

"So you were, in fact, hiding your drinking from your employer?"

"I wouldn't call it hiding."

"What would *you* call it, Ms. Quinn?"

"I'd call it being discreet. What with all the busybodies in town, I didn't want Father to get a bad name for something I did."

"Would Father Devlin be mad at you if he knew you drank in the rectory? Would he, for instance, have reprimanded you?"

I glanced over at Father.

"I doubt it," I replied. "He understands everyone's got their weaknesses. Long's I got my work done and didn't overdo it, what I did in the privacy of my own room was my own affair."

"He sort of looked the other way then?"

"You might say that."

"In other words, he wouldn't pry into your private business, as long as you did your work and, as you put it, 'didn't overdo it,' correct?"

"That's right."

"And would it be fair to say, Ms. Quinn, you didn't pry into Father Devlin's private life either?"

"I respected his privacy. I didn't go sticking my nose in where it don't belong."

"Of course not. You minded your own business, correct?"

"Aye."

"Would you describe Father Devlin as a private person?"

I looked at Father again. He sat there with his elbows on the table, his hands folded, and his chin resting on his knuckles.

"Until you get to know him he is."

"And so you respected his privacy, correct?"

"I did."

"Now, Ms. Quinn, the rectory is quite large, isn't it?"

"'Tis."

"How many rooms?"

"I never counted 'em. A dozen, maybe."

"Is your hearing so good, Ms. Quinn, you could hear *everything* going on in a house that large with your door shut?"

"I never had any problems with my hearing."

"But do you expect us to believe that in all those rooms it isn't even *possible* for you to have missed something while you were in your room with the door shut, especially after you'd had a few drinks and, on occasion, even a sleeping pill? Do you?"

"Very little went on under that roof I didn't know about, one way or the other."

"But it is *possible*, isn't it?" she asked, those dark eyes leveled on me.

"I suppose," I replied, grudgingly.

"So it's possible for you to have been in your room while Father Devlin entertained boys upstairs in his room?"

"Objection, Your Honor," said Mr. Leo. "Calling for speculation on the part of the witness."

"I'll withdraw the question," said Lassiter, who walked over to her desk, picked up one of Father's photo albums they'd taken with the search warrant, and brought it over to me. "Ms. Quinn, you testified earlier that to your knowledge Father didn't own a Polaroid camera, correct?"

"That's correct."

"Could he have owned one that you didn't know about?"

"I never saw one, that's all I know."

"Have you ever seen this album before?"

I looked at the thing.

"Yes," I replied. "It's Father Devlin's."

"Who took the pictures in it?"

"That'd be Father Devlin. Mostly."

"See that picture," she said, pointing to a photo in the album. It was of three skinny young boys in St. Luke's basketball uniforms. Their legs were pale as grubs. "Do you recognize them?"

"This here's Kyle Sanderson," I said. "That looks like one of the Santanelli twins. I don't know who the other one is."

"That's Russell Roby," she said, the lines around her mouth more pronounced. "Do you know who took the picture?"

"I couldn't say."

"But it *was* in Father Devlin's album and you just said he took most of the pictures."

"Most. Not all. I probably took some myself."

"Would it surprise you to know that that was taken by a Polaroid camera?"

"Like I said, I never knew Father to own one."

"But he may have owned one, correct?"

"Objection, Your Honor," said Mr. Leo. "The witness has already answered the question."

"Sustained," said the judge.

"All right, Ms. Quinn. Let's go back to when you first came to work for Father Devlin," said Lassiter. "Of all the people he could have hired for his housekeeper, do you feel you were the most qualified?"

"What do you mean?"

"Did he hire you because you were the best person for the job?"

"I couldn't say. I'm not one afraid of hard work and I know how to keep a clean house."

"I'm sure you're a wonderful housekeeper, Ms. Quinn. But by

your own admission, you were an alcoholic, had just had a nervous breakdown and tried to commit suicide. Certainly Father Devlin could have hired someone with, let's say, fewer personal problems. Wouldn't you agree?"

"I never claimed to be perfect."

"Then why did he hire *you*? Was he just being kind?"

I paused, glanced over at Mr. Leo.

"I suppose. He's always looking to lend a helping hand to those that need it."

"That's precisely my point, Ms. Quinn. Father Devlin took you in, gave you a job, helped you get your life in order, correct?"

"Yes."

"Would you say that you owe him a debt of gratitude for all the compassion he showed you?"

"Indeed, I do. He saved my life."

"Really? He *saved* your life?"

"In a manner of speaking, yes."

"Ms. Quinn, would you consider yourself a loyal person?"

"I do."

"And are you loyal to Father Devlin?"

I could see where she was headed.

"I am. And I'm not ashamed of saying it neither."

"That would be perfectly understandable, your feeling a sense of loyalty to someone who has done so much for you." Lassiter walked over to the jury and paced in front of them. I could feel sweat trickling down my back, my throat turning dry as a cinder. I was dying for a drink. "You said you owed Father Devlin your life, correct?"

"Yes."

"What would you do for him—as a measure of your gratitude?"

"I don't know. I guess I'd do whatever's in my power to do."

"Whatever's in your power to do," she repeated, seeming to enjoy the taste of my words in her mouth. "For instance, would you work for him for nothing?"

"If he needed me."

"Would you give him money if asked for it?"

"I don't have any. But if I did I'd give it to him."

"If he needed a kidney, for instance, would you give him one of yours?"

"I would."

"So in other words, you'd do just about *anything* for him, because of what he did for you."

"I suppose, I would."

Lassiter paused for a moment. She seemed to be interested in the crocheting the woman in the jury box was doing.

"Ms. Quinn, would that include lying for him?"

"I never said that," I replied.

"But would you? After all he's done for you, if you knew you could help Father Devlin by lying, would you?"

"No, ma'am." I glanced over at Father Jack. "I swore to tell the truth and that's what I aim to do."

"Have you *ever* lied for him?"

"No," I said.

"Never?"

"Not to my knowledge."

"Not even a little white lie?"

I paused for a moment, then said, "I can't think of any."

"You can't think of any. Ms. Quinn, you testified earlier about a cross you allege Russell Roby had stolen from Father Devlin, correct?"

"That's right."

"When you saw Russell Roby wearing it, you assumed he'd stolen it?"

"Yes."

"Why did you assume that?"

"Why? Because it was Father's, that's why."

"Did Russell Roby admit to stealing it?"

"No, not at first. He lied. Said it was his."

"How do you know it wasn't his, Ms. Quinn?"

"Because it was Father's, like I already told you. His own mother gave it to him the day he was ordained."

"But how do you *know* that? That it was Father's, I mean. For example, did it have his initials on it?"

"No."

"Well, was there some other clear identifying mark on it? A date of birth, for instance? Or the date Father Devlin was ordained?"

"No. Nothing like that. It was just a plain gold cross."

"But somehow you were able to recognize this plain gold cross when Russell Roby was wearing it as being the very same one owned by Father Devlin?"

"Aye, that I could."

"But wasn't it possible the two crosses just looked similar?"

"It was one and same."

"You're sure? You have no doubt about that?"

"None whatsoever. I had a good look at it. I'm positive."

"I see. Now before the day you confronted Russell Roby about stealing the cross, did you ever see Father Devlin wearing it?"

"I might've."

"You might have?"

"Yes."

"But you're not sure?"

"No, I can't say one way or the other."

"The cross didn't have his name on it and you're not sure you'd ever seen him wearing it before. Then how can you be so certain it was his?"

"Because," I said, "Father told me."

"Oh," Lassiter said, smiling again, those lines around her mouth cutting deep into her face. "So Father Devlin *told* you it was his?"

"Yes."

"And naturally you believed him?"

"Why shouldn't I? He told me his mother had given it to him for his ordination. That it was very special to him."

"So naturally you believed Father Devlin was telling the truth and that Russell Roby was lying. You took the word of a priest over that of a boy who'd been in trouble."

"Of course. And besides, when I told him I was going to go to the police he begged me not to. Why would he do that if it was his?"

"Why, indeed? Could he have been afraid of something else?"

"I don't know what you're getting at."

"Ms. Quinn, did it ever occur to you that Father Devlin might have been the one who was lying about the cross?"

"No."

"You already testified you'd do whatever was in your power to help him. Are you lying for him now, Ms. Quinn?"

"Certainly not!"

"I'll remind you, you're under oath."

"I'm telling you the truth."

"He didn't tell you to say the cross was his?"

"He did not!" I said, starting to hot under the collar. "He didn't say a blood—" Don't go losing your temper now, Maggie Quinn. Mr. Leo had told me she'd try to get my goat and make me say something I shouldn't. "He didn't say anything to me."

"Do you know what perjury is, Ms. Quinn? It's telling a lie while under oath. And do you know you can go to jail for perjury? So I ask you one last time, Ms. Quinn, was it Father's cross or not?"

I looked at her, then over at the jury. "It was Father's. I swear on the grave of my son, it was his."

"And you believe that simply because Father Devlin told you?"

"No, that's not all," I said.

"What proof, besides Father Devlin's word, can you offer this court that it was his and not Mr. Roby's?"

"I found it once up in his bedroom."

"You found it?" Lassiter said. "In Father's bedroom?"

"Aye."

"Where?"

"I was making Father's bed and I found it on the floor."

"You found it when you were making his bed?"

"Yes. I brought it to him and that's when he told me he'd been looking for it. That he'd lost it."

"So you were making Father Devlin's bed and you found this cross and naturally you assumed it was Father's, correct?"

"That's right."

"And how do you think it got there? In his bedroom?"

Mr. Leo stood up and objected, but the judge overruled him.

"I don't know," I replied.

"Well, do you think it might have slipped off Father Devlin's neck when he was sleeping, for instance?"

"I suppose it could've happened like that. Most likely."

"Can you think of any *other* way it could have ended up there?"

Again Mr. Leo objected, more vehemently this time, and again the judge overruled him. Lassiter had this smug expression that made my heart sink.

"No," I said. "I surely can't."

"You can't think of *any* other way the cross could have wound up in Father Devlin's bed?"

"No, ma'am."

"Ms. Quinn, what if Russell Roby *were* telling the truth?"

"But he wasn't."

"For the sake of argument, let's say he was telling the truth. That the cross *was* his. Can you now think of another way it might have ended up on the floor in Father Devlin's bedroom?"

I felt my face flush. I glanced over at the jury. The woman with the crocheting had stopped and was staring right at me. I saw what Lassiter was trying to do, what she was trying to get me to say. Why hadn't I thought of that before? Was it because I wouldn't *let* myself think that?

Mr. Leo objected once more and once more the judge overruled him.

"You mean to tell us, Ms. Quinn," she said, adding on a dry little laugh at the end, "you can't conceive of any other way that cross could end up under Father Devlin's bed?"

"No, I *can't*," I said, sounding surly even to myself. It was the first and only time while on the witness stand I knew I wasn't telling the whole truth.

"I submit to you, Ms. Quinn, that you know as well as everybody else in this courtroom that Russell Roby *was* telling the truth, that it was *his* cross, and that it slipped off *his* neck when he was in Father Devlin's bed."

"Objection, Your Honor," shouted Mr. Leo. You could hear this buzzing going around the courtroom. People whispering and talking. The judge whacked his gavel and things quieted down. "I move to strike that last statement by the prosecutor."

"Sustained," replied the judge. "The jury will disregard the district attorney's last statement. If you have a question, Ms. Lassiter, ask it. Otherwise move along."

"Sorry, Your Honor," said the D.A. "Now Ms. Quinn—"

"That's a damn lie," I hissed at her. "It was Father's cross, just like I told you."

"Ms. Quinn," the judge said, leaning over toward me, "please withhold your comments except in response to a question."

"Earlier, Ms. Quinn," Lassiter continued, "you said you were able to recognize the cross as belonging to Father Devlin, correct?"

"That's correct," I replied.

"Do you know where Father Devlin's cross is now?"

"No. I can't say I do."

"Well, does Father still have it? This article that was supposedly so *special* to him?"

"I would imagine so."

Lassiter walked over and stood behind Father. Father Jack continued looking straight ahead.

"If Father Devlin were wearing it now, would that surprise you?"

I hesitated, not knowing what she was getting at. "No," I replied.

"And if he *were* wearing it at this very moment, wouldn't that prove *he* was telling the truth and that *Mr. Roby* was lying, just as you maintain?"

"Aye," I said. "It would seem to."

"So in other words, if he had that cross on him, in this courtroom today, it would prove beyond a reasonable doubt that it was his and that Mr. Roby had stolen it, just as you contend. Isn't that correct, Ms. Quinn?"

I watched Father, trying to read his expression. But he just stared at some point on the front wall, his face impassive.

"Why, yes. I would imagine so."

"With the court's indulgence, Your Honor," Lassiter said. She walked over to where Russell Roby sat. She leaned over to him and whispered in his ear. Then he reached down into his shirt and lifted something off his neck and handed it to her. The courtroom starting buzzing again, only louder this time. Several times Mr. Leo cried, "Objection, Your Honor!" I felt my heart pounding as Lassiter approached. I watched as she extended her closed fist to me. I watched as she opened it and showed me what Roby had given her. Sitting there in the palm of her small, neat, well-manicured hand was a gold cross. She picked it up by the chain and swung it in front of me, like she was trying to hypnotize me.

"I now ask you, Ms. Quinn, is *this* the gold cross you found in Father Devlin's bedroom?"

"I . . ."

"Your Honor!" cried Mr. Leo. "This is outrageous."

At this point they all started talking at once—the judge, Lassiter, Mr. Leo. Their voices swirled around me as I stared at the cross.

". . . can't say for sure," I said.

"Well, is it or isn't it the same one?" Lassiter continued.

"Objection, Your Honor," Mr. Leo shouted.

"Sustained. The jury will . . . "

"I don't know," I replied.

"But just a little while ago, Ms. Quinn . . . "

"*Objection*!" cried Mr. Leo.

". . . you said you had no doubt about recognizing the cross."

"Sustained," the judge said. "Ms. Lassiter . . . "

"And now you can't . . . "

The judge frantically whacked his gavel several times. "Ms. Lassiter! I warn you, that'll be enough."

"No more questions, Your Honor," she said.

"I move for a mistrial, Your Honor," Mr. Leo cried.

"Motion denied," said the judge.

"But, Your Honor—"

"Sit down, Mr. Manzetti."

"You can't keep letting her get away with this crap."

"So help me, Mr. Manzetti!" Judge Askins warned, pointing his gavel at him. "One more word and you'll be in contempt. Counselors, I want to see both of you in my chambers immediately. The court's going to adjourn till nine tomorrow morning."

I don't recall much of anything after that. I don't remember leaving the courtroom. I don't remember talking to anyone. I sort of recall some reporters coming up to me, snapping my picture and asking me questions, but I don't remember what I said or if I said anything at all. I don't remember getting in my car and driving home. It was all a blur. The only thing I do remember was that cross swinging in front of my face. I remember that, all right.

• • •

Late that night Mr. Leo called.

"You told me it was his, Maggie," he said, his voice oddly restrained.

"It was," I said. "I thought it was."

"But you made it sound like there wasn't any doubt about it. Like you knew for a fact."

"Father said it was his."

"Why didn't you tell me you found it in his bedroom?"

"You never asked."

"Never asked! You didn't think that might lead people to a different conclusion?"

"I didn't think . . . I mean, I found it in his room. Father told me it was his. What was I to think?"

Mr. Leo was quiet on the other end for a moment.

"Forget it, Maggie."

"Where do you think they got it? That cross?"

"Who the hell knows? Lassiter could've picked it up in any five-and-dime jewelry store. It was a cheap trick but it worked."

"I should've just said it wasn't the same one. I don't know why I didn't. I knew in my heart it wasn't. *Couldn't* be."

"It might as well have been the same one as far as the jury was concerned."

"I really screwed up, didn't I, Mr. Leo?" I said.

"*I* was the one who screwed up. It was my fault. You don't go in blind like that. I should've known better. It was a stupid fucking mistake. I handed it to Lassiter on a silver platter."

"Now what do we do?"

"*Do?* Nothing," he said. "It's all over."

"What do you mean, it's all over?"

"Lassiter offered us a deal. Father pleads guilty to indecent assault. They drop the rape charges."

"You took it?"

"It's a good deal. All things considered, it's a very good deal."

"He's going to jail?"

"Yes. Maggie, he could have gotten twenty to life," Mr. Leo explained. "And not in any county jail either. Hard time, in a place like Cedar Junction. This way with time off, he could be out in two years. A free man."

"Free to do what though?"

"To go on with his life, that's what."

"His life was being a priest."

"Look, Maggie, I don't like losing either. But Lassiter offered us a good deal. A damn good deal. Do you know how rough it can be in the state pen for someone convicted of raping a child? And they've agreed to let him serve his time out of Adams County for his own safety."

"Mother o' God," I cried, still trying to swallow it all. "And it's all on account of me, isn't it? That damn cross."

"Don't go blaming yourself, Maggie. We could've ridden that out. I could've glossed things over on redirect. What really put us in the hole was the testimony about those pictures of Justin Blake. That really hurt. Even with that though, I still thought we had a fighting chance."

"Then why did you quit?"

"It wasn't my idea."

"*Father* decided to plead guilty?"

"I laid it all out for him. It still came down to his word against theirs. And even if we lost there was a very good chance we could win an appeal and get a new trial. All that stuff about Blake, it should never have been allowed in. No way in hell. Lassiter must have been worried about that too. That's why she put a last-minute deal on the table. I explained to Father that if we took the prosecution's offer we'd forfeit our chance to appeal, but if we didn't and the verdict went against us he could spend a good part of the rest of his life behind bars. In the end, it was his decision."

"Do *you* think he should've given up?"

"That's hard to say. I wouldn't be the one doing the time."

"Does it mean he admitted . . . doing those things?"

"In the eyes of the law, yes. He's a convicted felon now."

I waited for something more. I suppose for Mr. Leo to say Father still maintained his innocence, that he'd taken the deal only because he had no choice—like a man with a gun to his head. Or to say something about the other stuff. The Blake business. The cross. Any of it. But he didn't offer a thing. Even now he was playing his cards close to the vest.

"Frankly I think he was just tired, Maggie," he added. "All the publicity, it took its toll. He just wanted it to be over with."

"And now what?"

"What do you mean?"

"Is it? Over with?"

I heard that clucking sound in the back of his throat and I didn't like the sounds of that at all. I'd got to know him well enough to realize it meant he was holding back something.

"For now," he said.

For now? I thought. What did that mean? I wanted to ask what was beyond now, what lay out there on the distant horizon. But at the same time, I didn't want to know. I wanted to leave the future alone.

"I wish I never even mentioned that bloody cross."

"Don't go blaming yourself, Maggie. We gave it our best shot."

"I just feel I let the both of you down."

"You told what you thought was the truth. And maybe it was. Who knows. Least this way Father can be out in two years. That's something to take comfort in."

"Cold comfort," I said.

"Take care, Maggie. Maybe . . ." Yet he didn't finish his thought.

After I hung up, I stood in the kitchen staring out the window. Through the darkened trees I could make out the illuminated steeple of St. Luke's, shiny and white, pointing toward the sky like a pale, gaunt arm. To the left of that, well off in the distance, I made out the looming, shapeless darkness of Pelham's Overlook.

Part III

16

What is faith after all but a need to believe in something we can't see, something which the heart alone tells us is true. I suppose even in my darkest hour after my son's death, I never truly lost my faith. Not completely. Somewhere in my heart of hearts I still believed, I still had faith in God's infinite mercy and love. And no matter what they said, I still believed in Father. The Father Jack I knew was a good and decent man. Nothing they had said in that courtroom had altered that.

I was pouring Father Martin his decaf coffee after dinner one evening, a couple of days after Father Jack had been sentenced. Martin was reading the newspaper, as was his habit. I was starting to get used to his ways. He liked to sit in the dining room and peruse the paper over coffee. He never ate in the kitchen with me, the way Father Jack used to. I guess he thought there should be some distance between a priest and the hired help, which was fine by me.

"I'm certainly glad that's over," he said. I don't know as he was just speaking out loud or what. We didn't have much in the way of conversation. He might say it was a nice day, and I'd say indeed it was. Or he might tell me he didn't like his eggs the way I'd made them or so much starch in his shirts, and I'd say, yes sir, I'd see to that in the future. Tonight, he didn't have to say what *that* referred to. I knew.

"Is there anything else you'd be needing tonight, sir?" I asked.

"I think I'm all set, Miss Quinn."

"Then if you don't mind I'm going to turn in. I'm not feelin' up to snuff."

"Of course," he said. "Tomorrow, I'd like you to begin packing up his things."

"Packing whose things?"

"Why, Father Devlin's, of course," he replied with a bit of a laugh, like it should have been plain as the nose on my face.

"What of his would you like me to pack up?"

"Everything. You can begin with the bedroom. I plan on moving into it right away. It'll give me more space." Martin had been sleeping in one of the guest rooms, down the hall. Now with Father Jack gone, I guess he planned to make himself to home. "We can store his things in the basement for the time being. If you need a hand have Stanley help you."

"But . . ." I began.

"What is it?"

"Nothing. I'll get on it first thing tomorrow."

The next day I drove down to the Falls Tavern and got some boxes from Reuben Belliveau. Then I started packing Father's things. It near broke my heart to have to do it but what choice did I have? I packed his clothes, his books, his records and CD's, all his papers and notes, the sermons he'd written over the years, his basketball trophies, his favorite coffee mug—every last thing. Right down to the pictures on the walls, his toothbrush, the prescription bottles in the medicine cabinet. Martin insisted it all be cleared out. I guess he wanted no sign, nothing of Father Devlin's to remind him of the whole affair. Father Jack's photo albums, which the police had released after the trial, I placed in the corner of my closet. I didn't want them to get all moldy down in the basement.

Father's valuables, his jewelry and such, which he'd kept in the box on top of his bureau—those things I brought over to his office in the church, figuring to lock them away in the safe there. I didn't want anything to happen to them. The jewelry box was black lacquer, with a hand-painted scene showing a mountain waterfall. I'd bought it for him at the Christmas bazaar. Before I put the box in the safe, I lifted the top and casually poked through its contents. I told myself I was just seeing what was there, in case something later turned up missing. There were rings and cuff links, tie pins and bracelets. A college ring from Holy Cross. A St. Christopher medallion. A silver rosary with a small crucifix. No gold cross though. And just what did that prove, I thought.

While I was over there, I started removing the books from his bookshelf, packing them in boxes, too.

"How's it working for the new fellow?"

I turned to see Stanley leaning on a mop.

"He's got his own way of doing things," I replied.

"You ask me that Martin's another odd duck. Least maybe this one won't go buggering little boys."

"Don't you have work to do?" I said to him.

"He say anything about keeping us on, Maggie?"

"Not to me, he didn't. I don't exactly have his ear. I might give my notice in any case."

Which was true. Now that Father was away in prison, I'd given some consideration to quitting. I hadn't thought it through, what I'd do for a living, but I knew staying here, working for Martin, living in The Falls, wouldn't be any picnic, not with the way things had worked out. Everybody was angry with Father, and because I'd supported him, with me as well. Every time they saw me, I'd remind them of Father Devlin.

"Huh!" Stanley exclaimed. "Where the hell you gonna go?"

"Someplace else. Away from here."

"What are you doing?"

"Martin wants me to clean out Father's things."

"Looks like he won't be setting foot inside this church for a while. Me, I think I'll just stay put."

Funny thing was a few weeks later Martin caught Stanley shooting up in the basement of the church and cashiered him on the spot. I didn't shed any tears. No sir. I'd never liked the man. Good riddance. Though that wasn't the last we'd hear of him. Like a bad penny he'd turn up again.

Late one night, I lay in bed unable to sleep. I kept twisting and turning like a worm on a hook. Finally, I got up and went into the kitchen and made myself a cup of tea, added a bit of Jameson. When I'd finished that I poured a second one, this time leaving out the tea. Except for the furnace kicking on every once in a while, the house was stone quiet. What was on my mind was that blasted cross, had been ever since the trial. You see, in a way I still blamed myself for the way things had turned out. I should never have even brought it up in the first place. That was so bloody stupid of you, Maggie. Like Mr. Leo had said, Couldn't you see how it'd look, finding the thing under Father's bed like that. How others might look at it. Of course, I didn't put any stock in the notion that it was Roby's. Still and all, I had to admit it looked bad. Very bad. Like I was lying or Father was lying, or the both of us were.

I racked my brains, trying to sort it all out. Trying to make heads or tails of it. The cross I'd found under the bed had been Father's. I knew that. Father had said it was. But what of the one Roby had in court? That had to be another. Hadn't Mr. Leo said for all he knew Lassiter had gone out and bought one that looked like it? Surely that would explain things. Yet something didn't set right with me, was like a seed stuck between my teeth. I couldn't ignore it. Why hadn't I ever seen Father wearing it? When that Lassiter had asked me if I had, I couldn't say. Perhaps I had. I couldn't really remember though, and the thing is I've always had a good memory for details. Paying attention to details was my strong point, you might say. While I sat there pondering things, an idea come to me. Maybe some old photograph of Father would show him wearing the cross. Which would prove once and for all it was his. Of course, I thought. Why hadn't I thought of that before?

Excited by the prospect of clearing things up, I went into my closet and got the photo albums out. I sat on my bed, spread the albums out, and started going through them one by one. I saw pictures of Father dressed in his vestments and some in his collar and others in lay clothes. In several he was wearing the large wooden crucifix someone had given him for his birthday, and in one or two I saw him wearing the smaller silver one with the rosary beads. There was even a photo of him performing a marriage ceremony for Brenda O'Leary, in which a heavy Celtic cross hung from his neck. I looked and looked. I went through all the albums, slowly, carefully. But when I finished, I hadn't found a single photo showing him with the gold cross. Not a one.

Other times—pausing while I was ironing a shirt of Father Martin's, or while sewing a button on or scrubbing out the toilet—I'd get to thinking about different things. For instance, what Roby had said at the trial. How supposedly I'd gone up to Father's room and knocked on the door that time and asked if everything was all right. Which was just plain rubbish. Or Lassiter asking how I could have heard things with my door shut. She'd made it seem like I'd known something was going on, known about it and looked the other way. That I would lie to protect Father.

But I tried to put all that behind me. As my mum had always done, I tried to look on the bright side of things. A half loaf is better than none and all that. The Irish way of doing things. I thought with Father in jail, at least all those that had wanted to see him strung up from the nearest tree would be satisfied. They'd had their pound of flesh. I thought maybe now the cameras and the reporters would finally stop hounding him and let the poor man get on with his life, such as it was. Though I wasn't so naive to think it'd be all rosy from here on out, I felt that when the dust settled somehow he'd get through this. We would get through this. And while I'd considered moving on, or at the very least taking a new position, I decided to stay put. For Father's sake if nothing else. In my heart I felt it was still *his* church, *his* home. I wasn't going to let the bastards run me off, wasn't going to slink away with my tail between my legs, which to my mind would only prove to them I'd been lying. The future? I left it vague in my mind, floating out there in a haze, like the bluish mist that covered these mountains on a hot summer's day. I even thought that the Blake business would just go away by itself, like an ache which, if you pay it no mind, you wake up one fine morning and it's gone.

For several weeks, I put off going down to see Father. I figured I'd give him a chance to settle in, get his sea legs under him, so to speak. I told myself he needed time to adjust, without me there pestering him. It wasn't till early November that I finally went down. Nervous as a bride, I was. I'd never been inside prison walls before, had never smelled anything the likes of that god-awful stink. Not to mention those snotty-nosed guards giving you the evil eye and the other prisoners gawking at you and whispering. The worst though came when I finally laid eyes on Father, in that vomit-orange prison suit, his unshaven face already painfully thin. His complexion an ashen color save for a purplish bruise flowering under his right eye. And it was right then that I first used that trick, biting the inside of my cheek, to keep from crying.

"What happened to your eye, Father?" I asked.

He touched it gingerly with his hand. "Oh, I had a little accident."

I didn't pursue it. I hated to think what it must've been like in there for a man such as himself, someone used to his privacy, to his quiet and his book at night, someone like that rubbing shoulders with every class of common criminal. And I remembered what Mr. Leo had said about it going hard in jail for someone convicted of diddling children. Even on that first visit I could see the change in him, as if prison life had already settled into his skin and muscle and bones, and it was like he himself had retreated deep inside the protective shell of his body, the way a turtle would when sensing danger. Only his eyes, the same soft, pale blue, reminded me of the man I'd known.

For most of the hour-long visit, we fumbled for topics of conversation, almost like we were complete strangers. There was so much to talk about, yet so much to be avoided. We nibbled about the edge of things, cautious as mice around a trap. I asked how the food was. He spoke of parish affairs, how I was getting along with the new priest.

"He'll take some getting used to, that one," I said.

"Give him a chance," Father offered. "He's stepping into a bad situation."

"He wants everything done different. It's like starting all over."

"It took you what, seventeen years to get used to me?" he joked.

"Eighteen," I said, smiling.

I asked if I could bring him anything from home. I didn't tell him about his belongings being packed up and stored in boxes in the basement. I figured there'd be plenty of time to tell him that. This first visit anyway, I wanted things to go smoothly. I wanted it to be the way it had been between us, as much as that was possible given the circumstances. As I sat there struggling to come up with safe things to talk about, I realized one of the reasons why I'd put off coming: shame. I was ashamed to see Father reduced to this. I was ashamed of what they'd done to him. I was ashamed of bearing witness to his fall. And most of all, I was ashamed of my own part in helping to put him here. I wanted to say something, to apologize, I suppose, though I was reluctant to bring up the trial, the past, all of that. Funny, but it was Father that brought the subject up, almost like he'd read my thoughts.

"You mustn't blame yourself, Margaret," he said.

"How's that, Father?" I asked.

"Manzetti was here the other day. He said you thought it was your fault for how things turned out."

"I surely didn't help you any."

"Nonsense. You did your best."

"I was a nervous wreck up there on the witness stand. That Lassiter got me all balled up."

"You did just fine, Margaret. I was proud of you."

"All that about the cross though. You can't tell me that didn't hurt you, Father."

"Maybe it did. But it wasn't your fault. You told the truth."

"Aye, Father. That's what I been telling myself. But when that woman got through with me it didn't sound much like the truth, did it?"

"Don't worry about it. As long as we know, Margaret. That's all that counts."

He reached across the table and patted my hand.

"Thank you, Father. I can't tell you how relieved I am to hear you say that."

I was glad we'd got that business out of the way. I guess I'd been worried how he'd react when he saw me. That he'd blame me for bringing up the cross in the first place, for him ending up here. I'd wanted to start with a clean slate, wanted to be able to put all of that behind us and move on. Now I was hoping we could. And yet, something was still the matter. I couldn't put my finger on what it was but I felt it nonetheless. Like an irritation that, left unchecked, would turn into a blister if you just ignored it.

When it was time to leave, he gave me the titles of some books he wanted from his library. I said I'd bring them when I came next week.

"*Fad saol agat*, Father," I told him. Which means long life to you in Irish.

"God bless you, Margaret," he said, hugging me. "It was so good to see you."

"And you, Father."

I told him to take care, to try and write if he got the chance. I started for the door. I'd taken only a couple of steps, when I turned around and came back.

"There's one other thing, Father," I said. "About that cross."

"What about it?"

"I've been doing a lot of thinking on it. That one they had in court. That must've been some other one, I imagine."

"I would imagine so," he replied.

"Wouldn't be too hard to lay your hands on one like that is the way I figure it."

"Probably not."

"To tell you the truth, I doubt I could even have picked out yours, not after all this time."

He nodded, but not so much as if he agreed as it was that he was merely impatient for me to get to my point.

"Mr. Leo thinks it was just a trick. He says Lassiter could've gone out and bought one just like it in any jewelry store. To make folks think it was the same one."

Father rubbed his unshaven face. There was a look in his eyes, a cool blue gaze of recognition, one that saw right through me, that penetrated straight and clean to the heart of what I was really getting at like a scalpel in a surgeon's hands.

"I lost it," he said.

"What?"

"My cross. I lost it. Isn't that what you wanted to know?"

"Oh . . . no," I said, trying to pretend it wasn't. But of course he knew otherwise. "I'm sorry, Father. It's just . . . "

Father pursed his lips the way he did when he was disappointed about something. I felt embarrassed for even bringing it up now. More than embarrassment, I felt I'd betrayed him.

"Forget I even brought it up, Father," I offered. "It's not important."

"No," he said. "You have a right to know. I lost it. Up at the lake. Years ago. I was swimming. It must've slipped off."

"I knew it had to be something like that," I replied. "Mr. Leo should have put you on the stand, Father. You could have told the bloody bastards the truth—pardon my language."

"I wanted to. He didn't think it was a good idea that I testify. In retrospect, maybe I should have after all."

"A body could drive himself crazy with what-ifs and should-haves. It's over anyway. That's what we have to be grateful for, I suppose."

"You're right. At least it's over."

I hugged him once more and then turned and left the prison. I was glad I hadn't said anything about going through the photo albums looking for a picture of him wearing it. As I drove home that day, I recall thinking, Why, of course. He'd lost it.

• • •

Not counting myself and Father Duncan, and occasionally Mr. Leo on matters pertaining to his case, no one else came to visit him. Didn't see hide nor hair of his "good friend" Pete Beaupre or Judy Moran or any of the other birds who'd been his supporters and loyal parishioners. I don't know if it was his pleading guilty or the stuff that came out about Justin Blake that turned them against him, but when the trial was over they all abandoned Father quicker than rats jumping a sinking ship. On a later visit, when Father asked me if I'd heard from Pete, I said, "*Och*! He's made himself scarce, that one. And who'd have thought it, too?" But Father said you had to see it from his point of view, that it had to be hard remaining his friend. That we couldn't hold it against him. Pete was a businessman, Father said, and he had to think about how it would affect his livelihood. Who would want to buy a house from someone who continued to support a man like himself? I wasn't nearly so forgiving. It was a couple of months after the trial that I ran into Pete at Claude's service station out on 38. I'd stopped to get some gas after going over to Montville for groceries.

He came over and said to me, "Maggie, how's Jack doing?"

"As well as came be expected, I suppose," I replied curtly.

"Would you give him my best?"

"Your best?" I said, almost choking on the word.

"Maggie, you know I'd go down and see him if I could."

"So why don't you? He was your friend, for heaven's sake."

"He's also a convicted child molester."

"You know him. You know he couldn't have done that."

"But I don't know that. Not any more. He pleaded guilty."

"He only did that because they were going to put him away for the rest of his life."

"And who knows what else he may have done?" he said, though he didn't expand on that.

"No matter what," I said, "you don't turn your back on a friend in need."

"I stuck my neck out for Jack. You know that. We all did. We didn't betray him. He betrayed us."

"Go see him, why don't you, Pete. He could use a little cheering up."

"I'd like to. I would. But I can't afford to. I have to live here."

"And we have to live with our consciences, too."

There was a loyal few in town who did stick by Father. Father Duncan, of course. And Leah Bettancourt and Joan Kosnik might drop by the rectory and give me a book for Father, ask how he was doing. Once or twice Dina Cerutti stopped by for a visit. The two of us would share a cigarette like old times and chat for a bit. One or two others perhaps. But that was it. Most hated Father for bringing this down on The Falls. Half of them would've liked to stone him to death on the town green, while the other half just wanted to wash their hands of him. They wanted to put him out of their minds, pretend Father Jack never even happened. The nearly quarter of a century of his good work, his dedication and caring, all the things he'd done for this town, all the people he'd helped—it didn't count a fiddler's fart in their book. And the Church? Why, they were only concerned about their own neck. They quickly settled out of court with those Robys, gave them a pile of money, and sent them on their way. Overnight, Father's good name became mud around these parts. It was removed from everything associated with St. Luke's: the plaque with his name in the new annex of the church was taken down; on the parish letterhead "Father Devlin, Pastor" was changed to "Father Martin, Pastor"; the name of the scholarship he'd set up was renamed, as was that of the children's shelter over in Montville. They wanted to pretend that Father had never existed.

Folks turned not only against Father but myself as well. I'd worked for him and lived under the same roof and testified for him. So they shunned me, too. One time I bumped into Cindy O'Connell on Main Street. I hadn't talked to her in months. She was hauling her shopping cart down the sidewalk and we found ourselves in front of the CVS.

"How are you, Cindy?" I said, hoping we might let bygones be bygones. "Could I interest you in a cup of tea?"

But she gave me a look that would cut a stone.

"I hardly think so," she said icily.

"Maybe some other time then."

"He pulled the wool over everybody's eyes, that one. Even yours."

"He didn't pull the wool over my eyes," I replied.

"So you knew he done those things?"

"He's innocent."

"That's why he's in jail, I suppose. How blind can you be, Maggie?"

Still and all, I kept telling myself somehow we'd get through this. Somehow the truth *would* prevail in the end, just like Father used to say: *magna est veritas et praevalebit.* Yet I didn't like to think too far ahead, beyond one Tuesday to the next. What would happen to Father down the road, after he got out? Where would he go? What would he do? What would *I* do? I figured we'd cross those bridges when we came to them. For now, I thought only of those Tuesdays when I could go and be with him. That one hour a week was what I waited for, what I lived for. The rest of the time I played this game with myself: I pretended that *I* was in prison too. Just like Father. While I went about my chores, I made believe I was locked up, a prisoner just biding my time, and the hour a week I spent visiting him was the only moment I was free at all. I tried to make that be enough, tried to content myself with an hour. That and with the thought that at least the worst of it was behind us.

17

Of course, it never rains but it pours, and the worst of it wasn't over. No sir, not by a long shot. Oh, things did quiet down there for a spell. But it was a misleading sort of quiet: like I said, kind of like being in the eye of a storm, when the air gets so heavy and still and smells like electricity and you just know it's coming. I fell into a pattern of doing my job, minding my business, praying, looking forward to my Tuesday visits with Father. I was lulled into believing we were over the hump, that it could only get better. Yet it wasn't long before the bad news started up again, and this time it kept right on coming. Father wasn't in the prison but a couple of months when word come he'd had a heart attack. They said it was a mild one, but it laid him up in the hospital for a couple of weeks. And when next I saw him, as God is my witness, he looked ten years older: gaunt and haggard, the breath coming hard to him. He made me think of my mother in her last days before her heart gave out. I thought, *What have they done to you, Father?*

And then the Blake business started up again. For a few months after the trial, it was mostly confined to rumors making the rounds, which isn't unusual for a place like The Falls. I tried to pay it no mind. You might overhear two people in Hodel's talking. "I can't believe he'd do that," one would say, and the other would reply with, "Me neither. But they say he took those *pictures*." Someone else might say, "I remember that boy being over to the rectory *all* the time," and then he'd sort of raise an eyebrow. Once I was in Pelkey's Hardware, where Father Martin had sent me to buy a bag of rock salt. It was winter then, and he worried some old lady would slip coming up the walk and sue the parish for more money, which Martin said we could ill afford. As I was paying for the salt, I ran into Edie Horvath. She still had a bug up her arse about the way I'd turned on her in church that time. "The Blake boy used to deliver our paper, Ma," she said. "Such a sweet child. I sure hope they catch the s.o.b. did that to him."

Father wasn't in jail six months when you started to see things cropping up in the newspaper about it, about what folks in town used to refer to as "what happened up on Pelham's" or "the Blake business." Even before all this, you only had to say Pelham's Overlook or mention the boy's name and most people knew what you were talking about it. The Falls hadn't another murder in recent memory, so even after all this time people remembered it. The first article in the Springfield paper was just a small piece in the local news section but it was enough to get the ball rolling.

BOY'S MURDER REOPENED

(Montville, May 5, 1994) The Adams County D.A.'s Office has officially reopened the fifteen-year-old homicide case of Justin Blake, the murdered Hebron Falls youth. According to Assistant D.A. Miles Redmond, his office will go forward on the case. "While no unsolved murder investigation is ever closed," Redmond said, "as cases go this one was pretty cold." He stated, however, that new evidence warrants his office taking a fresh look at it.

On the evening of November 7, 1978, the twelve-year-old boy was reported missing by his parents. The next morning police and volunteers scoured the woods on both sides of Pelham Road, where the boy's bike had been found. They eventually located his body below Pelham's Overlook, a wooded, mountainous area known locally as a "lover's lane." According to investigators the boy had plunged seventy feet from the sheer cliff face, landing on rocks below. An autopsy conducted by Dr. Evan Mercurio, Adams County Medical Examiner, was able to determine strangulation as the cause of death. Authorities believe Blake had been strangled earlier and then thrown off the cliff to make it look as if he had taken his own life. Although state and local police had some leads at the time, even questioning the boy's father, no suspects have ever been arrested.

However, new evidence, including testimony which emerged during the recent Father Devlin sex abuse trial in Montville as well as a reexamination of physical evidence taken from the crime scene, may shed light on the case, prosecutors are hoping. "While it would be inappropriate to comment on the specifics of an ongoing investigation," said Redmond, "I can say that forensic advances unavailable fifteen years ago may provide new clues into solving this case." When asked if Father Devlin was a suspect in the investigation, Redmond would only comment that, "We will follow the evidence wherever it leads us. No stone will be left unturned."

A few weeks later another article appeared, this one at the bottom of the front page.

PRIEST CONSIDERED SUSPECT
IN ALTAR BOY'S DEATH.

(Montville, May 23, 1994) Prosecutors have confirmed rumors that Father John Devlin, 54, is a suspect in the recently reopened case of Justin Blake, an altar boy who was brutally slain fifteen years ago. Devlin, a Roman Catholic priest and former pastor of St. Luke's Church, is currently in jail for sexually abusing two former Hebron Falls youths. Sources within the D.A.'s office have also confirmed unpublished reports that the state is seeking to obtain blood samples from the priest in order to conduct DNA tests. Prosecutors are hoping to match the priest's blood with samples taken from the crime scene. Blood was found that didn't match Blake's blood type. Investigators have long speculated that a struggle took place between Justin Blake and his assailant and that the blood found at the scene could very well be that of the murderer. Prosecutors are hoping a DNA match of Devlin's blood could place the priest at the murder scene. The Adams County District Attorney's Office has obtained a warrant which would force Father Devlin to surrender a blood sample to the Commonwealth. "If he didn't do it, he has nothing to worry about," said D.A. Shelly Lassiter.

However, Leonardo Manzetti, Father Devlin's counsel, intends to fight the D.A.'s request in court, arguing that taking blood would be in violation of his client's constitutional rights. Mr. Manzetti said, "My client is well within his rights to refuse giving his blood." Manzetti maintained his client's complete innocence in regard to the Blake murder, and even went so far as to say that Father Devlin was willing to take a polygraph exam to support his claim. Such exams, often called lie detector tests, are usually not admissible as evidence in the state of Massachusetts. Manzetti called the investigation of his client a witch-hunt motivated by political considerations. He said that Father Devlin was being railroaded because of his beliefs and because of shoddy investigative work. "The police are trying to pin the murder on my client simply because they have failed to do their work. If they had, they'd be out looking for the real murderer." Devlin is currently serving a four-year jail term at the Holden County House of Corrections for indecent assault.

That was the first I was to hear of the blood business. Over the next year, though, I'd hear more and more about it, as the case wound its way from one court to the next. It was so important, in fact, Mr. Leo said without a blood match, Lassiter probably would never indict Father. You'd see things in the paper or catch them on the television news. Headlines like "DEFENSE REFUSES TO SURRENDER BLOOD SAMPLES" and "JUDGE TO HEAR MOTIONS IN BLAKE CASE." Or you'd hear on the evening news something like, "Battle lines drawn over blood samples."

Then one night I saw on the news how they'd dug up that boy's body. They showed Hillcrest Cemetery, a tractor with a backhoe. They showed them lifting the coffin out of the ground. They were going to do another autopsy. I couldn't believe it. Digging him up like that. Why couldn't they just let the poor child rest in peace, for heaven's sake? No, they had to be disturbing the dead, and for what? I thought. Afterward, that Andrea Ladd spoke to the boy's father,

Warren Blake. She had him standing in front of the church, even though I can't say when I'd last seen him inside. Blake told her how he always thought Father Devlin was a little "odd." But he was a priest, he said, so he overlooked it. He explained how Father used to take his son places, let him hang out over at the rectory. He said he never thought too much about it until once when Justin came back with bruises on his arms. Blake said he spoke to the priest about it, but that Father just denied it.

"If I'd only known then what I know now, I'd never let my boy near that pervert," Blake told Andrea Ladd. "It tears me up inside to think what he did to Justin."

Why that bloody two-faced bastard, I thought. If anyone, it was him that hurt his son, not Father. It wasn't any secret around town that Warren Blake took his hands to the kids, that he had himself a violent temper. And now he was trying to pass that off on Father.

• • •

A few months after this, two detectives showed up at the rectory. They weren't the same ones as before though. These two said they were "from homicide," said it like it was a place, the way you might say you were from The Falls.

"We'd like to ask you a few questions, Ms. Quinn," said one, a tall, lanky fellow with a pencil-thin mustache and sloping shoulders.

"I already told you people all I know about those Robys," I replied.

"This isn't about the Robys, ma'am," explained the other detective, also tall but more stoutly built. Tweedledee and Tweedledum, I thought of them as. "We'd like to ask you about Justin Blake."

So it'd come to that at last, I thought.

As with the other two, we sat in the den and they asked me questions. I tried to breathe regular, not to get nervous. They wanted to know if I recalled the Blake boy, how often he came around, if he spoke to me much and about what, the sort of relationship he'd had with Father. This and that. I told them what I knew. That Justin used to come around, that he was a nice boy, quiet, reserved, kept to himself. That he and Father were close. As soon as I said that I could see Tweedledee's eyes light up.

"Close?" he said.

"What I mean is they were good friends."

"Did Father take the boy places?"

"He would."

"Where?"

"Different places. Justin used to go with him on his rounds. Or he'd help Father and then Father'd bring him for an ice cream."

"Did Father Devlin ever take boys up to Pelham's Overlook?" asked the other, Tweedledum.

"No," I said. "Why would he do that?"

"Do you know if Justin ever went up there?"

"I believe so. He mentioned he'd been up there."

"Did he say with whom?"

I thought for a moment. "Other kids. They'd ride their bikes. Sometimes him and Derek would go up there."

"Derek?"

"His brother. They used to watch the sunset over the mountains. Justin liked doing that."

"Did Father ever take Justin up there?"

They were slippery as a pair of eels, these two.

"I just told you I never knew Father to go up there. With Justin or anybody else for that matter."

Then they began asking what I remembered about the night Justin died. Where I was and what I'd been doing and did I recall the sort of night it had been, and a dozen other things I didn't see the point of, to tell you the truth. If I didn't know better, I'd have said they thought me a suspect too. Which maybe they did, I don't know.

I said, "I told everything I knew to that other fellow that was here right after it happened."

"Detective Guilbault?" Tweedledee asked, looking at his notes.

"Might be. I don't remember his name. A young fellow, with reddish hair. He come round asking questions a few days afterward. You ought to ask him."

"But we'd like to hear it from you, ma'am. Do you recall when Father got home?"

"It was late."

"How late?"

"I don't know to the minute, if that's what you mean. It was a long time ago," I said, pausing. I knew they were trying to get me to say something they could use against Father. Just like those other two. Trying to trip me up, get me tangled up in my own words. *Careful, Maggie.*

"So you're *not* clear about the time frame anymore?" asked Tweedledum.

"No. I mean, yes. Sort of."

"Do you recall if it was it before midnight?"

"Yes, I'd say it was."

"You'd *say* it was? You don't sound too sure about it?"

"I'm sure," I said. "It's just like I told Detective Guilbault. I was here and Father come home and it was before midnight."

"You're sure?"

"I told you I'm sure."

"Is there anything else you can tell us about that night?" "No," I said. "That pretty much covers it."

"Thank you for your time, ma'am," they said.

As they were going down the steps I asked, "Is Father Devlin charged with anything?"

"No, ma'am," said one of them. "Not yet at least."

After they were gone, I went into my bedroom and shut the door. I took that picture out of my purse, the one I'd found up in the attic. The one of Justin and Father. I looked at it for a long time, feeling that old ache welling up in my chest. I could remember the boy coming over, sitting at the kitchen table, drinking a glass of milk and eating some cookies. The lad never had two words to say. *Cat got your tongue,* I'd tell him. He'd smile shyly at me, the same sort of smile as he had in the picture. *With love, Just,* it said on the back. With love, I thought. I happened to glance at the photo of Eion on my nightstand, the one of him sitting on a horse. Such handsome lads, the both of them. And both taken before their time. Such a shame, I thought. A crying shame.

A knock on the door interrupted my thoughts.

"Miss Quinn," Father Martin said. I put the picture back in my purse and opened the door.

"What did they want?" he asked.

"They wanted to ask me some questions about Justin Blake."

"The boy that was killed?"

I nodded. Though it was a warm spring day, I felt goose bumps sprouting on the backs of my arms.

"Why were they asking *you* questions?" Martin asked.

"I don't know. I guess because I was working here when it happened."

Martin chewed on his lip, the way he had a habit of doing when he was nervous. He stared at me like he wanted to ask something more but didn't dare.

"I thought the damn thing was over," he said.

"Aye. Me, too."

18

Some things the memory guards the way you would a fragile orna-
ment or a delicate piece of expensive crystal. They're not for every-
day use. Your memory keeps those things covered with tissue, put
away somewhere for safekeeping. And when you do take them out,
you're careful as a mother with a newborn babe. That's how my
memory was of Justin. As of something so delicate, so fine and glistening, so precious and so painful, too, that I handled it only with
the utmost caution. Yet unlike with those Robys, I didn't have to go
rummaging through my mind to bring up his memory. I knew right
where it was, just had to go and carefully take it down from the
shelf, unwrap it, dust it off. Now and then, I'd be going about my
work and into my head would pop some little thing I recollected
about him. How the light caught his blond hair, making it shimmer
rainbow-like. Or how his small, frail voice warbled when he'd ask,
"Is Father Jack around, Ma?" Or how he used to help me hang the
wash or work in the garden. And when I'd try to give him a quarter
for his services, don't you know he wouldn't want to take it. That's
the sort of lad he was.

"Go ahead, love," I'd say to him. "Buy yourself a treat."

I'd muss his hair, and he'd give me that skittish smile of his and
say, "Thank you, Ma."

And when I thought of him I felt that ache in my breast.

His mother worked evenings and his father spent a good bit of
his free time at the gin mill, so Justin pretty much came and went as
he pleased. The sort of boy that didn't get a lot of supervision, if you
know what I mean. Would stop by the rectory looking for Father a

couple of times a week. He was here so much I took to calling him Father's shadow. "Well, would you look who's here," I'd say as he got off his bike and came in the back door. "If it ain't Father's shadow." He might've stopped by before going over to Mass with Father or to help him with a car wash. Or maybe he'd just stopped by, without any reason whatsoever. If Father was busy in his study, I'd have Justin sit in the kitchen and keep me company.

"Can I be fixing you something eat?" I'd ask.

"No, thanks, Ma," he would reply, polite as always.

"Get out with you. Boys your age are always hungry."

So I'd pour him a glass of milk and cut him a piece of strawberry-rhubarb pie I'd just made. He always looked on the scrawny side and I had this urge to fatten him up.

"Doesn't that mother of yours ever feed you?" I codded him.

"She works," Justin replied, not one to say a thing against his own blood. He was loyal like that. Never did I hear him speak an ill word about his family, not even about that good-for-nothing father of his.

The Blakes lived across the river, on the east end of town in a ramshackle house in need of painting. They weren't poor exactly, but with the father's drinking, the mother had to work. Her name was Nancy. A petite, twitchy, once-pretty woman with large, doelike eyes that never met your own. Like Justin in that. She worked the swing shift over in the cabinet factory in Montville and so was usually gone when Justin got home from school. At church, she sat way in the back and never came up for communion, even if her own son was there assisting Father Jack. But she had her reasons, I suppose. On more than one occasion, she showed up to church with sunglasses to cover the handiwork of that husband of hers. She kept to herself mostly, not unfriendly so much as timid, the way women with that sort of husband often are. I felt sorry for her.

Warren Blake never attended church, like my da in that regard. The man drank—which, coming from me, I know, is a bit like the pot calling the kettle black. Still and all, he drank, and when he did, he turned mean, had a reputation for being ill-tempered. Around town there was talk of fighting at the Blake household. The man used to show up half in the bag to CYO basketball games, to watch his older boy, Derek, who played for Father Jack's team. Derek was quite a player, one of Father Jack's best, though even he could never please his old man. From the stands, Mr. Blake would be yelling his bloody head off, embarrassing his son. He was especially hard on Justin, as the boy wasn't much good at sports. Justin was more your quiet, studious sort. Soft, you might call him. A child prone to "accidents." There was a broken arm one time and a busted collarbone. A kid like that, you always wondered when he told you he'd slipped on some ice. Was he just protecting his old man? Suffice it to say, the child had problems at home, which was why, I suppose, he liked to hang out here.

I poured myself a cup of tea and sat down opposite him. As usual, he didn't look up from his plate.

"Cat got your tongue, Justin?" I asked.

"What cat?" he said. It was our little joke.

"Eat up. There's more where that come from."

Justin was small for his age and delicate-looking as a piece of bone china. A pale complexion, a few freckles sprinkled over his nose, bangs falling in his face. Blue-gray eyes that kind of glittered when he smiled, though he didn't smile often. Quiet and kind of shy, he had this serious, reserved manner most of the other boys his age lacked. I don't mean to say he was one of those precocious little brats that's too smart for his britches. No sir. He was regular enough in most ways. Just that he was sweet, genuinely sweet without really trying. A boy who liked flowers and sunsets and would sit around keeping an old bird like me company. A darling lad, really. Sometimes looking at him I'd get to thinking about my Eion. It was only natural, I suppose. The both of them with that blond hair, though Justin's was a shade lighter. Both with those blue eyes, a pretty smile. I'd ponder what might have been, the way any mother who's lost a child would. What my Eion might have grown into had he lived. Maybe a boy like Justin. It was a double-edged thought, to be sure, one that made me both sad and happy at once. A sweet ache.

"What's the matter, Ma?" Justin might ask when he'd catch me staring at him.

"Nothing," I said. "You made me think of someone is all."

Justin had been an altar boy. He'd show up at the rectory with his things stuffed in a grocery sack for Mass, his cassock and surplice unwashed and wrinkled, his shoes scuffed. I could only wonder how a mother would let her child go out looking like that, and to help serve Mass no less. So I'd take his things and throw them in the wash, and while I was at it, put a shine to his shoes. I didn't mind. Besides, Justin was always so grateful for it. "Thanks, Ma," he'd say. It'd been some time since I'd had occasion to wash a child's clothes.

"Don't we look sharp," I'd exclaim as he came out of the bathroom wearing his clean things. "Here, straighten out your hair."

Waiting for Father, we'd sit and have us a little chat, though Justin, at least at first, was a lad of few words. Yet, as he got to know me, he opened up a bit more. Would talk about his Boy Scout troop or some teacher at school. Or about his older brother, Derek. Justin idolized him. He was always going on about him. Derek this and Derek that. A star basketball player at the high school. An honor student. A good-looking boy who dated the Apple Festival queen. When I first come to work here, Derek, an altar boy as well, used to drop by to help Father serve Mass, shoot baskets with him out in the driveway, afterward come in for some milk and cookies. But then he stopped coming around, got too big for his britches, the way many of the boys do. One minute they're these sweet little angels in their surplices, and the next they're shaving and smoking and got nothing but girls on their minds. Like his old man, Derek didn't even attend church anymore. The only time I'd see him was when he'd stop by in his car to pick his little brother up after Mass. He wouldn't even come in and say hello.

Except for Derek, Justin didn't like talking much about his home life. Was like pulling nails. I recall asking him once about a split lip he had. He said his father had been teaching him how to box, said the man didn't want him to grow up to be a "pantywaist." That was one of the few times I can remember him saying anything regarding his old man. However, Father Jack, who counseled kids like Justin all the time, was well aware of the "problem." After Justin got the broken arm—"falling down the stairs," was how the lad explained it, his eyes not meeting yours—Father, not one to use foul language as a rule, got so mad he said, "I'd like to break his goddamn neck." Meaning, of course, Mr. Blake. Yes, Father was well aware of Justin's home life, and he was always looking to do what he could for the boy. And Justin knew Father's door was always open.

Take this one time. I'd returned early from a trip to Boston, where I'd driven Cindy O'Connell to see a sick relation. I'd no sooner come through the back door when I heard this faint noise. I couldn't tell where it was coming from so I followed it. Finally, I realized it was coming from Father's study. The door was shut. Out in the hall, I overheard Father say, "It's all right. I won't let it happen again. I *promise* you." And then a child's voice, tremulous from sobbing, said, "He'd kill me." It was Justin Blake's. I didn't want it to seem like I'd been eavesdropping, so I slipped into my room and quietly shut the door. After a while, I heard Justin leave. *He'd kill me,* he had said. It wasn't hard to figure out they must have been talking about Mr. Blake. No doubt Justin had come to Father and told him about another incident. Now he was afraid if the old man found out.

A couple of times things got so bad at home Justin ran off. Once they found him in a bus station down in Hartford. Another time he showed up at the shelter over in Montville looking for a place to stay. And once, Father even let him sleep in the spare room downstairs. When Father called the Blakes the next day to say their son was there, Mr. Blake was fit to be tied. I remember Father and him having words about it in the kitchen when the man stopped by to pick his son up.

"Who the hell do you think you are?" Warren Blake yelled.

"I'm just trying to help, Mr. Blake," Father explained.

"We don't need your damn help. He's my kid. I'm warning you—keep your fucking nose out of our business," Blake said, storming out of the house and slamming the door. Imagine using that language with a priest? But that's the class of man he was.

We didn't see Justin after that for months. Didn't come around, didn't go to church. *The old man's doing,* I thought. But then one Sunday morning, the boy just showed up carrying his robes in a bag.

"Well, well, well," I exclaimed. "Look what the cat drug in."

"My mother said it was all right to come," was all he said. It brought to mind my own mother putting her foot down with my da about me going to church.

Like I said, Father sort of took Justin under his wing. He helped him if there was a problem at school, took him places, spent time

with him. There'd be Father Jack at the kitchen table after school going over a math problem with the boy, or in the backyard teaching
him how to shoot a basketball. Or he'd let Justin tag along with him
when he visited someone at the nursing home. Anyone with eyes in
his head could see Justin enjoyed being around Father Jack. They
had this special bond, those two. In the few years I knew him, I could
see the child start to flower under Father's guiding hand, to come out
of that shell that he'd put up around himself because of his old man.
He began to speak up, to be more outgoing. I recall Justin telling me
once he wanted to be a priest when he grew up.

"'Tis a hard row to hoe," I told him. "Only a few have the calling."

"I want to be like Father Jack."

"Do you now? Can you say the Nicene Creed from beginning to
end, no mistakes?"

"Sure," he said. "*I believe in one God, the Father almighty* . . . "

I sometimes got the feeling it wasn't *only* Father that Justin came
to see. Even if I told him Father was off somewhere and wouldn't be
back, he'd often hang around anyway. The child would tag along after me like a puppy while I did my work. He might help me fold
laundry or run an errand on his bike to the center of town, or give
me a hand out in the garden. By the way he acted around me, I got
the impression he was sweet on me. You know, the sort of crush kids
get on an adult. Why, I remember having one on Mr. McGinty, our
milkman. Justin brought me some flowers one day—some marigolds
and lilies of the valley.

"These are for you, Ma," he said.

"Oh, how sweet of you, love."

I thought it was cute, the way he felt. Though of course I never
mentioned it to him as it would've shamed the pants right off him.
But I did tell Father.

"I have a secret admirer," I said to him.

"Who?"

"Justin."

"Justin?" he said.

"That'd be my guess, sir. Have you not seen the puppy-dog look
on the child when he's around me?"

"I didn't even know he was interested in girls yet."

"I'm hardly a girl," I said. "But didn't yourself have a crush on an older woman when you were a lad?"

"I can't remember, it's been so long."

"'Tis only natural. A boy that age."

Justin was a bit of a loner. Didn't seem to have many friends. The other boys didn't care for him. Especially the ones like that Villandry and his ilk, foulmouthed, ill-bred little urchins, the kind always getting into trouble. They teased and made fun of him. They taunted him. They called him names—pansy and momma's boy and worse. Because he had this gentleness about him, a softness the others didn't have and which they mistook for weakness. What's more, they knew he was Father's favorite and that made them jealous.

I was over to the community center one time, and I heard this racket coming from the boys' bathroom. A door banging, somebody screaming bloody murder. So I went running in there and found several boys had little Justin in one of the stalls. They held him by the arms and legs and was trying to stick his head in the toilet bowl. I asked them what they thought they were up to. I felt like boxing their ears for them. "Would yous like to try that with me?" I told them. Like the bullies they were, they slunk off with their tails between their legs. All except one. He turned on Justin and said, "You wait, Blake. You just fuckin' wait."

Justin's face was beet-red, and he still had tears in his eyes. I got a paper towel and started to clean him up.

"Are you all right?" I asked.

He pushed my hand away. "Would you just stay out of it?" he said.

"I only—"

"Just mind your own damn business."

Then he took off, running out the back door.

This surprised me, coming as it did from Justin, who was usually so sweet. Until, that is, I'd had a chance to chew on it a bit. You see, he only wanted to fit in. He was still a regular boy, and he just wanted to be one of the gang. That's why he didn't want me to interfere, why he went along with their teasing, why he'd laugh when they taunted him or punched him on the arm. I had to give him credit though. He was never one to come running to Father or me. No sir. Took his lumps and kept quiet about it. Yet when I happened to witness some cutting remark, some casual cruelty that's in the nature of boys, why, it broke my heart. I wanted to grab hold of those little bastards by the scruff of the neck and shake the living daylights out of 'em. What it was, don't you know, I just wanted to protect him, the way you do for your own. I didn't want to see him hurt. I only wanted what was best for him. That's all. That's all I ever wanted.

•   •   •

Then one night Justin didn't show up home. At first, I figured he'd just taken off again, like he had those times before. But the next day, we heard they'd found his bike. It was in a ditch off Pelham Road, up on the mountain west of here. Not only that but there was blood on the handlebar. And just a little ways off, where the dirt road goes in to Pelham's Overlook, they came across a sneaker—just the one—which Mrs. Blake identified as Justin's. That's when things started looking not so good. The police brought in dogs. Volunteers helped out—people from the parish, his Boy Scout troop, friends of the family. Father Jack, too. They combed the woods up on Pelham's Mountain. Over in the community center we set up coffee and doughnuts for those that were searching for the boy. We prayed he'd be found safe and sound. We tried to keep our spirits up. Maybe he'd just taken off again. Maybe he was hiding in the woods. Maybe, we thought, he was hurt and waiting for help to come. It had turned cold up in the mountains yet Justin was a healthy boy, and we crossed our fingers that somehow he would've survived the night. But as the hours passed and there was still no word, our fears grew worse.

In the afternoon I went back over to the rectory to get some more coffee. I was in the kitchen when Father came in the back door. I still remember the look on him. His skin was a pasty-white, and he had the most doleful expression I'd ever seen. His boots were covered with mud, but he didn't even bother wiping them as he shuffled over to the window above the sink and looked out, up toward Pelham's.

"Father," I asked, "did they find the child?"

He nodded.

"He's all right, isn't he?" I asked, despite already knowing in my bones that it was otherwise.

"He's dead," he replied in a monotone.

"*Dead*! Dear God in heaven, say it ain't so, Father."

But I knew it was so. I went over to him and hugged him, began sobbing. Right then, Father was too far gone for tears. The shock of it, I imagine. He stood there limp as a rag in my arms.

After a bit I managed to get out, "How?"

He told me how the searchers had come across his broken little body at the bottom of Pelham's Overlook. At first, they were thinking it an accident. A lot of kids went up there to drink and horse around. There'd been accidents up there before, though nothing like this. Maybe, some said, he wasn't alone. Maybe other boys were with him and they did something stupid, like boys are apt to do when they get liquored up. Perhaps they got too close to the edge, challenging each other, some silly game. That's what people were saying at first.

But it wasn't long till another rumor made the rounds. An ugly rumor it was, too. This one had Justin taking his own life. Some said he'd been depressed about things at home. It was even whispered in some circles that a boy who knew Justin said he'd told him he couldn't stand it anymore and was going to do "something." Which people took as meaning he aimed to kill himself.

A few days later we were in the kitchen, Father and I. I was making his breakfast and he was sitting there writing something in his calendar. The morning's paper lay unread on the table. When I'd brought it in earlier I saw the headlines: BOY'S DEATH POSSIBLE SUICIDE. Father remained silent.

"You don't think he'd do such a thing, do you, Father? Take his own life."

"I don't know," he replied, his manner somewhat abrupt.

"I knew that boy. He wouldn't of done that. He had too much on the ball for that. Father . . . Father?"

When I turned from the stove, I caught the back of him hurrying down the hall and into the bathroom. I heard him in there being sick. When he finally returned to the kitchen, he come over to me, dropped to his knees, put his arm around my waist, and started sobbing. Sobbing like a baby.

"Oh, God," he cried. "Oh, God."

"It'll be all right, Father," I said to him, stroking his head. As a priest, he'd certainly seen his share of death, but never had I seen him like this before. The boy's death hit him awful hard. He was so fond of him. The both of us were.

It wasn't but a few days later, we heard the official story.

BOY'S DEATH RULED A HOMICIDE

(Hebron Falls, November 11, 1978) The Adams County Medical Examiner has determined the death of twelve-year-old Justin Blake to be a homicide, it was announced yesterday. Following an autopsy, Dr. Evan Mercurio said the cause of death was asphyxiation. "Most likely someone strangled the boy with his hands," Dr. Mercurio told reporters. There were marks about the boy's neck that were "consistent with strangulation," Mercurio said. "Due to the fall, the severity of the boy's injuries at first prevented us from determining cause of death."

Authorities believe Blake was strangled first and then his body was dragged and thrown off Pelham's Overlook to make it appear a suicide. However, state police investigators found blood splatters on the handlebar of the boy's bike as well as some on a sneaker, blood which didn't match Blake's. It is believed that Justin fought with his assailant, and that he managed to cut him in the scuffle before being overcome. According to the autopsy report, Blake had not been sexually molested. Nancy Blake, the mother of the slain boy, said, "People liked Justin. He was a good boy. What reason could anybody have for doing this?" At this point, police have neither a motive nor suspects and are urging anyone with information to contact the state police.

Strangled! I thought. Who could have done such a thing? Who could have strangled the life out of that lovely boy with his bare hands, and then chucked him off the cliff like that? What sort of monster could have done such a thing?

As the police didn't release the body right away, the funeral was delayed some time. Even so, Father and myself went over to the Blakes, to pay our condolences. I brought a pot of stew and some homemade tomato sauce. With three mouths still to feed, the missus would surely not be up to cooking for quite some time. There was a bunch of people there when we arrived, friends and relations. Mrs. Blake was in the kitchen with some other women. As you might well imagine, the poor woman was beside herself with grief. "Why would anyone want to hurt my baby?" she cried. "He was such a good boy." I tried to comfort her. I said the worst thing in the whole world had to be losing a child, but that with God's help she'd get through this. I told her to pray, which was frail comfort in times like that but you offer what you can.

That's when I heard words coming from the living room. Mr. Blake was yelling at Father. He said Father had turned his own son against him, said Justin was never the same after he started hanging around him, disrespectful and sneaky. Everyone was looking at him. It was a terrible ugly scene, the like of which I'd never witnessed before. The missus tried to quiet him down, saying, "Please, Warren. For the love of God, don't do this." But the man was beyond the beyonds. He even threatened Father.

"*You* turned him against me, you son of a bitch," the man cried.

"Mr. Blake, I . . ." Father began.

"If it wasn't for you, he wouldn't be out who knows where. He'd have been home where he belonged," he said, jamming a finger into Father's chest. For a moment I thought he was going to hit Father, but some of the men, including his own son Derek, stepped between them.

"You'd better go, Father," the older Blake boy said. He was now taller even than Father. A man.

"Derek, I only wanted to help," Father said, looking at him. "You know that."

"Just go, Father. *Now.*"

I had a good mind to tell Mr. Blake, if anybody turned his son against him it was himself, pure and simple. Yet Father, shaken by what Blake had said and not wanting to cause a scene during their grief, just turned and left.

"He had no right to say those things," I told him out in the car.

"I never meant to cause any problems."

"Don't you worry, Father. You did all right by that boy."

The next day Mrs. Blake stopped by the rectory to apologize for her husband's behavior. Father wasn't home, but I invited her in and had her sit down at the kitchen table. I made her a cup of tea, added some honey and a bit of brandy, which is what my mum used to give me when I was feeling poorly. Pale as a ghost, she was, her eyes with dark circles under them. Maybe she was already sick even then with the cancer. Who can say? She said her husband had no call to act the way he did. She said Father was always a kind and decent man, and her son was very fond of him. She appreciated how Justin had someone he could go to, someone who understood him.

"He didn't have many friends," she said. "Justin isn't . . . *wasn't* like other kids."

"He was a fine lad, Mrs. Blake," I said. "Father and me thought the world of him. A lovely boy. Had himself a heart of gold."

"Warren felt he should've been with kids his own age. But I thought it would do him good. Spending time with Father Jack."

"They were fast friends. I used to call him 'Father's shadow.' Because he'd follow Father Jack around so."

Mrs. Blake laughed through her tears, turning her young and pretty for a moment. I could see Justin in her then, in her eyes and the shape of her mouth.

"My husband was jealous that Father and Justin were so close. Warren didn't understand our son. I think that's why they fought."

"Did Justin ever tell you he wanted to be a priest, Mrs. Blake?"

"He *did?*" she asked, her face brightening momentarily.

"Aye. I'm surprised he never mentioned that."

"Justin didn't tell me much of anything lately. We used to be so close."

"I wouldn't take it to heart, Mrs. Blake. That age, boys don't talk to their mothers much."

"He used to tell me everything. I don't know what happened. Maybe my being gone so much."

"You raised a lovely boy. Have no doubt on that score, Mrs. Blake."

"He always seemed so frail," she said, stirring her tea and then taking the spoon out and staring at her reflection in it. "Derek could always stand on his own two feet. Even when he was little he could take care of himself. And watch out for Justin too. At school, if any-

body gave Justin any problems they had his brother to deal with."
She bit her lip at that thought. "That's why Justin looked up to him.
But lately even the two of them weren't getting along. I don't know. I
guess we weren't a very happy family."

"Nonsense," I said. What else could I say?

"I should've paid more attention to what was going on. I guess I
wasn't such a good mother. If I had been maybe . . . "

Tears trickled down her cheeks, and she dabbed her face with a
napkin. She had the sort of looks that were fragile, subject to the
whims of bad luck, a lack of love, too many night shifts.

"Don't go blaming yourself now, Mrs. Blake. You did the best
you could. There's just no making sense of some things," I offered.
"It's God's will and we're to accept it." It made me think of what my
mum had told me after Eion's death. That God worked in mysterious
ways.

"Oh my little boy," she moaned. I got up and went around the
table and hugged her. I told her things have a way of working out.
She said how Justin always spoke well of me, was always going on
about Ma Quinn and what a good cook she was. Which set me to
blubbering, too. After a while I said, "I know what you're going
through. I lost a boy, too, Mrs. Blake."

She looked up at me, surprised. So I told her about my Eion, all
of it, the whole story. I told her how no matter if you were to blame
or not, when you lose a child you take on the guilt anyway. It's only
natural. For not protecting him. For not being a better mother. How
no matter what you did, no matter how good or bad you were, how
careful or careless, you'd brought this child into the world and it was
your responsibility to see that he stayed here, safe and sound, until
he was an old man and died in his bed.

"Don't you worry, Mrs. Blake," I told her. "Your little fellow's
out of danger. He's at peace now."

Still, Mr. Blake, spiteful man that he was, wouldn't let Father say
the funeral Mass for the boy. It wasn't even held at St. Luke's, where
Justin had been an altar boy, but over at St. Catherine's in Montville
and some other priest performed the services. Father didn't think it
wise that he should go, afraid of Mr. Blake causing another scene. As
if the boy's death wasn't enough, Father had to suffer those vile

things Blake had said and now wasn't allowed to go and pay his last respects. Why, it cut Father to the quick, don't you know. In all my living days I'd never seen him so down in the mouth. He stayed up in his room, wouldn't come down for meals.

• • •

For several weeks, Justin Blake's murder was in the papers and on the news. The police interviewed people. They had some leads. Someone had spotted Justin riding his bike west on Coffin's Bridge that afternoon, and they thought he'd been with another boy. Others said they saw a dark blue van with out-of-state plates cruising slowly along Pelham Road earlier. And a few people remember a stranger with blond hair who'd bought a coffee in the Falls Café and then drove off in what one person described as a dark-colored van, another as a pickup truck. In the paper he was even referred to as the "blond-haired stranger." Rumors buzzed around town. People were on the lookout for a dark van, a blond male. Parents, who'd normally thought The Falls a safe enough place, kept a closer eye on their children. Police received a call saying a van had been spotted outside the grammar school. Several kids reported a stranger who'd stopped in his car to ask them directions. And there was even one sighting by a couple of teenagers necking up at Pelham's Overlook of a man and a little boy. The man wasn't driving a van, but the car was dark, and they thought he might have been blond. But nothing came of it.

It wasn't long after the funeral that that fellow from the state police came around. Detective Guilbault. He had reddish hair and a soft baby-faced complexion that didn't look as if he even took a razor to it yet. He and Father and myself sat at the kitchen table, I remember. He was quite respectful to Father when asking his questions. You see, this was years ago. Things were different then. A priest was a figure that commanded respect, even from the law.

"Can you think of anybody who might've had a reason to hurt him, Father?" the detective asked.

"No. He was a good kid," Father explained, shaking his head in disbelief. "Everybody liked him."

"Not everybody," I said. "Some of the kids didn't like him."

"Why?" the detective wanted to know.

"They thought he was . . . I don't know. Too nice."

"Too nice?"

"You know how boys at that age are. They like to pick on those that are a little different."

The policeman asked for the names of the boys that teased him, and I told him I thought it wasn't anything really. Just boys having a bit of fun at someone else's expense.

"We'll still need to check it out," Detective Guilbault said. "Did Justin ever tell you about problems at home, Father?"

"Yes," Father said. "But some things he told me were in confidence, I'm afraid."

"We're investigating a murder, Father Devlin. Anything you could tell us might help catch his killer."

"What someone tells a priest in the confessional or in a counseling session is private."

I looked over at Father, wondering why he just didn't tell the detective what he was after. Why protect that good-for-nothing Blake?

"There was fighting," I said. Father glanced at me. "It wasn't any secret the boy knew the business end of his father's belt."

"So his father hit him?"

"I'll say. We saw the bruises," I added. "Didn't we, Father?"

Father nodded. He sat there rocking himself back and forth.

"Mr. Blake said that his son ran away on several occasions and that you allowed him to stay here. Is that true, Father?"

"He showed up here once," Father replied. "I let him stay the night, to let things cool down."

"That Blake fellow come over here afterward and gave Father hell," I added. "When Father was only trying to help."

"If you knew the boy was being abused, Father, why didn't you call someone? Social Services."

"I thought things were getting better at home," he said. "I counsel a lot of troubled kids. I thought we could handle it."

"Father Devlin, did Justin ever tell you he was afraid of Mr. Blake? That his father had threatened him?"

"Warren Blake was a lousy father. But in his own way he loved his son. He wouldn't have done this, if that's what you're thinking."

"Right now, we have no leads, Father," explained the detective. "We have to investigate every angle and see where it leads." He flipped back through several pages in his pad before asking his next question.

"When was the last time you saw him alive?"

"Let's see. That would have been the Wednesday before . . . before he died," Father explained. "Yes, he helped me at the church after school. We were setting up tables for bingo. And then I gave him a ride home afterward."

"So you didn't see him on Friday?"

"No," Father replied.

I hesitated for a moment, then said, "I did. I saw him that Friday."

"Where?" Detective Guilbault asked me.

"Why, he sat at this very table. I gave him some cookies and milk."

"Do you recall when that was on Friday?"

"It was after school. Around four, I'd say. I was getting supper ready." I glanced over at Father at the mention of supper, but if he recalled its significance he didn't give any indication. "Justin stayed for a bit and then he got on his bike and took off."

"Did he say where he was going?"

"I don't think so. He just thanked me for the cookies and took off."

Detective Guilbault referred to his notes again. "Mrs. Blake was under the impression Justin was meeting you that day, Father," he stated. "She said something about helping you with a paper drive?"

"Paper drive?" Father said, frowning. "That couldn't be. We finished that a couple of weeks ago."

"That's right," I tossed in. "I told her that when she called here looking for the boy."

"Do you think he could have been lying to his mother? About where he was going."

Father shrugged. "I guess it's possible."

"That doesn't sound like him," I said. "A straight arrow, that boy. I never knew him to lie."

"Don't take this the wrong way, Father. It's perfectly routine," said Detective Guilbault. Still, he seemed embarrassed to have to bring the subject up. "I need to know where you were Friday night."

"Why do you want to know that?" I asked.

"Like I said, ma'am, it's just routine."

"Let's see," Father explained. "I went over to the shelter in the afternoon. I was there until around seven or eight, I'd guess. Then I had an emergency over at Windham Hospital."

"What kind of emergency?"

"Rudy Lessard was very ill," Father replied. "I had to perform the last rites. I stayed with the family for a while and then headed home."

"And what time did you leave the hospital?"

"I don't know. I'd say about an hour after Rudy passed on. Around eleven."

"And you came straight home?" the policeman asked.

"Yes."

"And what time did you get back here?"

"My guess would be around eleven-thirty, I'd say," Father replied. "Margaret was here." Father looked over at me, the way he might've if he'd been asked where the mop was kept or how much last month's grocery bill had been. "Wouldn't you say it was about eleven-thirty, Margaret?"

I turned to the detective. "I don't see why you're wasting your breath here when you could be out looking for that fellow who done it."

"It's just routine, ma'am."

"Routine?" I said. "If I didn't know better—"

"Margaret," Father Jack broke in, "the officer's just doing his job."

"That's right, ma'am. Do you remember when Father got home?"

I didn't like what all these questions were getting at. I didn't like them at all. I looked at the detective. "It's just like Father said," I replied.

"I think that should do it," the fellow said, getting up and shaking Father's hand. "I want to thank you for your time."

"Of course. Anything we can do to help."

"By the way, Father. Please don't take offense at my questions. It's just that . . . "

"Don't worry. I understand completely, detective."

"My mother would've twisted my ear if she thought I was being disrespectful to a priest."

Both men laughed. Like I said, it was a different world back then, one in which a priest's word was sacred, his conduct above suspicion.

As Detective Guilbault got up to leave I said to him, "You make sure you catch the bastard what done that to Justin."

"We're sure going to try, ma'am."

They questioned dozens of people in town. They talked to Justin's classmates and to his neighbors and his friends. They spoke to some of those boys that used to pick on him. The police put up pictures of Justin around town and in the paper, asking that if anybody knew or saw anything to please come forward. Some even started up a fund to offer a reward for helping to catch the boy's killer. They had a few leads. They brought one or two people in for questioning, though they were never called suspects. They spoke to one man with blond hair, but as it turned out he was just visiting his brother and wasn't even in town the night Justin died. I read they even asked Mr. Blake some questions, yet that too went nowhere. They didn't have any evidence connecting him to his son's death. Nothing ever came of it. Nothing ever came of any of it.

The story about Justin's death slowly faded, receded in people's minds. Fewer articles appeared in the paper, and as time went by, you heard less and less about it around town. Oh, now and again you might overhear someone in the Falls Café say, "That was a crying shame about the Blake boy," and someone else would ask, "I wonder if they'll ever catch the guy," and another person would toss in, "You know what I heard," and then their voices would trail off to a whisper. A few years after the murder we got our hopes up with talk about a boy coming forward saying he knew something that would help them solve the case. But that fizzled out too. And then, maybe eight, nine years back, there was even some talk that they'd found the so-called "blond-haired stranger." But it turned out to be just that—*talk*.

After Justin's death, you hardly ever saw Mrs. Blake around. She stopped going to church, going anywhere in fact. It wasn't long before we heard she'd taken ill. Cancer. As they say, when it rains it pours. Right before she passed on though, she came to church one last time. Down to skin and bones she was, the cancer having gone right through her. It wasn't two years after Justin that the poor woman passed away. I went to her funeral. I told myself she was at least with her boy now. A few times I saw her other son, Derek. In Hodel's I happened to bump into him once. It was a couple of years after his brother's death, maybe a few months after his mom had passed on. I asked how he was doing. He said fine. I said he'd had his share of grief and then some. He just nodded. When he graduated, I heard he'd moved away, and I never saw him again. Occasionally you'd spot Warren Blake around town, usually coming out of some gin mill. He looked awful, the drink having ruined him altogether. Though I'd never liked him for the way he treated Justin, or Father, you'd have to be a hard-hearted soul not to feel a touch of pity for the man.

As time passed and the memory of Justin's death receded, everybody felt they'd never catch his killer. Once in a blue moon, you might see something in the paper, say, on the anniversary of his death. An article about the murder. Justin's picture, the one of him in his altar boy robes, smiling, looking happy. Opening the same old wounds, raising the same old questions. But that's all it was: questions. Never answers. Whoever'd done it and why and where he was now—we'd never know.

Or so we thought.

19

For *months after* the Roby trial, rumors about Justin Blake's murder swirled around town. There were things in the paper and on the television. There were statements by the authorities. First they said Father was just being questioned. The police and prosecutor's office kept denying it was any more than that. After several months, they finally admitted he was being considered as a suspect. Then it wasn't long before they confirmed he was *the* suspect in Justin Blake's death. In the paper there were things about how the D.A.'s office was battling Mr. Leo to get their blood samples. About the younger Roby's testimony regarding those pictures of Justin.

And every couple of weeks, don't you know, a fresh rumor would make the rounds. That the prosecution had some new piece of evidence, that they'd found something when they did the second autopsy on the boy's body, that somebody had come forward to swear he saw something or other. Sometimes I'd get a phone call at the rectory in the middle of the night. I'd run and pick it up, thinking it might be something important about Father, that—I don't know—something bad had happened. His heart perhaps. But the person on the other end would say something awful about Father, calling him a murderer or a pervert, saying he was going to rot in jail, and then hang up. Or worse, they'd call and not say a bloody thing. Sometimes I'd get those notes I'd find stuck under my windshield wiper or in the mailbox: *Just fry the son of a bitch.* Each new piece of gossip, each new article or phone call, seemed another nail in Father's coffin. But that had been going on for well over a year now. I tried to pay it no mind. Tried to remain optimistic. Besides, Mr. Leo kept reassuring us the prosecution didn't have a case.

One night Mr. Leo had stopped by the rectory. As it turned out, he lived north and west of here, up near the Vermont line, and so had to drive Route 38 through Hebron Falls on his way home. Now and then he'd stop by in the evening. We'd sit in the kitchen, and I'd pour him a cup of coffee, if he was hungry, fix him a bite to eat. He'd drop in as if only wanting to talk about the case, which of course we did. But sometimes it seemed it was just to talk, period. I learned he was unmarried though twice divorced, had no kids, lived in a run-down farmhouse he was slowly renovating himself. Without a warm meal or family calling him home, he was usually in no particular hurry to leave. It didn't appear he had any social life to speak of, though as I've remarked previously I did have my suspicions about him and that secretary of his, Gina Demarco. Sometimes, if Father Martin was gone, I'd even break out the Jameson from the liquor cabinet. I enjoyed Mr. Leo's company—about the only companionship I had of late. We'd become friends over the course of the past year and a half. We'd sit in the kitchen, chatting about this and that. He'd talk about going up to visit his Irish grandmother in Boston when he was a boy, and I'd relate stories about growing up in Galway. Eventually though, we'd get round to the subject that had brought us together in the first place—Father Jack.

This one evening, I recall Mr. Leo had been excited about some small victory in the larger legal battle he'd been waging on Father's behalf. It had to do with the blood business. Lassiter had fought him through the courts, trying to force Father to surrender a sample so it could be tested for DNA. At each step, Mr. Leo would fight back, filing his own motions to block her motion. Right then, the issue was before the Appeals Court, which would decide if they were going to let the State take some blood from Father for their tests.

"We have the sons of bitches on the run, Maggie," he said to me, those yellow eyes of his getting large as a cat's when hunting. He downed the rest of the drink I'd poured him. "We'll kick some ass now."

The drink had loosened his tongue, so I decided to pour us both a second. Father Martin was at some ecumenical meeting down in Holyoke. However, before I refilled our glasses, I went over to the window and gave a quick look out just to make sure Martin's car hadn't pulled in. I had to be careful, for the man was watching me like a hawk. He thought we had to be, as he put it, "above suspicion," that we couldn't give cause to anybody to start gossiping. I know he checked the level of the bottles in the liquor cabinet in the study to see if I was nicking any. But as he was a teetotaler himself and never let a drop pass his lips, I'd top the bottle off with water and no one would be the wiser.

I wasn't sure what Mr. Leo meant, who the retreating sons of bitches were whose arses we were supposedly going to kick. With Father rotting away in a jail cell and the business about the Blake boy very much hanging over our heads, I found it hard to imagine we had *anyone* on the run. But that was Mr. Leo for you: a scrapper, a cocky barroom brawler, someone who wouldn't've had the sense to throw in the towel even if he were getting his brains knocked out.

"You don't think Lassiter will indict him then?"

"If she had anything solid she'd have brought it before the grand jury by now. My guess is she's just shooting in the dark and hoping she gets lucky with the blood tests. So as long as we can block them from obtaining blood samples, there's little risk of an indictment. And as long as there's no indictment I doubt any court will agree to the blood tests without probable cause. It's a catch twenty-two."

Mr. Leo finished his second whiskey, a little too fast, I thought, which put him in a more somber mood. His eyes grew dark, the yellow shading toward khaki brown. He seemed to ponder something. Like a chess player, he was always thinking two or three moves ahead of you.

"But on the other hand," he explained, "Lassiter's got political ambitions and politicians don't necessarily decide to prosecute a case based on its merits. They look at whether it'll be good for their image."

"So we just keep blocking them from taking the blood sample?"

"That's the general idea."

"I wouldn't know my arse from my elbow about these things, Mr. Leo. But it seems to me the simplest thing would be just to let 'em have their blood."

Mr. Leo blinked once, reminding me of as a cat warming itself in the sun.

"No way."

"Why not? Wouldn't that prove they had the wrong man?"

He smiled at me.

"It's not that simple, Maggie. A trial is a lot like a prizefight. You concede nothing. You make them pay for everything they get. They land a jab, you counter with a body punch. They want to hit you in the kidneys, you hit 'em in the balls. It wears them down after a while. Sometimes you win with a knockout. Sometimes you win on points. The key is to win."

"And what about wearing Father down?" I said. "How much more do you think he can take?"

"Don't worry. I have his best interests in mind."

I debated with myself whether to ask what I would ask him next.

"Do you have your doubts?" I finally asked. "About whose blood it is?"

He didn't say anything for several seconds, just stared down at his drink. When he glanced up, he gave me one of those looks I'd seen him shoot a witness on the stand, that see-right-into-your-heart sort of look. A look that said he was perfectly capable of reaching right into your hidden-most place and just grabbing ahold of whatever it was he wanted. Thank God we were on the same side. Lassiter made me uncomfortable, she even unnerved me a bit. But if Mr. Leo had been on the other side, he'd have scared the living daylights out of me.

"Of course not," he said at last.

"That's *not* why you're stalling?"

"Absolutely not. For one thing, DNA isn't one hundred percent accurate."

"I thought they say it's like a fingerprint."

"That's what people think anyway. At best, it's only a probability. Like betting odds. A few years ago Massachusetts used to allow lie detector tests to be admitted into evidence. They said it was scientific. But then the supposed 'experts' couldn't agree that it was a valid test anymore. They said it depended on a lot of variables. The types of questions. The person giving the test. The mental state of the person taking it. Now you can't use a lie detector test as evidence of guilt. But I know of several cases back in the eighties where people were convicted primarily on the basis of lie detector tests. The same might be true of DNA. Who knows? The point is, why should we voluntarily submit to it and make ourselves vulnerable when we don't have to. A tie goes to us."

"You can't keep fighting them forever, can you?"

"Why not? I'll do it for as long as I can."

"Then what?"

"We'll cross that bridge when we get to it."

"Is that Father's feeling, too?"

"I'm his legal counsel and he's following my advice."

"And yet, you don't think they have case, right?"

"I never thought they had one. Not a strong one anyway. The only reason they focused on Devlin in the first place was that he was an easy mark. Especially after the Roby trial. For sixteen years the police didn't get off their asses. They haven't even looked at any other suspects. Warren Blake, for instance. Or that blond guy they saw around town. They'd come up with nothing—zilch—in sixteen years. And now they're looking for somebody to hang the crime on. Without a DNA match or an eyewitness, they got diddly-squat."

A tie goes to us, I thought.

• • •

So when Mr. Leo called me the Thursday before Good Friday, I wasn't prepared to hear what he had to tell me.

"I got some bad news," he said. "We lost our appeal, Maggie."

"About the blood?"

"Yeah. It means we're going to have to surrender a sample."

"That's not so bad," I said, trying to look on the bright side. I told myself it was actually good news, that it would once and for all show it wasn't Father's blood they'd found up there. "It'll only prove they had the wrong fellow all along."

"There's more though. You sitting down?"

"No."

"Sit down then. Lassiter's decided to proceed without waiting for the tests."

"What do you mean 'proceed'?"

"She's going to bring the case before the grand jury tomorrow. She plans to indict him for the murder of Justin Blake."

Jesus, Mary and Joseph! I thought. So it had finally come to this. I was standing in the kitchen, looking out the window. It was windy, the air gusting in sudden, angry bursts. The trees, naked and gray, seemed to shudder. I looked up the mountain behind St. Luke's, up toward Pelham's Overlook. I could see a portion of the rock face jutting out above the pines. I suppose I wanted to see something "in" it, the way you do a cloud in the sky—to give it meaning. But it was just rock, gray, mottled with lichen. Dumb.

I said, "But you always told me they needed a positive match *before* they would charge him."

"I guess I was wrong. Evidently Lassiter feels she has enough to go forward without it. They do have motive. Some circumstantial evidence. As well as the Robys' testimony—that is, if I can't get it excluded. She must feel pretty damn confident the DNA will match. Otherwise she's still going out on a limb. Either that or she's got something up her sleeve."

"Like what?"

"Who knows."

"Did you tell Father yet?"

"Yes. I met with him this morning."

"How's he taking it?"

"All right. He was half-expecting it anyway."

"Are you going to need me to testify again?" I asked.

"I might. I don't know exactly what the prosecution has. We'll have to see during discovery. Oh, one other thing, Maggie. Lassiter's going for first-degree murder. We don't have the death penalty so that means life without parole. She'll pull out all the stops."

Life without parole, I thought after I hung up. I had this picture in my mind of having to go down to see Father for the next twenty, thirty years perhaps. An old lady going to visit an old man in jail.

On the news, I saw that the grand jury did indeed indict Father for first-degree murder. They showed him at his arraignment wearing his orange prison suit, being led handcuffed into the Superior Court. He had his head bowed while reporters shoved their microphones at him and asked if he had killed Justin Blake. It was starting all over again. Would it never end? Would it just keep going and going? Father paused on the steps of the courthouse for a moment. He glanced about himself, looking dazed, his eyes squinting in the bright sunlight. *Tell 'em, Father*, I thought. *Go ahead. Tell the bloody bastards.* But all he did was turn and continue walking up the steps into the courthouse.

After the arraignment, a beaming D.A. Lassiter said, "We're confident the results of the DNA tests, together with the strong circumstantial case we've built, will prove that Mr. Devlin murdered Justin Blake in cold blood. We will show that Mr. Devlin had a sexual relationship with the boy, a relationship that soured and eventually led Mr. Devlin to strangle the boy to keep from being exposed. After sixteen long years, we hope finally to be able to bring the boy's murderer to justice and to give closure to the Blake family." Mr. Leo tried to put on a good face in public. On the news he said he was pleased with the court's decision. "I'm confident the blood tests will finally exonerate my client," he said. "It will show once and for all that it isn't Father Devlin's blood and that my client was nowhere near the boy on the night he was killed." But he wasn't fooling me. I knew how much he'd worried losing the fight over the blood.

Things quickly went from bad to worse. Like last time, Mr. Leo, thinking we couldn't get a fair trial in Adams County, tried to get a change of venue. And just like last time the judge, only another one this time, a Judge Eberhardt, denied it. A few weeks later, an article appeared in the paper:

SLAIN ALTAR BOY'S TRIAL SET FOR JULY

(Montville, April 26, 1995). The murder trial of Rev. John Devlin, former pastor of St. Luke's Church in Hebron Falls, has been rescheduled for July 24, according to Assistant District Attorney Miles Redmond. Yesterday both sides filed motions in Superior Court before Judge L. Clayton Eberhardt. The prosecution requested that Judge Eberhardt grant a continuance while the State awaited DNA test results on Devlin's blood. ChemTech, a forensics lab in California, is currently conducting tests which the prosecution believes will provide a match between Devlin's blood and blood collected from the 1978 murder scene. The prosecution recently won a lengthy court fight over the blood samples, paving the way for tests.

Several pretrial defense motions were also argued before

Eberhardt by Devlin's attorney, Leonardo Manzetti. Included was a motion requesting access to all results of tests conducted by the State thus far. Manzetti was seeking results of previous testing done on blood samples taken at the murder scene. Blood found on the murdered boy's bike and on his sneaker didn't match Justin Blake's blood type, leading authorities to believe it may be that of the boy's assailant.

Manzetti also hoped to secure results from an autopsy performed on the boy's exhumed body. Redmond had been quoted as saying "important new evidence" emerged from that autopsy which will "significantly" strengthen the State's case. Manzetti accused the prosecutor's office of dragging its feet on making those results available to the defense. Lastly, Manzetti filed motions that several parts of the State's case be excluded from the trial on the grounds that their prejudicial value to his client would outweigh their probative value. Specifically, Manzetti was asking that portions of the Roby brothers' testimony, including that relating to the supposed existence of pornographic photos allegedly taken by the defendant of the slain child, be deemed inadmissible in the trial. Eberhardt said he would take the motions under advisement.

Then Father Jack's heart started acting up again. He collapsed at the prison, and they'd had to rush him to a hospital in Springfield. It was another heart attack, this one a bit more severe. I went to see him there. He was hooked up to all these tubes and monitors, and he looked just awful. Frail and weary, an old man lying in the bed. I wasn't going to say a thing about the new trial. The poor man had enough on his mind. Yet it was Father who finally brought it up.

"I suppose you've heard, Margaret," he whispered hoarsely.

"Aye, Father, I have. Don't talk about it now. Save your strength."

"I'm sorry."

"Sorry?" I said. "For what?"

"For dragging you into this again."

"Nonsense. Just get well, Father."

20

On a sunny morning, I got in my car and headed over to Montville to meet with Mr. Leo. His secretary had called the day before to say he needed to talk to me about some things concerning the case. She didn't say what he wanted, just that it was important. As I drove by the Falls Café, I could just picture what everyone inside was buzzing about. And in front of the post office I saw Jo Pratt standing there jabbering with Cindy O'Connell. A couple of worse busybodies you couldn't hope to find. You knew what they were going on about. What the whole bloody town was talking about. Parked in front of the offices of the *Falls Sentinel* was one of those television trucks. Ever since Father had been indicted, reporters and television people had once more swooped down on this "sleepy little town," as they liked to call it. Not just the ones from Massachusetts this time but those from the national news, from as far away as New York and Chicago and California. They were queuing up to get their blasted stories. The sex abuse trial had been one thing. But there'd been plenty of other priests accused of fooling around with kids. Now, though, they'd hit the jackpot: a handsome, outspoken priest who was accused not only of sex abuse and taking dirty pictures but murder thrown into the bargain. Why, if you listened to some of the things that were being said about Father, they had him guilty of everything under the sun—from practicing Satanic rituals in the rectory to drunken orgies up at his cabin to the murder of some little girl over in North Adams. Some clever reporter dubbed him "Father Jack and Mr. Hyde," and many began calling it the Father Jekyll Murder Trial.

You'd see Father's face splattered everywhere, in newspapers and magazines and on the evening news. Once, when I was getting a fill-ing replaced at my dentist's over in Montville, I opened up a *People* magazine and there he was! "FATHER JEKYLL STANDS TRIAL FOR MUR-DER OF ALTAR BOY," the story's headline read. They had pictures of Father Jack when he was a boy, and one of him with his mother after his ordination, and another of him handcuffed and in his prison out-fit being led out of court. And there was a picture of Justin, too, decked out in his white altar boy robes, his blond hair flopping in his eyes, a hint of a smile. The one they always used because he looked so innocent and sweet and pure in it, like an angel, so that it made you all the madder. How could anybody have done that to him, it made you think. The worst they could do would be too good for a fellow like that. But for me, seeing the two of them side by side, and knowing how close they'd been, why it near broke my heart.

Things around here were crazy. I never saw the like of it. People showed up from "Hard Copy" and the Geraldo Rivera show, and from the evening news programs. You'd see these reporters, micro-phone in hand, standing on the corner talking with folks, or in front of St. Luke's or over on the steps of the Montville courthouse. There'd be people from town on the news, offering their two cents: *I think Father Devlin . . .* or *You ask me . . .* One night I saw Joe Abruzzi talking to a reporter. He was standing with a bunch of his TORCH cronies, his car dealership sign prominent in the back-ground. He said, "We only want justice. In the Bible it says an eye for an eye." There were posters around town insisting that the death penalty be brought back in Massachusetts for just this sort of terrible crime. In editorials in the *Falls Sentinel,* Father was called every sort of name: sodomist, pervert, murderer. One woman, Mrs. Grady, went so far as to say they should just take him out and hang him, don't bother with a trial, after what he did to that boy. And then there were the phone calls. They'd call the rectory, usually late at night. The gutless bastards would never give their names. They'd say something awful about Father, a few might allude to some sort of vague threat, and then hang up.

One of the few voices of reason in town was Mel Bassinger, the publisher of the town newspaper. In an editorial he advised against what he called "mindless vigilantism." "Now is the time for the citizens of Hebron Falls, Catholics and non-Catholics alike, to remain calm and let justice do its work. Father Devlin, who has done so much for our community, deserves his day in court."

I was hounded by calls from people wanting to interview me, asking me to say what I knew, offering money for my story. Reporters and television people. One newspaper offered me *twenty-five thousand dollars*! Another fellow was looking to write a book about it. He come knocking on the rectory door, wanting to talk to me. Said he wanted to tell the truth about Father's story. I was sorely tempted, let me tell you. Not for the money, but to give Father's side of things. Yet I didn't trust him. I'd already seen how those newspaper people could twist things around. Besides, Father Martin had given me clear orders. I wasn't to open my mouth to reporters. If anybody asked about Father Devlin, I was to refer them to a Church spokesman, that Father Wozniak. Martin was worried about bad publicity for the Church.

•   •   •

I picked up the bag containing the barm brack I'd made and climbed the three flights of stairs to Mr. Leo's office. I was a half hour early, so before going in, I slipped into a dingy bathroom at the end of the hall. I'd worn a light print dress that stopped just below the knee and a scarf about my neck. I looked in the mirror and rearranged the scarf this way and that. Finally I took the thing off altogether as it looked silly on me, like I was trying to put on airs. My complexion was quite pale, and my eyes had dark circles under them. Not having any rouge with me, I used the trick my mum had taught me. Gave myself a couple of good slaps to bring some color to my cheeks. I wanted to make a good impression, you see. I wanted to show Mr. Leo I was in good shape and not on the drink—which wasn't true, but what he didn't know wouldn't hurt him, I figured—and ready to give it another go if he needed me to testify.

Nobody was at the desk in the front office so I took a seat and waited. From down the hall that led to Mr. Leo's office, I could hear a voice coming out in short, strained bursts. "If the asshole calls again . . . tell him we'll go to court . . . And for Christ's sakes . . .

proofread your work." Gina Demarco came walking down the hall muttering to herself. She looked like a child who'd just got herself a good scolding. Her face registered surprise when she saw me sitting there.

"Oh, Miss Quinn," she said. "How long have you been here?"

"Not long," I said.

"Mr. Manzetti wasn't expecting you till ten. But I guess he can see you now." Then she lowered her voice and gave me a roll of her eyes. "Just watch out. He's got a bug up his rear end today."

I smiled at her. "Thanks for the warning."

Mr. Leo was lying on the floor, on his back, when I poked my head in. He had his shoes off and his toes were hooked under the ratty couch. He was doing sit-ups.

"Hope I'm not disturbing you," I said.

"Maggie . . . come in," he said, craning his neck to look up at me. His face was flushed, his breath labored.

"Your secretary said it was all right."

"Have a seat . . ." he explained, continuing to do his sit-ups. "Trying to get ready . . . for the trial."

"You aim to wrestle that Lassiter, do you?" I asked.

"If I have to."

He did another fifty before stopping. Then he rolled over on his stomach and did a couple of dozen push-ups, slowly, his arms trembling with the last few. Finally, he got up and walked over to his desk in his stocking feet, sat down, and folded his hands behind his head. He was nearly out of breath and sweat was sliding down his neck into his collar.

"I haven't been to the gym in weeks. Gained ten pounds."

"It looks good on you."

"A guy my height can't carry an extra ten pounds. So how've you been, Maggie?"

"Fair."

Though I'd spoken to him a few times on the phone, he'd not stopped by the rectory in a while. The only time I saw him anymore was in the newspaper or on the evening news, talking about the case.

"You're getting famous," I joked. "I see your puss everywhere."

"More than I'd like actually," he replied.

"Here," I said, handing him the bag.

"What's this?"

"Brought you some barm brack. Thought you might like to try it."

He broke off a piece. "*Umh*. That's very good. Sort of like a fruit cake. Thanks."

"Figured I'd bring it since you don't have time to stop by anymore."

"I've been meaning to," he said. "Really, I have. Just that I've been busy as hell getting ready for the trial."

"How's Father?" I asked. "I haven't been down to see him in a while. I've been kinda busy, too."

"Physically he's fine. He's out of the hospital and seems to be progressing nicely. I wish I could say the same about his case."

"That bad, is it?" I asked.

"Well, not *all* bad," he explained. "Actually, I do have some good news. Judge Eberhardt has ruled in our favor that the prior sex abuse convictions can't be used in the Blake trial."

"That's good for us?"

"Very good. It means they won't be able to use most of the Robys' testimony. It's considered prior bad acts. In other words just because you did something once, it doesn't necessarily prove you're guilty of doing the same thing again. With one exception, Eberhardt excluded everything related to the Robys' testimony. Which means that a significant link in the chain tying Father to the murder just went away. The abuse speaks to the issue of motive. If they can't prove Father Devlin had a history of sexually abusing kids, there's no reason why he'd have killed Justin Blake."

"What's the exception?"

"The pictures. He ruled that Robert Roby's testimony about having seen pictures of Justin Blake would be admissible. And that, of course, could really hurt us."

"But there are no pictures," I said.

"That was exactly my point. Eberhardt didn't agree though. So he's going to allow Roby to testify to having seen them. And that brings us back to motive again. The prosecution will argue that if such pictures did exist, then Father Devlin sexually abused not only Roby but Justin Blake as well. They'll try to paint a picture showing that Father was afraid he'd be exposed and that he killed the kid to keep him quiet."

"That's ridiculous."

"Maggie, you never saw anything around the rectory?"

"Like what?"

"Pornography. Pictures of boys. Anything at all."

"No sir."

"You kept his house. You're sure you never came across anything like that? Stuffed away in a corner. Hidden in his underwear drawer."

"I know every corner of that house. I never saw anything of that sort. No sir, I did not."

"Good. There is one more piece of bad news, however."

I felt a sour feeling in the pit of my stomach. What I feared was he was going to say it was about the blood tests. That they'd come back positive. That it *was* Father's blood they found up on Pelham's after all. Despite having told myself and Mr. Leo it would only prove him innocent, I guess all along it was the thing I secretly feared the most and didn't even know it. Just like that time with the lump in my breast.

"Is it the blood tests?" I asked.

"Hell, not *that* bad," Mr. Leo replied. "But bad enough. I've just learned that the prosecution has a new witness. Someone who's willing to say he remembers seeing Justin Blake leave St. Luke's on the evening he was murdered and get into Father Devlin's car."

"And who would that be?"

"He used to work for Father. You probably know him. Stanley Derenzy."

"Dear God in heaven!" I cried. "That good-for-nothing bastard!" I'd not seen hide nor hair of the man since Martin had given him the sack. Someone had seen him over in Montville, bumming around. Wouldn't you know it, I thought. Him turning up out of nowhere like that.

"So you *do* know him?" Mr. Leo asked.

"Indeed I do, the lying sack of shite. He worked for the parish till Martin canned him. How did he get his nose in this?"

"He was busted for narcotics. He told the police he had information about the Devlin case. So the D.A.'s office offered him a deal in exchange for his testimony. Does he have anything against Father?"

"He never liked him, I know that. Don't ask me why. Was Father picked him off the street, gave him a job. I wouldn't think he could remember that long ago, his mind being so pickled."

"I've read his deposition. He says he remembers seeing Justin get in Father Devlin's car that evening."

"Does he now? How come I never heard him say a word about it before this. It seems kinda funny, him just getting 'round to remembering. When it can do him some good."

"Evidently the prosecution thinks enough of his testimony to drop the narcotics charges."

"What did he say?" I asked.

"He says he was bringing the garbage out to the dumpster behind St. Luke's and saw the Blake kid leave the church and get into Father's car. Friday, the day of the murder."

"*Och*. He could've mixed it up with some other day that Father gave the boy a ride. He was always giving him rides."

"He says he remembers it was a Friday evening because he was putting the garbage out for Saturday pickup and the next day the kid was dead. He says Justin got into a gray Buick Le Sabre."

"Everybody knew Father drove a gray Buick in those days. What's that prove?"

"He even remembers Father opening the trunk of his car and putting the kid's bike in it. And that the boy was wearing a green windbreaker with a hood. Which is what they found him wearing."

"Huh! He could've read all that in the papers."

"I suppose. I still don't like it. Any eyewitness, even a druggy scum-bucket who's testifying to save his hide, is dangerous. You never know how a jury's going to react."

"All right. Even if Stanley's telling the truth—that Justin got in the car with Father *that* day—what's it prove? Only that Father gave Justin a ride someplace. So what? Like I said, he was always giving the boy rides. I don't see what the big deal is."

"The big deal, Maggie is that it could place the Blake kid in Father's car on the day of the murder. Not only that . . ." Mr. Leo began but paused as he hunted around on his messy desk for something. He pushed things this way and that, lifted papers and file folders. "Jesus Christ," he cursed. "I can never find a goddamn thing. Oh, here we go," he said, picking up a manila folder. "I've read over the report Detective Guilbault, the investigating officer, made back in 'seventy-eight. Now regarding his interview with Father Devlin, he says Father told him he didn't see Justin at all that day. The last time he saw him was on a Wednesday, two days before."

"So? Maybe Father just forgot."

Mr. Leo winced as he drew his lips tight over his crooked teeth.

"That's too convenient. You see how it looks. It gives the appearance that he was lying. That he was trying to put distance between him and the boy on the day he died. Believe me, the prosecution will hammer us on this."

"Can't you hammer back? Show that Derenzy is nothing but a liar. Or that he mixed up what day he saw Father give him a ride."

"Of course, I will. I'll paint him as a sleazeball who'll say anything to cut himself a deal. When I get through with him, he'll wish he'd done his time. But still, eyewitnesses always make me nervous. They're the weakest link in the chain of evidence but they're also the most dangerous. I'd feel a whole lot better if we had one of our own."

"What does Father say about all this?"

"He's sticking by his version. He said he doesn't recall seeing Justin that day at all. Now according to Guilbault's report, you told him you saw Justin at the rectory on Friday, the day he was killed?"

"I did."

"Do you remember when he left?"

"I don't remember exactly. It was still light out, I know that much. He was on his bike, and I wouldn't have let him ride if it was dark."

"Did you see him in Father's company at all that day?"

"No. He came after Father'd already left."

"You're sure?"

"Positive."

"And where was Father ~~was~~ that day?"

"As best I can recollect, he said the noon Mass, then came back and worked in his study for a bit. Later he went over to the shelter. After that he got a call from the hospital and had to go over there. Didn't get back till that night."

Mr. Leo made that clucking sound and drummed his pencil against his cheek. He wrote some things down on a pad, then looked at what he'd written like he was adding numbers in his head.

"All right. We can go any number of ways with this Derenzy guy. We can play it that he's lying to save his neck. That's he's got something against Father. That he's confused and it was some other kid he saw or even another day—*blah blah blah*. We got some leeway to work with that," he explained. Mr. Leo reminded me right then not so much of a man of the law, trying to arrive at the one and only truth, as he did a cook, one willing to adjust ingredients—add a pinch of salt, a touch of basil—to suit the tastes of whoever was going to swallow it. "Our biggest worry is that four-hour window of opportunity."

"Window of what?" I asked.

"A window of opportunity. The coroner's office estimated that the boy was murdered sometime between midnight and four A.M. That's the four-hour window I mean. What we need to do is shut that window. Shut it up tight. We take away his opportunity to commit the crime. Do you follow me?"

"Sort of. How do we do that?"

"We show that Father Devlin couldn't have done it because he was somewhere else during those four hours."

Mr. Leo was looking at me again in a way I didn't like. Those yellow cat-eyes of his burrowing right into my skull, feeding on my thoughts.

"An alibi. Isn't that what you call it?" I asked.

He smiled.

"Exactly. I've spoken with Father and I've read over Guilbault's report. The report has Father saying he got back around eleven-thirty. We know he was at Windham Hospital until around eleven. He gave the last rites to a . . ." He shuffled some papers around in the folder.

"Rudy Lessard," I said.

"Yes, a Mr. Lessard. Anyway, this Lessard died at nine-forty and the family back then was able to verify that Father was there until almost eleven P.M. or so. It's about thirty-five minutes from here to Hebron Falls. I drive that route every day so I know. If he came straight home, it fits that he'd have gotten back about eleven-thirty or so. Just like he said."

"Then what's the problem?"

"The problem is we need something to corroborate this. In his report, Detective Guilbault says you were home that night and were able to back up Father's statement that he was home at eleven-thirty. Is that correct?"

"If that's what it says there, then that's what I must've told him."

"You don't sound too sure."

I thought of my conversation with those detectives from homicide, Tweedledee and Tweedledum.

"I'm pretty sure. You got to understand, Mr. Leo, it was a long time ago."

"Maggie, if you want to help Father, you'll need to do a lot better than pretty sure. Juries don't like pretty sure. They're going to want some reassurance they're not setting free a murderer. The prosecution will argue that if he was out after midnight, even a few minutes after, he could have been up on Pelham's Overlook. It's only a ten-minute drive up there and back. I've timed it. He'd have had the opportunity."

"Opportunity?" I said, and then realized my mistake.

"The time needed to drive up there, strangle the kid, give him the heave-ho off the cliff, and get his ass back to the rectory."

I felt myself recoil, like he'd slapped me in the face. The way he'd put it, so coldly, so matter-of-factly. As if that poor boy's death didn't matter in the least, as if he was just another angle to be played, just another link in that chain connecting Father to life imprisonment. For a moment I saw Justin floating through the air, like in that dream I sometimes had, of a boy in a white surplice jumping off a roof, floating down, then changing into a beautiful white bird and flying off. Only he didn't change into a white bird. He smashed into the rocks below. I'd gone to the funeral. They'd had to have a closed coffin on account of the way poor child looked. I don't know as I'd ever thought about it quite like that before, but when I did, right then, sitting in Mr. Leo's office, what I felt more than anything was outrage. I felt anger, sharp and scalding in my stomach like a knife turning.

"He was somebody's child, don't you know," I said.

"I didn't mean it to sound like that."

"He wasn't just another piece of your damn evidence. He was a lovely boy and some bastard killed him."

"I understand how you feel. I do. Really, I do. I used to be an assistant D.A. My job was putting bastards like that away. Only now, my job is to make sure they don't put an innocent man away. You believe he's innocent, don't you, Maggie?"

"Of course, I do."

"Then I'm asking for your help. The problem is, if we can't place him, with some degree of certainty, *in* the rectory *before* midnight, the prosecution will make the case that he had the opportunity. I just want to neutralize Derenzy's testimony." Mr. Leo lifted up his tie and tried to scratch out an ink spot with a fingernail. "Dammit. I just bought this tie, too."

"Alcohol," I offered.

"What?"

"For the spot. Try rubbing alcohol."

"Oh. Maggie, all I'm asking you to do is say you remember telling Detective Guilbault that Father Devlin was home by eleven-thirty. That's all. It *was* a true statement, correct?" Mr. Leo asked.

"It was," I replied. "Then."

"*Then*? What the hell's that supposed to mean?"

"It was true when I said it."

"You lost me."

"At the time I said it, I must've thought it was true. Otherwise I wouldn't have said it."

"And now you don't think it's true? Is that what you're saying?"

"No, not exactly."

"Christ, Maggie," he said, "don't get subtle on me. Juries don't like subtleties. They like meat and potatoes. They like evidence served up black and white with clearly defined edges. No gray. If it was true then, it's still true. You just have to stick by what you told him."

"I'm just saying—"

"What?"

"That . . . well—"

"Well, what?"

"Would you kindly shut up and let me finish then?" I said, getting mad.

Mr. Leo got up, came around, and sat on the edge of his desk. I looked down at his feet. He had a hole in one sock, allowing his big toenail to poke through. He reached out and patted my knee.

"Sorry," he said. "Go ahead."

"It was a long time ago, that's all. I know I said that but . . ." I could see he wanted to reach into my mouth and pull the words out, yet this time he waited for me to finish. "That night—the night Justin died—isn't so clear in my mind anymore. I mean some of it is. I can remember some things clear as day."

"But some of it isn't?"

"Aye."

"And you're not sure anymore that he was home by midnight? Is that what you're telling me?" Mr. Leo's shoulders kind of sagged downward into his chest as he said this. Even the corners of his mouth seemed to wilt.

"I don't know. It's hard to put into words."

"Try."

"It's like this, you see. I do remember saying that to the detective. And I want to think it's true. But I'm not one hundred percent sure anymore."

He gave me that courtroom stare of his.

"Did you *lie* to Guilbault? Is that what this is all about?"

"No! Of course not."

"Maggie, you have to be completely honest with me. Are you sure you didn't lie then?"

"What I told him was the truth. At least, I think it was."

"You *think* it was? What's wrong, Maggie?"

"Nothing's wrong," I said.

"You're sure acting like something's wrong. I don't want to go into this blind like with the cross and have my head handed to me again."

"It's just that it was so long ago. And . . . "

"And what?"

"Well, I'd had a few that night."

"Oh, Christ. Were you drunk, Maggie?"

"No, not really. It's just that things are kind of hazy in my mind."

"That's great. That's just fucking great."

"I'm sorry. You wanted the truth."

"Maggie, I'm trying to do my best for Father Devlin. But I can only work with what I have to work with. And right now I don't have much. Let me lay it out for you. Forgetting about the blood tests for a minute, number one," he said, counting off the strikes against us on his fingers, "they have a witness who will say he saw that boy get in Father's car earlier that evening (afternoon?). Number two, if they can get a jury to buy that then it'll suggest he was lying to Detective Guilbault about not seeing the boy that day. Number three, they have another witness who's going to say he saw nude pictures Father took of the murdered boy. Number four, Father was out that night. If we're not able to come up with a reasonable alibi that he was here with you from midnight to four, the prosecution is going to try to convince a jury that he'd have had the opportunity. Now if they can do all that, we're going to be in deep shit, Maggie. I'm just looking for a little help anywhere I can get it. I thought you cared about Father Devlin?"

"Of *course* I care for him. He's a . . . dear old friend. And I'd do anything I could to help him. You know that."

"All I'm asking you, Maggie, is to stand by what you told Detective Guilbault. That's all. If Father was here with you by midnight, then he couldn't very well have been up on Pelham's Overlook, could he? You believe he didn't kill that kid, right?"

I looked up at him. He had his arms folded over his broad chest and he was staring at me for all he was worth. His X-ray vision burrowing into my heart. I wondered what he saw there.

"I already told you, no," I said. "I mean, yes. I believe he didn't."

"It's just that you seem to be waffling all of a sudden."

"I'm doing nothing of the sort. It's just . . . All right, let's say I could testify that I remember Father being home by midnight. After how Lassiter made me look like a liar last time, what makes you think a jury's gonna believe me this time?"

"You let me worry about that. Their eyewitnesses are far from unimpeachable. And you have something they don't, Maggie."

"What's that?"

"Integrity. Who's not going to believe that pretty Irish mug of yours?"

"Save your bullshite for the jury, Mr. Leo," I said.

He smiled.

"But here's the thing, Maggie. If I'm going to use an alibi defense, I have to formally notify the prosecution. And I have to do it pretty damn quick. Otherwise Eberhardt won't allow it. I hate to put you in this position a second time, Maggie. But you just might be our best shot of saving Father from a life sentence."

"Christ Almighty," I exclaimed. "Nothing like putting the pressure on me."

Mr. Leo laughed, showing his crooked, coffee-stained teeth.

"Do you think you can get up there and convince a jury Father was home with you before midnight?"

"I don't know. Maybe."

"All right, that'll be it for now. Here's what I want you to do. I want you to go home and sleep on it."

"Sleep on it?"

"Yes. I want you to try to remember every little detail about that night. Concentrate. Really try to focus. You'd be amazed what will come back to you."

"Like retrieving memories?" I said.

"Yeah, right," he replied, a sneer on his face. "I want you to write everything down for me. Better yet, here," he said, picking up the tape recorder on his desk and handing it to me. "Use this. It might help you to remember things. Jog your memory. But if you do, just don't share it with me."

"Why?"

"Because then legally I'm obligated to share it with the prosecution and I'd prefer not to do that. It's just for yourself, understand? Put down every little detail. Even if it doesn't seem important. I'll call you in a couple of days. Okay?"

I nodded, swallowing a mouthful of air that tasted of old socks. "And one other thing, Maggie. Stay off the booze this time."

"I'll try."

"I don't want you to try. I want you to do it. I'm going to need you sharp and clear on the stand. I'm counting on you. Father's counting on you. All right?"

• • •

That night, after my jobs were all done and Father Martin didn't need me, I went into my room and sat in a chair. From my nightstand, I picked up the photograph of Eion, the one of him wearing that cowboy hat and sitting on a horse. In it he was about three and a half. He was in need of a haircut, and he was smiling as he held the reins. He seemed like a happy child. I like to think he was anyway. I wondered if he'd have grown into a happy boy. Or would he have resented me for his not having a father? Would he have turned into one of those moody, sullen teenagers? Would he have gotten married and what sort of girl would she have been? Would she like me? Trying to figure all that from just this picture of my son seated on a horse.

From my pocketbook I got out the tape recorder Mr. Leo had given me, and fiddled with it till I got the hang of the thing. I turned it on but didn't know what to say, how to start, where to begin. I felt like I was back in school again and the nuns had given us a test. Had asked us, say, to write a theme on the nature of divine love or the fifteen Mysteries or about some moldy old saint, and don't you know my mind would go all blank as it usually did. I'd sit there forever it seemed, not knowing what to say. Like now. Only now it wasn't about some saint dead for a thousand years, some fellow that meant about as much to me as the man in the moon. No sir. Now it was about a lad I had known and loved. And it was about Father, too. Both of them. *You owe it to them*, I thought. To tell what you know. To tell what happened as best you can.

You were mad at Father for not calling, I said into that tiny black thing I held in my hand. Then I stopped. No, that wouldn't do at all. What sort of way is that to begin? So I rewound the tape, paused, thought some more. My throat felt dry as ashes. I could feel the blood shooting out of my heart, could feel the pulse in my neck throbbing, surging up into my head where it went *dong . . . dong . . . dong*, like the tolling of a church bell. I began taping again. *The last time you saw Justin was on a Friday.. . .* That was better but still I didn't know where to go from there. I waited for more to come but not a word slipped out of my mouth. So I rewound the tape yet again, but this time I played it back. *The last time you saw Justin was on a Friday*, I heard this vaguely familiar voice say. The way your voice sounds on tape, yours but not yours. Sort of like reading an old love letter you'd written long ago when you felt a certain way and now you couldn't hardly remember that feeling anymore. It was just words now. I hadn't the foggiest notion why I'd said *you* instead of *I*. I just did and it sounded somehow right. As if another voice inside me was doing the talking and I was just listening. Now what? I pressed Record and heard myself add . . . *the day he was killed.*

21

The last time you saw Justin was on a Friday, the day he was killed. Little things stick in your mind, as they do right before misfortune strikes. You were making salmon, remember. You were still old-fashioned like that, didn't like to make meat on Friday, especially for a priest. Fridays it was always fish, your doing, not Father's. You'd go over to the fish market in Montville because Hodel's never had a very good selection. And salmon was one of Father's favorites. You made a nice meal—baked salmon with roasted potatoes and asparagus, and for desert a pumpkin chiffon pie. You even got down the good china and set the table in the dining room. No special occasion. Just a quiet dinner for the two of you. You tried to do that every once in a while. All week long he'd be running here and there, tending to others' needs. And you felt he ought to have some time when someone catered to him. You'd take the phone off the hook—in those days you didn't have an answering machine—and you'd sit there and chat and catch up on things. Perhaps later Father and you would take your coffee and go into the den and listen to some music, maybe play a game or two of Scrabble. That's the way you'd planned the evening. But as they say about the best laid plans and all.

You remember Justin stopping by after school that day, just like you'd told the detective. It had just turned cooler, autumn weather, and he had the hood of his jacket up when he come in. His cheeks were rosy from riding his bike. You gave him some cookies and milk, and he sat there while you got supper ready. You told him Father was over to the shelter and wouldn't be back till later. The boy was in a quiet mood, quiet even for him. To tell the truth, you weren't really paying too much attention. How many times had he come over like this, would sit at the table and not say two words together. You're certain he didn't say anything about helping Father with the paper drive, because if he had you'd have thought that odd and would've remarked on it. Justin stayed for a little while and then said he had to go. He didn't say where. At least you're pretty sure he didn't. The only thing you do remember him saying was, Thanks for the cookies, Ma. Just that. Then he went out the door, got on his bike and took off.

Sometimes you would stand at the door and just kind of watch as he pedaled down the driveway, across West Street, and lickety-split over Coffin's Bridge toward the center. You enjoyed watching him. Had so much energy, the way kids his age do. His strawberry-blond hair streaking back with the wind, his legs going a mile a minute. A young, healthy lad brimming with life. It was like looking at a colt or a puppy, enjoying the body God gave him. Something inside you always ached a bit when you watched him like that, but it was a sweet ache just the same.

Yet you didn't watch him this day, the last time you'd see him. You were too busy getting supper ready. For years after it happened, you'd get this odd notion in your head. Why did you let him go, Maggie? Why couldn't you have stopped what it was you were about and gone to the door? You could've called to him. Wait, Justin. Come back. Stay for supper, why don't you? There's plenty. Father won't mind. Or maybe you could have asked him to run an errand for you, and by the time he got back it'd be getting on toward dark and you'd have had to put his bike in the trunk of your car and give him a lift home, as you had on a number of occasions. Something. Anything rather than let him go. He'd have been safe here. And things might have turned out different. Who's to say? If you'd only done something, why, maybe he'd still be alive. You know it doesn't make any sense at all feeling like that. It wasn't your fault. It's not like you could see into the future and know what was waiting out there for him. Still and all, that's what you felt. It's like what Mrs. Blake would feel afterward, that she could've protected him and didn't. The thing is, there's no making sense of what the heart says is true.

As it got past suppertime, you began wondering where he was. Father, that is. He said he'd be home from the shelter by five and here it was already half-six. Then seven. Then half-seven and still no sign of him. The salmon in the casserole dish was getting dried out and hard. You turned the oven to low, figuring to keep his supper warm, figuring he'd be home any minute. He knew you were making a nice supper and said he wouldn't be late. You'd better not be, Father, you warned him. Though, of course, he'd been late before. In fact, if you'd had a nickel for every time he was late you'd be wealthy. Every time he had to pay a sick visit or bring some kid to the doctor's office or listen to some old lady's bedside confession way out in the boondocks. He didn't exactly have the sort of job with banker's hours. Something was always coming up last minute like. Some problem needing his personal attention. Many's the time you'd be stuck holding his supper till ten or eleven o'clock at night, sometimes even later, without so much as a phone call from him. In your position, you had to expect that. He was a priest. His family was his flock. But the truth was, sometimes it made you mad. Sometimes it made you good and mad, all right. As if you had nothing better to do than sit around and wait on him hand and foot. Here he'd be thinking about everybody else's needs, and you, why, he wouldn't so much as pay the courtesy of a phone call when he was going to be late. You had no right to feel that way. You were nothing more than his housekeeper, and he didn't have to answer to you. But that's how you felt. That's the way of it. And this night, when he was late, you were mad at him for not calling.

You phoned over to the children's shelter, figuring he might have got held up with something and lost track of the time. But the resident counselor they had in those days—you forget his name—told you Father had already left, though he didn't know where. Well, to hell with him then. You sat at the kitchen table and went ahead and ate without him. It wasn't the first time you ate supper alone and for sure wouldn't be the last. You poured yourself a drink, too. You put the good china away and you took his supper out of the oven and threw it in the garbage. Serve him right. He could go hungry for all you cared. You go out of your way to make him a special meal and this is the thanks you get. You poured yourself another crapper of whiskey and then you went in and took your bath, like you always do. Afterward you got into your nightgown and headed into your room. You brushed your hair and did your toilet, and then got down on your knees and said a prayer for your mother and for Eion, too. When you were finished you put your bathrobe on as it was getting chilly, and you went into the kitchen and made yourself a cup of tea. You added a bit of whiskey, to take the chill out of your bones. And after that, you poured yourself another drink and went back into the den. You turned the stereo on and listened to some music. Though you were tired, you didn't want to go to bed and leave the house unlocked. You didn't like to do that. You figured you'd wait up for Father and see what it was this time.

Later in the evening, the phone rang. You figured it'd be him. You were about to give him hell, only it wasn't him. Who it was was Nancy Blake, Justin's mother. She was phoning from work, looking for her boy. She told you her son Derek called her to say Justin hadn't gotten home yet from helping Father with the paper drive. Paper drive? you said to the woman. The paper drive had been over for a couple of weeks. Mrs. Blake said that's what Derek told her. That Justin would be with Father Jack stacking newspapers. You told her Justin must have been mistaken. You explained that he had been here earlier, but that he'd left hours ago. No doubt he'd be home by and by. But you told her you'd call her if you had any word about her son. She thanked you and hung up. You didn't give it another thought. Not till the next morning.

You remember going back into the den and sitting down. You sat there looking up Main Street, waiting for Father's car. You had another drink or two. Then more after that. You forget exactly how much you had. You were in one of your moods. You started thinking about the past, about Eion and all that. From that point on things aren't so clear. They get a bit hazy in your mind. Somewhere along the line you must've dozed off in the chair. When you woke, the house was real quiet except you heard water running. You sat there for a moment trying to figure out where the sound was coming from. You realized finally it was coming from upstairs. The upstairs shower. Father must be home, you thought. After a while, you heard the water stop and the door open and footsteps padding down the hall. You thought he might come downstairs and look around in the fridge for something to eat, the way he sometimes would late at night. You'd be damned if you'd fix him anything. But he didn't come down, and so after a while you went up. His door was shut, and you knocked on it. He didn't answer directly, so you rapped again, harder this time

You said something like, Father, I know you're in there.

Margaret? he said through the door.

Aye, Father, it's me. So you got home finally, you said, not making any attempt at covering how mad you were. You were in a foul, stinking mood, for sure, the way you get when you'd had a few too many.

I was held up, he replied.

Have you not heard of a telephone?

I guess I forgot.

Forgot, did you? And did you forget about the meal I planned? It was ruined entirely. I had to throw the thing out. Salmon. Your favorite.

Sorry, Margaret, he said through the door.

Sorry! Here I go and plan a nice supper and everything, you told him. You could've at least called and said you're going to be late, Father.

You're right. I should've called. Forgive me.

You said something to the effect, I know you're a big important man and all, and I'm just paid help, Father. I know I'm nothing more than that to you. Just some drunken souse you took pity on. But I got feelings, too, don't you know. Here I am sitting home on my arse keeping your supper warm. Would it be asking too much for you to pick up the bloody phone for once and say you were going to be late? Would it now, Father?

He was silent on the other side of the door for a moment. Then the knob turned and the door opened just a crack. You could see that his chest was bare, his hair glistening from the shower.

Some things came up, he said.

Did they now? you replied sternly. So what was it this time?

I was at the hospital visiting Rudy.

Rudy Lessard, a friend of Father's, had cancer. He'd been sick for a while. He wasn't expected to live long.

Oh, you said, changing your tune. You were visiting Rudy, were you?

Yes.

And how is he?

He passed away, Father said. I had to administer the last rites. His eyes, you recall, had that faraway look to them, the way they got when he'd been at the bedside of a dying person. And suddenly you felt lower than low for having pestered him about not calling. Here a friend had passed on, and you were going on about him not calling.

That's a shame, you said. A young fellow like that with a family and all. And Eileen, how's she taking it?

She was holding up all right when I left. I don't think it really hit her yet.

I'm so sorry, Father, you said. Are you coming out?

No. I'm tired.

Can I be getting you something? Perhaps some brandy. Fix you right up.

No. I'm just going go to bed. Good night, Margaret, he said, closing the door.

Good night, Father.

You started to go downstairs. But you felt terrible about the way you'd behaved. Just terrible. Who the hell did you think you were, after all? Talking like that to a priest, to Father Jack of all people. So you turned around and came back, thinking to apologize. You were going to knock when you heard him in there, speaking in an undertone. A whisper. Praying you figured, the way you sometimes could hear him in there praying, and you didn't want to disturb him. You felt bad enough already. So you headed back downstairs . . .

I stopped the tape recorder at that point. The thing felt heavy and hot in my hand, substantial as a gun. My mouth tasted like I'd been eating chalk. I wanted a drink in the worst way. Yet I needed my mind clear. I had to try and remember what happened next. You see, that was the important part. The part Mr. Leo wanted me to think about.

. . . so you headed back downstairs. You remember that much. No doubt you would have locked up, as you do every night, and then gone around and shut off all the lights except for the night-light over the stove. The cup you'd been drinking out of you'd have washed and put away, as you can't stand to leave dirty dishes in the sink overnight. More than likely, being the creature of habit you are, you'd have set up the coffee for morning, too, seeing as Father always liked his cup first thing. Then you'd have brushed your teeth and put cream on your face and climbed in bed. Before shutting off the light on your nightstand, you'd have set the alarm clock for six, same as always. You always got up at six. Especially this night, you'd have made sure to set it. You'd had a few too many and like as not you would oversleep. And the next day would be a busy one. Getting things ready for Rudy's funeral. There'd be flowers to order and arrangements to be made at the church and things to bake for after the funeral. Yes, you'd certainly have checked the alarm clock. And if you had, wouldn't it make sense that you would have noticed what time it was? No doubt you did and didn't even remember. Of course. After all, it wouldn't be till three or four days later, when that detective fellow showed up asking where Father had been, that it would seem important to anybody but me. Not till the three of yous were seated at the kitchen table and Father turned to you and asked what time he got home. *Wasn't it half-past eleven, Margaret?* That's when it would seem important. Only then. And when you agreed with Father, when you told the detective it was just like he'd said, you thought it had to be the truth, didn't you? It had to be. You thought you must've looked at the clock and it had to have been before midnight, otherwise why would Father have said that? That's what you must have been thinking . . .

I turned the tape recorder off. There were other things I suppose I could have said, other things that came to me. But I figured I should stop there. That's what Mr. Leo wanted to know. What time Father got home. Anything else didn't matter.

22

I was washing the windows in the rectory office at the front of the house, the vinegary smell making my eyes water. I don't use Windex or none of that. No sir. Just a bit of vinegar, as it gets the glass squeaky clean and for half the price, too. Father Martin had given me a long list of jobs to do. Wanted the house cleaned from stem to stern, he did, like he was expecting the pontiff himself to drop in. He didn't say why, though I was to find out shortly. I no longer took much joy in my work, not the way I used to. Now it was just a job. Out the window I could see Mrs. Mueller across the street. She was pretending to water her flowers but really looking over here.

That's when I saw this big white car pull into the driveway. Two men got out and walked up to the front door. I recognized both. One was Father Wozniak, the other was the one with the slippery eyes. The church lawyer fellow. I showed them in and then told Father Martin, who was upstairs in his room. He instructed me to make some coffee and bring it to his study.

"Here you are, sir," I said, setting the tray on his desk. "Anything else you'll be needing?"

"Would you have a seat, Miss Quinn," said Martin. "We'd like a word with you."

Martin made the formal introductions, which he hadn't done last time.

"This is Reverend Wozniak, director of communications for the diocese. This is Mr. Hibbert, our legal counsel. And you know Miss Quinn."

"With Reverend Devlin's trial coming up we thought we should have a chat," said Wozniak. "So we're all on the same page."

"The same page, sir?" I asked.

"That's right. The Archbishop has set up a commission to investigate clerical misconduct, not only in this parish but in all of Massachusetts. So this sort of thing doesn't happen again. They'll be looking over our shoulders. Searching in all the corners for dirt."

So that's why Martin had me scrubbing the place.

"I keep a clean house," I told him.

"I was speaking metaphorically, Miss Quinn," Wozniak explained in a teacherly fashion.

"There'll be a great deal of media attention," chipped in Father Martin.

"I thought there already was," I said.

"Even more," said Wozniak. "We're going to be under close scrutiny. Our every move is going to be placed under a microscope. We have to make certain everything we do and say is going to project the right image."

"And that we speak as one voice," Hibbert added.

"Exactly," Wozniak said. "We know we can count on your cooperation, Miss Quinn."

"I'll do what I can," I offered.

"This is a very delicate situation for the diocese," Hibbert explained. "An altar boy was murdered. Naturally, our heart goes out to the boy's family and to the community. And like any organization we have to assume a certain amount of responsibility for the behavior of one of its members."

"You mean Father Jack, don't you?"

"Yes."

"That's *if* he was guilty," I said. *If,* I thought to myself. Why had I said that? I could recall Mr. Leo saying in our very first meeting, *Everything's an if. That way there's no surprises.* Was I afraid of surprises? I wondered.

"Of course," Wozniak said. "And we hope and pray that the trial will prove him innocent.

"The diocese's reputation has already been severely damaged," said Hibbert. "And there are financial issues at stake as well. Following the criminal trial it's quite likely there will be a wrongful death civil suit brought against us by the family. The Catholic Church's pockets are deep but they're not bottomless, I'm afraid."

The other two soberly nodded their agreement.

"So what is it you want from me, Mr. Hibbert?"

"I would just like to ensure that you are sensitive to this very delicate situation."

"Sensitive?" I asked.

"What Mr. Hibbert means," Father Wozniak cut in, "is that we're concerned about how we're portrayed in the media. With the upcoming trial, reporters and TV people will be snooping around. They could make an already bad situation worse."

"It's the way they operate, Miss Quinn," Hibbert explained. "Believe me. Their only concern is selling papers or getting ratings. They don't care who they hurt to get a story. I've dealt with them long enough to know how unethical most of them are."

Nothing like the pot calling the kettle black, I thought to myself. Here they were trying to cover their backsides. It was just like Mr. Leo had said. The Church was looking out for number one.

"We're concerned about them approaching you," Hibbert said. "Trying to interview you."

"Some may even offer you money to talk with them."

"They already have," I said.

"They have!" Hibbert exclaimed. "Who?"

"I don't know their names. One fellow offered twenty-five thousand dollars to tell him what I knew."

"How come you didn't inform me?" Martin asked, his eyes widening.

"Didn't see any reason to. I didn't say a word to him."

"That's good, Miss Quinn," said the lawyer. "Not only could it hurt the diocese but it might hurt Father Devlin as well. You wouldn't want to do that now, would you?"

"No."

"We're also concerned about a backlash against the Church," the blond priest explained. "Tempers are running high. The diocese has already received some threats. We wouldn't want to do or say anything that might worsen tensions." He glanced over at Martin in a way that suggested he must have told him something about me having a big mouth, that they had to watch out for me.

"Is Manzetti going to call you as a witness again?" Hibbert asked.

"I dunno. Maybe. Is that all?"

"We'd like to thank you for your time," said Father Wozniak. "And we want you to know that no matter what happens to Father Devlin, you can stay on at St. Luke's for as long as you want."

I got up and started for the door. "Oh, Miss Quinn," the lawyer fellow said. "Is there anything else that we should know about?"

"Like what?"

"Except for Father Devlin, you've been here longer than anybody else. Is there anything that might leave the diocese vulnerable to further litigation."

"I don't know what you're getting at."

"Let me be blunt then. Are you aware personally of any other, shall we say, indiscretions committed by Father Devlin?"

"Oh, I see," I replied. "You mean like did I keep tabs on the lads Father was diddling? Or what I saw while I had my nose pressed to the keyhole. Is that the sort of thing you had in mind, sir?"

"This is hardly a matter to joke about, Miss Quinn," Martin said.

"What kind of person do you take me for that I could know something was going on and not say a peep? Now if you don't mind, I have work to do," I said and left the room.

• • •

Later that morning, Wozniak, Hibbert and Father Martin got in the white car and left. They were running scared, you could see. I thought how they wanted me to be careful about what I said, not to talk to a soul. To be "sensitive"—that's the word they used. The lawyer fellow had asked if I knew of any other "indiscretions" by Father. *Indiscretions*, I thought. Like murdering a child? They were afraid I knew something and was going to blow the whistle on the lot of them. That's why Wozniak said I could have a job here as long as I wanted. Who were they kidding? I didn't come up the river on a bike, no sir.

I was sorely tempted to hit the drink, indeed I was. But I'd told Mr. Leo I wouldn't and I was aiming to keep my promise, as best I could anyway. If I had to get on that stand again I wanted to look sharp, like Mr. Leo said. I didn't want to let him down. *Father's counting on me*, he'd said. So I kept busy. I scrubbed and cleaned like a house afire, going from one job to the next without taking a breather. I washed the windows. I vacuumed the drapes. I hung the rugs out on the line and gave 'em a good thumping, which raised my spirits a good deal. For each time I'd smack the rug, I'd picture that Hibbert fellow.

Later that afternoon, I got cleaned up and headed over to the church. I hadn't been in a while. I took the path through the woods as I didn't want to run into anybody. I saw the new fellow out in front cutting the lawn, the one they'd hired to replace Stanley. He was a heavyset older gentleman with a head of silver-white hair. He seemed nice the few times I'd met him. He waved when he saw me and I waved back. I thought about Stanley. How the stinking cur was going to testify against Father. Going to swear he saw Justin with him the evening he was killed, and Mr. Leo saying how bad that would be for Father. Why would he do that? Why would he come up with such a thing after all these years? Except to save his own neck.

The church was empty. Funny, there was all this going on but the church itself hadn't a soul in it. I lit three candles, one each for my mum and Eion, and another for Justin Blake. Then on the way out I knelt and prayed before the statue of the Blessed Virgin. I said an "Our Lady of the Sacred Heart" as well as a "Hail Mary." I asked if she could help Father in his time of need. And while she was at it, if she could help me, too. After that, I headed back through the woods.

As I walked along, I thought how it was two years. Just two years before when it all started. It might as well have been a million. How everything had changed—Father in jail, now on trial for murder, the town all torn apart. How my life had changed, too. I thought about what'd been on my mind for several days. Could I get up on that witness stand and swear before God that Father had been home by midnight? That he was with me? It seemed like the simplest thing in the world to do. *Father's counting on you,* Mr. Leo had said. Christ, you're making a mountain out of a bloody molehill, Maggie Quinn. A few minutes one way or the other, what difference did it make? What are you getting so particular for? You know he's innocent. Of course you do. You know the class of man he is. And how much he loved that boy. Why, it's crazy to even consider he could have harmed a hair on his head. Not a hair. So why not say it's just like you told that detective fellow? All's you had to do is stick by what you said. That's all. You believed it to be the truth then, so why not believe it now?

When I got back, there were two messages on the answering machine. The first was from Gina Demarco. She said Mr. Leo wanted to talk to me. I didn't need two guesses to know what *that* was about. It'd been a couple of days since I'd met with him at his office. I was sure he wanted to know what I remembered, if I was going to be able to testify for Father.

The other message was from Reuben Belliveau, over at the Falls Tavern. Said to call him. What could he want? I wondered. I'd not stopped in there for a couple of months.

"Reuben," I said when he answered. "It's me. Maggie Quinn."

"Hello, Maggie. Listen, it's probably nothing. But Warren Blake was in here last night."

"Yeah?"

"He was drunk as a skunk and saying all sorts of crazy things."

"Like what?"

"That Father Devlin would pay for what he did to his kid."

"You know him. He's nothing but a big talker."

"You're probably right. But I know you had some trouble over there during the first trial." He meant the rock somebody had thrown through the window. "I thought you should know."

"Thanks for calling, Reuben."

"No problem. How are you holding up?"

"Just fine," I lied.

"Anything I can do, you let me know, Maggie."

When I hung up, I thought, *Warren Blake.*

• • •

The next night, I was sitting alone in the kitchen eating a late supper of chicken noodle soup and crackers. Father Martin had been invited to dine with the Abruzzis and a few other muckety-mucks in town, so I had only myself to cook for. Martin and the others were going to discuss the "Devlin situation," no doubt. I was sitting there reading the paper. With the trial now only a couple of weeks off, an article about it appeared nearly every day. The headline today read, WITNESS TO PLACE MURDERED BOY IN PRIEST'S CAR. Below that they had those pictures of Father and Justin, side by side. Justin appearing like an angel in his altar boy robes, looking so young and fine and innocent, so pure. On the other hand, Father in his collar but with his brow furrowed and his eyes looking uneasy, his lips parted like they'd caught him in the middle of saying something. That's when the doorbell rang.

I got up and went to the front door. When I looked out the window, my heart kind of flattened out, like it was a piece of dough that a rolling pin had run over. It was Warren Blake. *What's he doing here?* I thought about the warning Reuben had given me, and how the man had always made me a bit uncomfortable. I thought of that time years before, in the Blake living room, when he looked like he was going to hit Father. As I was all alone I considered just not answering the door. He'd go away after a while. But I guess I was curious. And you know what they say curiosity did to the cat.

"Yes," I said, pretending I didn't know him. "Can I help you?"

"I want to talk to Father," Blake demanded. He looked like he'd been drinking. His eyes were loose and glassy, and I could see that he swayed a bit as he stood there gazing up at me. His face was flushed, and up close like this I could see how the years of being on the drink had taken their toll. He looked like an old man, though he couldn't have been more than fifty-five or so. When I glanced out at the road I saw a pickup truck parked at the curb with someone sitting behind the wheel.

"Father Martin's out," I said.

"Not him. It's Devlin I came to see."

"What? He's not here."

"Where the hell is he?"

"In jail, of course. Where've you been?"

"Jail?" he said. "I heard they let the bastard out. For the trial."

"Well, they didn't."

"You sure he's not here?" he said, looking over my shoulder and into the hallway. For a moment I had a funny feeling he might try to push by me and have a look for himself.

"I told you, he's not here. Now if you don't mind," I said, making to shut the door.

"That son of a bitch killed my kid."

I knew it made no sense at all trying to reason with a drunken fool. Still, I wanted to try. I guess I wanted him to know the truth.

"He didn't kill your son, Mr. Blake."

"Sure he did. The bastard killed him," he cried, waving a fist at me. "And he's finally gonna pay."

"You're wrong there, Mr. Blake. Now go home, why don't you."

"He couldn't just kill him. No. He had to *destroy* my son."

"He didn't do it."

"How the hell do you know he didn't?"

"Because I know Father, that's why."

"If I had him here, I'd strangle the fuckin' bastard with my bare hands," he cursed, using his hands to demonstrate. He gritted his teeth and his loose eyes strained as he choked an imaginary Father Devlin. He looked scary, like he was capable of anything. I knew it was a mistake having opened the door.

"Go on home, Mr. Blake. D'you hear me?"

"I could kill him and not bat an eye."

"I'm going to shut the door now."

Yet he grew calm all of a sudden, looked so pathetic I couldn't bring myself to close the door on him. He was quiet for a several seconds, and the night closed in around us like a tight-fitting glove. "Oh, Justin," he moaned. It was a cry filled with such anguish it sent a shiver up my spine. You'd have had to have a heart of stone not to feel for the man, *even* for someone like him.

"'Tis hard to lose a child, Mr. Blake," I said to him. "But carrying on like this won't bring him back."

He grabbed ahold of the wrought-iron railing to steady himself.

"I had to go and identify him," he said. "Christ, he was so banged up I couldn't even recognize him. My own kid and I couldn't say it was him or not."

He started to sob, and his face seemed to shatter into fragments. He wiped his eyes with the back of his sleeve. You could see he didn't want to give in to the crying. He wanted to hold on to his pain, not give it away. Maybe he figured it was all he had left of Justin. I moved away from the safety of the door, letting the screen door slap behind me. I walked down several steps until I was close enough to reach a hand out and touch his shoulder.

"I'm sorry, Mr. Blake."

"Do you know what that's like? Do you have *any* idea?"

"It must of been hard," was all I said.

"Wanna know what the worst part was? Them thinkin' *I* could've done it. Me! His father. The dirty sons of bitches."

"I'm sorry, Mr. Blake. Truly, I am," I said. "But Father Jack wouldn't have hurt your boy."

"No?" he replied.

"He loved Justin."

Blake let out with a drunken laugh that made my skin crawl.

"Loved him!" he scoffed. "Huh! That's fuckin' good. He loved him, all right. His perverted goddamned love. I suppose he loved those Robys too. Bad enough my boy was murdered. That was bad enough. But to think that fuckin' pervert was . . . *doing that to him.*"

He paused, looked out toward the truck. The person there waved to him as if to say, Let's go, but Blake stayed put. When he turned around, I could see tears rolling silently down his cheeks.

"Nancy," he said, "when she'd tell me Just was out with Devlin again, I used to wonder about it. Sure I did. The presents, spending all that time together. Why the hell's he hangin' out with a twelve-year-old boy? But back then, hell, you didn't hear all this shit. Priests doing that stuff to kids. Besides, Nancy was real Catholic. She thought it was great. Derek had been an altar boy, so she wanted Justin to be one, too. She thought helping Devlin would keep Just out of trouble." Mr. Blake wiped his eyes with the back of his hand again. He shook his head. "But the more he hung around with that bastard the more he couldn't stand me. All's he talked about was Father Jack this, Father Jack that. He'd get mouthy with me. Not show me any respect. After a while, I got so damn sick and tired hearing him goin' on like that, I said, 'If you like him so goddamn much why don't you go live with him then?' But I didn't think . . . I thought they were just . . . friends."

"That's all it was, Mr. Blake," I said. "Just friends."

"That son of a bitch'll get his," Blake said, his eyes turning suddenly fierce again.

The person who'd been waiting in the truck got out and came up the walk. A man about thirty, I'd say, wearing a baseball cap.

"Let's go, Dad," he said, putting his hand on his father's shoulder.

"Derek?" I asked, gazing into the darkness. "Is that you?" I'd not seen him in a dozen years or more. He looked so different I barely recognized him. He'd gotten married, I'd heard, had a child, then got divorced. He was heavier, his face fuller but not in a healthy way. Puffy, bloated almost. He didn't look good. Yet there was something oddly familiar about him. Maybe it was just the resemblance to his brother. He still had Justin's pretty eyes and nice smile.

"Hi, Ma," he said, showing me that smile.

"Your father ought to be in bed, Derek."

"Let's go, Dad," he said.

"He murdered your brother," Blake cried, poking his finger into his son's chest just like he did to Father that time. "Don't you care? Don't you even fuckin' care?"

"Come on, Dad," he said, ushering his father toward the truck. He helped him in but then came back up the walk.

"I'm sorry about that," he said. "I shouldn't have driven him here."

"No harm done," I said.

"He never got over Justin's death. Now with the trial it's eating at him again."

He looked at me, still handsome in a way, broad-shouldered, tall, taller than what Justin would have been. But there was enough of a resemblance between the two to suggest what Justin would have looked like as a man. Derek's face appeared that of someone who'd had his share of bad times too. His eyes looked so sad, the way Justin's could at times.

"I understand," I said.

"All those years my brother's death was all he thought about. All any of us thought about. It just ripped our family apart."

"I feel sorry for your loss, Derek," I said, as if it had just happened. And with it only now coming to trial, I suppose in a way it had. I guess with his brother's killer still out there somewhere, they could never really put their grief to rest. Never close the book on it.

"Good night, Ma," he said.

Then he headed out to his truck, got in, and took off. I shut and locked the door. I felt my hands trembling. I felt that pounding in the back of my head. I knew I was going to break my promise. I had no choice, you see.

23

A few days later I woke with a raging hangover. I dragged my sorry arse out of bed and went over to my bureau. From the bottom of my underwear drawer I removed the fifth of Jameson. I poured a little in a cup I got from the nightstand and downed it straightaway. Just to ease the commotion in my head a bit. It was after nine o'clock. I hadn't set my alarm, and I found myself still in the skirt and blouse I'd worn the night before to the Falls Tavern. I reeked of smoke and booze. I vaguely remembered Reuben Belliveau driving me home. I'd told him about Blake stopping by. He said if I was worried I could stay at his hunting cabin up in the mountains, till the trial was over. Maybe it wasn't such a bad idea, I thought.

Father Martin knocked on my door, as it wasn't like me to sleep this late. I guess he was worried about me. "Is everything all right, Miss Quinn?" I told him I was sick, had a touch of the flu. He asked if he could get me anything, and I told him no, that I just needed to rest. *Is everything all right in there, Father?* That's what Russell Roby had testified that I'd said.

Though it was broad daylight and I was behind on my work as it was, I lay back down on the bed and closed my eyes. There was a dizzy sort of buzzing going off inside my head. Like a hornet's nest had been stirred up in there. It'd felt that way for a couple of days now. Ever since Warren Blake's visit. I'd wake up in the morning and there'd be that buzzing, starting low at first but then rising as the day went on until it fairly drove me crazy. What it reminded me of was that blasted bee in the courtroom. Bzzzzz, my head went as I did the ironing. Bzzzzz, as I vacuumed. Bzzzzz, as I hung the laundry on the line. Though I'd promised Mr. Leo I'd stay on the wagon till the trial was over, I needed a little something to get me through each day, and then more at night to fall asleep.

Mr. Leo had called several times. He wanted to know if I was going to be able to testify on Father's behalf. I'd told him I just needed a little more time to think about it. He said it'd been almost a week, that with the trial fast approaching he was running out of time. "I can't say just yet," I said. "I've had a lot of things on my mind, Mr. Leo." "All right, Maggie, but I need an answer soon. Very soon." In the evenings, I'd get in the car and go for long rides, just to clear that buzzing from my head. As I drove those curvy mountain roads, I'd hear Mr. Leo say, *Father's counting on you.* Or, *What's the matter, Maggie?* Or, *You believe he didn't kill that kid, right?* Last night when I got back late in the evening, Martin told me that Manzetti had stopped by to see me.

"He left his home number," Martin said, handing me a piece of paper with a Vermont number on it. "He wanted you to call him."

I took the number and headed for my room.

"He said it was urgent. Is there something I should know about, Miss Quinn?"

"No sir," I replied.

"Are you sure?"

"Nothing as concerns you, Father."

I was certain the buzzing in my head had something to do with all that was going on. With Warren Blake's visit and Mr. Leo's wanting me to testify and the upcoming trial. All of it coming together, preying on my mind. Sometimes I'd lie in bed at night unable to sleep despite the booze, the pills. Other times, I'd fall asleep but wake in the middle of the night from some dream. Now and then it'd be the one with that voice calling out to me. In it, I'd go running from room to room, trying to figure out its source. But I could never find my Eion. I could never save him. I'd wake with my head buzzing like mad, my mouth dry with what I could only call fear. I couldn't get to sleep again. I'd just lie there in bed, wide awake, staring off into the close, stuffy darkness of my room. Outside in the night I'd hear the whirring of the crickets and it would sort of blend with the buzzing that went on in my head.

Sometimes, I'd get up and just like in that dream I'd wander the darkened house like a ghost. Thinking. About this and that. About that night. Trying to picture it in my mind, don't you know. Trying to get it straight. What I'd done after I left Father's door and come downstairs. Did I look at the clock? Did I go right to sleep? Once, I even went so far as to climb the stairs and stand silently outside Father Martin's door, hoping that would help bring it back to me. Retrieved memories, I thought. Other times I'd try to recall if Justin had said anything more that afternoon, where he was going, who he was seeing. I remembered what his mother had told me, that Justin said he was helping Father with the paper drive. Why had he told his brother that? Why did he lie? It wasn't like him. What was he doing that he didn't want his mother to know about?

Now and again, staring into the darkness, I'd picture the two of them together, Justin and Father, like in that picture I had of them. Having fun. Going places. Maybe playing catch out in the backyard or Father playfully tousling the lad's hair. Friends. Just good friends. And as I recollected those happy scenes, those pleasant memories, I was hardly aware what it was I was really doing: searching my mind for memories. Looking for something that on the surface didn't mean a thing, but when you scratched the surface there might have been something else entirely underneath it. A seemingly innocent word. A friendly gesture or harmless glance between the two. Something that wasn't what it appeared, something that meant more than met the eye. Though what that something might be, I hadn't the foggiest.

Or I'd get to thinking about that cross. I thought I'd put that behind me, I thought that Father's explanation had settled things. But I was wrong. It would start to bug me again. One night, I even went through the albums again. This time I got the magnifying glass from the kitchen and looked closely at some of those pictures. Looking to see if I could find one, just one, of Father wearing that cross. Maybe I'd missed it before. Maybe it was there and I just hadn't seen it. Just one. I even went down into the basement and looked through the boxes down there. I picked up framed photos, took them out of their glass cases, and looked at them closely. But I couldn't find a one showing Father with that cross. And though I told myself it didn't mean anything at all, it still left me uneasy. It wasn't that I didn't believe Father. It's just that—I don't know—maybe I doubted myself. Maybe I just wanted to prove how foolish I was acting.

• • •

One evening after the supper dishes were washed and put away, I went out and got in my car. Partly I just needed to get out, partly I was avoiding Mr. Leo. I didn't think where I was going. Just drove aimlessly around, letting the cool night air blow against my throbbing temples. I wasn't consciously heading for it but I ended up there just the same. Up on Pelham's Overlook. Don't ask me why, I couldn't tell you. I'd never been up there before. Never had any reason to. But I just wanted to see it for myself. The place where he'd died. Call it a morbid curiosity. Call it what you will. I've read how a murderer will sometimes go back to the scene of the crime. Who knows why? Was my reason similar somehow to that?

There's a dirt lane that goes in off Pelham Road. I parked the car and walked in. The way was littered with beer bottles and fast-food refuse, assorted other debris. Along the edges of the path grew ferns, while tree limbs hung low over the ground, creating the effect of a tunnel. I came out into a clearing. Here there was more garbage, as well as evidence of recent campfires. Kids still frequented the place, to drink and neck and hang out. Most of them probably couldn't have told you a boy died up here, it had happened so long ago. I walked over to the edge. It was sunset, a beautiful view of the mountains. I remembered how Justin told me he used to like to come up here with Derek. How they'd sit and watch the sun set over the mountains. This is what Justin used to see, I thought. Below, you could make out The Falls, a miniature place, the black snake of a river meandering through the valley, Coffin's Bridge. You could even see the white steeple of St. Luke's, though the rectory was obscured by the trees. Then I looked closer in, to the rocks directly below. There were bottles and cans, even a few garbage bags kids had thrown over the edge. That's where they'd found him. Somewhere down there. And perhaps right where I was standing, in this very spot, I thought, some bloody bastard had thrown the boy off, with no more thought than he would that garbage. I shuddered as I considered that. Why in blazes are you doing this to yourself, Maggie Quinn. Why?

While I stood there, a memory came to me. It was shortly before Justin died. A few weeks maybe. I remember it was a warmish, sunny autumn day. The sort of fleeting Indian summer we get up here in the mountains, a last reprieve before cold weather sets in for good. I was out in the backyard hanging clothes. The day was so lovely and fine your heart kind of seized up in your chest. The mountain was ablaze with color. That wonderful smell of fresh-washed laundry mixing with the pungent tang of autumn. That's when Justin happened to come riding up on his bike. He got off and went up to the back door and knocked. He must not have seen me behind the clothes, and I didn't call to him, not right away anyway. I kind of just watched him, catching him unawares you might say.

I found myself doing something I'd done a few times before. Well, more than a few times, I suppose. I know it was wrong of me. Or if not quite wrong, at the very least I had no rightful business to be doing it. Only misery and sadness could come of it, I sensed, as it was wishing for what I couldn't have and that was something I didn't like to do. You see, what it was is I pictured all this—the laundry on the line and the yard and the great big house and everything inside, every last chair and picture on the wall, every spoon and glass and speck of dust even—all of it as mine. Everything belonging to me. Thou shalt not covet, the Bible says, but that's just what it was. I coveted it all. I desired it. I made it mine, at least in my imagination. That wasn't all though. I even pictured the boy standing there, just home from school, waiting for a snack, as mine, too. My child. I would ask him how his day had gone and he would share it with me. And if truth be told, I even imagined the man of the house, who was off at work now like any other, as belonging to me, too. And though I never did anything—not a word, not so much as a gesture—that you could say was inappropriate, in my heart of hearts I sometimes let myself think of Father Jack as my husband. As my lover even. I pictured the two of them, Father Jack and Justin, as mine. Not just friends but husband and son. My family. Mine. Was that so terrible? Does that make me a bad person? Just for wanting a piece of happiness. Looking back, I suppose it does.

Another moment or two slipped by before I called to him. "Justin."

He came walking over to me. Without even being asked he picked up some clothes from the laundry basket and started to help me hang them.

"So how goes it, love?" I asked.

"All right," he replied.

But I could tell something was up with the boy. I'd gotten so I could read his moods.

"What's the matter?" I asked.

He shrugged. From the basket he lifted one of Father's black shirts and sort of held it up to the light, before hanging it on the line.

"I hate him," he said.

"Who?" I asked, startled at the emotion behind his words.

"That bastard."

"Your father's got his problems."

"Not him," he replied. "Derek."

"Derek! Did the two of yous have a fight?"

He nodded. Then he put a wooden clothespin in his mouth, chewed on it for a moment.

"I hate the stupid bastard."

"Those are pretty strong words, Justin. You were always so fond of your brother, too."

"He's just like all the rest of them."

"Brothers fight," I said. "That's normal. Do you want to tell me about it?"

He screwed up his mouth.

"Give me a hand with this sheet, would you, love?"

He took one end and I took the other and we hung it on the line. He didn't say anything for a long while. I figured I wouldn't pry. I figured I'd let him tell me whatever it was he wanted to in his own good time. Then, without realizing it, he picked up one of my brassieres and when he recognized it, he glanced over at me. He turned five shades of red, and I had to suppress a laugh.

"I'll take that," I said.

We worked in silence for a while. At last he said, "He thought I was going to tell something."

"Your brother?"

He nodded.

"You mean like a secret?"

"Yes. But I wouldn't. I wouldn't."

"Did you tell him that?"

"Yes. But he doesn't believe me. He said if I ever told . . ." but his voice trailed off. I thought of asking him what it was but decided not to. I decided it wasn't my business. That it was just between the two of them.

"I've made an apple pie. Are you hungry?"

He gave a halfhearted nod. After a while he said, "Can I ask you something, Ma?"

"Why, of course."

"Does God . . . does He forgive everything?"

"That He does, love."

"Everything?"

"Every last thing."

"Even if it's really, really bad?"

I thought what's a twelve-year-old boy do that's really bad. Maybe he'd stolen something or his mother had caught him reading a girly magazine. Or perhaps he'd touched himself and thought he was going to burn in hell for it. Something along those lines. Father used to tell me about some of the things he'd heard the kids say in confession. Not the serious stuff, mind you, but the funny things. We used to have a good laugh about it, he and I.

"Did you rob a bank, lad?" I said, trying to make light of it. But I could see he was dead serious. "Don't you worry none. He forgives everything. Even if it's really, really bad. Just ask His forgiveness. You do it all the time when you make confession."

He nodded.

"It cleans the soul. Makes you feel like a shiny new penny."

"Why do we have to make confession anyway?"

"Why? That's how you say you're sorry for your sins. That's when you have God's ear. He can hear a pin drop."

"Why can't I just tell Him then?"

"Because we're Catholic and that's how we do it. We're supposed to tell our priest. That's one of the sacraments. Of course, you know that already."

"But why?"

"Oh, love, you're getting awful deep on me. You ought to be asking Father Jack these questions. Not me. He's the one you want."

He had a look to him like he was debating saying something else. At the time, I figured if I didn't say anything, just gave him some space, he might have told me what it was. If I'd just kept quiet and waited.

"Tell you what, love," I said. "How about you come inside and I'll cut you a piece of pie. And if you're not as bad as you're letting on, there might even be some ice cream in it for you." I put my arm around him, gave him a hug. "How does that sound? Nothing so bad a little pie and ice cream can't cure, eh, love?"

He nodded, fell silent as we finished hanging the laundry.

A few weeks later he was dead. I didn't think much about the conversation at the time, though now and again over the years it would come back to me. As it did now. Standing where his murderer had stood, I couldn't help but wonder what the secret was his brother didn't want him speaking of. And what it was the boy was so nervous about confessing. What had he done he thought so bad even God Himself with His infinite mercy wouldn't forgive him? And above all, what was he trying to tell me?

24

After giving the guard my name, I took a seat in the waiting room right in front of the television set they had bolted to the wall. One of those morning exercise shows was on. A toothy girl in glossy, skintight shorts was doing exercises to tighten her bum. She said as how all us "girls" wanted themselves a tight bum. I glanced around the room. Only a handful of visitors were here this early, a little after nine on a hot, humid morning in late June. Though the room was air-conditioned, I could still feel the sweat trickling down my neck, soaking my blouse. Every now and then, I'd look up and catch one of the guards giving me the eye through the glass of the guard station. *Would you look who's back?* I pictured him saying. *Thought she gave up on him.*

I hoped the wait wouldn't be long. It wasn't a Tuesday, and I had to get back to my work. I told Martin I'd broke a tooth, that I had to go to the dentist. Besides, I was kind of anxious to see Father. I hadn't been down for a while. Three or four weeks. The longest I'd ever gone between visits. He must've been wondering where I'd been. Thinking perhaps I *had* given up on him. I could tell him I'd been busy. Which was certainly true. Martin had me going a blue streak, getting ready for the Archbishop's commission. Scrubbing and cleaning, and tidying up after the painters and workmen he'd had come to spruce up the rectory. But it wasn't *just* that I was busy. No sir. Truth was I was nervous. About seeing Father.

Like always, I brought him some things—clean socks and toiletries, some gum and mints. I didn't bake anything though. Hadn't the time. I brought him some books, too, thought he might want something to occupy himself till the trial began, now just a few

weeks off. I'd grabbed ahold of some out of the boxes in the basement. One was a book about the saints. It had all these stories about
St. Thomas More and St. Bosco, St. Teresa of Avila and St. Catherine, even some I never heard of. I thought he might want to read
about them. What they had to go through, the suffering they had to
endure before their glory. But as I sat there thumbing through it,
coming upon one horrible story after the next, reading about this
one getting themselves burned and that one boiled, another drawn
and quartered, the more I wondered if it was such a good idea after
all. Bringing a book like that to someone in Father's situation. It was
just plain stupid. So I slipped the book in my handbag.

I was sitting there looking at the television, watching Miss Tight
Bums do her exercises. But all the while I was thinking, *Why are you
so blasted nervous?* It's just Father Jack. What's the matter with you?

That's when a voice behind me said, "Hey, stranger."

I turned to see Mr. Murphy smiling down at me. He was dressed
in the same blue work uniform.

"Why, hello there, Mr. Murphy," I said, shaking his hand.

"I thought maybe they released your father."

"No, no. Not yet. How've you been?"

"Had me a bad cold there for a while but I'm over it now," he
said, taking a seat next to me.

"Summer colds are the worst," I said. "And how's that grandson
of yours doing?"

"Junior's fine. With time off, they gonna let him out in August. If
he keep his nose clean, that is."

"I'm glad to hear that."

"And how about your father? His time must be getting short."

"'Tis," I replied. "Won't be long now."

We talked for a while, about his grandson and a job Mr. Murphy
had lined up for him when he got out.

"It's union scale," he explained. "Good money to start."

"I hope he learned his lesson," I said.

"If he didn't, I ain't too old and he ain't too big for me to take
him over my knee," he joked.

After a while my name came over the loudspeaker.

"Well, you take care now, Mr. Murphy. And give my regards to
your grandson."

"I will."

When I stood up, he did as well. He shook my hand and said, "In case I don't see you again. It was a real pleasure knowing you, Miss Quinn."

"Likewise, Mr. Murphy," I replied.

"I wish you the best of luck in the future." He said *future* in such a manner I realized suddenly he'd known about my little secret all along.

"Why, thank you, Mr. Murphy."

• • •

The visitors' room was nearly empty. One family sat at a table next to the vending machines. By the looks of it, they were having themselves a little birthday party. They had a cake with candles and those little pointed hats, and were singing "Happy Birthday," only in Spanish. I glanced around. Father Jack was seated at a table over near the windows, which looked out onto the courtyard. As he was facing the windows, he didn't see me right away. For a moment I just kind of stood there and watched him, as if letting my eyes get accustomed to seeing him in the flesh again. He was still way too skinny. But it didn't appear that he'd lost any more weight since I'd last visited. And his hair was at least combed and neat-looking. He was clean-shaven, too. Despite his heart problems, in some respects, he looked more like the old Father I'd known than at any time since coming here. I stared at him for another moment or two, the way you might look at something you're so used to seeing—say, a room you've cleaned a thousand times—but then all of a sudden it's like you've never seen it before at all.

"How are you, Father?" I said, trying to sound as regular as I could.

"Margaret," he cried, standing up and hugging me. "It's so good to see you."

He smelled of the Old Spice aftershave I'd brought him another time. Why, I could hardly detect that prison odor on him and that was surely an improvement.

"And you, Father," I said. Then I quickly added, "I've been awful busy. That Father Martin's got me hopping." I was going to tell him about Martin wanting me to get the place spotless but then he might want to know why and I'd have to tell him about the Archbishop's investigation and I didn't want to start out on a sour note. "Sorry I've not been down."

"Don't worry about it, Margaret," he said, sensing my guilt. "I figured you must have been busy. I've missed you though."

When he said that, I had to fight back a sudden pressure behind my eyes. I bit the inside of my cheek, the metal taste of blood souring my mouth. "Here," I said, handing him the bag. "I brought you some things."

"Thanks."

"And how are you getting along, Father?"

"Much better, thank you."

"You're looking well. Right as rain, I'd say."

"I'm not so tired anymore. Sit down, Margaret."

We sat facing each other. He smiled at me, then reached across the table and took both of my hands in his. I'd forgot how big and strong his hands were.

"Your hands, Margaret. Why, they're freezing." He began rubbing them.

"I think I'm coming down with something."

"Your eyes do look a little tired," he said. I couldn't say whether he suspected I was on the drink again or not. "Don't let him work you too hard."

"Martin's a fair man, all things considered."

"I imagine he's under a lot of pressure getting ready for Cardinal Stone's commission?"

"So you knew about that, eh, Father?"

"Yes. How's your garden?"

"Don't hardly have time for it these days. What with one thing and another. Like I said, I been busy."

"That's too bad. I know how you like to garden."

"Maybe when everything simmers down a bit."

I didn't say *trial* but that's what we both knew I meant.

We chatted about this and that. Little things. The youth dance. The clothing drive. The choir. Father Duncan. Safe subjects. The usual harmless topics that passed for conversation between us during these visits. Avoiding the others, giving them a wide berth. I suddenly realized how good I'd gotten at that: avoiding what needed to be avoided. I wondered how I'd been able to visit him week after week and talk so little about his situation. About the Robys. About Justin. Beyond offering something vague like, "Don't you worry, Father. Mr. Leo's doing his best." Or, "Nobody believes any of that rubbish." I realized how good I'd got at pretending there was nothing wrong, that nothing had changed. Just get through the hour somehow or other, was my thinking. Then go home and try to forget about it. Do the same thing the next week and the week after that. There was no future, just a string of those Tuesdays like beads on a rosary.

"You wouldn't have a cigarette, would you, Margaret?"

"A cigarette?" I asked. "What would you be wanting with one of those?"

"Can I bum one off you?"

"Get out, Father?" I said, thinking he was codding me. But then I could see he wasn't. "Don't tell me you smoke now?"

He nodded.

"Unfortunately I've picked it up. You pick up all sorts of bad habits in this place."

I gave him a cigarette and took out one for myself. I watched as he inhaled, drawing the smoke deep into his lungs like an old pro. It came as a bit of a surprise. The old Father couldn't abide smoke. Yet I suppose I had to expect some changes in him after his time in here. Hadn't I changed as well?

"You'll never guess who stopped by the rectory the other night," I said. I can't say why I'd brought it up. "Warren Blake."

Father's hand stopped with the cigarette in front of his lips, the smoke curling up before his squinting eyes.

"Blake?" he said. "What did he want?"

"Oh, nothing much really."

"Margaret, he must have wanted *something*."

"He was three sheets to the wind. Carrying on."

"About what?"

"I didn't pay him much mind. You know him, Father."

"Did you call the police?"

"What for? His bark is worse than his bite," I replied. I thought how I *had* been a little afraid of him at first. How he'd threatened Father. "Mostly I felt sorry for him. He seemed kind of pathetic."

"He is pathetic. But dangerous, too."

"I was thinking about what you said. That he was a lousy father but he loved his son."

"When did I say that?"

"To that detective who came around after Justin's death. I suppose it's true, too. About him loving his son. He looked just terrible."

"I still wouldn't trust him. Especially when he's been drinking."

"His son was there with him."

"Derek?"

"Yes. He talked some sense into him and then drove him home. You remember him, don't you, Father?"

Father nodded, took another drag on the cigarette.

"I want you to promise me if he comes back, you'll call the police."

"I doubt he'll be coming back though. He just wanted to blow off some steam."

I looked over at the family. They'd already blown out the candles and were now cutting the cake. The mother was handing out pieces on paper plates, and the kids were hollering and laughing. They looked like any regular family you might see on the outside. Except I couldn't help but notice how the boys wouldn't leave their mother's side. Seemed shy with their father. Probably on account of their not being around him that much. When I glanced at Father I saw he was looking at them, too.

"Remember the parties we used to have, Father? Christmas and Fourth of July. And St. Paddy's Day, too. Remember our sing-alongs?"

"How could I forget?" he replied, a faint smile hovering about his lips.

"We had us some good times, didn't we, Father?"

"We certainly did."

"Seems like so long ago."

I took a drag on my cigarette, trying to cover the metal taste in my mouth. "Lately I've been thinking an awful lot about those days," I said. "Must be I'm getting old."

Father pursed his lips. "Those days are long gone, I'm afraid."

"That's a fact. No sense crying over spilt milk." I paused for a moment, wondering where I was headed. *Just what the hell do you think you're doing, Maggie?* "But you know, Father, Mr. Leo's sort of put a bee in my bonnet."

"What do you mean?"

"Why with all his questions about back then."

"What kinds of questions?"

"This and that. Mostly about that night." Father knitted his brows, like he hadn't a clue what I was talking about. "You know. The night . . . Justin died. But I'm sure he's told you all about it already."

"He doesn't tell me much of anything. What did he ask you?"

"About what I remember."

"Why?"

"I guess he's figuring he might have me testify again. Like I didn't botch things up enough the first go-round. But he thinks that since Stanley—oh, you must've heard about him, didn't you, Father?"

"Yes."

"The bloody stinkin' liar. After all you did for him, too. I never trusted him. No sir."

"What does Manzetti want you to testify about?" Father asked.

"I guess Mr. Leo's a little worried. About Stanley saying he saw Justin get in the car with you that night. Though who's going to take his word over yours, I told him. But Mr. Leo's of the opinion Stanley's testimony might hurt you, Father. So he thinks it might be a good idea if he can prove you were home with me. An alibi."

Father remained perfectly still as I told him this, his eyes fixed on some distant point out the window behind me, a cloud perhaps. The pupils had that honed-to-a-fine-edge look they sometimes got, though the blue was all chalky, making his eyes cloudy at the edges.

"Anyways, he says all's we got to do is shut down this 'window of opportunity,' as he calls it, and we're in good shape. I don't claim to understand it all but the gist of it is, since they figure Justin was killed after midnight, if Mr. Leo can prove you were home with me before then it wouldn't matter what Stanley said. He'd just be blowing wind out his arse, pardon the expression. So Mr. Leo wants to shut that window. He wants me to testify that you were home by half

eleven. Which makes a good deal of sense. Don't you agree, Father
. . . Father? Are you listening?"

"Of course," he said, though he continued to gaze out the window. I wasn't sure if this meant he was listening or that he agreed it made sense.

"So Mr. Leo's been calling and putting the pressure on me to say I'll testify for you. Which, of course, Father, you know I'd do. But the thing is I been racking my brains trying to remember that night. Mostly I'm pretty clear on it. How you come home and took a shower and all that. But there's just a couple things I can't seem to get straight in my mind."

"Such as?"

"Well, like what time it was you got in."

Father cocked his head, gave me a kind of sideways glance. "Remember, you told that police officer—"

"Detective Guilbault."

"Right. You told Detective Guilbault I was home from the hospital by eleven-thirty."

"Aye, Father."

"So you *do* remember after all."

"Well, actually, the way I remember it, 'twas you told him that."

"What do you mean *me?*"

"*You* said that, Father. That you were home then."

"But you agreed with it, didn't you?"

"Yes, I suppose I did."

"Then what's the problem?"

"The problem is Mr. Leo wants me to be positive. And I'm pretty sure I can say you were home by then but it was so long ago. And the thing is, well, I'd had a few earlier that evening and things got kind of hazy. You know me when I'm like that."

Father continued staring at me, searching my face.

"You *don't* think I was home before midnight, Margaret?"

"No, no. It's not that exactly."

"What is it then? What's the matter, Margaret?"

"It's just that I'm having a bit of trouble remembering. I remember waiting up for you and falling asleep in the den. And then getting up when I heard you in the shower. I remember we talked through the door. I was mad at you for being late. I made supper and you didn't call. Remember that, Father?"

"No."

"It doesn't matter, I suppose. Anyways, you told me about Rudy, how you were over at the hospital with his family. After that I must've gone to bed. That's where I draw a blank though. I'm not one hundred percent sure I remember what time it was."

"But when I told the officer I was home around eleven-thirty you agreed with me."

"That's true. But you see, Father, I'm starting to wonder if I really remembered that or . . . "

"Or what?"

"Or if I was just going along with you."

"*Going* along with me?"

"Yes, Father. I didn't like what he was getting at with all his questions. And I figured if you told him that, then that's what it was. That's when you were home."

"So you *don't* recall what time I got in?"

"No, it's not that. It's more I'm just not sure. What I'm thinking is I could've looked at the clock in the kitchen. Or the one in my room without even knowing it. The one on my nightstand. You know how a body'll do that. Look at something and not even recall they did. The more I chew on it, the more I'm feeling that's what it was that happened. I looked at it and that's why I could back up what you told that officer. But I kind of wanted to hear your thoughts on the matter, Father."

"My thoughts?"

"Yes. Mr. Leo wants me to be one hundred percent positive I can say you were home with me."

Father leaned back in his chair, folded his arms across his chest.

"What are you asking me, Margaret?"

"Oh, just trying to sort things out in my mind is all," I replied.

"If you don't remember, you don't remember."

"I was thinking maybe you could help me, Father."

"Margaret, I can't help you remember something you obviously aren't sure about anymore."

"I'm mostly sure, you see. Just not one hundred percent, the way

Mr. Leo says I have to be if I'm to get on that witness stand. I thought maybe if we talked it over a bit I might get it straight in my own mind."

Father took a long drag on his cigarette. He blew the smoke straight up into the air.

"Are you asking if it's all right that you lie for me?"

"Of course not, Father. I wouldn't do that."

"Margaret, what's *really* the matter?"

"Nothing, Father."

"I know you well enough to tell when something's bothering you. It's not just about what time I got home, is it? What's the matter?"

"Nothing, really. It's just that . . . well, there's some things don't sit right with me."

"Like what?"

"Your cross, for instance."

"I thought I explained that to you already."

"Yes, you did. You said the one I found in your bedroom was yours."

"It *was* mine."

"But that one they had in court, it looked just like yours."

"Do you know how many crosses like that there must be? Thousands. Millions."

"I know, Father. But you see how that might look."

"I told you my mother gave it to me for my ordination. I told you I lost it up at the lake. I *told* you all that." I could detect the growing annoyance in his voice.

"Of course, Father."

"Then what's the problem?"

"I never seen you wearing it. Not once."

"So? Maybe you did and you can't remember. Just like you can't remember things about that night. It was a long time ago."

"Yes, that's true. That's exactly what I been telling myself. But the thing is I was sort of looking through your photo albums and there's not a single picture showing it on you. Not a one, Father."

"You *looked* through the albums?" he said, wincing, as if I'd pricked him with a needle.

"I was curious. That's all."

"You didn't believe me. You thought I was lying, didn't you?"

"No, Father. It was just for my own piece of mind."

"And did it give you piece of mind, Margaret?" he hissed at me, suddenly angry.

"Please, Father. Don't be like that."

"How the hell am I supposed to react? You don't believe me either."

"It's not that, Father. Really it's not. I believe you. I *do*. It's just . . ."

"What does that prove, that there were no pictures of me wearing that cross? I didn't wear it very often."

"But there's other things, too, Father. Things that got me to wondering."

"Like what?"

"That time I come home once and found you and Justin in your study together."

"What time? What are you talking about, Margaret?"

"One time I got home early from bringing Cindy someplace and when I come in the rectory, I overheard you and Justin talking. The two of yous were in your study."

"Yeah, so?"

"The lad was crying. And I heard you say, 'I won't let it happen again'? I recall that very clearly."

"And what did you think I meant by that?"

"At the time I assumed you were speaking about his father. That the boy was afraid of the man and you were going to protect him."

"And now?"

"It's not that I *don't* believe that. It's just . . . I don't know."

He crushed his cigarette out in the paper ashtray. For several seconds he stared intently at his hands, the palms flat on the table, the fingers splayed the way you might hold them if you were going to trace the outline of your hand on a piece of paper. He looked from one hand to the other, like his hands were things he'd never seen before. When he finally glanced up I could see the chalky blue of his eyes, the sharp, in-focus centers of which were locked on my own. The color had drained from his face. He leaned across the table toward me, so our heads were just a few inches apart. I could smell the smoke on his breath.

"Oh, my God," he whispered, his tone oddly flat. "You think it's true, don't you?"

"Think what's true, Father?"

"That's what this is all about, isn't it? Why you suddenly don't remember what you told the detective. Why you're looking through the albums and wondering if the cross was mine. You think I did it. You think I killed Justin."

"*What*!" I cried. "Why, that's the craziest thing I ever heard!"

"You do, don't you?"

"Of course not! I didn't say any such thing."

"But that's what you're thinking. I can see it in your eyes. You think I killed him."

"Get out with you, Father," I scoffed. "Have you lost your mind? You know I wouldn't think that."

"No?"

"Of course not."

"Then what *are* you saying, Margaret? What are all these questions *really* about?"

"I don't even know myself, Father."

"How could you think . . . ?" But he broke down then, put his face in his hands and started to cry. I could see his shoulders quaking, heaving with his sobs. I didn't know what to do, what to say. I felt numb. I reached across the table and put my hand on his shoulder but he shrugged it off.

"Please, Father," I said. "Don't be like that."

When he looked up at last, his eyes were red, glazed over. Tears rolled freely down his gaunt cheeks and fell onto the table. They left big dark splotches on the surface.

"Margaret, you *know* me."

"Aye," I said. "I do."

"What sort of man do you think I am?"

"I always believed you to be a good man, Father."

"Then do you really think I could do something like that? To *any* child, let alone Justin."

"I'm sorry, Father. It's just . . . I don't know."

"*You* of all people should know how much I loved him."

"I know you were fond of the lad."

"He was special. We had a special friendship. But that's all it was. Nothing more. It was innocent and pure, and they've all tried to make it into something ugly. Ugly and vicious."

"I'm sorry, Father."

"I thought you knew that. *You* of all people."

I put my hand to my mouth and started crying myself. I couldn't help it. After a while, I reached across the table and touched his shoulder again. This time he let my hand stay there.

"He was a darling child," I said.

"Yes, he was."

"And I know how much he meant to you. How he looked up to you. Remember, I used to call him your shadow, Father? Remember that?"

He pressed his palms into his eyes, as if trying to stop the tears from flowing.

"Then how in the name of God, Margaret, could you think I'd ever hurt him?"

"I don't know, Father. I just don't know."

He wiped his face with the back of his hand. The gesture made me think of Warren Blake crying that night. Both of them so broken up by Justin's death, even after all these years. From my pocketbook I took out a handkerchief and gave it to him.

"I know how you cared for that boy. I know you could never do anything to hurt him."

"He was like a son to me. The one thing I thought I could count on, the one thing that kept me going in here, was knowing you believed in me. I could take the others thinking what they would but I always felt at least you were on my side. At least *you* knew the truth."

"I'm sorry, Father," I said. "I swear I'll never bring it up again."

I stroked his face, felt the tears burning my fingers like hot wax. He clasped my hand tight against his cheek, then turned his face into my palm and kissed it. Neither of us said anything for a long while. We just sat there in silence.

Finally he said, "I'm sorry, too, Margaret. I know how it must have looked. If I were you, I'd probably have my doubts."

"I shouldn't've said those things, Father. I had no right."

"No, you did. I sometimes forget this has been rough on you, too."

"That it has, Father. That it has."

"I want you to know, Margaret, that you've always been a dear friend."

"As you've been for me, Father."

One of the guards looked at us, then pointed to his watch to indicate the hour was over. "Well, I guess I should be going."

I gathered my things and we walked to the door of the visitors' room. The family with the birthday party had already finished their cake and were now cleaning up, throwing stuff in the garbage can.

At the door I said, "Take care of yourself, Father."

"You, too," he replied, hugging me again. I could almost feel the heart in his chest beating through the prison uniform. When we parted, he held my hands and gazed into my eyes. "I've been thinking, Margaret. Maybe when this is all over you and I . . . "

"You and I what, Father?"

He hesitated for a moment, and when he finally spoke I thought it wasn't what he intended to say.

"Maybe we can finally get that hot-dog stand," he said, smiling at our tired old joke.

"*Och*," I exclaimed. "I almost forgot. And just what do you know about running a hot-dog stand?"

"It can't be any more difficult than running a parish."

"And who do you think was mostly responsible for that?"

"*You*," Father replied, laughing. He paused for a moment, and in that time his face quickly lost its momentary gaiety. "All the while I've been in here I never let myself think about what I'd do if I ever got out."

"Don't worry about that now, Father."

"The only thing I've ever been, ever wanted to be, is a priest. What will I do?"

"Just take it one step at a time."

I was going to say something else but figured I'd said enough for one visit. Instead I just said good-bye, walked down the hall and headed out of the prison. Though I didn't know it then, it would be the last time I'd ever see the place.

25

A couple of days later, I called over to St. Catherine's. I asked the secretary there when Father Cetrone, the pastor, heard confession. The woman, who had a Boston accent, told me he conducted the Sacrament of Reconciliation from four to five o'clock on Saturdays and by appointment. As it was a Thursday, I asked if I could make an appointment. For when, she asked. When I told her that day, she said Father Cetrone was quite busy but that she'd look in his appointment book. When she came back on she told me he had an opening later that afternoon at five. I said that would be fine. She asked if I wanted a face-to-face confession in his office or the traditional kind in the confessional. I told her the traditional kind would do.

As I drove over to St. Catherine's, I thought about the conversation I'd had with Mr. Leo on the phone the night before. "Maggie, where the hell have you been? I've been trying to reach you."

"I've been busy, Mr. Leo."

"Why haven't you returned my calls?" Over the past few days he'd left several more messages on the answering machine, each one more urgent than the one before. "I need an answer."

"I know, I know."

"We can't fart around anymore. Either I submit your name as an alibi witness or not. I don't have any more time."

"I'll let you know tomorrow."

"Christ, Maggie. You've already had a week and a half to think about it."

"Tomorrow, Mr. Leo. Tomorrow, I promise."

There were a couple of old folks praying in the front pews when

I got there. I took a seat in the back of the church. I could recall when I was little the nuns marching us off in a straight line to confession, giving us a good clip on the ear if we misbehaved or didn't do it right. Very serious business, it was. While I waited for Father Cetrone to arrive, I thought of Justin. He'd been on my mind a lot lately. I thought of that time out at the clothesline, him asking me why he couldn't just tell his sins directly to God. How I'd tried to explain the importance of confession to us Catholics. That God, of course, knew our sins but that we still had to confess to a priest to receive absolution. I wondered what it was his brother had been so angry with Justin about, what secret he feared the boy would tell. I wondered also what had been so bad that he didn't want to go to Father Jack with it, and if the two things had been somehow connected. Most of all I wondered why I hadn't pursued it. *Maybe he was trying to tell you something.* And just maybe you didn't want to hear it.

I recognized Father Cetrone. I'd seen him a few times before. He'd conducted Mass at St. Luke's once or twice and Father Jack had had him to dinner. He was an elderly man, late sixties, with white hair and jet-black eyebrows. He was a decent sort, with a good sense of humor. Father Jack liked him though he thought him too old-fashioned, too much a believer in Church dogma, as he put it. After he closed the door of the confessional I went over and entered the other side. Father Cetrone slid the little door back. I paused for a moment, out of practice the way I was. Then I said, "Bless me, Father. I confess to Almighty God, and to you, Father, that I have sinned. It's been . . . oh, I don't know, at least a coupla years since my last confession."

"What's kept you away, my child?" he asked.

"I don't know, Father," I said.

I started with little things, cursing and having impure thoughts, to get the hang of it. The easy stuff. Then I moved up to the bigger ones, missing Mass and taking the Lord's name in vain and having malice in my heart. Hating people like Abruzzi and Mrs. Mueller and those Robys. And the drinking, too. Once I got the pump primed, so to speak, the going got a bit easier, the sins coming out of me one after another. I didn't stop, just kept right on confessing. When I was done though, the funny thing was I didn't feel much better. Didn't feel clean or shiny and new, the way you're supposed to when you leave the confessional. I finished by saying, "For these, and all the sins of my past life, I am heartily sorry."

Maybe because he sensed I wasn't done, that I'd left something unsaid, Father Cetrone asked, "Is there anything else, my child?"

"No, I think that about does it."

"Are you sure?"

"I think so." He started to give me absolution but I said, "Wait, Father. There is something else."

"Can you tell me about it?"

"It's not something I did, Father."

"Is it something someone else did?"

"No, no. I didn't mean it like that. It's not something I did *yet*."

"It's a sin you *plan* on committing?"

"That's the thing, you see. I'm not altogether sure."

"Of course, you can't confess to a sin you're *going* to commit. To make a perfect confession, you must be sincere about never committing that sin again."

"I know, Father. The problem is, I don't know if it *is* a sin."

Father Cetrone was silent on the other side for a moment.

"Would you like to talk about it?"

"Let's say I've been asked to say something was one thing— black, for instance. And I'm pretty sure it was black. Almost positive in fact. But then again, maybe it wasn't. Maybe it was a dark, dark gray and I only think it was black because it was a long time ago. And maybe even I *want* it to be black and that's coloring my thinking."

"So you're not sure whether you'd be telling the truth or not. Is that it?"

"I'm pretty sure, Father. Just not one hundred percent."

"Are you looking for advice on what to do, my child?"

"No. Well, I suppose I am."

"You need to search your conscience and tell the truth, to the best of your ability."

"I had a feeling you'd say that."

"It's the best advice I can give you."

"But what if I say I don't remember and the thing really *was* black? Which I believe it was and in my heart even know it *had* to be. And if I don't say it somebody's life might be ruined. Somebody who means a great deal to me. What about under those circumstances, Father?"

"Pray to God, my child. Ask Him to help you see your way to the truth."

"Thank you, Father."

"I'm afraid I haven't been much help."

"No, Father. You have."

• • •

That night, I was washing the supper dishes. Father Martin was working in his study. Out the window the lightning bugs flickered on and off, and the crickets were making their infernal racket. My head was filled with its own racket, which I'd found the booze didn't make go away entirely, just kept it at a tolerable distance. Over and over I thought about the visit I'd paid Father Jack. *How could you think me capable of that?* he'd said. *You of all people should know how much I loved him. He was like a son to me.* I thought about what Father Cetrone had told me, that I had to search my conscience and pray to God to help me see the truth. And I thought about Justin too, what he'd said to me and how I might have been able to help him. I was thinking about these things when I heard someone speak from the darkness just beyond the screen door. Spinning toward the sound, I dropped a saucer, which shattered on the floor.

"Maggie," the voice said. It was Mr. Leo.

"You scared the daylights out of me," I said, letting him in.

He wore a wrinkled dress shirt, open at the collar, no tie. His face was sweaty, pink as an undercooked pork roast. His hair was sticking up, like he'd been driving with the windows down. I went and got the broom and the dustpan, and started sweeping up the pieces.

"We need to talk."

"Sure enough. Just not tonight though. I'm not feeling so good. Some kind of flu bug."

"Dammit, Maggie," he said. "Are you drunk?"

"I've had a few."

"I thought you were going to stay on the wagon until it was over."

"Just a few."

"Look, I could *make* you appear in court. I could serve you with a summons. Though I won't. It's up to you. But either way I need to know your answer—*tonight.*"

I dumped the pieces of the saucer into the garbage.

"All right. But not here. He's home," I whispered, meaning Father Martin.

"Let's go get a coffee."

Mr. Leo suggested the Old Mill Restaurant, about a dozen miles west on Route 38, a touristy sort of place way up in the mountains. Mr. Leo drove fast, with one hand on the wheel, seeming to take his anger out on the road. The tires screeched on the curves and the diesel engine clattered noisily on the inclines. Out of the corner of my eye I could see the muscles in his jaw working, clenching and then releasing. It was still warm out, and I had the window down. The breeze felt good. The night smelled of pine and mountain laurel, a sad sort of smell.

"Were you *trying* to piss me off, Maggie?"

"No."

"What were you doing then, not answering my calls?"

"I needed time."

"We're running out of time."

I thought he was going to ask me right then if I'd made a decision, but he didn't. Instead he drove in silence for a while. I figured it was some strategy of his. Take his time and wear me down. Let me stew for a bit. The act of driving seemed to have a calming effect on him though. After a while he began to slow on the curves, didn't punch the gas when the road straightened out.

"You might be interested to know you're not the only one who's having troubling remembering things," he said, glancing over at me with his usual poker face.

"How's that?" I asked.

"Evidently Robert Roby told some *Globe* reporter that he wasn't sure about his testimony in the first trial."

"Not sure? About what?"

"I don't know all the details yet. But from what I understand, he's having second thoughts now about what actually took place between him and Father Devlin."

"You mean he's saying Father *didn't* do those things?"

"He didn't go that far. But I guess he's having doubts. About what he remembers. He was quoted as saying that he thinks Father may have kissed him a few times. He doesn't know if it went beyond that."

"What about the pictures?"

"I don't know. If the story's true it certainly impugns his credibility as a witness."

We arrived at the restaurant and parked the car. It was a log cabin situated on the side of a mountain which overlooked North Adams. The city's lights sparkled in the darkness below. Inside the restaurant, we got a booth off by ourselves. The waitress was a young girl with buck teeth, who kept blowing a strand of loose hair out of her face. Mr. Leo ordered a cup of tea for me and a beer and an open-faced turkey sandwich for himself.

"I didn't eat supper yet," he said. "Sure you don't want anything?"

"I already ate."

"That'll be it," Mr. Leo said to the girl.

"Hey, I know you," the waitress said. "You're that guy. The one who's defending the priest, right?"

"That's right."

"I saw you on TV. Do you think he killed that kid?"

"If you wouldn't mind, miss," Mr. Leo said. "I'm kinda hungry."

After the waitress left, he said, "I told you, if I'm going to use an alibi defense, I have to submit your name to the prosecution."

"I'm sorry. My mind's been going every which way. First that Blake fellow coming to see me."

"He *what*!" Mr. Leo said in disbelief.

"He came to see me."

"The son of a bitch—"

But the waitress arrived back at our table with the drinks. As soon as she was gone Mr. Leo whispered, "Blake came to see you?"

"Aye. He came by the rectory."

"What for?"

"He wanted to talk."

"Did he threaten you in any way? Is that why you're nervous?"

"No, nothing like that. He just . . . I don't know. Wanted to talk."

"Did he ask you about the case?"

I shook my head.

"No fucking way he should be contacting you. Wait till I talk to Lassiter. You sure he didn't threaten you? Because if he did I'll have his ass in jail faster than he can blink. Intimidating a witness."

"He didn't intimidate me. He just wanted to talk about his boy."

"You didn't say anything about the case, right?"

"No, of course not," I said. I took a sip of my tea. It was too hot, and I burned my lips. I felt my eyes water with the pain. "I don't know, but seeing him brought it all back."

"Brought what back?"

"That boy's death. How much it hurt everybody, I guess. How much it tore apart this town. *Is* tearing it apart." I paused for a moment. "With Roby saying he's not sure, will you still need me to testify?"

"I'll need you *ready* to testify. I don't like to count on what the prosecution might or might not do. I like to have all my ducks lined up."

"And all I have to do is say he was home by midnight, right?"

"Right."

"Just that?"

"You just have to stick by what you told Detective Guilbault. Say it was true then and to the best of your recollection it's still true."

"And that's all you want from me?"

"That's it."

"All right, I will."

Mr. Leo leaned forward. "Are you sure?"

"Yes."

"Are you *positive*, Maggie? One hundred percent?"

"Yes. For all the good it'll do."

"You let me worry about that. Now the D.A.'s going to try to rattle you, Maggie. Just like last time."

"Let her. I know what I'm saying."

"She's going to try to break you down. It'll be a lot tougher than last time. This is a murder trial. The stakes for both sides are bigger."

"I know what I'm saying," I repeated.

"You'll have to be convincing. You'll have to look the jury right in the eye and make them believe you. You think you can do that?"

"Aye. But you won't put me on the stand unless you absolutely have to, right?"

"That's right. Only if I have to." Mr. Leo sipped his beer, staring at me over the glass. Those flecks of dark in the iris shaded his eyes. "Maggie, you're not hiding anything from me, are you?" he asked.

"No."

"I don't want any surprises this time. You're sure?"

"I'm sure."

Afterward he brought me home. In the driveway he said, "I'm sorry about putting you on the spot like this again. But I don't want to go in there without some insurance."

"Anything so you can win, right?" I replied, an edge to my voice.

"Don't you want to see Father cleared?"

"Of course, I do. You know that."

"Then what's the problem?"

I shrugged, glanced out the window at the night. The darkness had this grainy feel to it, like an old pot that had been scorched black.

"Maggie, I thought that's what we've been fighting for these past two years. Trying to keep an innocent man from going to jail."

"I know."

"You wanted that every bit as much as I did."

"I did want that. I *do*."

"Then what the hell's the matter? You seem like you're having second thoughts."

"About what?"

"I don't know. Everything, it seems."

"No, of course not," I said, perhaps a bit too quickly. Even to my own ear my denial had a hollow ring to it.

"Then what?"

"It's just that I've been thinking a lot about the boy. About Justin."

"What about him?"

"Sometimes in all this, he seems to get lost in the shuffle. Like we forget about him."

"That's not our business, Maggie."

"Not our business? Why, of course, it is. Somebody killed that poor child. It's all of our business. Everybody's. Or ought to be. Yours. Mine. The law's. It *should* be our business that an innocent little child was murdered. That somehow we let it happen."

"That's nonsense, Maggie. We didn't let anything happen."

I thought about telling him of that conversation I'd had with Justin out at the clothesline. About that something he'd been afraid of. For some reason, though, I didn't. Maybe it was that I was afraid, too. Afraid Mr. Leo would look into me with those X-ray eyes of his and see something in my heart I didn't know was there.

"But we did, Mr. Leo. We did. We weren't watching close enough. Or we didn't pay enough attention somehow. Maybe we just didn't love him enough. I don't know. But it was our fault. All of ours."

"By testifying for Father you'll be honoring Justin Blake's memory."

"Will I? It almost seems like I have to be for one or the other. Father or Justin. Like I have to choose between the two."

"No one's asking you to choose, Maggie."

"But that's the way it feels sometimes. Like being *for* the one, I have to be *against* the other."

"You just have to tell the truth, Maggie. That's the best way you can help Justin."

"That's what I been telling myself. Just tell the truth and let the cards fall where they may."

"Look, what happened was a terrible tragedy. I'm not saying it wasn't. Don't you think I feel bad for the kid? But that's the prosecution's job, to look out for the rights of the victim. My job is defending my client to the best of my ability."

"And if your client *was* guilty."

"But we both know he's not."

"Let's say some other client then. Not Father. The one who did kill him. Would you still defend him?"

"Since you're speaking hypothetically, yes, I probably would."

"Even if you knew he killed the boy?"

"Yes."

"How could you do that?"

"That's the way the system works."

"It doesn't seem right somehow."

"What's the alternative? Should we take him out and hang him from the nearest tree? Would you prefer that, Maggie?"

"I only want to see justice done. I want to see whoever done that to Justin punished."

"So do I. But sending an innocent man away for life isn't going to be justice. It'll only be another tragedy."

I started to get out. He reached over and took hold of my arm just below the elbow.

"Maggie, we both want the same thing."

"Do we?" I said.

"Yes."

"I certainly hope so."

26

On the Friday before the trial, you could feel the change in the weather, could taste it. Even early on, the air was thick and still, had an oily feel against your skin. It was supposed to be hot and humid again, yet with a storm front moving in from upstate New York by that night. You could feel it coming. In your mouth the air left a bitter taste, like ammonia. The sky had a peculiar greenish-purple tint to it, almost bruised-looking.

Throwing on my bathrobe, I went out to get the paper. I paused out at the sidewalk to glance at the headlines: "FATHER DEVLIN MURDER TRIAL OPENS MONDAY." They had those pictures of Justin and Father, the same ones that were always in the paper, side by side, like they were Siamese twins and nothing you could do, not even a trial, would ever sever them. I guess they'd always be linked like that, in people's minds if nothing else. For some, the altar boy and his priest. For others, most probably, the victim and his murderer. I had my head down reading and wasn't aware of Mrs. Mueller until I heard her dog start yipping.

"So," she said, walking toward me across the street. That little rat dog of hers was pulling on the leash, like it wanted to have at my leg.

"So what?" I asked.

"He's finally going to get his."

"Are you speaking of the trial?"

"It's a waste of good money, you ask me. What they ought to do is just take him out and stone him. Like in the Bible."

"And I suppose yourself would be the first to cast a stone?"

"He doesn't deserve any better. After what he did to that poor boy."

"That's for a jury to say. Not the likes of you."

"I heard you're going to stick up for that man again?"

"I'm going to testify, if that's what you mean."

"How can you, after what he did?"

"I aim to tell the truth," I replied, then turned and headed for the house.

"What do you know about the *truth*?" she flung after me. "He's an evil man! That's the truth!"

That sort of thing had become all too common during the weeks leading up to the trial. People would send hate mail. They'd say awful things about Father. A few even threatened him. One fool sent a cartoon drawing showing a priest hanging by a rope. At the bottom it said, "Kill the bastard." The phone calls got worse. This one guy would call late at night, wouldn't say anything at all. Just remain silent on the other end. I could hear him breathing. "Who is this?" I'd demand. Not a sound except for his breathing. "Who the hell is this?" Others would get their two cents in and then hang up before I had a chance to speak. Just last night some man called. I didn't recognize his voice. He said Father would get what was coming to him, if not in this life then in the next.

I sat at the kitchen table, sipping my tea while I finished the article about the trial. It said how both sides were ready and optimistic about their chances. Mr. Leo was quoted as saying his client was looking forward to his day in court. "Father Devlin has been slandered and vilified in the press. He has been unfairly tried and convicted in the court of public opinion. I am confident a trial based on fact, not innuendo and hearsay, will vindicate my client once and for all." They said Father had been transferred to the Superior Court jail in Montville to await trial.

The house was quiet. It was just me. Yesterday, Father Martin had driven over to Boston to meet with Cardinal Stone for a few days. Something to do with the investigation no doubt. A big pow-wow. He wouldn't be back till Saturday evening. He left me with some jobs to do and reminded me again not to talk to reporters.

Except to hang some curtains I'd washed on the clothesline, I stayed inside most of the day. By mid-morning the heat was something awful. It seemed to press down on the back of my skull, made that buzzing *inside* my head all the more pronounced. I tried to go about my jobs, hoping to lose myself in the work the way I did when something was troubling me. But it was no use anymore. Even a drink or two wouldn't stop that noise in my head.

As I hung the curtains in Father Martin's room, I got to thinking. This wasn't Father Jack's room anymore. Didn't even look the same, what with the new wallpaper and paint. None of his things around, none of his pictures on the bureau, none of his clothes in the closet. Everything gone. How surprised he'd be to see it all changed. But then I thought, What did it matter? He'd never know, for he surely wouldn't be coming back here. No matter how the trial came out, win or lose, he wouldn't be coming home. That was now as plain as the nose on your face, Maggie Quinn. To anyone not so dense, it would've been obvious all along. But what I'd done, you see, was let myself believe there was still a chance. I'd pretended that somehow or other, if he was acquitted of the murder, after he'd served his sentence he would be coming back here. After a few years, things would settle down and go on as before, or very nearly so. Without even admitting it to myself, that's what I'd been hoping, why I'd stayed on and continued working for Martin. Thinking somehow that our lives—Father's and mine—would return to what they had been. Which I realized now to be complete and utter foolishness. Just a fantasy. There was no way they'd ever let him come back. No way in hell. No matter what, he'd have to go away. Far away. Where no one ever heard of Father Devlin or Justin Blake or the Robys. This was no longer his home. Get that straight once and for all.

And since it was a time for realizations, I decided *I* would have to move on, too. I couldn't very well stay in The Falls, could I? Not after everything that had happened. I'd have to pack up my things and go away. Somewhere where people wouldn't be whispering about me or crossing the street when they saw me coming. Besides, there was nothing for me here anymore, nothing holding me. I was free, free as a bird. I could go somewhere else and start over. Start fresh. I'd done that once before, I could do it again. It would be easy. But then I thought, *Who're you kidding?* Nearly fifty years old, no savings to speak of. A woman who liked her drink. Just where would you go and what would you do there? Though I knew I'd have to leave, I also knew it wouldn't be easy. No sir, it would not.

Then I got to thinking about what Father had said, about us running off together. That old joke of ours about buying a hot-dog stand on the beach. Of course he was only kidding. He was always kidding like that. But the more I thought on it, the more I wondered, *Why not*? Why couldn't we go off somewhere together—the two of us? Neither of us could stay here. We were both outcasts. And as they say, misery loves company. Why *not* go somewhere together? Where no one knew us. Where at least we'd have the other to lean on. Someplace we might be able to start a new life, a life together. Of course, they'd talk. *Wasn't that just something, Ma Quinn and Father running off like that*, I could hear them now. *It wouldn't surprise me the two of them had been carrying on the whole time.* But let 'em. Before, I was always careful. I never wanted to behave in any manner so as to give them something to gossip about. Never in the slightest did I let my true feelings show through. We were just good friends. That's all. That was as far as I dared let even myself go. But now? What was stopping me? Stopping *us*? I was pretty sure Father felt as I did, but even if he didn't care for me in *that* way, I'd still go with him—if he'd have me. I could take care of him, look after him the way I done all these years. Things like this happened all the time. Priests leaving the ministry to get married. When I thought of it like that, it didn't seem so crazy anymore. In fact, it seemed like the most normal thing in the world. It seemed like everything *else* was crazy, but this was the *only* thing that made any sense at all.

In this way, for a little while perhaps, I was able to put the rest of it out of my mind—the trial and Mr. Leo, my visit with Father, the nagging questions that still plagued me. But not for very long. As I vacuumed or washed the kitchen floor or took the garbage out, I kept going back to it. I found myself trying to fit the pieces together, trying to assemble them so they made some kind of sense, sometimes even forcing them to fit though they didn't seem to want to. It was like gluing together some fragile knickknack that you'd broken while cleaning, and you were trying to get the pieces to stay in place but they kept crumbling apart in your hands. For instance, I thought about what Mr. Leo wanted me to do when I got on that stand. Just say Father was home by midnight. Just stick by what you'd told that detective, he said. That's all you had to do. It seemed easy enough. But was I *sure* he was home by then? What if I wasn't? What if I'd told the detective that just to protect Father? Then what? Or I'd think about what Father Jack had said, about me not believing him. *How could you think me capable of that?* he'd said. *You of all people should know how much I loved him.* Which was true. I, more than anyone else, knew just how fond he was of the lad, how much Justin had been like a son to him. And I'd think about the sort of man I knew Father to be and things would start to take a certain solid shape in my mind. They'd begin to make sense. But then, don't you know, I couldn't leave well enough alone. No sir. I'd go and wonder about something else, that cross, or overhearing Father and Justin that time in his study, and everything I'd so carefully put together would crumble into all these jagged pieces again.

I thought about the Blakes, too. For once, I considered their pain, what they'd had to go through. I could recall Nancy showing up here that morning to apologize for her husband. Blaming herself, thinking Justin's death was somehow her fault. And Mr. Blake, finally coming here years later, only with a different reason in his heart, looking for vengeance. I thought of him carrying that pain and anger and bitterness with him all those years. How it had eaten away at him, just as my own son's death had eaten away at me. I thought about Derek, too. How his brother's death had affected him as well. The sadness I saw in his eyes, the wound that had never healed.

And, of course, I thought about Justin. I thought about him all the time. As I washed the dishes or ironed clothes, he'd be right there by my side, as he was so often in life. I thought of that time out at the clothesline when we'd talked about God and confession. I thought about the last time I'd seen him, when he'd stopped by that afternoon. I wondered where he was going when he left. I wondered why he'd told his brother he was helping Father. What was he hiding? Why did he lie? And I wondered what his last moments on earth had been like. I couldn't stand to think he was scared or in pain, that he was all alone and frightened up there, with no one to comfort him. I couldn't stand that at all. Even my dreams were haunted by him. I'd have that one dream where a child's voice was calling out to me from some room, needing me, only it wasn't Eion's now. It was Justin's. I was sure of it. I'd say, *I'm coming, love.* But I could never get there, never save him. His voice was always just beyond my reach, in some other room, behind some other door.

Late that night, I locked up the house and changed into my nightgown. I took a sleeping pill, washed it down with some whiskey. Then I set the alarm and got into bed. Outside it had turned cooler. A wind had begun to blow. The buzzing in my head grew distant as the pill kicked in and I drifted off to sleep. I felt like I was floating in warm liquid: a fetus in the womb, protected, safe. But then I was awakened by the storm. Thunder shook the house, while rain slapped against the clapboards. Water blew in through my open window. I got up and shut it, though not all the way as the cool air felt good. I'd always liked the sound of the rain against my window when I was a girl. Yet beneath that sound, I caught something else. Another noise. A faint, grating sound coming from somewhere in the house, the kind that set your teeth on edge. I'm not usually the timid sort, not one afraid of the dark, but I must confess the sound made me a bit uneasy. I threw my bathrobe on and went looking for it.

It was coming from upstairs somewhere. I climbed the stairs to the second floor. At the landing, I paused for a moment, listening, trying to determine the source of the noise. I started walking down the hall. *Father's room?* I thought. I walked over, put my ear to his door. Yes, it was definitely coming from in there. Even though I knew Martin was still up in Boston, I knocked anyway, out of habit. Then I opened the door and entered. I glanced around, letting my eyes adjust to the darkness. It turned out it was just the wind banging the shade against the lamp on the nightstand. That's all it was. I went over and closed the window. I stood there for a moment gazing out at the storm. It was coming down cats and dogs. The driveway was a glistening black pond. The woods in back, lit occasionally by lightning, seemed to shudder in the wind. As I stood there, suddenly I thought I heard another noise, one very close by, in fact right there in the room with me. A voice. A child's soft fluttery voice, that of someone in pain. My heart leapt in my chest as I whirled about, searching the darkened room, staring into the corners. For several seconds I held my breath, listening. But there was nothing. Nothing at all. Maybe it had only been the wind. Or maybe it had just been in my head. Yet I thought, *It was like in the dream.*

I still don't know why I did what I did next. What we do can't always be reduced to a simple explanation. The heart is a strange creature, indeed it is, with a will of its own. It would seem odd later on, of course, in the light of day. In fact, come morning I would hurriedly change the sheets so Father Martin wouldn't suspect anything, a hair or my scent on his pillow. But right then, in the middle of the night, the storm raging outside, the thought of that child's voice there in the room with me, it didn't strike me as so odd. It seemed perfectly normal. I went over to Father's bed, pulled back the covers, and crawled in. I curled up on my side and fell sound asleep.

27

Sunday morning, the phone woke me. I got out of bed, my head woozy from the booze and the sleeping pill, and made my way into the kitchen. The sun was well up in the sky already, bathing the pines at the back of the property. The clock in the kitchen said five after nine. Good Lord! I hadn't ironed or set out Father Martin's vestments yet for nine-thirty Mass. He always liked his things hanging up over in the sacristy. He'd gotten back from Boston yesterday evening and I figured it might be him calling from the church, where he usually went to put the finishing touches on his sermon. It wasn't him though. It was Mr. Leo. What on earth was he doing calling me on a Sunday morning? I wondered. Then I felt myself stiffen, starting at my neck and working down my spine. Surely it meant something bad. Maybe Father's heart.

"What's the matter?" I asked.

"You going to church?" he said.

"Church?"

"I thought you'd want to go today."

"Why? What in blazes are you talking about?"

"I take it you didn't read this morning's paper?"

"I just woke up this very minute."

"So you didn't hear?"

"For God's sakes, what is it?"

"The reports on the DNA tests came in yesterday," he tossed out matter-of-factly. From his flat tone I couldn't tell whether it was good or bad news. Right to the end he was playing his cards close to the vest. "Actually it was Friday but the D.A.'s office only saw fit to share them with me yesterday."

I felt my knees go a little soft. "And?" I asked.

"Evidently the samples they had were in pretty bad condition. They were old, what they call degraded. Even with the new PCR test, they were only able to identify a part of the genetic DNA chain in the blood."

"Jesus, Mary and Joseph," I said, losing my patience. "Just tell me in plain goddamn English, would you?"

"Bottom line is they weren't able to make a positive match."

I remained silent, trying to let what he'd told me sink in.

"Did you hear me, Maggie?"

"I did. What does that mean for us?"

"What it means is that based on the tests they conducted comparing Father Devlin's blood to that found at the murder scene, they weren't able to come up with a match."

"So that proves Father wasn't up there?"

"Not exactly. But the next best thing. It means they can't tie him to the murder scene. That's not the best part. Get this: Lassiter has called a news conference for eleven o'clock this morning. She's going to drop the charges."

"Drop the charges!" I exclaimed. "You're not codding me, are you, Mr. Leo?"

"No. It's true."

"But what about . . . the rest of it? Derenzy and the other evidence they had?"

"I guess Lassiter was so sure the blood would put him at the crime scene she went out on a limb. Without it now, and with Roby waffling about his testimony regarding the pictures, what does she have? A druggie who's trying to save his own neck. Some circumstantial evidence. And with Father having an alibi, she probably realized she didn't have diddly-squat and decided she'd better cut her losses before she gets her ass kicked. And she doesn't want to do that with the election coming up next year."

Mr. Leo started that nervous clucking on the other end. I didn't say anything. It was too much to take in all at once.

"Isn't that un-fucking-believable, Maggie?" he said.

"Aye, 'tis," I managed to get out. "Praise be to God." I felt this sudden wave of relief sweep over me. I wasn't sure how much of it was for

Father, how much for myself, that I wouldn't have to testify now. I guess it didn't matter in the end. It was good news for both of us.

"You seem a little subdued," he said.

"I'm just so shocked is all. That it's finally over."

"Not quite."

"What do you mean 'not quite'?"

"I'm looking into the statements Roby made to the *Globe*. If they *are* true, I'll offer a motion to withdraw our guilty plea in the first trial. I think there's grounds for it. But that might mean another trial."

"Another trial? Jesus, no."

"That is, if Lassiter presses charges. She might decide she's had enough. I haven't talked to Father about that part yet. To see what he wants to do. But I'm sure he'll want to clear his name. And this time we'll win. We will, Maggie. We'll kick their asses but good this time."

I started to cry.

"I've called my own press conference for this afternoon. Would you like to be there?" Mr. Leo asked.

"Oh, I don't know. I don't think I should be there."

"Nonsense. Of course, you should. For his benefit as much as yours. He's going to need your support now more than ever."

"Well, if you think it's best."

"The press conference is at two. I'll pick you up at one. Wear something nice. Afterward, we'll go out and celebrate."

"Father, too?"

"No, he's still in custody. He'll be transferred back to the county jail for now. But if things go the way I hope, he could be out in a couple of weeks. Oh, by the way. We *did* both want the same thing. Maybe for different reasons. But the same thing."

After hanging up, I stood there for a moment, trying to let the dust settle. *Dear God in Heaven!* So there would be no trial after all. Father wasn't going to be charged with the murder. The tests didn't say it was his blood, just like I'd known all along. If Mr. Leo was correct, he'd be a free man soon, his name cleared. And I wouldn't have to testify.

I got out Father Martin's things, ironed them, then hurried over to the church. By the time I got there, people were already filing in. I slipped through the back door and went into the sacristy. Father Martin must still have been in his office for he wasn't there yet. I hung his things on the coat rack behind the door and headed back. Out in the parking lot, I bumped into Cindy O'Connell.

"Hear the news, did you, Maggie?" she asked, which made my jaw drop open that she actually spoke to me.

"I did."

"Isn't it just something? I been praying and praying to St. Jude. Why it's like a miracle."

"I suppose."

"The way they hounded that poor man. It was downright disgusting, you ask me."

I just looked at her, then said I had to be running along.

"We should get together sometime, Maggie," she called after me. "For lunch."

I walked home through the woods. The trees sheltered me from the bright sunshine. It was pleasant and cool in the shade, the smell of wild mint in the air. I took my time heading back, trying to let the news settle into me. It felt good to be out, my step light, the buzzing in my head still there but tolerable now, growing fainter. I thought how everything might work out after all. I wasn't sure how or when. Or where. I knew it still couldn't be here, of course. It would have to be somewhere else. Where they didn't know him. Where he could start a new life. Even if he couldn't minister any more, he could get a job doing something, an educated man like himself. Of course, it wouldn't be easy for him. I knew this business would follow him wherever he went. But he could settle into a new life, somewhere, somehow. And wherever he went and whatever he did, I would be there with him, if he wanted me, that is.

When I got back I figured I'd put my feelings down on paper. I didn't think I could do it in person, that it'd come out all wrong if I tried to tell him face to face. So I got a piece of paper and a pen, sat down at the kitchen table, and started to write. I'd never been much good with words but I knew I had to try to tell him what I felt. I began with *Dear Father Jack*, but decided to cross that out.

My Dearest Friend,

I've just heard the wonderful news. Praise be to God that our prayers have been answered at long last. No one knows more than I what you've had to suffer, the pain and humiliation. I can only hope that it will soon be at an end.

It is with difficulty, however, that I speak to you of another matter. I'm not much with words as you well know, but I speak this from the heart, which has its own brand of eloquence. If your troubles had not come upon you I would never have had the courage—nor the right—to confess to you my true feelings. I have ever cherished our friendship and would never think to do anything in the world to jeopardize that. You have been my dearest friend and companion. And if it were not for what happened to you—to both of us in a sense—I would gladly have taken my secret to the grave with me, believing myself quite fortunate simply to have known and served you. Now though I feel I must unburden my heart to you. The truth is my feelings for you are more than those of just a friend. I suppose I have always felt this way. Yet your collar was a constant reminder that what I felt could never be acknowledged, not to you, not to anyone. I suppose not even to myself. Now that you may soon be free to start your life over, however, I think it my duty to confess to you what's in my heart. It wouldn't be fair to either of us if I continued to deny it any longer. I don't mean to embarrass you or to make you feel uncomfortable in any way. And I would certainly understand if, upon reading this letter, you were to break off any ties with me whatsoever. But I must tell you the truth. As you have said, magna est veritas et praevalebit. And the truth is I love you. There, I've said it. Please forgive me.

Your faithful servant and friend,
Margaret

When I was finished I put the letter into an envelope and sealed it. I figured I would give it to him when I saw him and he could read it at his leisure.

• • •

I washed and blew dry my hair and then put on some makeup. I wanted to look nice for Father. I thought about wearing the red pantsuit but decided instead on my white, sleeveless sundress, with the square neckline and yellow daffodils on it. Father said he liked that. Mr. Leo picked me up and we drove over to the Superior Court in Montville. The afternoon was warm but not hot, the sky cloudless, blue as a newborn's eye. Vegetable stands along Route 38 were selling strawberries and I thought to stop and buy some on the way home. Maybe make a pie for Mr. Leo, to show my thanks for all his hard work. Like usual he was full of nervous energy. He clucked away and tapped the steering wheel with his hand.

"You look pretty, Maggie," he said.

"Thank you."

"I made reservations over at the Carmody House. To celebrate afterward."

"Sure."

"Have you given any thought about what you're going to do?"

"What do you mean?"

"Now. With your life."

"Oh, I don't know," I said. "Maybe I'll go someplace."

"That's a good idea. Get away for a while."

"No, I was thinking more permanently."

He glanced over at me.

"Want a word of advice, Maggie?" he offered. "Let the dust settle before you make any big decisions. Something like this distorts your perspective. Give yourself some time. Take a vacation someplace. This could be a new beginning for you but you don't want to jump into anything either."

A new beginning, I thought.

When we got to the courthouse I could see that a crowd had already gathered in front of the building. There were TV vans and reporters and people carrying cameras and microphones. I spotted that Andrea Ladd among them. She was all gussied up and talking to someone. And there were people holding signs. Some of the signs read DON'T LET A MURDERER GO FREE or WHAT ABOUT JUSTIN?—

things of that sort, which didn't much surprise me. I'd expected that. What did surprise me a little were the other signs, the ones supporting Father Devlin. Josh Pelkey carried a sign that said FREE FATHER DEVLIN NOW. Clifford Hodel, of Hodel's Market, had another that proclaimed FATHER JACK IS INNOCENT. In fact, a bunch of people from town had shown up. I saw several former altar boys: Jason Thibodeau and Jimmy Santanelli with his little boy. There was Margie Vasco, who sang in the choir, and Eileen Lessard, Rudy's widow, and Dina Cerrutti and her parents. I even saw Pete Beaupre standing there.

"Just keep your head down," Mr. Leo advised me as we got out of his car.

We had to push through the crowd, with those reporters shoving their microphones at Mr. Leo. We went in a side door and down a flight of stairs to the basement. It smelled of dampness, of sweating pipes down there. A guard escorted us to Father's cell. He was lying on a small cot, on his side, facing the wall. When he heard the guard opening the door he rolled over, stood up. He was dressed in regular clothes, the first time I'd seen him that way in almost two years. He shook Mr. Leo's hand, then turned to me and gave me a hug.

"Margaret," he said.

"I hope you didn't mind my coming."

"Of course not. I'm glad you're here."

"You're looking well, Father," I said.

And he did, too. He looked better in fact than he had in ages. As if the news of the charges being dropped had lifted this great weight off his back. His face seemed even to have some color and maybe it was just the light but his cheeks actually looked fuller. Mostly what struck me were his eyes. They didn't have that dull whitish glaze to them. They were clear and sharp, like they used to be.

"So how did you sleep?" Mr. Leo asked.

Father managed a weak smile. "Not very well, I'm afraid," he replied. "The accommodations weren't the best."

"Well, it won't be long now before you'll be sleeping in your own bed," Mr. Leo offered, patting him on the back.

His own bed, I thought. Just where would that be now? I looked over at the narrow cot Father had been lying on. It hardly seemed big enough for a man his size. As we stood there I remembered how I'd slept in his bed the night of the storm. It now seemed a very odd thing to have done. I felt embarrassed even thinking about it.

"I'm so happy every thing worked out for you, Father," I said.

"Me, too," he replied.

Mr. Leo then told us he had to make a couple of phone calls first.

"I'll be right back," he said.

The cell had no chairs so we had to sit on the cot. I glanced around the small room—toilet and sink in one corner, walls covered with graffiti, big chips of pea-soup-green paint flaking off. The bedsprings squeaked when you moved. I ran my hand over the covers. When I looked up Father was staring at me.

"Something the matter, Margaret?" he asked.

"No," I replied. "Just thinking is all."

"A penny for your thoughts?" He smiled.

I wondered if I should even bring it up, especially right then and there. Father had enough on his mind. *Besides*, I said to myself, *maybe I was just being silly*. The very thought of him wanting to be with someone like me. What was the chances of that? But on the other hand, I thought, *Why not? What do you got to lose?*

"Here," I said, taking the letter out of my pocketbook and handing it to him.

"What's this?"

"Just some things I wanted to tell you." He started to open the letter but I said, "No, not now. Read it when you're alone."

"You're sure?"

"Yes."

"All right," he said, folding it and stuffing it into his shirt pocket.

It was then that Mr. Leo returned.

"You ready?" he asked.

Father nodded.

"When we get out there, let me do the talking. Father, you stand there looking as innocent as you can," he said, winking.

The guard escorted us down the hall where several more guards were waiting. One of them put handcuffs on Father. It made me think of that time in the foyer of the rectory, when they first arrested him. It was just beginning then. Now it was almost over. I kept having to tell myself that. *It was almost over. Just be patient a bit more.*

Instead of the stairs, we took the elevator up. The four guards, Mr. Leo, Father, and myself—it was pretty crowded. We had to stand shoulder to shoulder. Father was opposite me. I glanced over at him. He stood there with his head bowed, looking down. With his hands held together by the handcuffs, he appeared to be praying. That or the way you might hold onto something with both hands, holding on for dear life. Though I sensed he knew I was staring at him, he didn't look up. A thought came to me then. I wondered if sometime or other, years from now, say, sitting together some night, Father reading, me sewing, I would look at him in just this way. I wondered, too, if I would break my vow and ask him something about all this, some question I still had. I liked to think I wouldn't, that I'd be able to put it all behind me. But who's to say?

When the elevator doors opened we headed toward the front of the courthouse. Through the glass you could see the people out there waving signs. Before we went out, Mr. Leo ran his hand through his long, curly hair, then checked his tie.

"Do I look all right, Maggie?" he asked.

"You look fine," I told him.

"All right, let's get this over with."

Then we went outside into the bright light of day. People started yelling things as soon as they saw us. You couldn't tell whether they were for or against Father. It was just so much noise. They had microphones set up at the top of the courthouse steps. A dozen cameras flashed as we came out. The crowd surged forward trying to get a closer look. A dozen or more police were holding them back. Mr. Leo raised his hands, waited for the crowd to simmer down. You could tell he was in his glory, just eating it up. He said some things, the sort of things I'd expect him to. About a "travesty of justice," about "vindication," about "redemption." I wasn't paying too much attention. I stood in the background, looking out over the crowd. When Mr. Leo was finished he grabbed ahold of Father's hands and lifted them high in the air, like they were the winners of some kind of sporting event. This was followed by more cheering and boos.

After that, the guards escorted Father down the courthouse steps and toward a waiting police cruiser out at the curb. The crowd was pushing and shoving, trying to get close to Father, trying to take his picture, ask him a question, get him to say something, spit at him perhaps—I don't know what. But he walked silently, head bowed. I waited above on the steps with Mr. Leo. I noticed the man with the baseball cap a second before he broke from the crowd. What caught my eye was the fact that he wore a jacket even though it was warm out. I thought, *What's he doing with a jacket, on a lovely day like this?* And right after that I thought: *Why, I know that fellow. That's the one was in the courtroom, the blond fellow.*

They say things go in slow motion when something awful happens. Don't you believe it. No sir. If anything, they speed up, go so fast you can't hardly follow anything at all. It was all just a blur. The fellow with the jacket lunged past the police and rushed up to Father. Then the noise came, making everything speed up even more: *bang-bang-bang-bang-bang-bang-bang-bang.* It almost seemed like the gunshots didn't stop. In the paper, I'd later read that he only fired three shots, but I'd swear it sounded like a dozen, which just goes to show how your mind can play tricks on you. Next, I saw Father reeling to his right, as if to look at the man in the baseball hat, before crumpling to the ground. Right after that, the police had wrestled the fellow with the gun down. It was Derek Blake. Justin's brother. And for the first time, I realized the man I'd seen in the courtroom was Derek. I don't know why I hadn't put two and two together before this moment.

By the time I reached Father, he was about gone. They let me at him. Maybe they thought I was a nurse. I was quiet and oddly composed, and maybe it looked like I knew what I was doing. I lifted his bloody head and rested it on my lap, the life flowing out of him and onto my dress. I wouldn't even try to get the bloodstains out. I would just throw it away. Father's eyes were wide open, the pupils large and flat as coins, and he was staring up at the sky. They were that same dull lifeless sort of blue as I remembered Eion's being when we'd pulled him out of the pond. The front of Father's shirt was a large red flower that seemed to be expanding, opening up its petals. When I touched it my hand came away wet. In the breast pocket, I saw my letter, unopened, also turning red.

Part IV

28

You can't even see the water from up here. No sir. Nothing but white puffy clouds covering everything like a layer of sheep's wool. The bloody plane is bucking and pitching like a pig who knows he's about to be butchered. My knuckles are white from squeezing the armrest. In my sneakers my toes contract with fear each time my seat drops out from under me. This was supposed to be good for me? Huh! Haven't flown in almost thirty years and I'm scared out of my wits. The first Dramamine I took before getting on the plane has about worn off, and my stomach is churning. The fellow next to me, an older gentleman in a suit, must be an old hand at it for he's snoring to beat the band. One of the stewardesses—flight attendants, they call them now—has been quite nice though. When she saw how scared I must've looked, she came over and struck up a conversation.

"Just a little turbulence," she said. "Nothing to worry about."

"Nothing for you maybe," I said. "How much longer?"

"We should be landing in Shannon in about an hour. Going home?"

"In a manner of speaking."

"Where are you from?"

"Massachusetts."

"No, I mean where were you born?" she asked.

"Galway."

"I've never been there. I heard it's pretty."

"Last time I saw it it was."

Ever since we took off from Logan, I've been having second thoughts. Wondering if this was such a good idea. Going back home after all these years. *Home*? I think. Still and all, I suppose I wanted to go, especially now that I had the money. Father, you see, had left me some in his will, from a life insurance policy he had. When Mr. Leo, who was the executor of Father's estate, told me about it, why, I nearly fainted dead away. He left half to the children's shelter, the other half to me. *Fifty thousand dollars*! What was I going to do with that sort of money? Mr. Leo's handling it for me. Put it in a special account that gets good interest. But first he left out enough for this trip. In fact, was him that put me up to it.

"It'll be good to get away for a while," he said.

"You think so?"

"Why not? Have some fun. You deserve it."

"There's nothing there for me anymore," I said.

"Your past."

My past, I thought. But I finally decided to go anyway. He had Gina Demarco call a travel agent and make all the arrangements. I'm to spend two weeks in Ireland. He said it would give me a different perspective on things. And when I come back? I asked. He told me maybe I wouldn't even want to come back. Maybe I'd like it so much over there I'd end up staying. Who's to say? Maybe he's right. What do I have to lose? In some ways I'm looking forward to it, seeing the old house and the street where I grew up. And I can't wait to see my friend Annie Harrigan, who I've not laid eyes on all these years. Talk to her, meet her family. Would she even recognize me when I knocked on her door? But at the same time I'm a bit uneasy about it, too, unsure it was such a good idea. How will it be to visit the graves, see my Eion's stone? Stirring things up from the past. My mum always said, Let sleeping dogs lie, which is good advice. Yet I always pictured going back sometime or other, though perhaps not like this.

Mr. Leo was nice enough to take time out from his busy schedule to drive me up to Logan. He's just taken on a big new case and he's quite involved with it. You'd never guess what. He's defending Derek Blake! That's right. He's going to be his attorney. Derek hasn't yet said why he did it, though at his arraignment he pleaded not guilty. When Mr. Leo called to tell me he was representing Derek, I guess he thought I'd be mad. That he was being disloyal or something. But the funny thing is I wasn't mad. Maybe surprised a bit. Maybe saddened, too. But surely not mad. I don't hold any bitterness in my heart toward Derek Blake. Maybe I should, but I don't. I can still remember his face that night when he came to take his father home. The pain in it. The terrible sadness in his eyes. The guilt, too. What I wish him more than anything is peace. Actually, in some way I still don't quite understand, Mr. Leo's defending the man who killed Father makes all the sense in the world. It was like those pieces I was trying so hard to put together finally fit somehow.

I told Father Martin I was leaving. I gave him two weeks, so he'd have time to get somebody else. I packed my belongings, cleared out my room. Reuben Belliveau let me store my things at his place until I get back. "You staying in town, Maggie?" he asked. I told him I didn't think so. Before I left the rectory, I went through Father Jack's possessions down in the basement. I threw away some things, gave others to charity. Donated all his books to the library. A few things—a crucifix, a seminary ring, some pictures—I kept for myself. In remembrance of him.

• • •

Father's funeral was a small affair. Only a handful of people showed up, which is what I expected. Father Duncan said the Mass. Mr. Leo was there, as was Joan Kosnik (Leah being sick, she said), Dina Cerutti, Petey Lindstrom, two old priests, teachers from Father's seminary days. Old Father Cetrone. A few others. Even Pete Beaupre made an appearance. He hugged me and said he was sorry.

"I liked him, Ma," he said. "I always liked him."

"He was fond of you too."

"No matter what they say, I can't believe Jack was a murderer. Not that."

"Just let it go, Pete," I said. "He's at peace now."

Of course some of those reporters didn't let it go. No sir. Not that lot. They hounded Father even unto the grave. They showed up outside St. Luke's, with their bloody Action News vans and their cameras and their microphones. They filmed us going in, and afterward they filmed them putting his casket in the hearse. I saw it on the television that night. Andrea Ladd was there. She ended her report by saying, "As one part of this bizarre and tragic story comes to an end, another one is just beginning with the arraignment of Derek Blake on charges of first-degree murder."

Least at the cemetery they gave us a bit of privacy. They stayed out at the road. The day was overcast and cooler. A slight breeze carried the smell of forsythia. Father Duncan gave a lovely graveside eulogy. He quoted a passage from Isaiah:

He was oppressed, and he was afflicted,
Yet he opened not his mouth:
He is brought as a lamb to slaughter,
And as a sheep before her shearers is dumb,
So he openeth not his mouth.
He was taken from prison and from judgment . . .

When he was finished, he said that no matter what Father's sins may have been, no matter what he'd done, he was in the loving and merciful hands of the Lord. Which is one thing I know for sure.

After the others left the cemetery, I dawdled behind, wanting a moment or two alone. I hadn't cried at all. Not a tear. Not in front of the courthouse holding Father's head, not later at the wake, not even standing here at his grave. I hadn't a tear left in me. I was all dried up inside, which I wasn't sure was a good or bad thing, but that's the way of it. I thought of the time in the jail cell, when I'd given him that letter. How he'd wanted to open it and read it right then, and how I told him to wait until later. I thought that might make me cry but even that wouldn't do it.

Then I wandered off searching headstones until I come across the one I was looking for. A small granite stone next to another. Side by side. One said Nancy Blake, the other Justin Blake. Father's and Justin's graves weren't a hundred feet apart. That too seemed fitting somehow. I said a prayer for him. Father's shadow. May you rest in peace. May the both of you rest in peace.

• • •

At the airport Mr. Leo and I sat and had a drink. He got a double scotch, while I ordered a tea. I'd been on the wagon for several weeks. I was making no promises to anyone. I was just taking it one day at a time. That's the way I knew I'd have to take everything from now on, one day at a time. One foot in front of the other, like Father used to say. Neither looking back nor forward, just living in the here and now, for that's all any of us really have when you stop and think about it.

"I think there was a good chance they'd have set aside the conviction in the Roby case," he said. "And given that Robert Roby recanted his testimony, I doubt Lassiter would have dared to retry him. He'd have been a free man in a couple weeks."

"Free to do what?" I asked. "All that hanging over his head?"

Mr. Leo raised his eyebrows in reply.

"Well, it's over at least," he said.

"*Is* it?" I asked, thinking about Derek and what was to come. His trial. What would come out in the wash there. But Mr. Leo wouldn't talk of that, his new client. He had new loyalties now, and I had to respect that.

"For Father anyway," he said.

"Do you think people believe he did that? To Justin. To those other two."

"Of course, some will. You can't do anything about that."

I don't think I'd ever asked him straight out what he thought. I guess I didn't want to know. The closest I'd come was that night out in the driveway. When I'd asked him if he could have defended someone knowing all along that he'd done it.

"Do you?" I said.

"Me?"

"Yes. Do you think he was guilty?"

"You mean the murder?"

"Of any of it."

"Maggie, what I think isn't worth a cup of coffee."

"But *do* you? I'm asking."

Mr. Leo slowly lifted his glass and took a sip of his scotch. His manner was that of someone who was searching through a box of things, looking for one thing in particular. He stared at me above the glass, his yellow cat-eyes narrowed, hinting at absolutely nothing. "Legally I think he was in the clear," he said. I knew that that was all I'd ever get out of him. And in some ways I was thankful for it, too.

"By the way," he said, "about your letter."

"Letter?" I said, then added, "oh, that."

"I'll try to keep it out of the trial. If I can. But I can't promise anything. It's evidence, after all."

"It doesn't matter," I said. "I put down what I felt. It's the truth."

"You never were able to tell him?"

"No."

"Do you think he knew?"

"Perhaps. I don't know."

• • •

The plane is plunging down into the bed of clouds. Looking out the window, you can't see ten feet beyond your nose, they're so thick. When I was a girl, the nuns used to tell us this was heaven. That God and all his angels lived up here. I'm squeezing the armrests for all they're worth, feeling my stomach drop out of me each time the plane bounces. My ears want to pop but can't. The flight attendant walks by, looks maternally at me.

"We'll be landing in twenty minutes," she says, touching my shoulder.

"Can I still use the john?"

"You'd better go now."

I get up and hurry down the aisle to the bathroom, weaving like I'm drunk. I go in and sit down and do my business. Then I throw some cold water on my face, dry off with paper towels. I take a second Dramamine out of my pocketbook. I draw some water into one of those pointy little cups and wash the pill down with it.

I'm wondering if I would have done it. What I mean is, if push came to shove whether I'd have said Father was home with me by midnight. I don't know if he was. He might have been. He very well might have been. Sometimes when I think about it, I'm almost certain I *did* look at the clock and *do* remember seeing that it was eleven-thirty. But other times, I'm not so sure. Other times I think I just talked myself into believing that. That I was just going along with what Father said, that I *don't* recall the time or when he got home. And I've been wondering a lot lately just what I'd have said if I had to get up on that witness stand. I guess it's one of those things I'll never know for sure.

From my purse I take out the picture. The one of Father and Justin in their robes standing in front of St. Luke's. Father is behind Justin, his hands resting on the boy's shoulders. Both are smiling, happy-looking in the picture. I turn it over. "*With love, Just,*" it says on the back. I guess I'd been hoping I'd come to some kind of understanding at last, that those pieces would snap together into a clear whole thing. That I would have no lingering doubts, no unanswered questions. That in my heart I would know the truth. But now I know it won't happen. Not now, probably not ever. So what I'm left with is trusting in what I do know for sure. That Father, the one I knew anyway, was a good man. That he loved Justin and could never do anything to hurt him and that Justin loved him, too. That's what I *do* know, and that will have to be enough.

I look at the picture one last time before sliding it carefully back into my purse. Only then do I return to my seat and buckle up. Out the window, I can see that we've broken through the clouds and are plunging earthward. And there below us, greener than my memories of it, is Ireland. Home.